HIGH PRAISE FOR
JOHN LESCROART AND

GUILT

Please turn the page for more extraordinary acclaim. . . .

GUILT

JOHN LESCROART

ISLAND BOOKS
Published by
Dell Publishing
a division of
Random House, Inc.
1540 Broadway
New York, New York 10036

This novel is a work of fiction. Names, characters, places, and incidents either are the product of the author's imagination or are used fictitiously. Any resemblance to actual persons, living or dead, events, or locales is entirely coincidental.

ISBN 0-440-22281-8

Reprinted by arrangement with Delacorte Press

Printed in the United States of America

Published simultaneously in Canada

September 1998

20 19 18 17

OPM

*To Al Giannini, Don Matheson
and—always—to Lisa*

ACKNOWLEDGMENTS

I am not a lawyer and never attended law school. Over the years, a lot of great human beings in this most vilified profession have contributed to the tone and verisimilitude of my books. For their help with this book, thanks to Peter J. Diedrich and Jim Costello.

Other valuable technical advice came from Peter S. Dietrich, M.D., M.P.H.; Dr. Boyd Stevens—San Francisco's coroner; Dianne Kubancik, R.N.; Bonnie Harmon, R.N.; Dr. Mark and Kathryn Detzer; Dr. Chris and Michelle Landon; Father Dan Looney. Bill Mitchell, Communications Director of the Archdiocese of San Francisco, was kind enough to show me the chancery office and expose me to a great deal of interesting arcana about the Catholic Church.

For their personal support, the usual suspects— Karen Kijewski, William P. Wood, Richard and Sheila Herman—have been there with unfailing goodwill, advice and generosity of spirit. Max Byrd is a terrific writer who's passed on some terrific advice. Also thanks to my brother Emmett for his faith; to Robert Boulware for postgame head straightening; to Jackie Cantor for everything; and to Andy Jalakas, a true believer. Finally, I'd like to thank my agent, Barney Karpfinger, for helping to make the dream a reality.

WE DO NOT SEE THINGS AS THEY ARE;
WE SEE THINGS AS WE ARE.

—TALMUD

PART ONE

1

Mark Dooher couldn't take his eyes off the young woman who had just entered the dining room at Fior d'Italia and was being seated, facing them, at a table ten feet away.

His companion for lunch was, like Dooher, an attorney. His name was Wes Farrell and he generally practiced in a different stratum—lower—than Dooher did. The two men had been best friends since they were kids. Farrell glanced up from his calamari, his baleful eyes glinting with humor, trying to be subtle as he took in the goddess across the room. "Too young," he said.

"My foot, Wes."

"All parts of you, not just your foot. Besides which," Farrell went on, "you're married."

"I am married."

Farrell nodded. "Keep repeating it. It's good for you. I, on the other hand, am getting divorced."

"I can never get divorced. Sheila would never divorce me."

"You could divorce her if you wanted to . . ."

"Impossible." Then, amending: "Not that I'd ever want to, of course, but impossible."

"Why?"

Dooher went back to his pasta for a moment. "Because, my son, even in our jaded age, when ninety percent of your income derives from your work as counsel to the Archdiocese of San Francisco, when you are in fact a prominent player in the Roman Catholic community, as I am, a divorce would play some havoc with your business. Across the board. Not just the Church itself, but all the ancillary . . ."

Farrell broke off a bite-sized piece of Italian bread and dipped it into the little dish of extra virgin olive oil that rested between them. "I doubt it. People get divorced all the time. Your best friend, for example, is getting divorced right now. Have I mentioned that?"

"Lydia's divorcing you, Wes. You're not divorcing her. It's different. God," he said, "look at her."

Farrell glanced up again. "She looks good."

"Good?" Dooher feasted for another moment on the vision. "That woman is so far beyond 'good' that the light from 'good' is going to take a year to get to her."

"At which time, you'll be a year older and forever out of her reach. Pass the butter."

"Butter will kill you, you know."

Farrell nodded. "Either that or something else. This calamari *milleottocentoottantasei*, for example."

"Or pronouncing it."

A handsome young man in a business suit—every male customer in the restaurant wore a business suit—was approaching the woman's table. He pulled a chair out across from her, smiling, saying something. She was looking up at him, her expression cool, reserved. Farrell noted it, and something else.

"Don't look now," he said, "but isn't the guy sitting down with her—doesn't he work for you?"

Wes Farrell was on his schlumpy way up toward Columbus and the North Beach walk-up out of which he ran his law business. Dooher lingered in the doorway at Fior d'Italia, then turned and went back inside to the bar, where he ordered a Pellegrino.

He sipped the bottled water and considered his reflection in the bar's mirror. He still looked good. He had his hair—the light brown streaked with blond, camouflaging the hint of gray that was only just beginning to appear around the temples. The skin of his face was as unlined as it had been at thirty.

Now, at forty-six, he knew he looked ten years younger, which was enough—any more youth would be bad for business. His body carried a hundred and eighty pounds on a six-foot frame. Today he wore a tailored Italian double-breasted suit in a refined shade of green that picked up the flecks in his eyes.

From where he sat at the bar, he could watch her in profile. She had loosened up somewhat, but Wes had been right—there was a tension in the way she sat, in her body language. The man with her was Joe Avery—again, Wes had nailed it—a sixth-year associate at McCabe & Roth, the firm Dooher managed. (McCabe and Roth both had been forced to retire during the downsizing of the past two years. Now, in spite of the name, it was Dooher's firm, beginning to show profit again.)

He drank his Italian water, looked at himself in the mirror over the bar. What was he doing here?

He couldn't allow himself to leave. This was something he thought he'd outgrown long ago—such an overwhelming physical attraction.

Oh sure, when he'd been younger . . . in college a couple of times . . . even the first few years of the marriage, the occasional dalliance, stepping out, somebody coming on to him, usually on a business trip or one of the firm retreats.

But that had stopped after the one crisis, Sheila getting wind of what was going on with one of them. She wasn't going to have it. Infidelity wasn't going to be part of their lives. Dooher had better decide whether he wanted to sleep around or keep the kids.

A hundred times since, he wished he'd let Sheila go, taking the kids with her.

But in truth, back then, fifteen years ago, he was already unable to risk a divorce, already working with some of the charities, the Archdiocese itself. There was big money there, clean work. And Sheila would have scotched it if things had gotten ugly.

He knew she would have. As she would today.

So he'd simply put his hormones out of his mind, put all of his effort into real life—work, the wife, the kids, the house. He would be satisfied with the ten-fifteen-twenty days of vacation, the new car.

Everyone else seemed to survive in that secure between-the-lines adult existence. It wasn't so bad.

Except Mark Dooher hated it. He never got over hating it. He had *never* had to play by the same rules as everyone else. He was simply better at everything, smarter, more charismatic.

He deserved more. He deserved better.

That *couldn't* be all there was. Do your job, live the routine, get old, die. That couldn't be it. Not for him.

* * *

He couldn't get the woman off his mind.

Well, he would just have to do it, that was all. He'd call up his fabled discipline and simply will her out of his consciousness. There was nothing to be done with her anyway. Dooher didn't trust the dynamic of lust, that hormonal rush and then the long regret. Well, he wasn't about to get involved with all that.

It was better just to stop thinking about her. Or at least not get confused, keep it in the realm of fantasy. It wasn't as if he knew anything about her, as if there could be real attraction.

In fact, if that turned out to be the case, it would be far more complicated. Then what? Leave Sheila . . . ?

No, it was better not to pursue it at all. He was just in one of his funks, believing that the opportunity that would give his life new meaning was passing him by.

He knew better. In reality, everything disappointed. Nothing turned out as you hoped.

He'd just suck it up and put her out of his mind, do nothing about the fantasy. He didn't even want to take one step, because who knew where that could lead? He'd forget all about her. He wasn't going to do anything.

It was stupid to consider.

Joe Avery looked up from the clutter of paper littering his desk, a legal brief that was already anything but brief. "Sir?"

Dooher, the friendliest boss on the planet, was in the doorway, one hand extended up to the sill, the other on his belt, coat open, sincere smile. "A Mardi Gras party. Feast before fast. Unless you've got other plans . . ."

"Well, I . . ."

"You'll enjoy it. Sheila and I do it every year. Just casual, no costumes, masks, taking to the streets afterwards, none of that. And pretty good food if you like Cajun. Anyway, eight o'clock, if you're free . . ."

Avery was young and gung-ho and hadn't spoken to Dooher more than a hundred times in his six years with the firm, had never spent any time with him socially. His mouth hung open in surprise at the invitation, but he was nodding, already planning to be there, wondering what was happening.

Dooher was going on. "If you've got other plans, don't worry about it, but you've paid your dues around here—you're up for shareholder this year if I'm not mistaken?"

Avery nodded. "Next, actually."

Dooher waved that off. "Well, we'll see. But come on up. Bring your girlfriend, you got one. Or not. Your call. Just let us know."

Then Dooher was gone.

2

A LONG WEEK LATER—PARTY DAY—AND IT WAS GO-
ing to rain.

Dooher had noticed the clouds piling on themselves out over the ocean as he drove out to his home in
St. Francis Wood.

He considered his neighborhood as the best of all
worlds. It was both the city and a suburb, but without
the blight of either. He had civilized neighbors. An ele-
gant, gracious canopy of old boughs shaded the streets
by day, enclosing them with what felt like a protective
security by night. Stands of eucalyptus perfumed the air
in the fall, magnolias in the summer.

The street was quiet, with large houses, widely
spaced. Most cars were in their garages, although—in
the few houses with small children—vans squatted in
driveways.

The afternoon sun gave a last glorious golden
shout through the clouds—and it stopped him for a moment as he turned into the drive in front of his home.

Like the other facades on the block, his old California Spanish hacienda was impressive, with its tiled front courtyard behind a low stucco fence, ancient magnolias on the lawn, wisteria and bougainvillea at the eaves and lintels.

Upstairs in the turret, Sheila's office, a light had been turned on, although it wasn't dark. Imagining her up there, Dooher felt a stab of what he used to call the occasion of sin—the frisson of excitement. One deep breath drove the thought away—after all, he had done nothing wrong.

He pulled up his driveway.

He parked in the garage and closed the automatic door behind him, then walked back down the driveway and into the house through the side entrance, as he usually did.

"Hello!" Cheerfully announcing his arrival.

He knew she was upstairs in the turret, probably talking to one of their offspring, which she did when he wasn't around. He'd seen the light on up there and knew she wouldn't be able to hear him unless he bellowed.

So there was no answer except the silent echoes of his own voice. "Hello." More quietly, with an angry edge.

He went over to the refrigerator—stuffed with party supplies—and pulled out a beer. Opening it with the churchkey, he remembered days when she'd meet him at the door, his drink in her hand, mixed. They'd sit in the living room and she'd join him and they'd have a civilized half hour or so.

In those early years, even after they had the kids, he'd come first for a long time. When had it ended exactly? He couldn't remember, but it was long gone. He took another sip of the beer, staring out the French doors into their backyard.

The wind had freshened in the long shadows. A first large raindrop hit the skylight over his head.

"I thought I heard you come in."

He turned. "Oh? I didn't think you had. You didn't answer."

She used to be very pretty—short, slim-waisted and high-breasted. She used to work at maximizing what she had. She still could look good when she put her mind to it, but at home—just for him—it never happened anymore. It didn't matter to her. Mark knew what she looked like underneath the clothes—slim waists and high breasts were in the past. She was forty-seven years old and in decent shape, but she didn't look the way she did at twenty-five. No one could or should expect her to.

Today she wore green sweats, green espadrilles. Her once luxuriant black hair was now streaked with gray—she loved the natural look—and cut to a sensible length, held back by a green headband. There had been nothing wrong with her face when he'd met her— widely spaced hazel eyes, an unlined wide forehead, an expressive, beaming smile. There was nothing wrong with her face now, except that he'd seen every expression it could make, and none of them had any power to move him anymore.

She was up next to him and put her cheek against his, kissing the air—friends. "I was on the phone, Mark. The caterers. They're going to be a half-hour late."

"Again? We ought to quit using them."

She patted at his arm. "Oh, stop. They're great people and they make great food. You're just jittery about the party."

She turned on the tap at the sink and filled a glass. He took a slow sip of his beer, controlling himself. She was having water. "You're right," he said. "It's nerves, I guess. You want to have a drink with me?"

She shook her head. "You go ahead. I'll sit with you."

"Are you going to drink tonight at the party?"

Challenging, she looked up at him. "If I want to, Mark. It's all right if I don't drink, you know."

"I didn't say it wasn't."

"Yes you did."

He tipped his beer bottle up, emptying it, then placed it carefully on the drain. "I'm sorry," he said. "You're right. I'm uptight. I'll go take a shower."

Sheila was sitting at her dressing table in the makeup room behind the bedroom, wearing only her slip, her legs crossed, putting the finishing touches on her face. Outside, night pressed a gloomy and oppressive hand to the window. The lights in the room flickered as wind and driving rain rattled the panes. In the bedroom, Dooher had dropped a cuff link onto his dresser three times. More rattling.

Sheila stopped with her blush brush and glanced over. "Are you all right, Mark? Do you feel okay?"

He got the cuff link in, turned it so it would hold, looked up. "I'm fine. It's nothing, maybe the weather."

Sheila went back to the mirror. "It'll be all right," she said. "Don't worry. Everyone will fit inside. It might even make it more fun."

Dooher made a face. "Fun," he said, as though the concept were foreign to him.

She turned again, more slowly. "Can you tell me

what it is?" An expression of concern. "Wes not being invited?"

Because of Wes Farrell's pending divorce from his wife, Lydia, Sheila had suggested with the force of edict that they not take sides. So they had invited neither. It was the first party they'd ever thrown that didn't include either of their mutual best friends.

Mark Dooher could not tell his wife that he'd had enough of the man he'd been pretending to be for so long. Something had to change, was going to change. "I don't think that's it. I've been known to have fun without Wes Farrell . . ."

"Not as much, usually." Teasing him.

"Well, thanks for that," he said. Then, as she began to apologize, the doorbell rang. Dooher looked at his watch. "That'll be the band."

He turned on his heel and left the room. His wife looked after him, her face wistful, saddened. She sighed.

The guests had been arriving through the teeth of the storm, and Dooher and Sheila were greeting the early arrivals in the spacious foyer. They'd hired a staff of five to handle the food and drinks and there was of course the band, cooking away early on the first of what would probably be twenty or thirty takes of "When the Saints Go Marching In."

Dooher's palms were sweating. He didn't know for sure if the woman in the restaurant had, in fact, been Avery's girlfriend. She might be anything to him—sister, cousin, financial adviser, architect. But he did know Avery was coming, bringing a guest.

He hadn't planned what he'd do after he met her. It all synthesized down to the simple need to see her again. If she wasn't with Avery tonight, he'd just . . .

But she was.

Dooher was moving forward, Sheila at his side, putting his hand out, shaking Avery's as the woman shrugged out of her raincoat, passed it to one of the staff, shook the wet from a French braid. She wore a maroon faux velvet dress with spaghetti straps. There was a tiny mole on the swell of one breast. Her body was already subtly catching the rhythm of the music. Avery was introducing her, first to Sheila, then . . .

". . . and this is Mr. Dooher, er, Mark, our host. Mark, Christina Carrera."

He took her hand and then—without consciously intending to—briefly raised it to his lips. A scent of almond. Their eyes met and held, long enough to force her to look down.

No one noticed. Other guests were arriving. He realized he was still holding her hand, and let it go, including Avery now in his welcome. "Thank you— both—so much for braving this New Orleans monsoon." He lapsed into a drawl. "Sheila and I had ordered a couple dozen degrees of humidity for . . . for *verisimilitude's* sake, but this is takin' it a bit farther than I'd hoped, wouldn't you say?"

He had struck the right tone. They laughed, at home, embraced by the host. Sheila had her arm on his, appreciating the return of his good humor. He nodded again at Avery. "Go on inside, get yourselves some drinks, warm up. Have fun."

Now that she was here, he could be gracious. After his earlier apprehension, an almost narcotic calm settled over him. There would be time to meet her, get to know her. If not tonight, then . . .

She was in his house now. He had her name— Christina Carrera. She would not get away.

* * *

They had remodeled their kitchen five years before, and now it was a vast open space with an island cooking area. A deep well, inset into the marble, provided ice and a continual supply of champagne bottles. Across the back of the room—away from the sinks—a twelve-foot table was laden with fresh-shucked oysters, smoked salmon, three kinds of caviar, crawfish, crab cakes, shrimps as big as lobster tails.

The band—cornets, trumpets, trombones, banjos and bass—was playing New Orleans jazz, getting into it. People were dancing throughout the downstairs, but here in the kitchen the swinging doors kept out enough music to allow conversation.

Christina was standing at the well, alone, pouring champagne into two flutes that she'd set on the marble. Dooher had seen her leave Avery with some other young people from the firm, take his glass and go through the swinging doors into the kitchen.

He came up behind her. "While you're pouring, would you mind?" He put his glass next to the two others on the counter.

She turned and smiled. "No, of course not." Her gaze stayed on him a second. "This is a super party. Thank you." She tipped his glass, poured a small amount of champagne, let the bubbles subside, poured again.

"A woman who knows how to pour champagne," Dooher said. "I thought it was a lost art."

She was concentrating on the task. "Not in my family."

"Is your family from around here?"

"No. They're from down south. Ojai, actually."

"Really? I love Ojai. I've often thought I'd like to settle there when I retire."

"Well, that'll be a long time from . . ."

"Not as long as you think . . ." She handed him his glass, and he touched hers. "When I think of the pink moment."

She laughed. "You *do* know Ojai."

The town was nestled in a valley behind Ventura, and many times the setting sun would break through the fog that hovered near the ocean and seem to paint the red rock walls of the valley a deep pink. The locals set great store by it.

Dooher nodded. "I tell you, I love the place."

"I do, too."

"And yet, you're here."

"And yet . . ." Her eyes glistened, enjoying the moment, sipping champagne. "School. USF." She hesitated a moment. "Law school, actually."

Dooher backed up, his hand to his heart. "Not that . . ."

"I'm afraid so." She made a face. "They tell me it's an acquired taste, though I'm done in June and I can't say I've been completely won over." She smiled over her glass. "Oops. I'm saying too much. Champagne talk. I should never admit that to a managing partner."

Dooher leaned in closer to her, dropping to a whisper. "I'll let you in on a secret—there are moments in the profession that are not pure bliss."

"You shock me!"

"And yet . . ." he said.

"And yet . . ."

A moment, nearly awkward with the connection. "Well, Joe's champagne's getting warm just sitting there . . . that, I take it, is Joe's glass?"

"The dutiful woman . . ." she said, softening it

with a half smile, but there was no mistaking it—some tension with Avery. But she picked up his glass.

"Are you clerking somewhere this summer? Have you applied with us?"

Most law students spent their summers clerking with established firms for a variety of reasons—experience, good pay, the inside track at a job offer.

Christina shook her head. "Joe would kill me."

"Joe would kill you? Why?"

She shrugged. "Well, you know . . . he's on the hiring committee . . . he thinks it would smack of nepotism."

"From the Latin *nepos*, meaning nephew. Are you Joe's niece, by any chance? Perhaps he's *your* nephew. Are you two related to the third degree of consanguinity?" He raised his eyebrows, humorous, but holding her there. "Love those lawyer words," he said.

She was enjoying him. "No. No, nothing like that. He just thinks it wouldn't work."

"Well, I may have to have a word with Mr. Avery . . ."

"No! I mean, please, it would just . . ."

He stepped closer again. "Christina . . . may I call you Christina?"

She nodded.

"Look, are you going to be a good lawyer?"

"Yes. I mean, I think I am. I'm law review." Only the best students made law review.

Dooher pounced. "You're law review and . . ." He put his glass down, started over more slowly. "Christina, listen, you're not doing yourself a favor, nor would you be doing our firm a favor, by *not* applying if you think there might be a good fit. A woman who is on law review and . . ." He was about to make some comment about her beauty but stopped himself—you couldn't be too careful on the sexual harassment score these days. "Well, you'll do meaningful work *and* you'll bring in clients, which is quite a bit more than half the ball game, although that's a dirty secret I should never divulge to an idealistic young student."

"Not so young, Mr. Dooher . . ."

"Mark. You're Christina, I'm Mark, okay?"

She nodded. "But I'm really not so young. I'm twenty-seven. I didn't start law school until two years after college."

". . . so you've already got practical work experience? Look, Christina, after what I'm hearing, if you *don't* come down and apply at McCabe & Roth, I will come out to USF and try to recruit you myself, clear?" He grinned.

Her champagne was half gone. "I should really watch what I say when I'm drinking. Now Joe is really going to be upset."

"I bet he won't be upset." He touched her arm. "Don't you be upset either. This is a party. I'm sorry, I didn't mean to push it if it's . . ."

"No, he will. He also said that there's no sense applying if we're going to get married because there's a policy against attorneys being married . . ."

"Are you engaged? I don't see a ring."

"Well, not yet, not exactly, but . . ."

Dooher pushed it. "Christina, Joe's a good attorney but this doesn't have to do with him. It has to do with what's best for your career. It's your decision. You come down and apply, and it'll go through channels from there, *capisce?*"

"All right."

"Promise?"

She nodded.

He clinked his glass against hers, and they drank.

3

H E AWOKE WITHOUT THE ALARM IN THE HALF DARK, listening to the water still dripping from the gutters. The digital clock on the nightstand read 5:30.

He and Sheila hadn't come up to bed until nearly two, but Dooher had always been able to wake up at any time he wanted, no matter how long he'd slept. It was a matter of control, of discipline.

And he had made plans for early.

Sheila slept on her side of the bed, the covers pulled high over her, and he slipped out and walked over to the window. It was cold in the room but the chill braced him. He stood, shivering, enjoying it.

The storm continued with no sign of letting up. His spacious back lawn looked gray and somber, mottled with soaking clumps of plant matter. The old elm's skeleton hung barren, the bushes in the rose garden reached out their swollen arthritic fingers—the whole place sepulchral within its enclosing hedges.

It was Ash Wednesday.

* * *

Abe Glitsky's eyes opened to blackness and he was suddenly all the way awake, sprung from fitful sleep by the jack-in-the-box mechanism that had controlled his metabolism over the past five months, ever since Flo had been diagnosed.

Unlike a jack-in-the-box, though, he didn't move. Pop went the weasel and the lids of his eyes shot open, but that was all that happened on the outside.

He lay there, listening in the dead room. His wife was breathing evenly, regularly. His head rang—an anvil for the staccato hammering of his heart.

Glitsky was a homicide inspector with the police department. He'd been getting through the days by doing what he had to do in five-minute increments on the theory that if he could just make it through the next five minutes, he'd be all right.

When the long vigil began, while he felt he still had some analytical powers left, he'd tried to make it through entire days at a time by force of will. He wouldn't think about what was coming, what would be. But his focus on those days would keep splitting up, disintegrating into pointillistic little nothings, the stuff of his life unconnected, separating.

Now he was down to five-minute intervals. He would function for five minutes, keep his focus. There were twelve five-minute intervals in one hour, two hundred and forty in twenty hours. He'd consciously done the math. He was doing twenty-hour days, on average. He was also into sit-ups, two hundred and forty sit-ups every day. A symbol.

He wondered how he could be so tired and not sleep, not be *sleepy* at all. He was never sleepy—tired beyond imagining, far beyond what he'd ever thought were the limits of his physical endurance, but his brain never slowed.

Sometime in the course of a night or post-midnight morning, the apparatus that was his body would shut down and he would lie unconscious for a few hours, but this never felt like sleep.

Last night—a blessing—the boom had lowered while he lay in bed next to his wife, praying for it.

Now—pop—he was up.

The digital changed—a flicker at the periphery of his vision, the only light in the room—5:15. Still deep dark, yes, but morning really. Far better than when the pop was 3:30, when he knew he was up for the day and it was still night.

He swung his legs off the bed.

At six-fifteen, Dooher was in the fifth row of St. Ignatius on the campus of the University of San Francisco because of a hunch that Christina Carrera would appear, as she'd implied jokingly when she'd said her good-byes last night.

Dooher realized that the odds might be long against her actually getting up and coming down to church for ashes, but long odds had never fazed him.

After all, what had been the odds, back when he was fifteen, that the baseball team he played for, from San Carlos, California, would go all the way to the Babe Ruth World Series? And then, beyond that, that Dooher would come up in the bottom of the seventh inning, two out, one run down, with his best friend Wes Farrell standing on second base? And that he would hit a home run to win the whole thing?

Long odds.

Or, when he'd managed the Menlo Park McDonald's in 1966 and '67 during his first two years at Stanford and decided to take the stock option they were offering to their "management employees" even though it lowered his pay by ten percent, to under three dollars an hour. He'd taken a lot of grief from friends about the thousand dollars he was throwing down the drain, but Mark had had a hunch, and when he got out of law school eight years later, that stock was worth over $65,000 and he and Sheila used it as the down payment on the home he still owned, which they'd bought for $97,000 in 1975, and was now worth well over a million.

Longs odds.

Kneeling in the pew, his knee jammed painfully into the space between the padding so it would hurt, some of the other riskier chances he'd taken came back at him. The time . . .

But, halting his reverie, Christina appeared in his peripheral vision. He lowered his head in an attitude of prayer. She was wearing jeans, boots, a Gore-Tex overcoat, and did not see him. She kept walking, her own head bowed. A couple of pews in front of him, she genuflected, stepped in and kneeled.

The Glitskys lived in an upper duplex on Lake Street, and Abe was in the kitchen, bringing handfuls of cold water to his face. A steady downpour was tattooing the roof, but a thin ribbon of pink hung in the eastern sky, off to the right, out the window over the sink.

The thing to do was get the chores started, but he couldn't move. The order of things didn't flow anymore.

How could he do this alone?

He wasn't going to ask that question, not in this

five minutes. It would paralyze him. He wouldn't think about it.

He depended on Flo—she was one of the world's competent beings. The two of them had split up their domestic duties long ago. Glitsky had always helped with heavy cleaning; he'd fixed things, lifted and moved, washed and dried dishes, organized shelves and rooms and closets. When the boys had been born, he'd changed diapers and heated baby food, but eventually their care—dressing them, feeding them, comforting them—had fallen mostly to Flo.

And now it was falling back on him.

How was he going to do it?

Stop it!

It wasn't that he minded doing more work, or even thought about the work. Flo was not someone who worked for him. She was his partner. In some fundamental way, he felt he was half her, she half him.

And their life together—his job, her competence, the boys—had taken every bit of both of them together. How could that continue with only half of them? It wasn't a matter of shaking the thoughts because they weren't really thoughts.

He was resting his weight on his arms and hands, which were planted on either side of the sink, fighting vertigo. The ground felt as though it were going to give way to an echoing abyss.

He raised his head and the strip of morning hadn't grown appreciably wider.

After mass, after the ashes, Dooher thought he would let Christina come to him, rather than approach her. Waiting on the steps outside, he watched the rain come down.

"Mr. Dooher?"

He turned with a practiced look of surprise mingled with curiosity, then took an extra moment to place who she was, exactly. He knew her, but . . .

"Christina," she said, reminding him.

"Oh, of course, Christina. Sorry, I'm not quite awake."

"I know. Getting up this morning was a little . . ."

"Hey, we're here. That's what counts in the eyes of God."

"The eyes of God," she repeated.

"Penance," he said. "Lent. Some people need Thanksgiving or Christmas. I need the reminder about dust to dust, ashes to ashes." He shrugged. "One of the occupational hazards of lawyers is that we tend to think that what we do on a daily basis is important."

"It is important, wouldn't you say? I mean, people's lives, solving their problems . . ."

He tapped the dot of ash on his forehead. "Eventually, it all turns to this." An apologetic smile, self-deprecating. "This happy thought brought to you by Mark Dooher. Sorry."

She kept looking at him. "You're an interesting man."

Glitsky had ten pieces of bread spread out on the counter. Five sandwiches. Two each for the older boys, Isaac and Jacob, one for the baby—no, he reminded himself, not the baby anymore, the ten-year-old—O.J.

"What are you looking at?" His youngest son didn't sleep much either—night terrors. Everybody in the duplex handled it differently. O.J. was wearing a Spider-Man suit he'd slept in, standing in the doorway to the kitchen. Glitsky had no idea how long he'd been there.

"I'm making lunches."

"Again?"

"Again."

"But you made lunch yesterday."

"I know. It's going to happen a lot. I make lunch, okay. And let's talk quiet. Nobody's up. What do you want?"

"Nothing. I don't eat lunch."

"O.J., you eat lunch every day. What do you want?"

"Nothing."

Outside the window, the trees of the Presidio behind their duplex had come into relief. Morning breaking slowly.

He wasn't going to fight his child over lunch. He would just make something and put it in the box, and either O.J. would eat it or he wouldn't. Glitsky was in his mid-forties. He wore green string-pull pajama bottoms and no shirt. Crossing the kitchen, he went down on one knee, pulled his boy onto the other one.

"How'd you sleep?"

"Good." O.J. had to be coaxed to give anything up.

"No bad dreams?"

"Nope."

"Good. That's good."

But the boy's arms came up around his father's neck, the small body contouring to Glitsky's chest. A moment holding him there—not really an embrace. An embrace might drive him off. "I know you don't want anything for lunch, but if you did want something, what would it be?"

Eye contact. A shrug. "Peebeejay, I guess."

It took a minute to process. "Okay, you get dressed. I'll make it."

O.J. wasn't ready to do that yet. He stayed on the knee. "But the way Mom does, okay?"

Glitsky took in a breath. "Okay. How is that?"

"You don't have to yell at me. It's not that hard."

"I'm not yelling. I'm whispering, in fact. And I didn't say it was hard. I'm sure it's not hard. I just want to know how you like it so I can make it that way, all right?"

"I said I didn't want one anyway." The eyes were clouding up, threatening to spill over. "Just forget it."

Glitsky didn't let him pull away. "I don't want to forget it, O.J. I want to get it right." He had to keep from slipping into his cop voice. This was his son. He loved him. "Tell me how Mom makes it," he asked gently, "would you please do that for me, buddy?"

"It's *easy*."

"I'm sure it is. Just tell me, okay?"

A pause, considering. O.J. stood, off the knee, and Glitsky straightened up. "Bread, then butter—you never put butter, but Mom always does. You got to put butter first—*then* peanut butter, over the butter. Then, on the other bread, the jelly."

"Butter, then peanut butter, then jelly. I got it."

"On the *other* piece of bread."

"I got it. But don't you close the sandwich when you're done, so that the peanut butter and the jelly are stuck together anyway?"

"But that's not how you *make* it. I could tell yesterday."

"But yesterday I didn't put on the butter first."

"Nope."

"Nope what?"

"Also you put the jelly straight on the peanut butter."

"I probably did, you're right."

Glitsky couldn't *believe* he was having this conversation. His world was coming apart, as was his son's, and here they were discussing a completely undetectable difference in the placement of *jelly* on a sandwich.

But he had no strength to tell O.J. this was stupid. Maybe it wasn't stupid. Certainly it wasn't any more stupid than all this talking about it. Perhaps it was O.J.'s cry for order as his universe devolved into chaos—jelly on the bread, not on the peanut butter.

One thing he could control.

He motioned his son closer and brought a hand down around his shoulders, then gave him a pat, sending him back to his room to get dressed. "On the bread first, I got it."

But he knew he didn't get it. The peebeejay was one thing, random and irrational, the first word in a whole new language that he had no ear for.

The other eight pieces of bread lay spread out on the counter. He couldn't think what he was supposed to do with them.

The rain continued steady as a metronome. The wind had let up and the drops were falling straight down out of black clouds. Miz Carter's Mudhouse had been serving high-octane java on California Street for forty years, and Dooher and Christina were in a booth by one of the windows. Miz Carter served her coffee in oversized, mostly cracked mugs, the product of some warehouse clearance sale of twenty years before.

"I really did try to become an ex-Catholic for a lot of years," Dooher was saying. "Stopped going to church entirely, even though I was starting to get some work for the Archdiocese. Hell, back then, a lot of the *priests* I was working with had stopped going to church. But it just wasn't me. I guess I need the ritual."

"I don't think that's it," she said. "You don't have to explain it to me. I think you just believed."

"That's the problem. I do."

"That's not a problem."

"Well . . ." He sipped at his coffee, moved food around on his plate.

"Why is that a problem?" she persisted.

Deciding to answer her, he let out a small sigh. "Well, as you know, we lawyers get used to defending our positions. It's a bit awkward taking a position that doesn't really have a logical framework. I mean, it's faith. It's there or it's not. But there's really not any *reason* to have it."

"Or *not* have it."

"But you can't prove a negative."

"But"—she pointed a finger at him—"there's no reason to prove it. It's personal."

"Well, of course, I know. But . . . it sets me apart, a bit, from my peers. It's old-fashioned, fuddy-duddy . . ."

"Come on. It is not. Not on you."

He pointed back at her. "Says you."

"Yes," she said, "says me."

"Okay, I guess that settles it. So what about you?"

"What about me and what?"

"Faith. Belief. Why you've got ashes on your fore-head here at"—he checked his watch—"seven o'clock of a rather inclement Wednesday morning."

She glanced down at her food, cut into her waffle, wiped it in syrup. She did not bring the fork to her mouth.

"Evasive action," Dooher said.

Still looking down, she nodded. "A little, I suppose."

"I'm sorry. I don't mean to push you."

She took in a breath, raised her head. Her eyes had a shine in them. "Penance, too, mostly. Figuring things out."

Dooher waited. "This isn't turning into the most modern of conversations, is it? Faith and penance. Sounds like the Middle Ages, or me and Wes on one of our retreats."

She seemed grateful for the reprieve. "Wes?"

"Wes Farrell, my best friend."

"Best friends, another not so modern concept."

Dooher studied her face—something was troubling her, hurting her. He kept up the patter to give her a chance to let the moment pass if that's what she wanted. "Well, that's me and Wes, a couple of throwbacks. We go on retreats, we call 'em, replenish the soul, talk about the big picture, get reconnected."

"You're lucky, a friend like that." A pause, adding, "Still believing in connecting."

He took a beat, making sure. She didn't want to avoid it after all, didn't want to be protected, insulated from whatever it was. Not today, not now. She had decided to get it out, and this was an invitation to him, to ask.

"It's really so trite."

She liked the way the corners of his mouth lifted slightly. "Trite happens," he said.

She leaned forward over the table. "You know last night when I let you believe I'd been in the workplace after college for a couple of years? That wasn't the truth."

She watched him for a sign—she wasn't sure of

what—displeasure, boredom? Ready to retreat at any provocation. He only nodded, patient and tolerant. Taking a breath, she went on. "He was a professor at Santa Clara, my adviser. Married, a great guy. You probably know everything I'm going to say, don't you?"

"Do you ever talk about this?"

"No. It's too . . ." She shook her head.

"I'm here," he said. "I'm interested and it won't go any further. If it would help . . ."

Through the expanse of window, a volley of rain raked the parking area, beat briefly against their portion of the glass, passed over. "He was going to leave his wife," she began. "I guess that's what I had the most trouble with when it was first starting to happen, that I was going to wreck his happy home. Except that he told me that Margie and he didn't love each other anymore, that he was leaving her anyway, it had nothing to do with me . . . and I guess I wanted to believe that."

"You're not the first person that's happened to."

She had turned in her seat, one leg extended on the bench, her elbow on the table, leaning over toward him. The waitress came to clear and they both sat silently, watching her remove dishes, wipe the table down.

"More coffee here?"

After it had been poured, Dooher prompted her. "It must have been painful. And not so trite after all."

She was biting her lip again. "You've only heard the short version—girl falls in love with college professor, who's going to leave his wife for her after she graduates . . ."

"Christina . . ."

She held up a hand. "Listen. It gets worse. Girl has best friend from childhood, let's call her Ginny, who's kind of the liaison between the two of them, covers for them with the wife, all that. Girl gets pregnant—professor had been childless with his wife, told girl he was sterile, low sperm count. Now accuses girl of sleeping with someone else—couldn't have been him. Dumps her just as she graduates."

Christina reached for her cup, took a quick sip, swallowed. She looked over at Dooher, met his eye. "Girl has abortion," she said. "End of story. See? Trite. And p.s., professor dumps wife and marries friend Ginny, just to tie it all up."

Dooher picked up his mug, holding it with both hands. He blew on it, glanced at the rain outside. "That's what the penance is for?"

She nodded. "I still don't know what to do with it. It's been almost five years . . ." Sighing. "It's so funny because I know better. I mean, I'm educated, reasonably smart. But, I don't know, it changed me, not just Brian's . . ." She looked embarrassed at the slip of the name, continued. ". . . Brian's betrayal, and Ginny's. Mostly the abortion, I guess."

Silence.

"So what did you do for the two years before law school?"

"I went home—down to Ojai. I moped around, let my mom and dad take care of me. And then one day my dad and I had a talk about how giving in to grief, too much, is really wrong. Well, that struck a chord, and I decided I had to do something, start living again. So I applied to law school, as if that's living." She gave him a weak smile. "Anyway"—she touched her forehead—"that explains the ashes, the penance . . ."

"The engagement to Joe Avery . . . ?"

That got a rise out of her. "I didn't say that. Why do you say that?"

Dooher shrugged. "I don't know. The connection just jumped into my head."

"Well, that doesn't make any sense . . . I like Joe very much. Love him, I mean. Don't look at me like that."

Dooher's voice remained measured. "I'm not looking at you any way. I just made an observation, that's all. I like Joe, too. Hell, I hired him. I shouldn't have spoken so frankly. I thought we were baring our souls here. I didn't mean to offend you. I'm sorry."

She softened. "I'm sorry, too. I didn't mean . . ."

"No, it's all right." He looked at his watch. "And it's time for me to go to work. Can I drop you back at school?"

Christina sat straight-backed, pressed against her bench. "Now you're mad at me."

Dooher leaned across the table. "Not at all. You're still applying to the firm? Today, tomorrow, the next day?"

"I said I would."

"But will you? Now?" He broke a smile. "After our first fight?"

Gradually, the face softened again. She nodded. "Yes."

"Then I'm not mad at you."

Glitsky closed the door, having just gotten the three boys off to school.

He stood a minute in the tiny foyer, closing his eyes briefly against the constant sting of fatigue. He could hear the voices of his sons.

But he didn't stand still for long. He had about a week's worth of work to do today, which was how he'd arranged it. He would just keep doing things—that was the trick.

Today, Flo was alive, and his boys were healthy and doing fine in school. That's what he would concentrate on. He had five homicides he was investigating, and he was also studying for the Lieutenant's Exam, which he hadn't even decided to take. But it was more busywork.

He looked at his watch. He had to go now into the kitchen, pour himself some tea, get his day moving.

"Abe?" Flo, suddenly awake, called from the bedroom.

"Yo." Hearty as he could manage. He was already across the living room, stopping in the bedroom's doorway. His wife had propped herself up and she was smiling at him.

"Get 'em off?" She meant the kids.

Glitsky saluted. "Out of here, on time and looking good."

She patted the bed and moved over so he could sit. "What time did you get up?"

"Actually, I had a pretty good night. Got up before the alarm, but not much, I think about six-thirty."

She searched his face, ran a light finger across the top of his cheek. "Your eyes have bags."

"That's just the way they look, Flo. I'm working on them as an investigative tool. Keep me from looking too friendly."

"Oh yes," she said, "that's been a real problem."

"You'd be surprised," he said, "witnesses thinking I'm all warm and fuzzy. I decided I ought to look a little tougher."

"Good idea. You wouldn't want your sweet nature to show through."

"People just take advantage. You wouldn't believe."

Glitsky's mother, Emma, had been black. His father, Nat, was Jewish. So Glitsky had a dark-skinned face with a hawklike nose. In spite of that, people tended to see first the uneven white scar that ran between his upper and lower lips. Even when his eyes didn't have valises under them, as they did now, his smile was a terrifying thing to behold.

He laid a hand on his wife's thigh. "So how's by you? You want some food? Coffee? Tantric sex?"

She nodded. "All of the above. I'll get up."

"You sure?"

"Unless *you* want the tantric sex first, but I'm better after coffee."

"Okay, I'll wait."

"You put on the pot," she said. "I'll freshen up."

He went into the kitchen. There, on the table, were the remains of the boys' breakfasts—empty bowls, cereal boxes, milk, sugar all over the table.

And his police reports—the five dead people and as much of their recent lives as Glitsky had been able to assemble. The most disturbing of the recent crop, a young woman named Tania Willows who'd been raped and murdered in her apartment.

The cereal in the cupboard. Sugar on the counter. Milk in the fridge. Got to clean out the fridge—if there's that much mold on the cheese, who knows what the meat drawer is going to look like?

Sponge that sugar off the table. The smell of the sponge. The thing had to be three months old. He should toss it but they didn't have another one. Where did sponges come from anyway? He couldn't remember ever having bought a sponge in his entire life.

And then, oh yeah, the coffee, the water boiling

now, and he still hadn't ground up the beans. He really should grind up a bunch all at once so he wouldn't have to do it every morning, but Flo liked the fresh-ground, and he wanted her to have . . .

At least he and Flo, this morning, that was a good wake-up. He'd just keep cheerful another few minutes, maybe a half hour, and so would she, and then that would be another morning, and if they just kept that up . . .

4

CHRISTINA'S SEVEN-YEAR-OLD TOYOTA HADN'T started and when it finally did, the windshield wipers refused to function. So she walked down the hill from USF, past St. Mary's Hospital. She was planning to cut through the panhandle of Golden Gate Park on this rainy Ash Wednesday; the shortcut would get her to work on time.

But she didn't count on San Francisco's seemingly endless capacity to provide local color. This morning's entry was a substantial coven of half-clad Druids conducting some sort of tree-worshiping ceremony, chanting and clapping and having themselves a hell of a good time.

Christina broke right trying to skirt them, but a tiny, thick woman of uncertain though recent vintage latched on to her. A shawl covered the woman's shoulders, she'd woven flowers into her hair, and she wore a long leather skirt, but her breasts were completely exposed. When it became clear that Christina wasn't about to join them, was in fact going to *work*, she segued smoothly from missionary high priestess to spare change artist.

By the time Christina got to Haight Street, where the Rape Crisis Counseling Center maintained its office, she was soaking wet and twenty minutes late for her appointment.

Her boss was a single, attractive thirty-five-year-old smart-mouthed pistol named Samantha Duncan, whose industrial strength convictions on the ongoing battle of the sexes served her well in her role here—counseling women who had been raped.

Her genuine compassion for these victims was unfortunately matched by her impatience with the healing process for the women, the legal process in identifying and punishing their attackers, and the administrative reality of having to depend on part-time volunteers to keep the Center functioning.

When Christina had first interviewed for the work, Sam had impressed her with her humor and passion. Then she had laid out the ground rules in no uncertain terms. "I know this job doesn't pay anything," she'd said, "but I need my volunteers to believe and to act like it's a *job*. I need you here when you say you're going to be here. I'm not very good with excuses."

Up until today, Christina had been punctual and dependable. Sam had a *fire*, a presence, and Christina admired the hell out of her and wanted to please her. She also wanted to prove that she wasn't a dilettante—this was her own very real commitment as well.

Many of the barriers had been broken already—Sam and Christina had gone out for coffee together two or three times, outside of work, talking issues and politics. Christina thought they were close to real friendship.

But Sam had a hair trigger regarding her volunteers, always ready to see signs of their lack of commitment in the work, and based on that, to bail out of personal involvements with her staff.

And this morning, as Christina shook the water off herself, it was clear that their tentative relationship had suffered a major setback.

Sam didn't exactly greet Christina with a smile. "Oh, here she is now. Christina, this is Sergeant Glitsky. He's with the police, investigating . . . well," Sam sighed, "you know about that. I'll let him tell you. Sergeant, nice to have met you." Sam didn't favor Christina with so much as a glance before she disappeared back into her office.

But Christina couldn't worry about Sam, not now, and she turned her attention to the man in front of her.

This guy Glitsky was in some kind of trouble, Christina thought. He appeared, even at a casual first glance, to be under incredible pressure, in the grip of some strong emotion he was struggling to keep under control. She noticed his fingers clenching and unclenching before he reached out and shook her hand. A surprise, it was a gentle handshake, his touch softer than she would have imagined.

The half smile he gave her didn't soften his *looks* any, though. "I'm investigating the murder of Tania Willows and Sam was telling me you had talked to her."

Christina nodded.

Tentative, embarrassed and unsure, Tania Willows had been their most recent tragedy—nineteen years old, just out to San Francisco from Fargo, North Dakota, she had come to the Center three times. She was being raped, she thought. She meant she thought it was technically rape. She didn't have a relationship with the guy, who was older. She was confused because she knew her assailant—he didn't jump out and attack her from behind some bush. So she wasn't sure if it was really rape.

He'd started coming by her apartment, gradually getting more aggressive, and then he'd force himself on her—she was sure of that—but she also seemed almost certain that it wasn't like he was going to hurt her or anything like that.

He never even hit her, though there was this sense of fear, that if she didn't . . . maybe she had somehow been at fault, leading him on—did Christina know what she meant? How it could be? Sending the wrong signals.

But she definitely felt forced, *was* forced—she had kept telling him no and he wouldn't stop—but otherwise Tania didn't think the person was like a criminal or anything, and really all she wanted was for him to leave her alone now. She didn't want to get him in trouble, maybe she shouldn't even be here . . .

And then four days ago, Tania's murder had been all over the news. She'd been raped in her apartment, tied and taped to her bed, gagged and strangled.

The Center had called the police at that time.

Christina found she had to clear her throat. Glitsky was asking her something, which she didn't catch. "I'm sorry . . . ?"

He showed no sign that he was bothered by having to repeat the question. "I was just wondering how much she might have told you about the man . . ."

Christina was sitting on the front edge of the ragged couch, leaning forward, her elbows on her knees, her hands folded in front of her. Her hair, still wet from the rain, hung in front of her face. "Almost nothing," she said. "She knew him. He lived near her, maybe in her apartment building. She definitely felt that if she moved she could get away from him, but she couldn't afford to move."

Glitsky nodded. "And she didn't want to press charges."

"I'd hoped we were getting to there, but no, not by . . . not in time."

"And no names, not an initial, a nick-name . . . ?"

She shook her head. "No, nothing, I don't think. I wish . . . I'm sorry."

"Did you take any notes I might look at. Maybe there was something . . ."

"I know I took some. I'll go check. It wouldn't have been much, but maybe . . ." The sergeant's face had clouded—he was staring blankly out through the fogged glass, out into the desultory traffic on Haight. "Can I get you anything?" she asked. "Cup of coffee or something?"

Glitsky didn't answer.

She touched his arm. "Sergeant?"

Back with her. "Sure. Sorry. Just thinking."

"Are you all right?"

Suddenly the face wasn't terrifying at all. What she saw was sadness. "I'm a little distracted," he said. "My wife's sick." Then. "Some tea would be nice, thanks."

It still wasn't noon.

Christina was just tired, she told herself. After all, with the party, she'd been awake until nearly two last night, then had her nightly argument with Joe. This morning, then, her ashes and the long, strangely emotional breakfast with Mark Dooher, her car not starting, the neo-hippie woman in the park, Sam's disapproval.

Then Tania Willows and Abe Glitsky with whatever his sorrow was—his sick wife.

Suddenly, the rain launching a new attack behind her back against her grimy window, the lights off as she sat alone in her tiny cubicle, something broke in her. She wiped the back of her hand roughly against her eyes —as a child would—trying to will away the tears, but they kept coming.

She was just tired.

This—the sudden collapse—hadn't happened in almost two years. She wasn't going to let herself think it was anything to do with the baby she'd lost, with her past. Not that again. That was behind her and she wasn't going to let it get to her anymore. It was the events of the morning, that was all.

She'd just toughen up. That was it, that was what she'd do.

Swiping again at her face, sniffling, she got up from her desk, pulling her Gore-Tex up around her face. The rain would hide the tears.

No one would see.

5

His Excellency didn't have to explain it all to Dooher, but if it made him feel better, Mark would let him go on—he was the client, and every hour was $350. They were sitting in the Archbishop's office, above the children's playground at Mission Dolores. Their informal meetings always took place here, in the serenity of the laughter of children that floated up into Flaherty's sanctum sanctorum.

Although the Archdiocese employed a full-time attorney of its own, its mandate was far too broad for one man to do it all, and so a lot of the work needed to be farmed out to private firms. And over the years, Dooher's firm had come to specialize in the Church's secular affairs—dozens upon dozens of slip-and-fall cases, liability, property management, personnel.

Dooher, personally, had gotten close to Flaherty not only for his ability to handle the tougher cases diplomatically and with dispatch, but because there was an unstated but perfectly understood ruthlessness in each of the men.

Both got things done. Sometimes what the Archbishop needed to accomplish was better handled outside of his office. Dooher was unofficial but de facto consigliere.

Also like Dooher, Flaherty was an athletic man who looked a decade younger than he was. Still, at fifty-seven, he was running about fifty percent in his squash games (non-billable) with Dooher. Here, in private, the Archbishop wore tasseled black loafers, black slacks, a white dress shirt. Dooher, deeply molded—nearly imbedded—into the red leather chair, had his coat off, his tie loosened.

"I don't know why these things always take me by surprise," Flaherty was saying. "I keep expecting better of my fellow man, and they keep letting me down. You'd think I'd learn."

Dooher nodded. "The alternative, of course, is to expect nothing of your fellow man."

"I can't live like that. I can't help it. I believe that deep down, we're all made in the image of God, so our nature can't be bad. Am I wrong, Mark? I can't be wrong."

Dooher thought it best not to remind His Excellency that he had predicted exactly what would happen back in the early stages of the decision-making process over the current lawsuit. But he'd been overridden.

"You're not all wrong, Jim. You've got to take it case by case."

Flaherty was standing by the open window, looking down over the schoolyard. He turned to his lawyer. "As neat a turn away from philosophy and to the business at hand as one would expect." He pulled a chair up. "Okay, where are we today?"

Reaching down for his props, though he didn't need them, Dooher pulled his briefcase from the floor, opened it, and extracted a yellow manila folder labeled "Felicia Diep."

Mrs. Diep had come to the United States in 1976 from Saigon, a young single mother with a substantial nest egg from her deceased husband in Vietnam. She'd settled in the lower Mission District of San Francisco, where she became a regular parishioner at St. Michael's Parish and, not incidentally, a longtime paramour of its pastor, Father Peter Slocum.

Over the course of the next twenty years, Mrs. Diep gave Father Slocum something in the order of $50,000 for one thing and another, and all might have been well had not the good priest decided to take his promotion to monsignor and move away from her, down the peninsula to Menlo Park.

He had abandoned her and she wanted her money back, so she decided to go to a young lawyer in her community named Victor Trang.

Trang wasn't in the medical field, but if he had been, he would have qualified as an "ambulance chaser." Barely making a living in his first three years after graduating from one of the night schools that taught law, he took the case, hoping for no more than his fee of one third of the fifty grand Mrs. Diep wanted.

He sued the Archdiocese for fraud—Father Slocum wasn't celibate as promised and he'd taken Mrs. Diep's money under false pretenses, promising her over the years that he would eventually leave the priesthood and marry her.

This was where Dooher got involved, though the case didn't much appeal to him. He'd served in Vietnam after college, and reminders of his hitch over there weren't particularly welcome.

Still, he supposed he'd better get used to it. There was getting to be so much of this Asian junk in San Francisco, ever-ready as it was to worship at the altar of diversity. The enemy had become mainstream American—he'd never understand it.

In any event, the Diep case hadn't begun as a big item on his plate. One of his associates took care of the preliminary motions in response to the lawsuit, then passed them up to him. (Distasteful as it might be to have to deal with these Vietnamese people, Dooher wasn't about to give one of his associates the opportunity for personal access to the Archbishop. He knew from his own experience where that could lead.) Finally, he and Flaherty had determined that they would offer ten grand as a settlement and if Mrs. Diep didn't accept it, the Archdiocese would go to court and take their chances.

So in the middle of the previous week, Dooher had called Victor Trang, conveying the settlement offer. He discovered that things had changed, and arranged this meeting with Flaherty.

The Archbishop's face did not exactly go pale, but he was rocked. He lifted his eyes from the folder. "Three million dollars?"

The lawyer nodded. "Trang's got nothing else to do, Jim. The Church has deep pockets so he went looking."

Flaherty was trying to read and listen at the same time. "Not very far, it seems."

"No."

"Slocum was sleeping with the daughter, too?"

"Veronica, now nineteen. That's Trang's story. To say nothing of several other immigrants whose names he didn't provide. He may be bluffing."

Flaherty closed the folder abruptly. "I know Slocum. It's possible Trang's not bluffing. This is nowhere near the first allegation."

This was not welcome news. Dooher leaned forward. "If you knew some of this, why'd you make him a monsignor?"

A crooked smile. "I didn't *know* it. They were allegations we'd heard. We thought we'd remove him from the temptation, put him where he didn't have the same freedom of movement, give him more responsibility."

A shake of the head. "And thereby change his nature?"

"I know, Mark, I know. My nature's the problem. I believe people. I trust them."

"Well"—Dooher slapped his palms on his knees—"that's why you've hired a top gun like myself. I trust no one." He pointed down at the folder, still on Flaherty's lap. "You get to the end of that?"

"No. I stopped at the three million."

Dooher took it. "Okay, I can give you the short version. It gets worse." He went on to explain what Trang had told him last week on the phone. The young upstart would be initiating a series of investigations with other immigrants in San Francisco to determine with what kind of frequency these clerical abuses were occurring. He expected to discover that the Archdiocese systematically condoned this kind of behavior from their priests. "He's calling it a policy of tolerance, Jim. He's going to amend the complaint to name you personally."

The Archbishop was back at his window, looking down at the children. "Can we have Slocum killed?" Quickly, he turned, hand out. "I'm joking, of course."

"Of course."

"But all kidding aside, Mark. What are we going to do?"

* * *

Flaherty wasn't having his best year.

Six months earlier, after an extensive two-year study by the Archdiocesan Pastoral Planning Commission had confirmed their predicted results—he'd finally bitten the bullet and announced the closing of the ten least financially viable parishes in the city. He knew that the Archdiocese would not survive into the twenty-first century if it didn't take steps now. The city had taken a hard line after the World Series earthquake and passed an ordinance that assessed the Archdiocese $120 million for retrofitting their unreinforced masonry churches. (Dooher had worked his magic to lower the bill down to $70 million, but it might as well have been $3 zillion for all the Church could afford to pay even that.)

The plain fact—and it broke Flaherty's good heart —was that the Archdiocese couldn't afford to keep the smaller parishes operating with attendance down at masses throughout the city—Holy Family Church out in North Beach, for example, averaged only seventy-five people, total, for four masses on Sundays. And there were really no significant private donations to offset the appallingly low Sunday offerings.

But after the closings were announced, a firestorm of protest had developed. Flaherty had even heard from Rome.

The problem that Flaherty had not foreseen (and Dooher had) was that perennial San Francisco two-headed serpent, ethnicity and money. Most of the parishes that had been closed were those in the poorest areas—Hunters Point, the lower Mission District, the Western Addition, the outer Sunset, Balboa Park. So Flaherty was widely vilified for abandoning the poor, and what had been a purely financial move had been totally misinterpreted.

Flaherty had also believed that the Catholics in the closed parishes would simply move to other buildings for their worship, and would be accepted in those new locales by the other Catholics who already worshiped there.

"That is truly an ecumenical theory, Jim, and in a perfect world, that would surely happen," Dooher had said. "But my prediction is that my fellow parishioners" —St. Emygdius, in St. Francis Wood—"are simply not going to offer the kiss of peace to the Vietnamese community from St. Michael's that's going to descend upon them. It's not going to happen."

Flaherty responded—as he always did—that people were better than Dooher gave them credit for. The Commission had made its recommendations—it had not been Flaherty's decision alone. The people would get used to it—it could actually be a force for growth, for advancement of the whole Catholic community.

"Well, yes, Jim, I guess you're right. It could go that way," Dooher had finally said, thinking *and I'm the king of Ethiopia*.

And now Trang was threatening to name Flaherty in a lawsuit contending that he tolerated fraud and licentiousness among his priests. Before all of these problems had begun, there was a rumor that he had been on the short list to be named a cardinal. He had confided to Dooher that he had dreams of being the first American pope. Now all of that, perhaps even his immediate survival as archbishop, was at stake.

He was at his desk now, moving items randomly,

nerves showing. "But Trang hasn't yet amended the complaint?"

Pacing, Dooher stopped. "That's why we're talking here, Jim. I need to head this off. The guy's obviously looking for press, make his name in the community, bring in some clients. I've got to talk sense to him."

"What are you going to say?"

"I'll just tell him we'd be grateful for his coopera-tion. He knows—*you* know there wasn't any policy here. We've got to get him off this, Jim, or at the very least you can forget about your red hat."

Flaherty pulled himself up in his chair. "How grateful?"

Dooher clasped his hands in front of him. "Settle for six hundred thousand, if it goes that high."

"Lord . . ."

"*And* a gag order. No press conferences. No 'con-science of the community' nonsense. Trang pockets two hundred thousand dollars. Mrs. Diep gets a nice return on her fifty grand and her broken heart. Everybody's happy."

The Archbishop shook his head. "I'm not. We start at six hundred?"

Dooher tried to keep his tone light. "Jim, this is Mark Dooher you're talking to. We start by offering to break Trang's legs. Hopefully we stop a long way before six."

Flaherty nodded. "A long way if you can."

Dooher bowed slightly from the waist. "I under-stand," he said. "I'll take care of it."

"You're not actually *seeing* her."

"Wes, I ran into her at church. That's all."

"At church. That's very good." Wes Farrell lowered his voice a notch. "The night after your party, which she happened to attend because her boyfriend got himself invited? Markus, we're running into a critical coincidence factor here."

Wes Farrell had his feet up on the desk in his small office. Behind him, through wooden slats, rain beat against the window. Dooher was continuing with the fairy-tale version of his story about Christina, and Farrell finally stopped him.

"This is all good stuff, Mark. I mean it. And because I am your long-standing friend, I believe every word of it. However, I will offer one word of advice, lawyer to lawyer."

"What?"

"Don't try it on anybody else. It sounds suspiciously like a rationalizing crock, although I know in my heart of hearts—because you would never lie to me—that it couldn't possibly be. How did she look?"

Dooher crossed his hands behind his head, considering. "Who, in your opinion, is the all-around best-looking woman in the world? Face, body . . ." An expansive gesture. "The whole schmeer. Everything."

Farrell thought a moment. "Demi Moore."

Dooher nodded. "Well, Demi Moore is a *dog* next to Christina Carrera. Even with wet hair and ashes on her forehead."

"I've never seen Demi like that," Farrell said. "Usually, when we go out, after she ditches Bruce, she dresses up, puts on some makeup, like that. Come to think of it, I wonder if she's why Lydia's divorcing me. If she found out about Demi and me?"

"That could be it," Dooher said.

"Those damn paparazzi."

Dooher cracked a grin. "Your fantasy life is much too rich for you to be a good lawyer."

Farrell pointed across the room. "Says the man who meets his associate's fiancée at church. What do you plan to do with her, if I might ask?"

A shrug, as though he'd never considered the question. "I don't know. I'm thinking of hiring her." At Farrell's expression, he added, "Just as a clerk. She's law review. Pretty sharp kid, actually."

Farrell pointed again. "I must tell you, this is fire."

"It's all innocent, Wes. I swear. Nothing's going on."

"So do yourself a favor and get another clerk."

"We're going to have ten other clerks. Christina's just going to be one of them."

Farrell scratched his chin. "Oh boy," he said. "Oh boy, oh boy, oh boy."

"I'm so worried about Mark. He's just not been himself."

Lydia Farrell—Wes's wife—threw an "oh, please" expression at Sheila Dooher over the rim of her china cup.

The two women were in the glassed-enclosed breakfast nook with the French countryside motif, above which the driving rain of the earlier morning had turned to a romantic Normandy drizzle. At the look, Sheila said, "Come on, Lyd, they're not all bad. Men, I mean."

Lydia put her cup down. "I didn't say they were. You know I don't think Wes has anything bad going against him. He's just got nothing going, period. Either direction. Against, for, sideways. Mark, I don't know."

"Mark's a good man, Lyd. That counts."

Once, in the very early days, Mark had subtly but very definitely come on to Lydia, his best friend's wife.

When she'd called him on it, he'd backed off, saying in his charming way that she must have misunderstood something, he was sorry. But she knew she hadn't misunderstood a thing.

She'd never mentioned it to Wes or to Sheila. On some level she was flattered, even amused by it—to have something on the great Mark Dooher, who obviously thought she was attractive enough to run that risk. Imagine!

But she had decided opinions about his inherent goodness.

Still, Sheila was her friend. They'd been through moves and children and schools and their husbands' careers together, and she deserved a listen.

"I'm sorry. You're right. Good counts. I'm just a little snippy today. I'm seeing Sarah"—her divorce lawyer—"tomorrow, and I want to be in shape. I'm always tempted to be so nice, let Wes have something I've got a legal right to. So Sarah told me, 'Start thinking hate thoughts the day before. Think of all the shitty things he's done, the times he hasn't shown up when he said he would, the dinners that got cold, the shirts you've ironed, to say nothing about . . . more personal things. You'll never regret it.' Sarah's a jewel."

"I never want to go through that."

"Well, I didn't either, dear, but divorce is like war. If you're in one, you'd better win. Still, you and Mark aren't going to get divorced."

"No, I don't think that . . ."

"But . . . ?"

"I didn't say 'but.'"

Lydia smiled at her friend. "Yes you did. So why?"

"Why what?"

"Why do you think your marriage is suffering?"

Sheila put down her cup, picked up the tiny spoon and stirred. After a long moment she answered. "Because Mark is."

"From what?"

Sheila took a moment phrasing it. She wasn't sure herself. "I think he's clinically depressed. With the kids gone now and all. I think he's lost." A pause. "I'm worried he might kill himself."

"Has he said that?"

"No. You know Mark, but he's made a few comments."

Lydia picked up her cup, sipped at it, eyes on Sheila. "Why would he kill himself? He's got everything."

"Maybe what he has doesn't mean anything. Or enough." Sheila's eyes were dry and she spoke calmly.

But Lydia had known her since college, and had learned that just because Sheila wasn't given over to histrionics didn't mean she didn't go deep. "How's he acting?" she asked.

"Silent. And he's not sleeping. His doctor gave him some pills but he won't take them. He was up and out by seven this morning when I got up, and we didn't get to bed until very late. Two-ish."

"Up and *out?*"

"Gone."

"To work?"

"No. I called. He didn't get in till after ten."

"I don't want to say . . ."

Sheila held up her hand. "No, it's not an affair. He doesn't have time. You don't go meet your lover at six in the morning someplace. Actually, he went to church—Ash Wednesday—for ashes. I asked and he told me."

"The good Catholic. Still."

"That's him. But the point is he's getting no sleep. This has been going on almost a year now. It's like he's afraid he's going to miss something—some excitement, I don't know. And then he's constantly disappointed when nothing happens."

"Are you two doing okay? I mean, personally."

Sheila wore a rueful look. "You mean our sex life, speaking of nothing happening . . ." Then, as though she'd said more than she intended, added, "It's great when we get around to it, which is about every four times the moon gets full, if that."

Lydia looked out at the drizzle, at her manicured lawn. She sighed. "That happened to Wes. The whole thing you describe. I tried as long as I could, but I just couldn't stand it. He wasn't depressed, I don't think. He'd just stopped loving me. I don't mean that's you and Mark, but that was me and Wes."

Sheila thought a moment. "I just don't believe that," she said. "I think it's deeper and if I could just figure out what it was, everything would get better."

Lydia took her hand over the table, patted it. "You know him better than me, Sheila. I'm sure you're right. I hope so."

Sheila really blamed herself.

That was her training as well as her inclination. She always blamed herself, for everything that went wrong—their kids, Mark's dissatisfaction. It had to be her.

She knew it couldn't be Mark, who didn't make mistakes—not the way other people did. Factual errors, even in casual conversation? Forget it. The man knew everything and forgot nothing. Sheila made lists to remember all of the many jobs she had to do every day or week. Mark just did them—all, and perfectly. He never needed a reminder. He never lost his temper. (Well, once in a very great while, and invariably when she had provoked him beyond the limits of a saint.) Mark Dooher performed his duties flawlessly.

So if something was wrong, and something was, it had to be Sheila's fault.

She thought it was probably the double-whammy of the onset of menopause and Jason—their baby—finally going off to school. Way off, to Boulder, where he could snowboard all winter long. And Mark, Jr., working now on that rig in Alaska, trying to make enough to pay the bills for a summer of his sculpting since his father wouldn't help him if he was so set on doing that kind of stupid art, and Susan in New York.

Well, at least Susan called every week or so, tried to keep them up on her life, though Sheila and especially Mark would never understand why she had no interest in men.

Sheila's hormones, too, had caught up with her, swirled her into the depression. She couldn't deny it and she couldn't blame Mark. She'd become miserable to live with, a hard truth to accept for Sheila Graham Dooher, who until she turned forty-five was one of the city's legendary partyers.

But as the gloom had begun to settle and she couldn't shake herself out of it, she felt less and less motivated to try. For over a year, everything Mark did she'd pick pick pick, losing her temper, poking viciously even at his perfection, his charming smile, his trim body, his own patience with her. She couldn't blame him for retreating into himself, his work, for not approaching her on sex. Whenever he did, she turned him down.

Then came the end of their nights out, or even the laugh-filled gourmet dinners at home with Wes and Lydia. In their places thrummed the somber pervasiveness of the big, empty house.

No wonder it had gotten to him, finally worn him down.

Which is what had finally woken her up. She hadn't intended to hurt Mark. She'd just been in her own funk, thinking somehow it would end. It was her problem and—a good Dooher all the way—she would suffer it in silence.

What she hadn't counted on was the long-term effect that her depression had on Mark. He had withdrawn, and she didn't know if she could get him back.

She'd decided she had to get over it, had finally gone to her doctor, and he'd prescribed the antidepressant Nardil, and it had worked.

The only drawback was that she couldn't drink while taking the drug, which meant no more cocktails with Mark when he came home after a hard day, no more sharing his passion—hers, too—for wine with dinner. No more getting a little silly and loose and rubbing up against him.

She might have just told him about the prescription, but she was afraid of his reaction, that his opinion of her would sink even lower. Doohers didn't need to take antidepressants, they *willed* their weaknesses away.

So she told him, instead, that she'd reached the decision that her depression was a result of her *drinking too much* and she was going to stop, cold turkey. That was the kind of decision a Dooher would make—an act of will to better yourself. Mark had to respect that, even if he didn't like it. It was far better, she reasoned, to give up drinking and treat her husband civilly than it was to have him consider her weak, "hooked," perhaps forever, on an antidepressant.

But it wasn't working. Mark was gone, and she wasn't sure he was going to come back. And it was all her fault.

6

JOE AVERY WASN'T MALICIOUS OR ABUSIVE. CHRISTINA didn't want to be overcritical. He had a lot of fine qualities.

But he was driving her nuts.

Joe would go into little routines with mind-numbing regularity to illustrate how, in spite of being a lawyer, he was actually a nice guy, not really a type-A kind of uptight dweeb. Fly-fishing, for example—how he was catch-and-release all the way, used only barbless hooks —that way those little fishies didn't feel a thing, probably enjoyed the exercise there on the end of his two-pound test. Keep their HDLs up.

Or the volunteer work with the Sierra Club. See? Even though he made money—and he wasn't ashamed of that, nosiree—he was sensitive to the environment.

Christina did volunteer work herself, so she could back him up here. It was important to have a broad spectrum of interests and involvements. You didn't want to lose sight of the big picture, which was a quality life.

Another of his big phrases—quality life.

Also, he had the habit of saying, "Look at the facts," followed by "That's very interesting." Both of which set Christina's teeth on edge.

When she'd first started seeing Joe, she'd been attracted by the sense of sweetness he projected. It had been nearly three years since her professor. And Joe had just happened.

He'd been the TA in her contracts course. After a few classes, some of the students started hanging around together afterward, going out for pizza, talking the ever-fascinating law talk. And then one night everyone else went home early.

She and Joe had closed the place, in the course of the night leaving contracts behind them, discovering a mutual interest in backpacking, skiing, the Great Outdoors. Christina also liked Joe's looks, his full head of black hair over a chiseled face. A cleft chin like her father's.

Joe and some friends were going out in the Tahoe Wilderness for five days over Thanksgiving. Would Christina like to come?

No push, no come-on. She'd liked that.

After a while, she came to recognize that she liked his manner and his personality in a lukewarm way that occasionally got up to a fair impersonation of heat. That was all right. Maybe it would change—she would wait. She didn't trust too much passion. She also desperately wanted to believe that the "like" could over time transmogrify into "love." It was why she had after all this time picked a nice person, someone whose company was if not thrilling, then pleasant, livable.

* * *

Joe was now at his desk at four in the afternoon, twirling a pen between his fingers, glaring at Christina, struggling to control his anger.

"I don't know why you're so mad," she was saying.

"I'm not mad. I just thought we'd already talked about this. I mean, you didn't even mention it last night, and now here you are, dressed to impress . . ."

She spread her hands in front of her. "Joe, this is a simple business suit."

"Yes, but every other applicant for summer clerk or anything else sends in a letter and a resumé. Then we review it and decide whether . . ."

"I know all that. Mark Dooher asked me to come down, so I thought it would be appropriate to dress nicely."

"Which on you doesn't—" He stopped himself, not wanting to say it, to admit that whether she liked it or not, her beauty was an issue, over and over again. "I'm . . . maybe I'm a little disappointed, is all." The pencil snapped between his hands, and he looked down at it in surprise.

"I don't know why you'd be disappointed. I really don't. Mark said . . ."

"Mark. You mean Mr. Dooher?"

Her lips tightened in frustration. "He said to call him Mark. He's a nice guy, Joe."

"He's a nice guy." Avery reeled himself in. "I lied," he said calmly. "I am really mad." He looked over Christina's shoulder, making triple sure his door was closed all the way. "Mr. Dooher is not a nice guy. Let's get that straight. Look at the facts. He is a hatchet man. He cut both McCabe and Roth out of here like so much driftwood after thirty years and . . ."

She was shaking her head. "Okay. He's tough in business. He's the boss, right? That comes with the territory. But he asked me to come down. What was I supposed to do?"

"I asked you *not* to come down. How about that? How about how comfortable I am with you going around feeling out the job situation here behind my back?"

"I didn't do that." The volume went up. "I told you, I ran into him at church. Jesus, give me a break, Joe. Don't be so . . . so . . ."

"So what?" Jumping on her, notching it up.

"So goddamn *controlling*, is what."

Avery sat back, lowering his voice almost to a whisper. "I'm controlling? If I am, I'm not very good at it, am I?"

"You shouldn't be. That's my point. This is *my* life and *my* career and if the managing partner invites me down for an interview, what do you expect me to do? Say, 'Oh, I'm sorry, I'm a modern woman and all, but my boyfriend would be so upset.' "

"I'm not upset."

"And you're not mad either, I suppose." Though she knew he was furious. "Damn it, Joe, you don't have any right to be mad at me." She grabbed up her briefcase.

"Where are you going?"

"I'm going to talk to Mr. Dooher." She hesitated. "To *Mark*."

This got him up, hand outstretched, nearly knocking his chair over behind him. "Whoa, whoa, wait a minute, Christina. Wait a minute!"

She paused, her hand on the doorknob. "All right, one minute. What for?"

He crossed around his desk, stopping an arm's length from her. "Look . . ." A long breath, getting his own control back. "Look, I'm sorry. Don't go to Mr. Dooher, not like this."

"Like what? Like all mad at you? Like I'll get you in trouble? I promise, I won't mention you at all."

"Christina . . ."

"I don't understand why you don't want me to work here, Joe. I thought you'd be happy. We could be together, see each other during the day, go out to lunch . . . I thought it would be fun."

He moved toward her, held her arms gently. "I know," he said. "I know. It would."

"So what's the problem?"

"It just surprised me, that's all. I thought we'd decided something else, and then just having this sprung on me . . ."

"This wasn't *sprung*, Joe. I didn't feel like I needed to ask your permission. I came down and here I am now, telling you. I'm not hiding anything."

"All right," he said. "All right, I'm sorry. I don't want to fight about this."

"I don't either."

"Okay, then." He stepped back. "Did you bring your resumé with you? A cover letter?"

She nodded, crossed to his desk, put her briefcase on it and snapped it open. Handing him the envelope, she asked him where it went now.

There was a look in his eyes that she didn't like very much. Then a half smile to back it up. He motioned with his head—follow me. On the floor next to one of the bookcases across the room was a cardboard box that had originally held a case of wine.

As the associate in charge of the summer clerk program, Avery received all the hopefuls' resumés, which a four-person committee reviewed once every two weeks. In the meanwhile, Avery "filed" the resumés in the cardboard box, which currently was two or three inches deep in them.

He dropped Christina's in on top.

"Okay," he said, "you're in the hopper. Next it goes to the committee." He reached out a hand and touched her sleeve. "After this it gets pretty objective, Chris. We'll just have to see what happens."

All that to drop her envelope in a box! She had been finessed.

Christina was so angry that she didn't even feel her reaction until she'd kissed Joe good-bye by the elevator banks and ridden the twenty-one floors back down to the lobby that opened onto Market Street. There, she stopped still, her heart suddenly pounding.

Though it was short notice, Victor Trang had been only too happy to come down for an afternoon meeting with Mr. Dooher, who was representing the Archdiocese.

As usual, Trang wasn't exactly loaded down with litigation and he was heartened by the almost immediate response represented by Dooher's call. Also, late in the day, he welcomed the excuse to leave his one-room office in the darkened back corner of a turn-of-the-century building near the Geneva Avenue off-ramp of the Junipero Serra Freeway—as bleak a setting as San Francisco offered.

As soon as possible, would he like to come downtown to the no doubt elegantly appointed twenty-first floor of the One California Building and discuss this matter? Why yes. He allowed as to how he could find the time.

He'd only brought the matter up with Dooher on the previous Thursday, and thought that this quick a reply boded well for a quick settlement, which was why he was in the game.

Mark Dooher wasn't drinking anything, but his secretary came in and served excellent French roast coffee in an almost translucent white china cup with a thin band of gold at the rim. Trang was sitting before a mahogany coffee table on an Empire-style couch, looking across Dooher's spacious office and out through the floor-to-ceiling windows.

The office, hanging here exposed above the city, was intimidating. The message it conveyed was clear— Dooher hadn't gotten here by losing very often. The weather had been dismal all day, and now wisps of dark clouds blew by in the strong wind, alternately obscuring then revealing the view—the Bay Bridge and Treasure Island, freighters and tugs on the water. The hills across the bay, in the distance, were hulking shapes of gunmetal gray.

Trang took a sip of his coffee, nodded, and smiled at his host. He was thirty-three years old. He'd been a U.S. citizen for fifteen years, and was used to Caucasian faces, but this one was unreadable—open, honest, apparently friendly, civilized and well-groomed. It was the kind of face that scared him the most, and the man who owned it sat kitty-corner to him, hands crossed, elbows on his knees, leaning slightly forward, getting right to the point.

"First, the Archbishop wanted me to convey to you that there is no intentional policy of toleration toward this kind of behavior in the Archdiocese. If Father Slocum had this relationship with Mrs. Diep . . ."

"He did, and with her daughter, too."

"*If*, as I say, if this went on with Father Slocum, it

was wrong and we deplore his actions. But," Dooher continued, "the larger issue—the whole question of officially looking the other way—that's a very sensitive area."

Trang nodded. "That's true," he said, "but it's equally true that many people have been substantially damaged."

Dooher winced at the legal phrase. Without "damages," there is no recovery. Trang was putting him on notice that he was here to talk turkey. "*Some* people *may have* actually suffered damages, Mr. Trang. For the moment, I thought we might stick with Mrs. Diep. She's your primary client, isn't she?"

Trang put his coffee cup down and smiled. For the first time, he had a sense that this was going to work. And if it did, he would be on his way. "Only until I file the amended complaint." Another smile. "Which I believe you've seen."

"Yes, of course. That's what I wanted to see you about. Needless to say, we'd prefer you don't make that filing."

Trang barely concealed his excitement. The Archdiocese was going to offer a settlement. He lifted his shoulders an inch. "Naturally, if we could reach some understanding here . . ."

Dooher smiled, nodded, and stood. "Good," he said, "I think we can." He walked over to his desk, where he picked up a leather folder and opened it. "I have here a check in the amount of fifteen thousand dollars as a settlement for Mrs. Diep's claims."

Trang's stomach went hollow. Ten seconds before, he'd been thinking in the millions, and now . . .

"Fifteen thousand?"

"It's a generous offer, considering," Dooher was saying. "I know Mrs. Diep feels that she's been wronged, but let's not pretend that she wasn't a willing participant in this whole unfortunate scenario. This is as far as we're going to go. I know the Archbishop. If I were you, I'd take it. That's honest advice."

Trang forced himself to remain seated, to keep his voice calm. "We were asking . . ."

"I know, I know, but look, Victor—you mind if I call you Victor?—look, let's not pussyfoot around. You and I know what you've been doing. You've been out beating the bushes trying to find witnesses or victims or whatever you want to call them to accuse priests of things that didn't happen, or are very difficult to prove. It's going to get ugly and it's going to take forever and p.s., you're going to lose. You're going to waste five years of your young life." Dooher was standing by the windows. "Come here a minute. Come here."

Obediently, Trang rose and crossed the room. The height was dizzying. The floor upon which they stood seemed to end, unsupported, in space. Dooher stepped to the window, his shoes nearly touching the glass. He motioned Trang up next to him, stood too close to him, threateningly close.

Dooher picked up the thread of the discussion. "You know, not a day goes by that I don't stand here looking down over the city reflecting on the frivolity of our fellow men. All these buildings, all this scrambling activity . . ." He leaned right into the window. ". . . all that humanity down on the street, tiny and busy as ants, doing so much that is frivolous. You know what I'm saying?"

"You are warning me about the dangers of bringing a frivolous lawsuit."

A beam lit Dooher's face. "That's exactly right, Victor. That's what I'm doing. Because I must tell you— this may be old news to you—that the courts are overworked as it is and extremely sensitive to frivolous lawsuits. Extremely sensitive. They smell frivolous and you got fines and even suspensions like you wouldn't believe. Bad stuff, very bad. Especially for sole practitioners such as yourself. Courts have been known to put 'em right out of business."

Trang straightened himself, moved away from the windows. "This lawsuit isn't frivolous."

"Mrs. Diep's may have some merit. We agree. Hence the fifteen thousand. Look." Dooher laid a hand on his shoulder, seeming to push him out over the city. "I was going to play hardball with you, Victor, and not make any offer. But when I told Jim Flaherty—the Archbishop—that you would be fined and have to pay our fees, and possibly be suspended from the bar and so on—well, he insisted I convey to you this warning and offer the really generous settlement. Myself, I hate to give away strategy, but His Excellency doesn't want you to suffer, and if you go ahead with this lawsuit, you're going to."

"That's a bald enough threat, Mr. Dooher."

"Not at all. It's friendly advice. Here, let's sit back down." Dooher was shepherding him back over toward the couch. "Over the years we've had hundreds of cases with litigants who viewed the Church as deep pockets. Some kid's skateboarding on the steps of one of our buildings and breaks his leg. Dad hits us for liability—okay, we settle, sometimes. But some greedy people have attorneys who don't stop there—they want negligence due to faulty maintenance, punitive damages, that kind of thing. These cases always lose."

Dooher picked up the check from the coffee table and dropped it in Trang's lap. "You know why they lose, and you know why your amended complaint will lose? Because if you ask for three million dollars, you enter the realm of bullshit, and bullshit walks in this town, Victor. I've seen it happen a hundred times. Whereas there, on your lap, is fifteen thousand real dollars—you take a third, right?—five grand for your trouble, ten for Mrs. Diep, and you get to spend your next five years a lot more profitably."

Trang felt as though he would be sick. What Dooher was saying just *couldn't* be true, this case *had to* be a winner. It was the best idea Trang had ever had. If this one couldn't make him some money, he wasn't going to survive in the law. His mouth was sandpaper. Looking down, he saw his coffee cup and grabbed for it. Cold. He swallowed, nearly gagging, trying to think of some response. "I can't take the check without consulting with my client."

The buzz at the telephone gave him a moment's reprieve.

Dooher picked it up, nodded, said, "Okay, let her come on in." He shrugged an apology to Trang as the door opened and one of those impossible women appeared in the doorway—at least Trang's height, her skin flawless, her teeth even.

One step in, she stopped. "Oh, I'm sorry, Janey said . . . I didn't mean to interrupt."

Dooher was coming forward. "It's all right, Christina. Mr. Trang and I were just about finished."

He introduced them. Trang shook her cool and firm hand with his own hot and damp one.

There was, from Trang's perspective, a long and awkward moment, eye contact between the woman and Dooher. She seemed overly self-conscious that she was interrupting, that there was another person in the room. It was clear she had expected a personal moment, and was somehow disappointed.

At the same time, Dooher's bravado faltered. She

was obviously one of his young associates, and yet it was clear that he was struck, tongue-tied, with her.

No, Trang thought, it was mutual, both of them somehow at risk. "I could step outside," he said.

Christina recovered. "No, really. It's just a short message." She was back at Dooher. "I just wanted to tell you that I left my resumé with Joe, as promised."

"Good."

She shrugged. "Joe says from here on it's out of his hands." She deepened the pitch of her voice, put on a stern face. " 'After this, Christina, it all gets pretty objective.' " A flash of that connection again between them.

"Objective works in your favor, Christina. I'm glad you let me know. We'll talk later?"

Trang thought he caught a note of panic in the question. It was nowhere near as casual as it sounded—Dooher desperately wanted to see her again, *needed* to see her again. He could put on any act he wanted in their negotiations, but here in this moment Trang was certain he glimpsed an underlying vulnerability.

But she kept it light, said sure, and apologized to Trang again before turning and leaving them.

When she'd gone, Dooher was lost another instant, staring after her. Then, as though surprised to find Trang still with him, he put on his smile again. The animation. "So, Mr. Trang—Victor—you want to use my phone, call Mrs. Diep now? Feel free."

But the woman's entrance had ruined Dooher's rhythm. He wasn't the same power broker he'd been. Suddenly the pushing to settle *right now* seemed overdone. It gave Trang some hope. Dooher wasn't as tough as the game he was playing. He could be beaten, and certainly Trang would never know if he didn't play it out at least a little further. "I think Mrs. Diep and I should confer in person."

Dooher shrugged. No show of disappointment. He was back in his persona. "Well, that's your decision. The check will be here until noon tomorrow. After that, the offer is rescinded. You understand that?"

Trang was standing. "Yes, I do. And thank you for the warning. I'll consider it very strongly."

A dim shadow fell across Sergeant Glitsky's desk and he lifted his eyes from the report he was pretending to read. A woman stood, back-lit from the fluorescents overhead. Wearily, he pushed his chair back, glanced up at the clock on the wall. Five minutes to five, and here's a random witness come to the Hall. His lucky day. "Help you?" he asked.

"I might have remembered something."

Glitsky had no idea who she was. He stood up. "I'm sorry, you are . . . ?"

She put her hand out. "Christina Carrera. Tania Willows? We met this morning at the Rape Crisis Center."

Glitsky narrowed his eyes. It was possible, he supposed. He really wasn't noticing women these days. The woman this morning wore jeans and a wet jacket and had soaking hair hanging down in front of her face. But he still didn't think he could have picked this woman out of a lineup as the person he'd interviewed in the morning.

He ran a hand across his forehead, assayed a broken smile. "Keen eye for detail. It's what makes a good cop." He sat back down, motioned she do the same, on the wooden chair by his desk. "So what did you remember?"

"I'm not sure it's anything. I was downtown applying for a job. I thought it would be okay if I stopped in without an appointment."

"It's fine," Glitsky said, then repeated, "What did you remember?"

"He has a tattoo."

In the distant future, Glitsky thought these days would be remembered as the Age of Bodily Mutilation. Everybody had a tattoo. Or a nipple ring, or at least something metal pushed through some erectile tissue somewhere.

But unless Tania Willows's rapist/killer had a tattoo of his full name with middle initial, it probably wasn't going be distinctive enough to help Glitsky identify him. But the woman, Christina, was going on.

"I don't know why I didn't think of it this morning, when we were talking." She touched her head. "It just wasn't here. There were a lot of other things going on. And then I was thinking about Tania, what had happened—waiting for the bus, and I saw this guy in an ad with a tattoo . . ."

"Okay."

She paused a minute, swallowed. "It was on his penis."

Glitsky pulled himself back up to the desk, sat up straighter. Okay, this might be something.

"*On* his penis?"

She nodded. "He asked her if she wanted to see his tattoo, and she said sure, thinking it was . . . I mean, you know. Not there. She never thought that."

Glitsky broke a rare smile. "The old 'come up and see my etchings' trick, updated for the romantic nineties. Did Tania happen to notice what it said?"

Christina shook her head no. "I'm sure she didn't. She would have . . ." She trailed off, but the pretty head kept shaking, looking down, embarrassed, Glitsky surmised, by the topic. Her eyes came up to his, and he saw that in fact she was trying to control herself, her laughter.

He knew exactly what she was thinking.

"Not Wendy then?"

"It's not funny," she said. "I don't mean to laugh. No, it wasn't Wendy, I don't think."

The Wendy joke: When the man got an erection, the tattoo read "Welcome to Jamaica. Have a nice day."

Suddenly, Glitsky, whose professional life was a litany of violent deaths, who hadn't slept more than four hours any night in the past month, who had little money, three young children, and whose thirty-nine-year-old wife was dying of cancer—suddenly something broke in him and he couldn't stop himself from laughing. Out loud.

The chief of Homicide, Lieutenant Frank Batiste, had come out of his cubicle to see if anything was wrong. Glitsky hadn't laughed here in the homicide detail in his memory. Maybe nowhere else either.

"You okay, Abe?"

Glitsky had it back under control, raised a hand to Batiste, looked over at Christina. "That never happens to me. I'm very sorry." His eyes glistened with tears. The fit had gone on for nearly half a minute.

"It's okay." Christina had lost it for a second or two herself. "It's supposed to be good for you."

Glitsky wiped his eyes, took in a breath, sighed. "Whew." Batiste went back inside his office. "Sorry anyway," he repeated. Then, unexpected, "I don't know what I'm doing here."

"What do you mean?"

"I don't recognize you four hours after our interview. I crack up over some rapist's tattoo. I ought to take a leave, come back when I'm worth something."

She didn't know how to respond to such a personal exposure, but felt she should say something. "You said your wife was sick. Maybe your brain is concentrating on her?"

Truly sobered now, Glitsky reached for the Willows file. "That could be it," he said.

"Maybe you should call her? See if she's feeling better?"

He waited, deciding whether he should say it. Denial didn't seem to help, so maybe admission once in a while wouldn't hurt. "She's not going to get better," he said. "She has cancer."

Christina sat back. "Oh, I'm so sorry."

He waved it off, opened the file, stared at it for a few seconds. "Was there anything else you remembered?"

7

OUTSIDE DOOHER'S WINDOWS, THE CITY LIGHTS glowed up through the clouds. He sat in his darkened office, elbows on the arms of his chair, his fingers templed at his lips. In the hallways, he could hear the occasional voice—all of the associates at Mc-Cabe & Roth worked late.

Dooher ran a tight ship. His crew—the young men and women who hoped, after seven years, to make partner and thus in theory secure their financial future—were expected to bill forty hours per week, fifty-two weeks a year. This left them no time during the "regular" nine-to-five workday to do administrative work, answer their mail, talk to husbands, wives, significant others, eat, take breaks (or vacations, for that matter), go to the bathroom, small details like that.

To bill eight hours, the associates had to work at least ten, and more likely twelve, hours every day. If they wanted their two-week vacation on top of that, they could count on working at least ten weekends a year. So at this time every day, the firm hummed along. Mark Dooher, who had overseen the downsizing and belt-tightening that had made the place profitable again, felt a profound satisfaction in what he'd wrought. People weren't necessarily happy, but they put out some serious work.

For which, he reminded himself, they were handsomely rewarded. And nobody had ever said a law firm was in business to make its members happy.

He rose and walked around his desk, stopping at the edge of the windows again to look out. Now, with the clouds, there was no view, merely a sensation of floating.

She'd left her resumé!

Telling him it was his move.

Joe Avery was at his desk, plugging away. Dooher knocked quietly at his office door and Avery looked up in surprise—two visits from the managing partner in two weeks. Unheard of.

"Still at it?" Dooher asked. "I thought after last night you'd call it early."

Avery struggled for the proper tone. "That was a good party, sir. I meant to come up and thank you earlier, but this *Baker* matter . . ."

Dooher waved him down. Shut the kid up. "I'm sure it's in good hands, Joe. I came down to pick up the summer apps file."

A worried look crossed Avery's face. "It's not . . . ? I mean, is there some problem?"

"Not at all, not at all." Stepping into the office, he closed the door behind him. "We're handing off your summer clerk duties to another associate, Joe. I think you're going to find yourself with more meaningful work."

"Sir?"

Dooher cut off the expected barrage of questions, raising his hand again. "I've said more than I should, Joe. Maybe I shouldn't have mentioned anything, but you might as well know. The summer clerks are going to have to get by without your involvement. There are bigger items on your agenda, and more than *that* I really can't say."

In another minute, he had the wine box full of resumés under his arm.

On his cell phone in the car, driving home, he left a message. "Christina. This is Mark Dooher. Just wanted to thank you for keeping me in the loop on your application. I'm proud of you. You made the right decision. If you need to talk to me, anytime, the number here in my car is . . ."

He left his home number as well.

Christina didn't hear Dooher's message. She'd talked to her parents in Ojai when she'd finally gotten home from her meeting with Glitsky, and then decided that her day—which had begun with ashes at six-thirty —was over. She was plain done in.

If the phone rang at this time of night, it would just be Joe anyway, and she *really* didn't feel like talking to him. So, with the sound turned down on her machine, she was snuggled under her comforter, in bed and beginning to doze.

The doorbell rang, and she heard Joe's voice. "Christina?" Then a soft knock. "Christina you there?"

She knew she could just lie there and pretend she was asleep, but she wasn't able to do it. Exhausted and angry, she grabbed her bathrobe, wrapping it around her. "One second."

Unhooking the chain, she opened the door.

"You're in bed already?"

"No. Actually I'm standing here in the doorway. You got a problem with that?"

"No. I just thought we might . . . what's the matter?"

"Oh, nothing. Not a thing." She whirled around, crossed the front room, snapped on the floor lamp and plopped herself down on the sofa. "You coming in or not?"

He closed the door after him. "Why are you so mad?"

She pulled her robe close around her, glaring up at him. "See if maybe you can guess."

He spread his arms, all innocence. "Chris. We had a misunderstanding, that's all. Your resumé's on file now."

"File . . . that's good. It really is."

"That's a fact. It's on Mark Dooher's desk at this instant, as we speak, in fact."

"In fact," she repeated.

He went on, oblivious: "He picked them all up tonight—they're giving the summer hires to somebody else."

"Why?"

"Because I'm moving up." He ventured a step closer. "Come on, Chris, don't be mad at me, not to-night. Tonight we should celebrate."

"I don't want to celebrate. I don't even know what we'd be celebrating. I don't even know if there should be a 'we' anymore. I really don't."

"Chris . . ." He sat on the far end of the couch. "I mean it, Joe. Okay, you're moving up, maybe, and I'm glad for you, but where are we going? Are we getting engaged? Are we getting married? I mean, what is all this? I don't get to apply to your firm because we *might* be an item someday . . ."

"We *are* . . ."

"No we're not." She held out her left hand. "You see a ring there? I don't. We're still trying to decide, Joe, aren't we? We're still looking at the *facts*."

He went silent. "How am I supposed to respond to that, Chris? You know it's—"

"No! You're just getting to where you think that after all the time you've put in on our relationship, it would be nice if it worked out, after all." She swiped at the angry tears that had broken. "But the truth is that you don't like how I act, how I *am*. You certainly don't want me working around you, that's obvious."

"But I do!"

"Which is why you didn't want me to apply . . . ?"

"That's not true. You *know* there's a rule about—"

"Stop lying to me! That's not it and you know it! We are, in *fact*, not actually engaged, you realize that? So there's no reason . . ."

"But we were going to be . . ."

She laughed. "Here's how that happens, Joe. Listen up careful now. One person asks and the other says 'yes.' Not too difficult. So how about it—do *you* want to marry *me*?"

"Chris, you know . . ."

"Goddamn it, Joe! It's a yes-or-no question."

"But it isn't! You keep saying you don't want kids, ever, and I don't think . . ."

Suddenly, she bolted upright on the sofa, kicking out at him. "Get out of here! I mean it, get the hell out of here."

* * *

The lifebuoy in Santa Barbara Bay had a deep-toned bell and it didn't seem to be far off—although the fog was so heavy she couldn't see it. She was trying to save her baby from drowning. And she couldn't see it, either. Didn't even remember if it was a boy or girl, though of course she knew. It just wasn't in her consciousness at that exact moment.

The tolling of the lifebuoy wouldn't stop, though. It was pulling her forward, toward it, through the water, which seemed to be thickening as she moved.

There was the baby, so close, just out of her reach, disappearing into the brine. "Wait! Wait! Don't . . ." Sitting up, now, in a sweat. Her eyes opened on the clock next to her bed: 2:15.

The tolling continued—her doorbell. She tossed off the covers and pulled her robe around herself again.

"Who is it?"

"It's me, Joe."

Still groggy, too tired for any more anger, she sighed, flicked on the overhead and opened the door, leaving the chain in place. Hangdog, he stood there, his hair damp as the coat of the suit he wore, hands at his sides. He'd been out walking around for a while, perhaps since he'd left earlier. "I'm a total jerk," he said.

"That's a good start."

"I'm sorry."

She stood looking at him through the crack in the door. Finally, she closed it, undid the chain and pulled it open. He came forward into her, wet and smelling of wool. She leaned into him, gradually bringing her arms up to encircle him. They remained that way a long moment before Joe let go of her, backed up a step and theatrically went to one knee.

"Joe . . ."

"No. This isn't a joke. I want to know if you want to marry me."

"Hypothetically, or what?" She didn't mean it to come out so harshly, but this hadn't exactly been the way she'd dreamed it (if in fact she ever had dreamed it about Joe Avery).

He wasn't going to be sidetracked by semantics. "No, not hypothetically. If I asked it wrong I'm sorry. I'm talking real life here. Will you marry me, Christina?" His hand grasped at the fall of her robe as his desperate eyes came up to her. "Will you please say you'll marry me? I don't think I could live without you."

It surprised her that it was not at all pathetic, as it might have been. He'd finally woken up, realizing he was going to lose her. She saw it in his face. He thought, at this moment, that he loved her. Maybe she could work on that, make it last. It struck her that this was the best she was going to do, and it wasn't that bad, not really.

At last, she nodded. "Yes," she whispered. "Okay."

She reached down and pulled his head close up against her. His arms came around her, clutched her to him.

8

ON THE MORNING OF ST. PATRICK'S DAY, MARK Dooher stood at the door to Wes's apartment and shook his head in disbelief.

"How do you live like this?"

Farrell surveyed his living room, which he persisted in calling his salon. It looked about how it always had since he'd moved in half a year ago, with the books and old newspapers piled on the floor, the television astride the folding chair, the forlorn futon in its unfinished oak frame.

Well, all right, this morning there were a few additions to which the fastidious—such as Dooher here—might object. His boxer, Bart, had spent a few delirious moments savoring the aromas of one of the used bath towels and had strewn its remains across the rug. And last night, Wes had ordered Chinese food and hadn't quite gotten around to putting away all the little cartons. And, come to think of it, there was the pizza delivery container from two—three?—nights ago on the brick-and-board bookcase. The paper plate on which Wes had served himself the reheated spaghetti he'd had for breakfast decorated the floor next to the futon, near his coffee mug.

And, of course, there was Bart himself—sixty-five pounds of salivating dog, lending a certain aroma to the digs, sprawling over half of the futon, chewing a nylon bone.

"Hey, do I make fun of your house when I come over?"

"I'm not making fun. I am truly appalled."

Farrell gave the place another once-over. "I think it's homey. It's got that lived-in feel. Realtors actually pay people to fix their houses up like this . . ."

Dooher was crossing the darkened yellow rug, negotiating some ambiguous stains. "I'm getting some coffee."

"So, Mr. Dooher, tell me again how you found all this out about divorce, one of which you are not getting."

They were in the kitchen, drinking their coffee by the window that looked out over the early morning traffic on Junipero Serra Boulevard. The old metal-legged table was pocked with cigarette burns at the edges of the Formica. Bart had come in to join them, settled on the floor under Wes's feet.

"Gabe Stockman."

"Who is?"

"Who is the official attorney for the Archdiocese."

"And this just came up in conversation?"

"More or less. Actually, we were on the golf course last week and he started talking about annulment. In the Church."

"Maybe *I* could get an annulment," Wes said. "Is there alimony with annulment? But why do you care about annulment? When last we spoke, you and Sheila were in a state of bliss."

"We are."

"That's not what Lydia says."

Dooher had his mug nearly to his mouth when his hand stopped with it, turning it around slowly. "Lydia?"

"We still do speak, you know. Mostly she's digging to find out the secret location where I've squirreled away my last two coins so that she can take them to rub together, but occasionally she does mention something human. And she told me that Sheila thinks the two of you are in trouble, that you in fact might be nearly suicidal which, if that were the case, would make me sad."

Farrell put aside the wise guy pose, rested his own mug on the table, his hands encircling it. This was his best friend and Lydia's information had worried him. It was why he'd asked Dooher over this morning to pick him up so they could drive downtown together for a game of squash and get a chance to talk. He wanted to find out if Lydia's information was true, and if so, if there was anything he could do to help. "Are you all right?"

"I can't say I'm in a state of bliss, but I'm fine."

"Which is why you're getting all the facts on annulment?"

"I don't want an annulment. I don't want a divorce. And I'm not suicidal." He pointed a finger. "Annulment came up and I thought since you and Lydia . . . I thought you'd be fascinated. I thought maybe it could help you somehow."

"How?"

"Well, the short answer is it can't."

"Great. That *is* fascinating."

Dooher was smiling. "Nevertheless, I thought there might be something in it for you, so since Stockman brought it up, I asked. But the bad news is that there's no annulment without a civil divorce. Which of course puts you back where you are."

"That's okay. Bart and I are happy here, starving and all." But Farrell the lawyer couldn't let it go, even if it didn't affect him directly. "I thought the only way you could get an annulment was if you never consummated the marriage, and somehow the existence of my children would cost me credibility there."

"The other way to get an annulment is if one of the spouses isn't psychologically capable of making a real commitment."

Farrell sat back in his chair, his hands outstretched. "Well, there you are! You have just described my soon-to-be-ex-wife. Psychologically, possibly pathologically, incapable of commitment, that's her all over."

"Wes, you were married for twenty-seven years."

"Twenty-nine, actually, but . . ."

"However many, that's going to count as a commitment."

"A mere twenty-nine years? Where I come from, that's barely going steady. My parents were together fifty-six years. Now *that's* a commitment."

"It's beautiful," Dooher said, "but twenty-nine years is going to count."

"Damn."

They had their three games of squash. Dooher won two, letting Wes take the second, 11–9, before creaming him 11–3 in the third. When they'd been younger, both had been roughly equal as athletes; they had, in fact, remained a double-play threat through high school. But in the past few years, and especially in the six months since he had been living alone, Wes had put on about ten pounds and, no surprise, it slowed him down.

They walked together down to the Hall of Justice, where Wes was having a meeting with Art Drysdale, the chief assistant district attorney, about a client of his, Levon Copes, who'd been charged in a rape/murder.

Farrell had originally thought the case had a chance to go to trial, and since the defendant was a middle-aged white guy who owned an apartment building, he had money to pay his lawyer. The initial retainer had been $45,000, the check had cleared, and Wes had hoped that if he played it right, the trial could carry him financially for a couple of years, even with Lydia chipping away at whatever she could.

Since his client's arrest, though, he'd read the discovery—the prosecution's evidence—and concluded that there must have been some mistake. There wasn't nearly enough, in his opinion, to go to trial at all, much less get a conviction. So Wes was going to try to talk Drysdale into dropping the charges altogether. It would be extremely unusual in a case like this, but, he thought, possible.

His success would be the best possible news for his client, if not financially for Wes. But he had no choice. He was a lawyer—if he could get his client off, he had to do it.

Dooher had listened sympathetically to all of this, then left Farrell at the Hall of Justice.

Now he was walking alone uptown the ten or so blocks to his office. The weather continued damnably Irish. The banshee was howling off the bay only a few blocks to the east, the cloud cover occasionally dipped low enough to become fog, and the soft drizzle ate into his bones.

Dooher was wearing a light business suit and no overcoat, but he didn't feel the cold. For the first time since she'd left her resumé, he was seeing Christina again. In fifteen minutes.

The engagement ring infuriated him.

The fucking chintzy little fifteen-hundred-dollar, quarter-carat trinket—he wanted to rip it off her finger, stomp it under his foot, slap her silly for accepting the stupid thing.

But he wasn't going to do that. He was going to smile and say, "It's really nice, Christina. I'm happy for both of you. Congratulations."

They were in a cafeteria down Market Street from McCabe & Roth. She'd left a message asking to meet him, and for her own reasons didn't want it to be in the office. She thought it might be awkward. She seemed embarrassed at the explanation, her head tilted to one side, not meeting his gaze. "I just thought that after our talk, after . . . everything you did for me . . ."

"I didn't do anything."

"Well, I certainly wouldn't have applied without you, and now with me and Joe . . ." She twisted at the ring, gave Dooher a hopeful look. "Anyway, now that we *are* engaged, there wouldn't be much point in going on with the application process, and I thought it would only be fair to come and tell you in person."

Dooher fiddled with his own coffee cup. "You know, Christina, not to get too technical, but the rule regarding personal relationships isn't exactly written in stone. It's devised more to discourage the associates. We've had two or three couples in the past."

He'd fired them, but he left that unsaid.

Forcing his easy smile, though his stomach churned, he risked reaching over and touching her hand lightly. "But again, I'm giving away the house secrets."

Her remarkable green eyes sparkled briefly. "They're safe with me. I'll take them to my grave."

"It's the only reason I tell you."

"And I appreciate it."

Their eyes met and held for an instant. Then Christina shrugged and the smile faded.

"The point is," he persisted, "that if it's not a problem for you and Joe personally, I don't think it would stand in the way of you coming aboard, if that's still what you'd like to do." Not only didn't he think it, he was the managing partner and it was a certainty. He'd see to it. But he was tiptoeing here, afraid to push too hard and scare her away.

"I don't know," she said.

"What don't you know?"

"Just . . ." Twisting the ring, round and round. "Just if I'd want to start with the rules being bent. I'd want to be like everybody else."

Dooher's chuckle was real. "Believe me, once the work starts getting given out, you'll feel just like one of the gang. Do you have any other offers yet?"

"No."

"Well, I'm just saying I wouldn't withdraw yet, on the theory that it's always a good idea to keep your options open until they get closed for you."

"I know that, in general, but . . ." A silence, then her eyes lit again, a feeble flame. "Damn you, Mark." The face lighting now. "This was supposed to be easy."

He sat back in his chair. "I'm *trying* to make it easy."

Shaking her head. "No, I mean just letting this whole thing go, but then here you are, Mr. Reasonable . . ."

"I'm not trying to stop you from letting it go, if that's what you want. I just want you to be dealing from the facts."

She seemed to jump in her chair. "Ahh! Don't say that word!"

"What word?"

"Facts. God, spare me from the facts."

A little came out about Joe, and Dooher told her, lightly, she'd better get used to it if she was going to marry him. "When's the happy day, by the way?"

She shook her head, not exactly the picture of hopeful expectation. "It's not final yet. We thought we ought to wait about a year . . ."

Dooher let out the breath he realized he'd been suppressing since he'd first seen the ring. A year? Plenty of time.

The world could change in a year.

On the third floor of the Hall of Justice, a gray-blue block of concrete and glass at 7th and Bryant, Chief Assistant District Attorney Art Drysdale was having a discussion with an assistant district attorney named Amanda Jenkins and Sergeant Abe Glitsky regarding a murder case: *People* v. *Levon Copes*.

Copes had a tattoo that did not, as it turned out, read "Wendy," but, more prosaically, "Levon."

Unfortunately for the cause of justice, Levon's arrest had come about after Glitsky had interviewed several residents of the building he owned and lived in (and where Tania Willows, his victim, had resided as well). He learned that Levon's tattoo was no secret—Copes talked about it all the time.

So Glitsky had a pretty good idea of the identity of Tania's killer from the beginning of his investigation. Finding other damning evidence hadn't been too hard. Fibers in Tania's bed that matched with clothes in Copes's closet; the same type of rope that had strangled Tania was in the building's basement, to which Copes had the only key; his hairs were in her bed.

So Glitsky had gone to the DA's office with his evidence. Normally Art Drysdale would have reviewed this and assigned a prosecutor. But Drysdale had been on vacation.

Which left Les McCann to handle administrative matters. McCann, a retired-on-duty drunk with seniority, had assigned the case to Amanda Jenkins, who was on record as saying that sex criminals were *worse than murderers*. In the Hall, it was common currency that she was perhaps not the soul of objectivity when it came to analyzing evidence in cases like *Copes*.

She had reviewed the file. She'd had a talk with Abe Glitsky. He told her about the tattoo, which had clinched the *fact* of Copes's guilt for her. Armed with that knowledge, she had gotten Les McCann's approval to go to the Grand Jury and seek an indictment, and Copes had been arrested.

This morning, though, Art Drysdale—home from vacation—got a call from Wes Farrell, who inquired if Drysdale had taken vast quantities of mind-altering drugs while he'd been away. Because based on the discovery Farrell had seen, there wasn't enough in the way of evidence to support a murder charge on Levon Copes.

What, Farrell wondered, was going on?

This was the question Drysdale now put to Jenkins. Her short dark green skirt rode high over legs that, while heavy, possessed some indefinable quality that tended to stop male conversation when she sat and crossed them. They were uncrossed now, her feet flat on the floor, hands clasped tightly on her lap as she was explaining to her boss all about the tattoo and her witnesses and so on.

"Okay, but so what?" Drysdale asked. Feet up on his desk, effortlessly juggling three baseballs as he often did, he appeared calm, though Glitsky knew him better and wasn't fooled. "I can't believe the Grand Jury indicted on this nonsense and I'm doubly disappointed in you, Amanda"—he stopped juggling long enough to point a finger—"for getting conned into this."

Glitsky, in a flight jacket and dark blue pants, leaned forward in his chair. His eyes flicked to Jenkins, came back to Drysdale. "I didn't con anybody, sir."

Drysdale palmed the balls in one hand and leaned over his desk. He knew all about Glitsky's home situation, was inclined to be sensitive on a personal level— but this was business, and Glitsky was, usually, one of the cops that the DA's office could count on. So he had a gentle tone. "Figure of speech, Abe."

"How 'bout this, Art? I didn't *get conned*, either." Jenkins's demeanor was severe as a sandstorm. "Abe didn't get around to the duct tape."

Silver duct tape had been used to bind Tania Willows's hands to the bed's brass railings, and on the inside, sticky part of one of the strips of tape, Glitsky had found a fingerprint that belonged to Levon Copes.

Drysdale sat back. "I know about the duct tape, but again, so what?"

"So that proves Levon Copes did it."

"And how exactly does it do that?"

Jenkins held her lips in a tight line. Furious at this inquisition, she held her voice in a monotone. "Copes pulls the tape"—she was pantomiming his actions—"and his fingerprint stays on the inside. This means not only was he in the woman's room, but he was in it when the tape got unwound, which was when she was tied up."

Drysdale nodded. "I was afraid that was the answer."

Glitsky spoke again, again wearily. "It's a good answer, Art. In fact, it's the right answer."

But Drysdale wasn't hearing it. "No. Sorry, guys, but how about if our landlord Copes came in to fix some pipes, started undoing this magical tape and left his fingerprint on it. Then he simply forgot to take the tape with him when he left. The next day, our perp comes in to do what he did, and there is the convenient tape. Why couldn't it have happened that way?"

God, it got tiring, Glitsky was thinking. There was always some other way it *could have* happened. He knew Drysdale was playing the devil's advocate. None of them doubted that Copes had left an incriminating fingerprint on the inside of the duct tape, but—the point—that wasn't good enough. Drysdale sat back, pondering his options. "The tattoo is what screwed this all up."

Glitsky, from a deep well: "The tattoo means he did it, too."

"Which is where you guys went wrong. You don't *start out* knowing that." He held up a hand. "Hey, I *believe* with all my heart that Levon Copes is our man. I don't see how in the hell we're going to prove it."

Suddenly, Glitsky let out a heavy sigh and stood up. "I thought the duct tape was pretty good. You titans let me know how it all comes out. You need me at the trial, if it gets to trial, I'm there."

The door closed silently behind him as he left the office. His co-workers sat, stunned, in the ensuing vacuum. Finally, Drysdale blew a little gust of air through puffed cheeks. "Abe's having a hard time."

"The duct tape *is* pretty good, you know," Jenkins responded.

Drysdale started juggling again. "You're dreaming," he said.

Glitsky had to get out of the Hall, out onto the street. He checked in at Homicide—no messages—then walked the windblown back stairway out to the city lot behind the building. He always had half a dozen witnesses on other cases he could interview. It was the constant in the job.

So he was driving west through the fog, toward his home—vaguely—and the Bush Street projects where . . .

He didn't know what bothered him the most, that he'd almost lost his temper in the office, or that Drysdale had been right. You really didn't want to start with a certainty about who'd committed what crime. If you did, as Abe had done in this case, there was a temptation to lose sight of the evidentiary chain—the sense of link-by-link accretion that eventually became the working blueprint a prosecutor would use to build a case that would convince a jury.

It was, by necessity, a slow and tedious process, where you questioned yourself—your own motives, your preconceptions, your work habits, every little thing you did—every step of the way. And it was best if the things you discovered *led you* to the only possible correct answer.

He slammed his hand, *hard*, against the steering wheel.

* * *

Glitsky couldn't say exactly why he stopped by the Rape Crisis Center. There really was no official reason. Maybe it was a human one—maybe he needed to talk to somebody. He told himself he was fostering good community relations, something the men in blue were always encouraged to pursue.

"Ms. Carrera said she would like to be kept up on the progress of things."

"She's not here right now," Sam Duncan replied. "But if it's not a secret, I wouldn't mind hearing about it. The progress, I mean. Would you like to sit down?"

He took the folding chair in front of her desk, turned it around, and straddled it backward. "It doesn't look very good."

Sam's shoulders sagged an inch. "Why doesn't this come as a shock? What's the problem this time?"

"You've been through this before?"

It was not quite a laugh. "I've been around rape and the law for about ten years. Does that answer your question?" She sighed. "So another creep's gonna walk?"

Glitsky temporized. "Maybe not. They might still go ahead. The prosecutor wants to put Mr. Copes away, the Grand Jury *did* indict. I'm going to keep looking." He paused. "I think the problem was that I did my job backwards."

She cocked an eye at him. "That's funny. I thought I just heard a cop admit he might have made a mistake. What do you mean, you went backwards?"

He explained it all to her—Christina and the tattoo, the evidence that really wasn't admissible. Finally he wound down.

"So this Copes? There's no doubt he did it?"

"Not to me, but that's never the point, as you probably know. The tattoo can't be mentioned. It's hearsay."

"This sucks. And of course he's got a million-dollar lawyer who's going to make a million more?"

"He's got Wes Farrell. He's good enough, but . . ."

She interrupted him. "I don't understand these defense lawyers. I'm serious. I don't understand how any human being can take a case like this. I mean, this man Farrell, he's *got* to know his client did it, raped and killed this poor woman. Doesn't he? He knows about the tattoo, all of that . . ."

"Sure."

"And he still . . ."

"Best defense the law allows. It's what makes our country great." Glitsky shrugged. "Maybe he needs the money. Maybe it's just a job. Murder cases pay."

"But if he *knows.* I mean, if you really, truly *know for sure*, how can you . . . ?"

"It's amazing, isn't it?"

"It blows my mind, Sergeant, it truly does."

Whistling, Wes Farrell took off his white shirt and tie in the cramped unisex bathroom down the hall from his law office. Farrell often thought he was too easily amused by stupid things, such as the T-shirt he had been wearing under his suit all day—green with gold lettering that read "Take me drunk, I'm home."

Okay. So he was getting divorced, his kids didn't see him much, his career generally sucked, but his life wasn't all bad. He had his health, and that was number one, right? Give or take a few pounds, he still had his body. Lots of acquaintances. And at least one true and great friend, Mark Dooher. How many people could say that much?

Plus attitude. He had attitude in spades, and that's what pulled him through in the here and now—that positive attitude, the vision that day-to-day life itself was okay, even fun.

And now, thank God, he had Levon Copes. He *loved* Levon Copes. Levon was a lank-haired, slack-jawed, sallow-fleshed, hollow-chested, low-life, weak-willed, inbred and brain-dead sociopath, for sure, but . . .

"All together now," he said aloud into the mirror, "DOESN'T MEAN HE ISN'T A NICE PERSON!"

Except that Levon really wasn't a nice person.

But Wes Farrell was going to forgive him for that. He wasn't going to forget about the heinous crime he'd undoubtedly committed. But he had to admire one thing about Mr. Copes—the man had a serious bank account.

Art Drysdale had not given up on the case—at least not yet. He'd told Farrell this morning that the district attorney's office was planning a vigorous prosecution, as it did with all indictments, unless, of course, Farrell wanted to cop a plea.

No, Farrell had responded, he would go to trial on this one, thanks. Because this one was a winner. Farrell knew juries and he knew San Francisco, and you needed a lot more than they had on Levon Copes to convict anybody of murder here.

So he might be going to trial, to a trial that he could win, and a drawn-out murder trial meant that he was going to wind up billing his client a minimum of $150,000 before it was all over. And his client would pay it, gladly; it was the price of freedom.

God, he loved Levon!

So now—tonight—Wes was going to celebrate, maybe even get himself some horizontal female companionship for the first time since his separation. There was no denying it. He felt some spark tonight, some sense of life. He wasn't sure where it had come from, but he wasn't going to jinx it by worrying it to death. The ride's here, boys! Get on it or get out of the way!

He was going to start at Ghirardelli Square, for the view, to remind himself of where he lived, of why San Francisco was the greatest city in the Western world. Heading downtown, he'd hit Lefty O'Doul's, put himself on the outside of some corned beef. Then perhaps a stop by Lou the Greek's, near the Hall of Justice, the watering hole for the criminal legal community, of which he was—thanks to Levon Copes—a member in good standing.

What a city on this night! The possibilities were endless. Flush as he was—out of Levon's $45,000 retainer, he had kept $2,000 in cash out of his checking account, before Lydia could even see it to grab—he was going to cab it everywhere he went, bar-hopping—the Abbey Tavern, the Little Shamrock . . .

By ten-fifteen, he'd had himself half a yard of ale, some outstanding mega-cholesterol food, three extended discussions with interesting people about subjects that had been totally engrossing even if now somewhat vague in his memory. His cabbie, Ahmal, was turning into his best friend—Ahmal had already cleared $140. He had parked the cab just around the corner from the Little Shamrock and would wait all night for Farrell's return.

Getting inside the door through the crush of people was a bit of a trial, but he persevered. He knew the place well. It was on his way home. Small, well-kept, without discernible ferns of any kind, it was the oldest bar in the city—established in 1893! There was often a crowd up front or at the bar, but he knew that in the back there was a mellower area, furnished with rugs and couches and easy chairs—just like a living room, though not just like *his* living room.

So he moved steadily, in no hurry, toward the back. They had waitresses working, which was unusual on a weekday—normally you just ordered at the bar—and he had a pint of Bass in his hand before he'd gone twenty steps. The jukebox didn't drown out the people here, and especially tonight it didn't. The place was bedlam. Only now could he make out "What a Fool Believes" over the crowd noise. He thought it was fitting.

And there she was.

Through the jockeying mass of humanity, he saw her sitting on the arm of one of the couches, leaning forward on her arms, sensual curves everywhere, and one leg curled under her. She was a grown-up, which was about as close as he could guess for her age—beyond that it didn't matter.

Something about her was knocking him out.

He looked away, took another sip of beer, checked for signs of how drunk he was and decided not very, then looked back at her. Yep, she still looked good—medium-length dark hair with red highlights, great skin. Her face was alive, that was what it was. Her smile lit up all around her.

He got himself a little closer. She was in conversation with a couple on the couch next to her, and suddenly the woman who was half of the couple got up—it was magic—and went into the adjacent bathroom. Wes moseyed on over.

She slid off the arm of the couch, into the empty place next to the other half of the couple, a good-looking man. Put an arm around him. Uh oh, maybe not . . . then she looked right at Wes.

"I love your shirt," she said. Then, "This is my oldest brother, Larry. He was fun when he was younger." She patted the arm of the couch and Wes moved up a step and sat where she'd been. "Wes," he said, sticking out his hand, which she took and shook. Over her head, he asked, "How you doin', Larry?"

"Larry's loaded. Sally's taking him home. Sally's his wife. She just went to the bathroom. I'm Sam. I'm staying."

As it turned out, she didn't stay all that long. Sam had apparently been waiting at the Shamrock for someone who looked just like Wes to walk through the door and save her from a night of aimless drinking. So another beer later for each of them, they were arm in arm outside, and there was Ahmal, parked on 9th where Wes had left him. This made an impression on Sam.

He paid Ahmal fifty more at her place, a downstairs flat on Upper Ashbury, and while Sam was getting out, told his good buddy the cabdriver to wait an hour more and if Wes didn't come back out, he could take off, and thanks for the memories.

The door closed behind them on a cozy space—a large open room with a low ceiling, old-fashioned brick walls, built-in and seemingly organized bookshelves, a wood-burning stove.

"You have a dog," he said.

A cocker spaniel was waking up, stretching in a padded basket next to the stove. "You're not allergic or anything, are you?"

"As a matter of fact, I myself own a dog."

"I knew there was something about you . . ."

"His name's Bart. He's a boxer."

She leaned over to pet her little darling. "This is Quayle," Sam said, "with a 'y,' just like Dan. You know, the brains of a cocker spaniel, so I thought, why not? Do you want another drink?"

"Not really. Would you like to come over here?" He held out his arms, and she gave Quayle one last pet, hesitated a moment, smiled, then walked to him.

She came naked through the door of the bedroom, a glass of Irish whiskey in each hand. "The funny thing," she said, "is I don't normally do this."

There was a blue liquid lava lamp from the sixties or seventies next to the bed. The windows were horizontal, high in the brick wall, at ground level outdoors.

Wes was under a thick down comforter, hands behind his head. He reached out for one of the glasses. "I don't, either."

She handed him his glass and sat on his side of the bed. He thought she was as comfortable with her nakedness as it was possible to be, and also thought that was as it should be. Her body was toned and lush, nice breasts with tiny pink nipples. He rested his hand on her thigh. "You can tell me the truth," she said. "It won't hurt my feelings. I can take it."

"That is the truth. I was married for almost thirty years. Now this."

"You mean, this is the first time since you were married?"

"That was it. Am I blowing my cover here as man of the world?"

"No, I'm just surprised."

"Why? It seemed natural enough to me. Pretty great, actually."

She gave him her smile again. "That, too. Me, too, I mean. It's supposed to be such a hassle to get it right, especially the first time."

"Maybe not."

She put her whiskey glass on the side table and slid in next to him, snuggling into his chest. After a minute, he could feel her begin to laugh.

"What's funny?"

"Well, the name thing . . ."

He thought a moment. "Your name isn't Sam?"

This made her laugh. "No, my name's Sam. I'm talking *last* names. You *are* at least Wes, aren't you?"

"Full disclosure coming up." He patted her back reassuringly. "Wes Farrell, attorney-at-law, at your service."

She groaned. "Oh, you're not a lawyer, not really?"

"Realer than a heart attack. We're everywhere."

"Wes Farrell . . ." she said quietly. "I feel like I . . ." She stiffened and sat up abruptly.

"What?" he asked.

"*Wes Farrell!*"

"*Au personne*, which means something in French, I think."

But the good humor seemed to have left her. "You're Wes Farrell? Oh my God, I can't believe this . . ."

"This what? What are you . . . ?"

"What am *I*? What are *you*?"

"What am I what? Come on, Sam, don't . . ."

"Don't you *don't* me." She was up now, grabbing a robe from a hook behind her on the wall. Pulling it around her—covering up—she turned and faced him.

"You're the Wes Farrell who's defending that scumbag Levon Copes, aren't you?"

"How do you know . . . ?"

"Don't worry, I know him." She was fully engaged now, slamming her fists against her thighs, the bed, whatever was handy. "I *knew* it, I just fucking knew it. God, my luck. I should have known . . ."

"Sam . . ."

"Don't *Sam* me either!" Walking around in little circles now. "I'm sorry, but this just isn't going to work. I want you to go now. Would you please just leave?"

"Just leave?" But he was already sitting up, grabbing his pants from the floor.

"Yes. Just leave. Please."

"Okay, okay. But I don't know why . . ."

"Because I can't believe you'd do what you're doing with Levon Copes, that's why, trying to get him off. I can't believe *this* is you. Oh shit!"

"It's my job," he said. "I'm a lawyer, it's what I do."

That reply stopped her dead. Suddenly, the energy left her. She let out a frustrated sigh and whirled around one last time. "Just go, all right?"

He had his shoes in his hands, his shirt untucked. "Don't worry, I'm gone."

It had been more than an hour, and Ahmal had gone too.

Mark and Sheila Dooher had said no more than a hundred words to each other all night. She had made the traditional New England boiled dinner that he normally loved, but he'd only picked at the food. At dinner, he'd been polite and distracted and then he'd excused himself, saying he felt like hitting a few balls at the driving range—he'd been playing more golf lately, an excuse to stay away from home longer, go out more often. He'd even asked her if she wanted to accompany him, but he really didn't want her to—she could tell—so she said no.

Now, near midnight, he was still up, reading in the downstairs library, a circular room in the turret, under her own office. When he got home from the driving range, he'd come in to say good night, kissed her like a sister, saying he had work to do. Would she mind if he went to the library and got some reading in, some research?

She couldn't take it anymore.

She stood in the doorway in her bathrobe. He'd lit a fire and it crackled faintly. He wasn't reading. He was sitting in his green leather chair, staring at the flames.

"Mark?"

"Yo." He looked over at her. "You all right? What's up?"

"*You're* still up."

"The old brain just doesn't seem to want to slow down tonight. So I thought I'd just let it purr awhile."

She took a tentative step or two into the room.

"What's it thinking about?"

"Oh, just things."

Another step, two more, then she sat sideways on the ottoman near his feet. "You can tell me, you know. Whatever it is."

He took a moment. "I played squash with Wes this morning. Went over and picked him up at the hovel he calls home. You know what he told me? That you'd told Lydia you thought I was suicidal. That our marriage was on the rocks." He leveled his gaze at her. "Imagine my surprise to get it from Wes."

* * *

He was being a good listener, leaning forward now, holding both her hands. He couldn't help but notice the hands. They really did age quicker than everything else —you couldn't fake hands. The hands gave her away.

He really wished she wouldn't cry, but she was. Not sobbing, but quiet tears. ". . . no looking ahead, no laughs."

"I know," he said. "It's my fault, too. I suppose I let your depression get to me. I shouldn't have done that. I should have said something."

"But you tried, and I pushed you away."

"I still should have . . ."

"It wasn't you, Mark, it was . . ."

"Wait, wait. Let's stop who it *was*. It doesn't matter who it was. We're talking about it now. We'll fix it starting now, starting today." He leaned over and kissed her. "We've just gotten into some bad habits. You feel like a nightcap?"

She hesitated, then decided. "Sure, I'd like one. Light, okay. One drink isn't going to hurt me."

"You're right."

She held on to him. "I love you, Mark. Let's make this work, okay?"

He kissed her again. "It will. I promise."

9

WES FARRELL EXITED THE CROWDED ELEVATOR INTO the familiar hallway madness—cops, DAs, reporters, witnesses, prospective jurors, hangers-on.

It was just after 8:00 a.m. and the various courtrooms wouldn't be called to order for at least another half hour. Farrell knew that a lot of legal business got done here in these last thirty minutes—pleas agreed to, witnesses prepped, lawyers hired and fired.

This was also the moment when negotiations about plea bargaining got down to tacks. If you were a defense attorney, as Wes was, and you had a losing case, you didn't really want to go to trial. But your client generally didn't like the prosecution's offer of jail time —*only* ten years just didn't tend to sound like a deal except when you compared it to twenty-five you'd do if you got convicted. Maybe somebody's mind would change and your client would get off with a fine. Maybe world peace was just around the corner.

So you played the game and hung tough for your

client, bluffing that you really would put the prosecutor's office through the time and expense of a jury trial. But at some point—such as now when you were in the hallway waiting for trial—this was when you folded your cards and took the plea.

But that wasn't Farrell's intention this morning. He wasn't here to run a bluff. He was here with the outrageous intention of talking the DA into dropping murder charges against Levon Copes right now or, failing that, to deliver the message that Levon was prepared to go to trial. Of course, Levon had already pled not guilty at pretrial, but that had been more or less pro forma.

This was different.

Wearing a black silk blouse and one of her trademark miniskirts, dark green today, Amanda Jenkins was leaning against the wall enjoying this morning's special entertainment. Decked out in fezzes and robes, a dozen or so representatives of the Muslim mosque were protesting the arrest of one of their members for bank robbery, and were performing a *hucca*—a ritual dance derived from the old whirling dervishes. They were jumping up and down and chanting "Just-us, just-us." Several uniformed cops were available to maintain a semblance of order, but it probably wasn't going to get out of hand. These things happened every week in the Hall. To Farrell, it was almost more amazing that no one seemed to think it was that odd.

He came up to Jenkins. "With a couple of instruments, they could take it on the road. It'd really go better with music, don't you think?"

She considered it seriously. "Accordion and tuba. Alternating bass notes. Oom-pa, oom-pa. It's a good idea."

They discussed variations on the theme until they

located an empty bench far enough away to hear themselves talk, and Farrell went into his pitch.

"You can't be serious," she said when he wrapped it up. "You're saying you expect us to simply *drop* this?"

"Like the hot potato it is. I don't really expect it, but you don't have a case, and your boss seems to know it."

"I'm sorry he gave you that impression and I'm sure he would be, too. I just talked to Art this morning before coming down here and he is totally committed to this prosecution."

This was a lie, but Amanda delivered it straight.

"Murder one?"

She nodded. "With specials." Meaning "special circumstances"—in this case murder in the course of a rape. The state was going to ask for LWOP—life in prison without the possibility of parole.

"So why are we having this discussion?"

Amanda straightened her skirt, pulling it down to within four inches of her knees, a move she was unaware of. It didn't escape Farrell's notice, however. Neither did the clearing of her throat. The woman was a nervous wreck. "You called Art."

"True. But then he'd called me back, said maybe we had something to talk about after all. If your best offer is life, I think all in all I owe it to my client to try to get a better deal." He paused. "Especially since you can't convict him, not on the discovery I've seen. He's gonna walk, Amanda, and you know it. Drysdale knows it. You guys fucked up."

"We drop the specials. You plead murder one straight up, twenty-five to life."

Farrell cast his gaze down the hallway, up to the ceiling. "How can I phrase this? No chance."

Amanda was trying to get *some* satisfaction out of

this. Drysdale had told her she was going to have to drop the charges, an extraordinary, once-in-a-lifetime decision in a rape/murder case. This just didn't happen, ever. Except now, it was happening, and Amanda was in the middle of it.

The only chip the DA wanted to play was to use its slight remaining leverage, if any, to avoid embarrassment in the press. Jenkins, who took this stuff personally, was hoping to salvage a little more.

"Wes, your client killed this woman."

"My client is innocent until you prove he's guilty."

"Oh please, spare me. What do *you* think? Really?"

"I just said what I think."

Jenkins took in a breath and held it for a long moment. "Murder two," she said at last. "Fifteen to life. He'll be out in twelve."

Farrell crossed his arms, gave her a worldly look. "Amanda, please."

"What?"

"When's the last time you went to a parole board hearing? Out walk five people who've read the police report, hate your client, and figure he's done it before. At least one is there from some victims' rights group. Your client comes in, says he's sorry—hell, he's *really* sorry—and they say thanks for your time, see you in another five years."

Amanda repeated it. "Still, he'll be out in twelve on murder two."

"He'll be out in twelve *weeks* if we go to trial."

"I guess we'll let the jury decide then. We're not going to simply drop these charges, Wes, and if we go to trial, it's One with specials. That's putting your client at tremendous risk."

Farrell nodded, stood up, grabbed his briefcase. "I'll discuss it with him. See you in ten seconds." He held out his hand. "I'll be in touch."

He'd gone about five steps when the prosecutor called after him. "Wes?"

He stopped and turned. He was almost tempted to go back and put an arm around her shoulder, tell her everything was going to be all right. This was just a job, a negotiation, nothing to take so seriously.

A vision of Sam from St. Patrick's Day—when it had been personal to her, too. What was *with* all these women?

Amanda Jenkins's eyes showed her concern, even panic. The woman was deeply conflicted, but she forced a weak smile. "Nothing," she said, "forget it."

"I had to *try*, Art."

"No you didn't, Amanda."

"Farrell's going to talk to Levon right now, this morning. Levon *knows* he did it. He's looking at LWOP if he doesn't plead. We've got some leverage here."

"We don't have the evidence. Farrell appears to have a pretty good understanding of that."

"He's *got* to convey our offer to Levon. If he takes it, we win. It was worth a try."

Drysdale picked up the telephone on his desk. "All right, you had your try. You got Farrell's number?"

She argued for another five minutes, but it did no good, so she made the call and told Farrell the People were moving to dismiss the charges on Levon Copes "to permit the time for further investigation."

*   *   *

Victor Trang made Dooher drive half an hour out to Balboa Street to meet in some dive named Minh's, decorated mostly in yellowing strips of flypaper that hung from the ceiling.

Dooher hated the smell of the place. He didn't see Trang right away—Dooher had to walk along a counter and endure the suspicious eyes of the proprietor, of the four other customers who sat hunched over their bowls.

Trang sat in a booth at the back, papers scattered around him, his calculator on the table so he'd look busy. There was a cup of tea in front of him, some dirty dishes still on the table, pushed to the side. He wore the same suit, the same skinny tie he'd worn the last time they'd met.

Dooher slid in across from him and Trang, punching the damn little machine, held up a finger. He'd be with Mark in just a minute. Finally—a whirr of number crunching—he looked up. There was a smile, but it lacked sincerity.

He began briskly enough. "I'll be filing the amended complaint next Monday, which gives us a week to reach a settlement agreement, if you're still interested. If not, I'll go ahead sooner."

Dooher tried to run his bluff. "I did tell you that our offer expired the day after we met. When I didn't hear from you . . ."

"And yet you're here."

"The Archbishop thought it was worth another try."

Trang stared at the ceiling behind Dooher. At last, he put down his pencil, brought himself back to the table. "Here's the situation, Mr. Dooher. First, I'd appreciate it if you'd stop insulting me with this talk about the Archbishop's concern for my well-being. I've got a lawsuit that's going to do his diocese a lot of harm and incidentally might smear him with the runoff. He knows it, I know it, you know it."

"All right." Dooher wore his poker face. "I didn't know you. I meant no insult. Some people hear the bluff and cave early."

Trang seemed to accept that. He shuffled some of his papers around, appearing to look for something specific. Finding it, he pulled the page toward him and read a moment. "I've got, let's see, twelve names here."

"Twelve people? You're telling me Slocum was involved with twelve people?"

Trang's self-satisfied smile remained in place. It was getting to Dooher. "I've got twelve people, so far, who are willing to allege a relationship with a priest in the Archdiocese. Three different parishes. It's a widespread problem, as my amended complaint contends. Clearly, there's a policy of toleration beginning at the very top . . ."

Dooher took the paper and glanced at the list. "All of these names seem to be Asian."

"That's correct. Most are Vietnamese."

"An interesting coincidence."

Trang shrugged. "These refugees came to this country as displaced people. They turned to their spiritual advisers to help them through the many adjustments they had to make, and many of these advisers— these priests—betrayed them, took advantage of their weakness and vulnerability." He shook his head at the tragic reality.

Dooher had a different interpretation. "We'd depose every one of these women. You understand that?" Telling Trang what he suspected—that the charges were bogus. Trang had recruited a dozen liars to trade their accusations for a fee—some tiny fraction of the settlement he hoped to get.

But Trang had another card. "They're not all women." Another meaningless smile. "This is San Francisco, after all." So now Trang had priests seducing young men as well, with Flaherty consistently looking the other way. "And of course there'd be depositions. My clients would want to reveal the whole truth, if only to warn others who might be in their position." He made a little clucking noise. "This is the kind of story that will be all over the newspapers, though of course we'd try to contain that."

This, Dooher knew, was the real issue. Trang was running a scam, pure and simple. He was threatening to foment a scandal. And what made it viable was that it wasn't *all* made up. Undoubtedly, Mrs. Diep and perhaps her daughter had been wronged by Father Slocum. Perhaps there was another victim, maybe two.

But *twelve*? Magically appearing out of the woodwork within the last few weeks?

Dooher didn't think so, but what he thought didn't matter much anymore. He had to contain this lunatic. It's what Flaherty expected him to do. It's what he got paid for. "Let's talk about Mrs. Diep for a moment, all right—the suit that's already been filed. She's asking for—"

But Trang was shaking his head, interrupting. "No, no, Mr. Dooher. That is in the past. I've uncovered a widespread problem that would, frankly, benefit from a public forum. Your Archbishop may have meant well, but many people have been damaged. And I think as we proceed that many other victims will come forward. Don't you think that's likely? It's the way these things often go."

Again, the smile.

Dooher knew he was right. Trang's plan was wonderful—he'd prime the pump with bogus victims. Then, once the issue made the daily news, everyone who had ever been kissed by a priest was going to stand up and ask to join the party.

"Which is why we would prefer you not to proceed."

A nod that perhaps Trang believed was dignified, magnanimous. He was going to be a good winner.

Dooher wasn't prepared to be a loser, however. Not to this little upstart gook. That wasn't going to happen. Not now. Not ever. "The Archdiocese wants to redress the wrongs it may have inadvertently condoned, Mr. Trang. That's why we're talking. These people"—he indicated the list on the table—"now they may feel betrayed, but I don't think there's much of a case that they've been substantially *damaged*. Mrs. Diep, yes. Her daughter, okay. We're prepared to give Mrs. Diep her fifty thousand, with another fifty to be distributed among"—he paused, a look of distaste—"among your other clients."

Trang sucked on his front teeth. "If you deduct my fees, that really satisfies no one completely. Thirty thousand among twelve people is an insult for what they've endured. You must know that. And Mrs. Diep will be still be out nearly twenty thousand in cash, plus the interest . . ."

Dooher held up a hand. "We'll pay your fees on top." This upped his offer to $150,000 or so. This situation was making his stomach churn with rage and impotence. *Three times* what Trang had been asking only last week and . . .

And he was still shaking his head no. "I don't think that figure addresses the seriousness of these charges, Mr. Dooher, the sense my clients feel that there should be some *punishment* so that the Archbishop will think twice before allowing these betrayals to occur on his watch. A hundred thousand is a mere slap on the wrist. He'd never feel it."

Swallowing his bile, Dooher folded his hands in front of him. "What do you want, Trang?"

It was a simple question. Palms up, Trang came clean. "The amended complaint asks for three million."

Dooher kept his face impassive. This had become personal, Trang playing him like some fish. But he wasn't going to flop for him. He waited.

"Perhaps I could convince my clients that half of that figure would be a reasonable compensation for their suffering."

A million five! Dooher knew that this wasn't close to what he'd been authorized to offer. And yet if he didn't get to some agreement they'd all have to go to court and the whole thing would become public. Even if most of Trang's clients were invented, the fallout would poison Flaherty. And Dooher would have failed in every respect. He could not let that happen.

"That's too much," he snapped. He grabbed the paper again, ran his eyes down the list. "I'll tell you what we will do, Mr. Trang. Final offer, and subject to a confidentiality agreement, no press conferences . . ." He was showing his temper, and paused a fraction of a second for control. This was his last card and he knew he'd better play it. "Six hundred thousand dollars."

Trang showed nothing. It was as though Dooher hadn't said a word. He was in the middle of lifting his cup to his lips, and there wasn't even a pause. He drank, put the cup down. "That is really excellent tea," he said. Then, as though it were an afterthought. "Six hundred thousand dollars."

Dooher let him live a minute with the number. Then he said, "A lot of money." He didn't say, *And two hundred grand for you, you slant-eyed little prick.* Which was what he was thinking.

"It is a lot of money," Trang agreed, "but it is also a long way from three million, or even one five. If I may, I'd like to take the offer under advisement. Speak to my clients."

"Of course," Dooher said, except he knew that Trang had nobody to discuss anything with. He decided he had to raise the stakes. "But this offer expires at close of business today. Five o'clock."

Trang digested that, then began gathering his papers, packing them into his briefcase. "In that case, I'd better be on my way. It's going to be a busy day."

The sun had come out for what seemed the first time this year, and that springtime sense of hope in the air prompted Christina to walk into Sam's office.

Her boss was sitting on the back legs of the hard chair, eyes closed, with her arms crossed over her chest, her ankles crossed on her desk. Sensing a presence in the doorway, she opened her eyes.

"I hate all men," Sam said. "Well, I don't hate my brothers or my father, but all the other ones."

Christina leaned against the door, smiling. "How do you feel about volunteer rape counselors?"

"I don't think they should be men." Sam shook her head. "I'm sorry about the other day. Sergeant Glitsky came by here and told me *you'd* come down to his office, outside of office hours, doing your job." She paused. "I'm a jerk as a person and a lousy boss, aren't I?"

"Which one?"

A nod. "I deserve that."

But Sam was trying to apologize and Christina

didn't think it was a moment for sarcasm. "Neither, really," she said. "Neither a jerk nor a lousy boss. You care a lot, Sam, that's all. That's a positive thing."

"Too much."

Christina shrugged. "Beats the opposite, doesn't it? I'm going out to get some coffee. You think the office will survive fifteen minutes without us here? Or should I bring you back something?"

Sam considered a moment, then brought her feet down off the desk and stood up. "I'll leave a note on the door."

They waited in line at an espresso place down the street from the Center. Sam's general theme on men had narrowed to the specific.

"Wes Farrell?" Christina was saying. "Where do I know that name?"

"He's Levon Copes's attorney."

"No, that's not it. I didn't know that before you just told me. I know that name from somewhere else."

Sam had omitted the details of her interaction with Wes Farrell, leaving it only that they'd met and she'd given him a piece of her mind.

"Maybe you saw it on one of Glitsky's reports or something."

"Maybe." Christina ordered a latte, her brow still furrowed, trying to remember. When they'd gotten served, they sat at a tiny two-seat table up by the window, in the sun. They shared the sill with two cats, and one of them purred up against Christina's arm. "Anyway," Christina said, "I didn't think last week was the greatest time to tell you—just when you were finally starting to believe that I was a real person who genuinely cared about the people I try to help, which I am."

"I know that now. I see that."

"Well, but . . . so now this is a little awkward, but I wanted to give you notice that pretty soon I'm going to have to stop coming into the Center, doing this."

A long dead moment. "Because of this Tania Willows thing?"

"No. Really because in about a month I'm taking finals, then graduating, then studying for the bar and working full time for a firm downtown, which I hear is about a hundred hours a week. Then *taking* the bar. I'm not going to have any time."

Sam stirred her coffee. Stopped. Her eyes restlessly scanned the street in front of them. "Damn," she said, finally, "this always happens."

"I know. I'm sorry."

"It's all right. I just get so tired of it, where it seems you finally get to where you might connect with somebody . . ."

"Then they leave. I know." Christina was holding her coffee mug in both hands, trying to keep them warm. "So you didn't convert Wes Farrell away from defense work?"

Sam made a face. "I was dumb. I just got mad at him. And it wouldn't have mattered anyway, whatever I did. Copes would just go out and hire another one. Fucking lawyers . . . oops, sorry."

Christina waved it off. "That's okay. I'm not a lawyer yet, and I'm not going to be that kind of one anyway."

"It's funny, because he seemed like a nice guy otherwise. A great guy, really."

"Who?"

"Who are we talking about? Wes Farrell."

Christina looked over her coffee. "You *liked* him, didn't you?"

"I don't know. I might have. Maybe I would have. I don't know."

"Call him up. Say hi. He's got to be in the book. Tell him he's making a mistake with Levon Copes but that you were too hard on him. You'd like to buy him a drink."

Sam shook her head. "I don't think so. I don't know if I want to buy him a drink." Sighing. "It's not that simple."

"But wouldn't it be nice?"

The conference room at McCabe & Roth was meant to intimidate. The dark cherry table was twenty-four feet long and the shine on its surface encouraged neither relaxation nor work. It was a table at which to sit. And listen. And be impressed. The subliminal message from such perfection was that to leave so much as a fingerprint upon it was to vandalize a work of art, so briefcases stayed on the floor, notes were taken on laps.

Coffee cups? Paper clips? Drinks? Food? Forget it.

At one end of the room, the floor-to-ceiling windows worked their power-view magic, while the walls were covered with heavily textured, light green cloth wallpaper. Original oils in heavy frames glowered. Sconced lighting kicked in when the blackout drapes were drawn.

After his debacle with Trang earlier in the day, Dooher was primed to win one. He'd had a bad day all around, in fact, with the Archbishop giving vent to his frustration that even his top offer of $600,000 had not been immediately accepted. Dooher still found himself smarting from the carefully phrased reproof. "It's really not like you, Mark, to let a beginner get the upper hand like that in your negotiations."

There had been nothing he could say. And now close of business had come and gone and he hadn't heard back from Trang, so the Archbishop's offer was no longer on the table. And Dooher knew it was all going to get much worse.

But for now, this moment, he was going to enjoy himself. He sat at the head of the conference table, and checked his watch—5:40. The other eight partners should begin arriving any minute.

He found himself smiling, thinking of David and Bathsheba, and of Bathsheba's poor first husband, whom David sent off to war, promoting him so that he would be at the front of the troops, leading the charge against the Philistines, a hero.

Alas, never to return.

"Joe, you may have heard rumors to the effect that the firm has been considering expanding into new market areas. Well, we're all gathered here now to put an end to those rumors. They're absolutely . . . true."

A polite ripple of masculine chuckle.

Joe Avery smiled nervously from his end of the conference table. Several of the other men looked his way, nodding and smiling. Dooher continued. "We've reached the decision that the first satellite office should be in Los Angeles. As you know, we do a lot of business down there—many of the cases you've been working on, as a matter of fact. We've all been impressed with the hours and effort you've put in over the years here, and we'd like to reward you now by asking you to put in some more."

Another round of club laughter.

"But seriously, and before we get to down to the nitty-gritty of what we're expecting down in LA, all of us wanted to take a minute and say congratulations. And, I should add—I'm afraid I've hinted at this to you before"—here Dooher included most of the partners around the table in a conspiratorial wink—"we kind of rushed your partnership through committee a little earlier than you might have expected.

"We'd like you to take the helm down in Los Angeles, Joe, open the office, get us up and running and put us on the map down there." Again, an inclusive gesture around the room. "Gentlemen. I've seen the future of McCabe & Roth and its name is Joe Avery. Congratulations, Joe."

Heartfelt applause. Joe Avery stood, beaming and basking in his colleagues' approval. And Dooher knew that even if it meant losing Christina, the fool wouldn't let this job get away.

10

ON THE NEXT THURSDAY NIGHT, DOOHER SUDDENLY stopped his reading in the library on the lower floor of the turret. His eyes raked the shelves quickly, all of his senses alert with an overwhelming prescience. Something was going to happen—he could feel it.

The telephone rang. He knew who it was and he trusted these things implicitly. Besides, the timing was about right—four days since Avery had been promoted. He picked it up on the first ring, resisting the urge to answer with her name.

Instead, he was as he always was. "Mark Dooher here," he said. The library doubled as his private office, with a personal phone that he answered in business tones.

A longish pause, then, "Mark, hi." Another breath. "It's Christina Carrera. I'm sorry to bother you at home."

"Christina!" Heartfelt surprise and enthusiasm.

"It's no bother. I wouldn't have given you my home number if I was going to get mad at you for using it." Dooher carried the portable phone across the room and quietly pushed the door closed. It was a little after 9:00 p.m. and Sheila was watching television in the kitchen, doing the dinner dishes. The closed door was a signal that he was working—she wouldn't disturb him. "To what do I owe this pleasure? What can I do for you?"

"I don't know, maybe nothing, I feel very awkward about calling you . . . but then again I've been awkward about everything lately."

As he listened, Dooher recrossed the room, went to his bar and poured a couple of fingers of bourbon, neat, into a brandy snifter. He was nodding, fully engaged.

". . . but I didn't know who else I could talk to. I think I need some advice."

"Advice is my business and my rates are reasonable—well, not completely reasonable. No one would respect me if they were."

He could almost see the relief in her face, her smile. Their banter—Mark's light touch—put her at ease. He was her friend and she was glad he was here for her. He heard it in her voice. "Okay," she said, "I'll pay."

"Good. Lunch on you." Then, more seriously. "What's the problem, Christina? The job again?"

This time, the silence continued for several seconds. He waited. "Really it's not so much the job. It's more personal."

"You're not in legal trouble, are you?"

"No! Nothing like that."

"But personal?"

"Joe," she said simply. "I just don't know what to do."

He sipped his drink, still standing by the wet bar. "We can talk, Christina, but if it's Joe, maybe this would be better discussed with him."

"That's what I'm trying to avoid. I don't want to always be so negative with him. Not when he's so happy with everything."

"It's the transfer I presume?"

A bitter laugh. "I almost want to blame *you*."

"For promoting Joe?"

"I know. It's stupid."

"No, not that. But this move has been in the works a long time. Certainly before I ever met you." This was not strictly true. The decision to open an LA office had been considered months before, but Dooher's decision to go ahead with it and then to appoint Avery was finalized over the last six weeks or so. In administrative matters, Dooher rode roughshod over his nominal partners—he ran his firm his way. It was making money and if the partners didn't like his decisions, one of them could try to do what he did—but without him. He and his business would go elsewhere.

"I know. I *know* that." She sighed. "God, I'm such a bitch."

"I haven't really noticed that. Are you being hard on Joe?"

"Not yet. I think that's why I needed to call you."

"For my permission for you to be hard on your boyfriend? I don't think so." He couldn't bring himself to call Avery her "fiancé." Also, he wanted to deliver the subliminal message—boyfriends were temporary and unsubstantial.

"I don't want to be a nag all the time. That's just it. I'm not an unhappy person. Don't laugh. I'm really not."

"I'm not laughing."

"But now, I can't seem to accept . . . if I talk to Joe, everything I say lately comes out like I'm not being supportive of his career. I probably shouldn't even be talking to you."

"You can stop saying that, Christina. I'm glad you called. I'm just not sure what I can do. The decision's already been made." The drink was kicking in—he eased himself down onto a barstool, relaxing.

"I guess I'm not asking you as the managing partner, Mark. And I don't know if I'm presuming. But you've been . . . I feel like you've been a friend, is that all right? And I need to have a friend who can talk about this, who can understand both sides."

"All right, then I'll take off my managing partner's hat." He lowered his voice. "I'm touched that you thought of me. And I really don't know if I can be any help, but I'm listening."

The good husband, Dooher was finishing a second drink at the table in the kitchen nook, confiding to his wife about the call. "So the poor kid's in a bind. What's she going to do?"

Sheila was drinking her decaf. "This is the really stunning girl from the party, isn't it? Christina?"

"That was her."

"And she called you?"

He pointed a finger, broke a sardonic grin. "Actually, the truth is she wanted me to leave you for her. Said she couldn't live another moment without me and I can't say I blame her. But I had to tell her I was taken." He reached across the table and took his wife's hand. "Happily."

"Are you?"

A reassuring squeeze, eye contact. "Completely, Sheila. What kind of question is that? You know that."

"I know, but lately . . ."

"Lately we haven't exactly been flying. Okay. We've pulled out of dives before. We're going to do it again." He shrugged. "Of course, she was devastated, but she's young. She'll get over it. Probably."

Sheila was shaking her head. "To think that someone who looks like she does could have problems . . ."

"People have problems, She. You did—we did—especially when we were young, trying to figure everything out."

"But I never looked like her."

"Not like, but every bit as good."

His wife beamed and covered his hand with both of hers. "You've got a half hour to cut this flattery out. I mean it." She let go of his hand, picked up her cup and sipped. "Aren't you glad we're not starting out now, you and I? I don't know how these kids do it. I mean, in our day, if you'd been transferred, I'd have gone with you, no questions asked. In fact, I *did* go. Berkeley, then waited through Vietnam, then LA, then back here."

"I remember. And you never complained."

She couldn't stop smiling at him. He was getting back to his old self, the little compliments, the kindnesses. "Well, complained sometimes, but never thinking I wouldn't go with you. Now—these girls nowadays —I mean women, of course, they're women—I mean she must be in her mid-twenties if she's getting out of law school—we had all of our kids by that age, do you realize that?"

"We were unusually wise and mature. Still are."

"But now look at what this girl is dealing with. And all because she wants her precious career. And what's a career? Who wants to have to *work* your whole life?"

"She wants to *be able to* work, Sheila. There's a difference. Maybe she'll need to. It's hard to say nowadays. It's a different world."

"I think it's a damn shame. I'd tell her to just go with her man, and the rest will take care of itself."

Dooher's face broke into a conspiratorial smile. "I don't think I could put it exactly like that. She'd think I was the last of the reactionary pigs. Well, maybe not the last."

"But you wouldn't be wrong."

"Maybe not, but I'm afraid in today's social environment it's one of life's little truths that she's going to have to discover for herself."

"So what's she going to do? What did you advise her?"

"I was punctiliously p.c.—told her, if it were me, I'd stay here and do a great job this summer, study for the bar and pass it, be supportive of what Joe was doing. If they're in love, it'll work out eventually, maybe sooner. Lots of people get separated by jobs, by life. The ones that are meant to make it, make it. It doesn't have to be a crisis."

She took his hand again. "You know, Mark, sometimes I forget what a romantic you are."

He shrugged it off. "I'm just trying to be a good boss. They're both valuable assets to the firm—if they're not happy they won't be as productive."

"Oh, and that's it? All this paternal advice is simply an ingenious management technique?"

"Essentially." He tipped up his glass. "Mostly."

She shook her head, smiling. "Yes," she said, "I'm sure." Motioning to his empty glass, she asked if she could get him another one.

He hesitated. "I'm not trying to be an enabler here, but would you consider joining me?"

She still wasn't anywhere near telling him about the Nardil, her antidepressant drug. She didn't think she'd ever get to there. But Mark was relaxed, in a sensitive mood, open to her. She'd gone back to her wine over the past few weeks and there'd been no ill effects. Now Mark wanted her to join him for a nightcap. If she said no, the mood would be gone, and she wasn't going to risk that.

Midnight.

Sam Duncan sat up abruptly, terrifying Quayle, who'd been asleep in bed with her. The dog yipped twice, then whimpered, and she reached out a hand to calm him, bringing him over the blankets onto her lap.

Petting the dog absently, she swung her legs over the side of the bed. She hated it when she couldn't sleep, and she'd made a resolution that she wasn't going to drink even a drop of anything to make her nod off. The last time she'd had a drink was St. Patrick's Day, and look where that had gotten her.

To right here.

The couple who lived in the unit above her— Janet and Wayne—were silent now, though from the sound of it, they'd had a hell of a good night. Actually, it had been like one of those scenes in the movies where the couple next door let out all the stops and just completely *went for it*. Perhaps Janet and Wayne didn't realize that Sam had come home. Maybe they didn't think sound carried that well through the old building. Regardless, they put on some show over pretty much the complete range of the audio spectrum—vocals, screams, thuds, creaking springs, sighs and moans, you name it. In the movies, it was often pretty funny.

For Sam, tonight, it wasn't. It was damn near tragic, she thought.

But she wasn't going to panic. She was a mature woman and if fate had not supplied her with a mate after all this time, she had dealt with it, made a successful life for herself. The men had come and gone, a few steadies, a fiancé once for a couple of weeks, but for the past four or five years, she'd simply decided to stop pursuing it, stop worrying about it, concentrate on her career and let whatever was going to happen in her love life simply happen. The problem was that nothing significant had happened.

Not until Wes Farrell.

She hadn't been with him more than two hours, but in that time—stupidly, without any reason or explanation—she'd felt more alive, simply *better*, than she could remember. There was just a whole different quality to the way they'd related—complete ease, immediate rapport, sexual attraction, attitude, humor. Of course, she'd been half in the bag. But the half that hadn't been thought it remembered pretty well.

And then he'd turned out to be . . .

Well, what, really? A guy who did a job she didn't approve of? Didn't it come down to just that? What was so bad about him? It wasn't like he was a mass murderer, a professional wrestler, a car salesman. And the violence of her reaction to what he did—though she hated with all her heart to admit it—might have had just a tad of a tiny bit to do with alcohol.

So she did the wise thing first—went completely on the wagon. Thought about the whole issue soberly and while sober. She was thirty-five. She hadn't been lonely before, but now, damn it, she was. Well, no, not exactly that. What she wanted was another fix of *him*.

Christina had said to look him up in the book, and after two days of struggling with herself, she had. There was a work number, on Columbus, no home number listed. And the number was there right now on the notepad on her bed table under the lamp.

"Shit," she said, flicking on the light.

What the hell, she was thinking. It's midnight. He's at home and I can just talk to the machine at his office, apologize for being such—no, not apologize, don't start on that note. I'd just like to talk with him. And she'd leave her number.

But wait. He knew where she lived, and if it had been important to him, he could have come by, rung the bell . . .

Except that, no, she'd thrown him out. He'd probably think, with some justification, that she was a nutcase. Even if he was tempted to come back, he'd think twice, maybe ten times—and decide he'd better not. She couldn't blame him. Also, if she was really, as he'd said, the first woman since his marriage, he'd be skittish. And again, she couldn't blame him.

It was going to have to be her.

I've got to find out if his marriage is over, she thought. That's got to come first. I'm not getting involved with a married man. I don't know him at all. This is dumb.

But she was punching the numbers and the phone had started ringing.

"Hello."

"Oh, I'm sorry. I must have the wrong number."

She was about to hang up. She wasn't prepared to really *talk* with anybody, certainly not with him. She was only going to leave a message. "Sam? Sam, is that you?" It stunned her. He recognized her voice?

She clenched the phone. She should just slam it down. Wrong number. Wrong time. Wrong.

"Sam?" he repeated. "Is that you?"

She sighed with frustration. "I wanted to apologize. No! Not apologize, explain. I thought I'd get your machine."

"You want, I'll turn it on, promise not to listen till tomorrow morning."

"That'd help. Are you still working, I mean at work?"

"If you ask questions, my machine won't be able to answer. It'll get all confusing."

"You're right."

"Also, I think you should know that I got my client—Levon Copes?—I got him off. If that's what you were calling about."

"You got him off?"

"They dropped the charges. The DA decided the evidence wasn't going to stick. He's out of jail."

She took a breath. "Well, that's not exactly what I called about. Maybe a little, but not mostly." Another pause. "Listen, if I promise not to get psycho on you, would you like to meet me sometime for some coffee or something?"

"Sure. I mean okay. I guess. Why don't you tell me when?"

"Would, like, about now be all right?"

PART TWO

11

SERGEANT PAUL THIEU, AN INVESTIGATOR IN MISS-
ing Persons who doubled from time to time as
a translator, rode in the passenger seat of Glitsky's unmarked green Plymouth, chattering away as though he
were on his way to a wedding or a party, instead of a
murder scene. Next to him, Glitsky kept his eyes on the
road—it was dusk and the fog clung around the car like
wool.

Actually, Glitsky was thinking that it wasn't so
bad hearing a voice with some animation in it. There
wasn't much cheeriness in the rest of his life, especially
around his house, where now they had a nurse coming
in every day.

Flo wasn't going to spend her last days in any hospital—they'd discussed it and the family was going to be
around her. Not that she was there yet, to her last days,
but they were coming. Also, Nat—Glitsky's father—was
spending a lot of nights on the couch in the front room,

taking up the slack with the boys, trying to keep things in some perspective, as if there could be any.

But Glitsky had his job. Going to it was a kind of relief. And Thieu, chatter or not, represented the beginning of what might turn out to be a more than normally interesting case.

By far the majority of homicides in the city were what law enforcement personnel referred to as NHI—"no humans involved"—cases. One person from the lowest stratum of intelligent life would kill another, or several others, for no apparent reason, or one so lame that it beggared belief.

Last week, Glitsky had arrested a twenty-three-year-old woman whose IQ soared into the double digits and who'd killed her boyfriend in a dispute over what television show they were going to watch. After she'd shot him, she sat herself down and watched all of *Roseanne* before thinking, well, hey, maybe I'd better see if I can wake old Billy up now. Which, with a bullet in his heart, proved an elusive undertaking.

But occasionally someone with a more or less normal life got killed for a real reason—the deadly sins did continue to reap their grim rewards. These were the cases homicide cops lived for. Glitsky and Thieu were driving to what looked like one of them now—an attorney named Victor Trang, who'd been stabbed in the chest.

"So the way I figure it there's no way I'm going to get to Homicide by moving up the list." Thieu was referring to the seniority list by which promotions in the SFPD were controlled. "The other guys up there—isn't this true?—they put in their fifteen-twenty and by the time they get assigned to Homicide, they are completely burned out. Then they discover they actually have to work weekends and nights if they want·results. But they don't want to put in that kind of time. Hell, Homicide's a reward, isn't it? But they can't be touched because of their seniority. And they still want the prestige of the homicide detail, so they take the job and then don't do it."

Glitsky shot him a glance. "I do my job, Paul. Other guys do their jobs."

Thieu didn't seem affected by Glitsky's lack of agreement. Certainly it didn't shut him up. "I'm not saying that, Abe. I'm not talking about you. You know who I mean."

A noncommittal nod. Glitsky did know who he meant, and Paul had perfectly analyzed the deadwood problem within the unit. It was not Glitsky's inclination, however, to bad-mouth anyone else in his detail. These things had a way of getting around.

"But the point is, I'm being the squeaky wheel. I want to *do* this. This is the action and I crave it."

Something in Thieu's enthusiasm for the work forced Glitsky to consider smiling. The idea of the thrill of the chase had slid away from his vision of his job over the years.

"And imagine this!" The gush went on. "I get this call in Missing Persons and we wait our three days and I just *know*. I know this is a homicide."

"It's a rare gift, Paul."

Thieu caught the intonation and realized he was pushing too hard. But who could blame him for being excited? When he got the call from the Vietnamese-speaking mother about her missing son, he'd had a hunch. In San Francisco, a missing person had to be gone for at least three days before it became an official police matter. And Thieu had gone by the book, waiting the full three days, but sticking with the story as it developed.

"So how many calls did you get in total?"

Thieu didn't have to consult his notes. A graduate of UCLA in police science, crew-cut and clean-shaven, he represented the increasingly new breed of San Francisco cop. He wore a light tan business suit and a flamboyant red silk tie that somehow worked. "His mother, his girlfriend, one of his clients."

"And how long was he missing?"

"This was in the first day, before it even got to us."

"Three people in the first day? This was a popular guy."

"Well, evidently that's a question."

Glitsky, driving slowly, flicked him a glance.

"I looked into it a little, did some background before he got filed officially as an MP." A missing person. "Something the mother said about a lawsuit this guy was working on."

"Which was?"

"Well, evidently he was well known, but not particularly liked—except by his mom and girlfriend."

"Why not?"

"Why not what?"

"Why wasn't he liked?"

"Oh. Well, appears the guy was a politician in the Vietnamese community here. Glad hand, big smile, full of shit." Thieu looked over at Glitsky, checking for his reaction, which was not forthcoming. He was watching the road. "That's not me speaking ill of the dead. It's what I've heard."

Glitsky was paying attention to Mission Street. They were now at the light on Geneva, which wasn't working. Traffic was a mess. The fog made it worse. Darkness was closing in fast.

So Thieu kept chattering. "Anyway, seems this guy Trang was always showing up at parties, gatherings, weddings, funerals, giving his card to everybody . . . a real nuisance."

"I think I met him," Glitsky said, straight-faced.

"Really? You met Trang."

Another sideways glance. "Joke, Paul. Not really."

Momentarily taken aback, Thieu slumped a little in his seat. Glitsky, perhaps oblivious to his passenger's distress, said, "The heck with this," and pulled his flasher out, putting it on the roof, turning on the siren. In five seconds, they were through the intersection, rolling. "So what did his mother say?"

Glitsky's rhythms put Thieu off his own—he'd lost the thread of what he'd been saying. "About what?"

"About some case he was working on that made you think there might be trouble, which as it turns out there is, if you define trouble as getting yourself killed, which I do."

"Well, apparently Trang was suing the Archdiocese of San Francisco for a couple of million dollars or something . . ."

"What for?"

"I don't know. Not yet. The mom said he was over his head, and knew it, but it was a big case. He was scared, she said."

"Of what?"

"I don't know. Just playing at that level, I think. The mom seemed confused about the Church and the Mafia and thought getting mixed up with one was like the other . . ."

Glitsky nodded. "I've heard worse theories. So he was scared. Did he get any threats anybody knew of, the mother knew of? Anything like that?"

"No."

"Well, there's a help."

As was often the case, Glitsky was the first of the homicide team to arrive. The body had evidently been discovered at around 4:15 p.m. by someone from Trang's weekly cleaning service, who, undoubtedly not wanting to call attention to his immigration status, had gone back to the main office and reported it to management. After suitable discussion, the company had called the police. Squad cars from Ingleside Station had confirmed the stiff.

Since they had a tentative identity for the victim, Glitsky had made a courtesy call to Missing Persons and asked if they had an outstanding MP named Victor Trang. Which had alerted Paul Thieu, who'd asked if he could tag along.

A couple of squad cars were parked in front of a squat, faceless, depressing building on a side street off Geneva. Two uniformed officers stood shivering four steps up in a little semi-enclosed portico, smelling of urine and littered with newspaper and broken glass. Identifying himself and Thieu, Glitsky asked them to wait until the coroner and the crime scene investigators arrived.

Then he and Thieu opened the door and entered the building.

Inside, two bare bulbs illuminated a long hallway, in which three doors were staggered on opposite sides. At the far end, the other two officers and either another plainclothes cop or a civilian stood in a tight knot, whispering. Glitsky was aware of his and Thieu's echoing, hollow footfalls on the wooden floors.

* * *

Though the other doors in the hallway were wood-faced, pitted and stained, with the lacquer peeling off, this one's top half was of frosted glass, upon which had been etched the name "Victor Trang" and, under it, in script, *Attorney-at-Law*.

"He had that door made special," the civilian said. His name was Harry something and he lived upstairs and said he managed the place.

Poorly, Glitsky thought.

Harry did have master keys for the building—the uniforms had located him as soon as they'd set up. It was a minor miracle, and Glitsky was grateful for it. "Must of cost him a thousand bucks, the door." Harry was trying to be helpful, talking to be saying something.

Glitsky ignored him and turned to Thieu, to whom the likely presence of a dead person was having the opposite effect than it was having on Harry. Thieu had stopped chattering. "You ever do this before?"

"No."

"You might want to wait then."

Steeling himself—it was never routine—Glitsky opened the door, flicked on the light. Fortunately, he thought, it had been cold in the office. Even now the room was chilly, but he could detect, before he saw anything, the distinctive smell. Something was rotting in here.

In Glitsky's experience, real life crime scenes tended to be prosaically ordinary, rarely capturing the *vividness*, the sense of evil and foreboding so favored by cop shows and B movies. This one, though, Victor Trang's office, came close.

Trang had evidently blown all of his appearances money on his door. Once he was inside, the office reverted to the form of the rest of the building and neighborhood. The long desk was an eight-foot slab of whitewashed plywood—in fact, Glitsky realized, it was another door, perhaps the original. At an "L" to the desk, a table held a computer and printer, the phone, an answering machine.

The walls were a flyspecked shiny beige that may once have been white, and they were absolutely bare—not a calendar, not a picture, not a Post-it. Behind the desk, a dark window, without blinds or curtains, was a black hole. There was a yellow couch along the side wall, a wooden library chair with a pillow seat, a folding chair set up facing the desk.

Slowly, taking it in as he moved, Glitsky walked around the folding chair—had it been set up for an appointment? Was it always where it was now?

He stopped. The chair behind the desk had been knocked over—he could see it now up against the back wall.

The body rested along the length of the desk in an attitude of repose, almost as though—no, Glitsky realized, *exactly* as though—it had been placed there. Carefully laid down.

Trang had been wearing an off-white linen suit, and now it was striped with red, in neat rows. There was a large bloodstain in the center of the chest, but it was roughly circular—it hadn't run down the front of his shirt. Therefore—strangely—it hadn't bled much until Trang was already on the floor.

Glitsky stood looking for a moment, letting it all sink in. He would wait until the coroner arrived, until he'd read the forensic reports, but his impressions were coalescing into a certainty. He knew what the red stripes were. It chilled him.

The killer had used a knife, then had held Trang

up in some death embrace, holding him up, maybe for as long as a minute, leaving the knife in, perhaps twisting it toward the heart. Then, with his victim good and completely dead, he'd laid him down carefully on the floor, finally pulled out the knife, then calmly wiped the blade off on Trang's suit—two or three swipes at first glance.

Glitsky had been a cop for twenty-two years, in Homicide for half of them. From the evidence of what he was seeing here, he thought he might be looking at the most cold-blooded, up close and personal murder of his career.

12

"MARK, ARE YOU ALL RIGHT?"
        Christina stood in the doorway, one arm propped against the frame. Her hair was down. She wore a navy blazer over a white silk blouse, two buttons open, just this side of demure. She wouldn't start her summer job until late June, but she'd been coming in regularly for the past couple of weeks—ever since Dooher had counseled her to be supportive yet independent—to help Joe get his workload organized for the move south.

She'd also gotten into the habit of stopping by Dooher's office after business hours, just before she went home. Daylight saving time had begun two weeks ago, and the office was above the fog layer, bathed in an amber light from the sunset. "Is something wrong?"

"No. Nothing's wrong."

"Something, I think." Moving into the room, she stopped behind the brocaded easy chair, hands resting on it.

He took in a deep breath, held it a moment, exhaled heavily. "The Trang thing, I guess. Can't get it out of my mind."

He raised a hand to his eye and rubbed. Weary and distressed. An apologetic half smile at Christina, a shake of his head. "What's the sense in it, huh? Here's a guy who's just getting started, prime of his life, perfect health . . . I don't know. You wonder. It rocks you."

"The big plan?"

"Yeah, I guess. The big plan."

"Maybe there isn't one."

"It's all random, you mean?"

"If it isn't, what's free will?"

He paused a minute, nodding as though in agreement. "That's a good lawyer question. I'll have to get back to you on it."

Her lips curved up slightly and she came around the chair, sat at the edge of it, pulling at her skirt, meeting his eyes, then looking down. "You do hide behind that, you know? That lawyer pose. The glib answer."

"I *am* a lawyer, Christina. If I'm glib, it's a line of defense. First we argue, then we deflect the direction words might be going, and on those rare occasions when it doesn't look like we're going to win, we . . . obfuscate. But I'm not hiding from you. I hope you believe that."

"I do. I know that."

He shook his head again. "I feel bad about Trang, but what's the point of belaboring it? Nothing's going to bring him back. It's the simple *fact* of it . . . of life being so fragile. I don't feel so glib about that. Not at my age."

"Your age again. How old are you, anyway? Sixty? Sixty-five? You couldn't be seventy." She was teasing him, trying to cheer him up.

"Eighty-three next month," he said. "But I work out." He pushed around some items on his desk. "Actually, since you're as young as you feel, I couldn't be a day over eighty-one." He shook his head. "Sometimes the world gets to me, Christina. I shouldn't burden you with it." Shifting around behind the desk, he flashed his self-deprecating grin. "You're just lucky, I suppose, getting to listen to my moaning."

"I do feel lucky."

"Well, I'm glad. I do, too."

"You do?"

He nodded. "Why do you think the managing partner takes fifteen minutes at the end of the day just to visit, risking not only the office gossip but the wrath of people who think they need my time?"

"I don't know. Part of me thought you were just watching out for me, after talking me into coming here, that I wasn't screwing up."

"I don't believe that."

"Well, a small part, but some . . ."

"None. Not the smallest bit. I don't take care of people professionally—you either do it here or you're out."

"No. You wouldn't . . ."

"I don't recommend you try me. But I have no worries about you. Not one."

She sat back in the chair. "Then I don't know why . . . ?"

"Yes you do, Christina." He leveled his eyes at her across his desk. The moment called for a matter-of-fact, intimate tone, and he got it. "You know, life goes along, and people get so they don't talk to people—I mean you talk, but it's mostly surface, but with you and me, maybe we got lucky that first morning, Ash Wednesday, you remember?"

"Of course."

"What I mean to say is this, it's not common—in fact, it's rare. And valuable. I value it immensely. You ought to know that. I'd hate to have me die suddenly like Trang did and have you not have known. This isn't business. You and me isn't business, okay?"

"Okay."

"And another thing, while we're on it—I'm happily married. My wife is a great partner and a wonderful person and not a half-bad cook. I'm not going to accept any gossip about you and me that this office is likely to put out, and I hope you don't either."

She was smiling now, with him. "I won't. I don't."

"Good. Now, how are things with your boyfriend?"

Abe Glitsky, in a pair of khaki slacks and a flight jacket, was walking down one of the muted hallways toward Dooher's office, accompanied by the night receptionist, an exceptionally attractive black woman of about twenty-five. She was explaining that Dooher's secretary had gone home—was Glitsky sure he had an appointment for this time, six-thirty? Normally, the receptionist was explaining, if she'd known that, she would have stayed.

"I made it with Mr. Dooher personally," he said, noncommittal. "Maybe he didn't mention it to her."

Glitsky was struck by the color of the light. The doors to several west-facing offices were open and the sun was going down over the cloud banks, spraying the hallway with crimson.

In almost every office he saw a young person hunched over a desk, oblivious to the sunset, to everything but what they were reading or writing.

Fun job.

Dooher was standing in his doorway, talking to yet another beautiful woman. Glitsky figured they grew on trees at this altitude.

"Sergeant Glitsky?"

She was smiling at him, holding out her hand, and he realized he knew her—from the rape clinic, and then that visit to his office. What was she doing here?

"Christina Carrera." Helping him out.

"Right. Levon Copes," he said. "And I'm still looking."

This seemed to register positively. "I'm glad."

The man with her—Glitsky presumed it was Dooher—stepped forward. Protectively? "You two know each other?"

Christina quickly explained while Glitsky checked out the man in his thousand-dollar pale gray Italian suit. The only wrong note was the hair—no gray, which meant the guy was vain and had a bottle of Grecian Formula hidden in the back of his sock drawer. Glitsky figured if he looked like Mr. Dooher, he'd be vain too. But he'd have to go some before he decided to dye his hair.

The receptionist had disappeared. Christina was asking if Glitsky was the only homicide inspector in town.

"Sometimes it feels like it."

"I don't know how you do it," Christina said. "Up until a couple of months ago, I never knew anybody who'd been murdered, and now I've met two—Tania Willows and Victor Trang. It's unsettling."

"You knew Trang?"

"I met him here in Mr. Dooher's office once. Still . . ."

"It is easier if you don't know them first." Glitsky

tried to mitigate the cop humor of what he'd just said by smiling, but his scar got in the way. "I know what you mean, though."

"It's terrible," Dooher said. "Christina here and I were just talking about Victor Trang, the waste of it."

"You were in Vietnam?"

Christina had gone away—Glitsky had no questions for her. He and Dooher went into the big corner office and they had more or less finished with the routine questions. Glitsky was still seated on the sofa, his tape recorder spinning silently on the coffee table. The receptionist had brought him a cup of tea, and it was excellent. With a slice of lemon yet. He would take the moment of peace until the cup was drained. They were hard enough to come by.

Dooher was volunteering information. It probably had no connection with Victor Trang, but Glitsky's experience was that a murder investigation led where it took you, and the most innocuous comment or detail could be the hinge upon which it all eventually turned. He sipped his tea, leaned back in the soft leather, waited for whatever was coming next.

The strange red sky had gone mother-of-pearl and Dooher had loosened his tie. He was drinking something amber without ice, pacing around, leaning on the edge of his desk, crossing to the easy chair, to the floating windows. Nervous, Glitsky thought. Which wasn't unusual. He knew that people—even attorneys—got jittery when they talked to homicide inspectors. It would be more suspicious if he wasn't.

"That's why I was surprised I found myself liking him. Trang, I mean." Dooher sighed. "I don't like to admit it, but it's one of the prejudices I've carried around all these years. Maybe it's genetic. My dad had the same thing with the Japs—the Japanese . . . *he* always called them Japs. Me, now, some of my best friends . . ."

Glitsky kept him on it. "So how'd you like it, Nam?"

"You go?"

He shook his head. "Bad knees. Football."

"Yeah, well, maybe you've heard—it sucked."

Glitsky had come upon that rumor. "You see action?"

"Oh yeah. We got ambushed and most of my squad got killed." He swigged his drink. "I still don't know why I survived and the other guys . . . and then the warm welcome at home, that was special." He looked over at Glitsky. "I was bitter for a while. Blamed it on the Vietnamese. Ruined my life, all that."

"Did they?"

Dooher took in his plush surroundings. "No, that was all youth, I suppose. Excuses. Look around, my life isn't ruined. I've been lucky."

Suddenly he snapped his fingers, went around his desk and opened a drawer, pulled something out and handed it to Glitsky. "These were the guys."

It was a framed color photograph of a bunch of soldiers, armed and dangerous, goofing and scowling. Dooher was in the front row, on the far right, with his captain's bars, his weapon propped next to him. "I had this up in that space in the bookshelves here till just before Trang came up here the first time. Then I realized it would be offensive to him. I guess I can put it back up now."

Glitsky handed it back. "They're all dead?"

"I don't know all. Three of us came home, i know

that. But I haven't seen either of the other two in maybe fifteen years."

The tea had cooled. Dooher went back around the desk and placed the frame in its former space, in full view now. "Anyway, they trained me pretty well," he was saying, "to hate 'em. Charlie, I mean."

"So what happened with Trang?"

"Like anything else. You finally meet one personally, get to know 'em a little, and you realize they're people first. I just put off meeting any of them for a long time. I *wanted* to keep hating them, you see? So the war would make some kind of sense. Dumb. It's so long ago now."

"So who still hated him?"

"Trang? I don't know."

"I understand he was suing you . . ."

Dooher had settled in the easy chair. He leaned forward, elbows on knees. "Well, that's technically accurate. He'd filed a lawsuit where some priest took money from a woman. He was amending the suit, that was all. Trying to get more. Hey, it's his job. Anyway, I represent the Archdiocese. The whole thing hadn't gone very far. That's just our business. Litigation. Personally, we were on good terms."

Glitsky didn't have any reason to doubt Dooher. He did believe that the killer was probably a tall, strong male, and though that described Dooher, he didn't have a patent on the build. "I'm wondering if he mentioned anything to you about anybody else—clients, colleagues . . ."

The attorney gave it a long moment. "Honestly, I can't think of anybody. I'll put my mind to it if you'd like."

"I'd appreciate that." Standing, Glitsky turned off his recorder and slipped it into his pocket. He handed

Dooher his card. "If something comes to mind, that's me, day or night."

Dooher accompanied him to the door, opened it for him. The cotton clouds out the window had begun to glow with the lights coming on in the streets below. "Do you have any leads at all, Sergeant? Who might have done this?"

"No, not yet. It's still early, though. Something may come up."

"Well, good luck." They shook hands, and Glitsky turned to leave as the door closed quietly behind him.

13

Wes Farrell and Sam had been going out for a couple of weeks now and hadn't yet moved into the "serious" phase, as they called it, of what they were also calling their quote relationship unquote. There was no plan as yet to escalate. Things were nicely physical. They were getting along, moving back and forth between their places, taking care of their respective dogs, although Quayle and Bart had yet to meet.

Wes was flirting with what felt like his first happy and carefree moment in about half a decade. It was the Saturday evening after a noon wake-up, followed by lovemaking and the Planetarium in Golden Gate Park. They'd sat in the plush reclining seats holding hands as the night sky came up indoors—Farrell learned more than he ever thought he'd need to know about the planet Neptune. Although you never knew—facts had a way of coming in handy.

They ended up sharing a short drink at the Little Shamrock, the bar where they had met.

It didn't hurt that the winter cold had lifted. Not that it was balmy, but anything above forty-five degrees seemed a gentle gift. The wind and fog were both gone, and here at dusk Wes was comfortable half-reclining in the chaise outside, wearing blue jeans and a sweater on Sam's tiny fenced-in deck, surrounded by potted greenery, in the cupola created by three large redwood trees. She'd handed him a perfect martini—gin had always been, to Wes, the harbinger of summer—and told him she'd be out in a minute to join him, as soon as she'd put the game hens on to roast.

Sam was making him dinner, a first step into the heretofore dreaded return of the domesticity that had failed him so miserably the first time around.

They had talked about the implications of the dinner and decided they could risk it. Besides, Sam had pointed out, it wasn't going to be just the two of them and Quayle. Nothing that intimate. Other guests would be there to buffer the raging magnetic attraction that was nearly ripping the skin off their bodies. There was going to be some lawyer woman from her office, Christina, and her fiancé, another lawyer, Joe. And Sam's brother—remember Larry and Sally?—would serve to balance out the lawyer ratio.

Wes sipped his drink. Sam thought he might be nervous meeting all these people in her circle at the same time. He supposed maybe one day long ago this kind of situation might have had that effect, but today there was nothing but a sense of the exhilaration of new beginnings. Hope. It was great.

The door creaked. A hand on his shoulder. The scent of her as she leaned over from behind the chaise, laid a soft hand against the side of his face.

"You know what I can't believe," she said. She came around the lounge chair, holding her own martini. Farrell loved a woman who drank like he did. He also loved the look of Sam—the way she had filled her glass right to the rim, slurping at it delicately to get that first taste, puckering her lips around it. "Um-um." She was wearing jeans, too. And a white sweater. And hiking boots. She looked seventeen.

He smiled up at her. "What can't you believe?"

"I can't believe that Pluto's going to be inside the orbit of Neptune for the next eleven years. So it's not Jupiter, Saturn, Uranus, Neptune and Pluto anymore; it's Jupiter, Saturn, Uranus, Pluto and Neptune."

"That wacky old solar system," Wes said. "Just when you think you got it all figured out." He moved his legs off the recliner, patted it with his palm, and Sam sat, the haunch of her leg tight up against him. He grinned at her. "The good news is that this is the kind of fact on which I believe we can make some money."

Larry and Sally arrived first. The sun was down and Wes was back inside with Sam—another round of gin poured and good smells emanating from the kitchen—everybody already getting along, laughing about St. Patrick's Day.

"Hey, the parts I remember were great." Larry, defending himself from his sister's mock attack.

"And how many parts do you remember?"

Larry paused, considering. "At least two."

"Including meeting Wes?"

He gave Farrell an appraising glance, shook his head. "I'm afraid that particular moment didn't make the cut. Where were we exactly? No offense, Wes."

"You had the T-shirt," Sally said to Wes. She was

as tall as her husband, with long dark hair that had gone about a third gray. Her friendly, attractive face showed more age than Sam's. She also wore nicer clothes, some makeup, dangling earrings.

"That's what did it," Sam said. "The shirt. I saw that shirt and read the message and said, 'Here's a guy I've got to meet.' "

"I thought it was how it fit me."

"That, too," she said. "That's what I meant."

"You guys." Sally was smiling. "No foreplay until after dinner. It's one of the rules."

"What shirt?" Larry asked.

Farrell recognized them both immediately. Shaking Joe's hand, taking in the woman—Christina Carrera. Yep, it was her, no doubt about it. Not looking any uglier either, he noticed. And it looked as though she'd found the right guy—Joe Avery was tall and thin, with an angular, clean-shaven face, shoulders a yard wide and no gut at all. It wasn't fair.

"You're at McCabe & Roth, aren't you?"

Joe included Christina. "We both are."

"Not quite yet."

"Close enough." Then, placing Wes. "You've been to the office . . ."

"No more than two, three hundred times. Mark Dooher's my best friend."

Christina snapped her fingers. "*That's* it." Explaining. "I *knew* I knew the name Wes Farrell. When Sam told me . . . it's been driving me crazy. You go on camping trips or something with Mark, right?"

"Occasionally. Retreats, we call them."

Joe Avery was looking a question at Christina, but Sam was coming up, kissing her on both cheeks, getting introduced to Joe. "Okay you lawyers, break it up. No professional talk until we've all said hello. At least."

The moment passed.

Sam and Sally were in getting dessert and Larry had gone to the bathroom.

Joe turned to Christina. "So how do you know about these retreats?"

"Mark told me about them, one of the first times we talked. I don't remember exactly. It just came up." She turned to Wes, hoping to deflect the line of questioning from Joe. "He said you guys go out and get recharged on life."

Farrell shrugged. "Mostly we drink," he said. Then, continuing to make light of it, "Get away from the day-to-day. Talk about what we believe in, in theory. Try to beat the burnout which you know, Joe, is a constant." Wes drank some more wine and smiled at Christina. "You'll find out after you've been at this business a year or so."

Joe shook his head. "I can't see it with Mr. Dooher . . . Mark. He doesn't seem like he's on the burnout track. He's always geared up."

"Joe, he's got to act that way." Christina, rushing to Dooher's defense, nearly blurted it out. "You don't want your managing partner moping around, making you feel like it's all so hard."

"Well, he doesn't do that, that's for sure."

"Yeah, but I think Christina's right. He acts tough, but if you know him . . ."

Christina laughed. "Don't tell me he's a pussycat. A gentle heart, maybe, but . . ."

"No way." Joe couldn't envision it. "Maybe with you guys, but I've worked for him a lot of years, and

Mark Dooher does not invite closeness." Joe looked around the table, perhaps realizing he was being too negative. He caught himself, nearly knocking himself over backtracking. "Although, lately, I must admit—I don't know exactly what happened—he's been fantastic."

"You got over the hump, that's all," Farrell said. "You proved yourself."

"Is that it?"

Farrell nodded. "That's Mark. He used to be too soft—one of the guys, you know. Didn't want to give orders, set himself above anybody."

Avery laughed. "Well, he sure got over that one."

"Joe!"

"That's a fact, Christina. Say what you want about Mark, being afraid to give orders isn't what he's about anymore."

Farrell stopped them. "You're responsible for ten people dying, Joe, it hardens you right up."

In the silence, Christina finally spoke up, "What do you mean, dying?"

Farrell made a face. He hadn't intended to bring this up. It was too personal. One of Dooher's true ghosts. But to drop it now would only arouse more curiosity. Better to downplay it—God knew it did relate to their discussion.

"Mark was in Vietnam," he said. "Platoon captain, about a dozen guys under his command. This being Vietnam, as you may have heard, the guys smoked some dope."

"Did they inhale?" Joe asked. "Mr. Dooher smoked dope?"

Farrell shook his head. "No, I don't think so. But his men did."

"So what happened?" Christina asked.

"So Mark knew how bad things were over there, and he knew the dope made it bearable for his troops—regular guys pretty much his age—so he made an unspoken policy that they had to be straight when they were going out on maneuvers, but otherwise he wasn't busting anybody for a little dope. He thought it was a reasonable rule and so everybody would follow it."

"What was a reasonable rule?" Larry, returning from the bathroom, didn't want to be left out.

Wes shortened it up. "My best friend happens to be the managing partner of Joe's law firm," he said. "We were talking about how he got to be such a hardass to work for. And the answer is Vietnam. He didn't exert his authority, didn't take charge. So his troops went out on patrol it turned out they were stoned to the eyeballs and got themselves ambushed and most of 'em died. I don't think he's ever forgiven himself for that."

"Jesus." Joe clearly wasn't used to stories like this one. "You get used to thinking in business terms, how maybe somebody beat him in a deal or something, but this . . ."

"No, this wasn't like that. This was real. So now he's more careful. He's got to be. Problem is—and I've known him my whole life—underneath he really does want to give people a break, but people, you cut 'em some slack once and next time they expect it again, so they don't perform as well as they might and that doesn't help anybody. So he's a bastard at the firm."

"He is not." Christina didn't like the language at all. "He is nothing like a bastard."

Wes held up his hands. "He's my best friend, Christina. We're a little free with what we call each other. He's been known to be less than flattering to me."

"Who has?"

Sam was coming back in with a large plate of cut fruit and cheeses. Wes rolled his eyes. They weren't going over this whole thing again. Enough Mark Dooher, already. "Nothing," Wes said. Then: "I've got five dollars that says Neptune is the last planet in our solar system." He winked at Sam.

"No, it's Pluto," Joe said.

"It *is* Pluto." Christina was sure too. Larry and Sally were nodding in agreement.

Wes extended his hand out over the table. "Five bucks," he said. "Just slap my palm."

"That was cruel," Sam said.

The guests had all gone home. She and Wes were having some port, sitting on the love seat they'd pulled in front of the wood-burning stove. Quayle was curled over her feet.

"Cruel but cool," Wes said, "and we did make fifteen dollars, and it could have been twenty if Sally had ponied up her own five."

"They're married," Sam said. "Married people never do that."

"I remember."

A piece of wood popped in the grate. Wes raised his glass to his mouth and realized he'd had enough tonight—gin, wine, port. Maybe for tomorrow, too. The silence lengthened.

"You all right, Wes?"

He brought her in closer against him. "I'm fine."

" 'Fine' isn't the strongest word in the dictionary."

"Okay, I'm ecstatic."

"This wasn't too much tonight—the family stuff, dinner at home?"

He had to chuckle. "I assure you, this wasn't anything like any dinner I've ever had with Lydia, at home or anywhere else. In the first place, you can cook."

"I'm not pushing anything," she said.

"I know, not that I couldn't handle a little of that, even. But it was fun. I had a great time. I enjoyed your brother and sister and thought your friend Christina was charming and lovely and I think you are fantastic, although I'm not absolutely sure I'm going to respect you in the morning."

She put her own glass down, took his hand from where it rested on her shoulder and placed it on her breast. "I hope not," she said.

"Let's go find out."

At about the same moment that Wes Farrell was enjoying his first martini that evening, Mark and Sheila entered St. Emygdius Church to attend Saturday night mass.

They walked together down the center aisle and chose a pew about ten rows from the front. There were more than fifty people in the church, a good showing. The congregation had come early to take part in the Reconciliation Service, which had for most Catholics replaced the old, often humiliating sacrament of Confession. Now, sinners were offered an opportunity to reflect on their weakness, privately resolve to do good, and then be communally absolved of any guilt without having to confront another human being or suffer the minor indignity of a formal penance.

Today, though, before the priest had come onto the altar to begin the Reconciliation Service, Mark leaned over and whispered to Sheila that he was going to use the real confessional, which was still an option. "I'm old-fashioned," he said. "It does me more good."

He didn't know what priest would be sitting in the confessional, but there was a good chance he'd know Dooher, and vice versa. All the priests at St. Emygdius knew him. Maybe not, though. Often a visiting priest would get the chore of Saturday confession.

Dooher would let fate dictate it.

He nodded his head, made the sign of the cross, stood up and opened the confessional door. The familiar smell of it—dust and beeswax—filled his soul, as did the comforting darkness. Then the window that separated him and the priest was sliding open. The man recognized him immediately.

"Hello, Mark, how are you doing today?"

It was Gene Gorman, the pastor, who'd been to the house fifty times for poker, for dinner, for fund-raisers, who got a bottle of Canadian Club every Christmas, who'd baptized Jason, their youngest.

Dooher paused. "Not so good, I'm afraid," he whispered. He let the silence gather. Then: "I don't want to burden you, Gene."

"That's what the sacrament's for, Mark."

Dooher hesitated another moment. Hesitation heightened the gravity of things. "Would you mind not using my name? Is there someone in the other stall?"

The confessionals at St. Emygdius, as in most Catholic churches, had three compartments—one in the middle for the priest, and one on either side of him for the repentants. This time the hesitation came from Father Gorman. Dooher heard him slide open the window on the other side, then close it. "No, we're alone. You can begin."

The old words, the ritual he so loved. Again he made the sign of the cross. "Bless me father, for I have sinned . . ."

14

JOHN STROUT, SAN FRANCISCO'S CORONER, WAS A
gangly southern gentleman of the old school. He
had a prominent Adam's apple, a perennially bad case of
dandruff in his wispy gray hair, poor taste in clothes and
a pronounced Dixie accent. He was also, rube or not,
one of the country's most respected forensics experts,
and now he was taking a morning walk with Glitsky
through the debris and detritus of south-of-Market San
Francisco.

It was Monday morning—sunny, breezy and cold.
Strout was, of course, a medical doctor, and—after a
lifetime of bad morning coffee and stale donuts—had
recently become a convert to the theory that a healthy
breakfast was the key to a long life and perhaps even
more luxuriant hair growth. Like all good converts, he
had found the truth and was going to spread the word
around, goddamn it. Like it or not.

So, whenever feasible, he'd taken to briefing cops
and DAs about his forensics reports over breakfast in

one of the city's eateries. It never occurred to him that discussing the finer points of often gory violent death, complete with color photographs, might not be particularly conducive to stimulating the early-morning appetite.

It did occur to Glitsky.

Strout had finished the PM on Victor Trang on the previous Friday afternoon, and Glitsky had—atypically, in Strout's experience, probably because of his troubles at home—said he'd be free to discuss the results first thing Monday morning. Let the weekend intervene. Why not?

"I'll just look at the pictures while we're walking here if you don't mind, John." With a show of reluctance, Strout handed over the folder, and put his now empty hands into the pockets of his greatcoat against the chill. "What do we have? Any surprises?"

"Way'll, as a matter of fact . . ."

Glitsky closed the newly opened folder. "What? I'll listen first."

"Surprise may be too strong a word, but the deceased here got himself gutted by a pigsticker of the first order."

"Pigsticker?"

"Knife."

"A pigsticker is a certain kind of knife?"

Strout's expression betrayed a certain intolerance. "Damn, you Yankees . . . pigsticker *means* knife. Generically. Victor Trang got stabbed by a big knife, is that clearer? And not just any big knife, something like a Bowie or my own favorite guess, a bayonet. Y'all familiar with the term 'bayonet'?"

Glitsky played along. "I've heard of it. Made by the Swiss Army people, right? Whittling tool."

"Yeah, that's it, 'cept the large version." Strout put

a hand on Glitsky's arm and stopped him as they walked. "Open the file," he said. The breeze gusted and they moved into the entrance of an office building, out of it. "The photos."

Glitsky followed instructions, flipping over glossies of the murder scene, the body as he'd found it, then as it looked from various angles stripped on the morgue table. Finally Strout put his finger on one. "There you go. That one."

It was an extreme color close-up that Glitsky recognized all too soon. The wound itself, after the area had been washed—long and wider than most knife wounds he'd been witness to.

"You see there?" Strout was saying. "Right at the top?"

Glitsky squinted, not clear on what he was supposed to recognize. Strout moved in closer, put his finger on the area over the top of the gash. "Right here. You see that half-moon? The little circle under it? Know what that is?"

Glitsky took a second, then guessed. "It's an imprint from the haft of the knife."

The coroner was pleased. "I must say, it is a pure pleasure to work with a professional. That's exactly what it is. The perp stabbed him so hard and so far up, the haft left this little fingerprint, which is pretty damn distinctive, you ask me. Actually cut into the skin above the blade area. I wouldn't put my name on it as a definite"—this was because he could never prove it for certain and some attorney might discredit his entire testimony if he wasn't one hundred percent positive and correct on every detail—"but between us, this could be nothing but a bayonet."

Strout reached inside his greatcoat and extracted a

folded brown paper shopping bag. "As a matter of fact . . ."

"You just happen to have one handy."

This wasn't as unusual as it might have appeared. Strout's office contained an impressive collection of murder weapons from throughout the ages—maces, crossbows, garroting scarves, sabers, handguns and Uzis. And, apparently, bayonets.

He withdrew it from the bag, hefted it affectionately, handed it to Glitsky. "I thought I'd cut my steak with this at breakfast. Make an impression on our waiter. But look."

Abe was already looking. It was, as Strout had noted, a pigsticker of the first order. Where the blade met the handle of the knife was an oversize steel haft with a half-inch circular hole through the metal.

Strout was pointing again. "That's where it connects to the mount on the rifle." Then back to the picture. "It's also why there's that kind of double circle —the top of the haft, then the punch-out area . . . couldn't really be anything else."

"How common are these things, you think?"

Strout shrugged. "Way'll, they ain't exactly Carter's Pills, but anybody wants could get ahold of one. Army/Navy stores, gun clubs, mail order, good old paramilitary-type boys saving our country from the government . . . your guess is as good as mine. Round here they probably wouldn't be as common as, say, in Idaho or Oregon, but you'd find 'em."

"Also, ex-army," Glitsky said. Suddenly, he experienced a small jolt of connection. Mark Dooher. Vietnam and his dead troops. He closed his eyes, trying to revisualize the photograph he'd seen in the attorney's office, whether there might have been a bayonet mounted on any of the many weapons displayed. He couldn't see it, couldn't bring it back.

But Strout was going on. "Actually, Abe, that might be a tougher nut. If memory serves, they take your weapons away when they muster you out. Course, you could smuggle 'em . . . people probably been known to."

Rubbing his thumb over the bayonet's blade, Glitsky nodded. "I don't think so," he said. "That would be illegal."

After his Monday morning breakfast meeting with John Strout, Glitsky had planned to get right on the Trang investigation—murders that didn't get solved in the first couple of days very often never did. But when he'd come back to the office, there had been another homicide. He had been on call *last* week, so normally this would have been someone else's problem, but this week's inspector had called in sick and gone salmon fishing, and Glitsky appeared just as his lieutenant, Frank Batiste, had despaired of finding an inspector to assign.

Apparently, a fry cooker who'd been fired from a Tastee Burger in the lower Mission had returned to the scene of his humiliation and gone postal—a new expression Glitsky loved. The ex-employee naturally killed none of the people with whom he had a gripe. He did, though, by mistake before he killed himself, end the life of a seventeen-year-old high school student who'd stopped in for a hot chocolate. This new homicide brought Glitsky's workload to seven active cases, and put him inside and around the Tastee Burger for the rest of the day.

Now it was just before noon on Tuesday and finally he was at Mrs. Trang's clean but cluttered apartment with Paul Thieu, his enthusiastic interpreter.

Victor's mother had been Glitsky's first choice of where to begin asking questions, but like so many others of his plans lately, this one hadn't panned out. He had respected the fact that she had been too distraught to talk in the immediate aftermath of her son's death. Then there had been the wake and funeral. This morning was the earliest they could get together.

The apartment was a study in lace. Every smooth surface was covered with some type of crocheted *thing*— a doily or hankie or tablecloth. There was lace over the back of the overstuffed couch that Glitsky and Thieu were directed to, lace over the coffee table, on the end tables under the lamps and photographs, on the television set, under the phone on the little hall table. A feeble sunlight struggled to pierce a veil of weblike lace drapery covering the front windows.

Trang's mother was petite and weathered, with flat gray hair and a shapeless tiny body, made more so by its enclosure in an oversize men's black business suit, over the shoulders of which she had thrown a crocheted white shawl. She offered them small flavorless cookies of some kind and coffee—near boiling, chicory-laced and appalling to Glitsky's taste, but Thieu sucked the first cup right up, black, and accepted a second. She sat still as a rock at the coffee table, responding to his opening expressions of regret in a patient and compliant way, without any interest. Her life, along with her son's, was apparently over.

But now, finally, he was getting to it. "And the last time you saw your son was?"

He waited for Thieu to interpret, listened to the woman's flat inflection as she answered, trying to piece something in advance from sounds alone, but the tonality was too flat. Thieu nodded to Mrs. Trang, then turned to him: "She saw him the day before he was killed, but talked to him that night, that evening, after dinner sometime. She's not sure exactly what time."

Glitsky pretended to scribble on his pad and kept his face impassive, his voice low and conversational. "Paul, would you please just say the words she says, exactly? Don't tell me what she says. *Say* what she says."

The younger man nodded, then swallowed, suitably chided. "Sorry."

"It's okay." He sat forward on the couch, spoke directly to the mother. "Mrs. Trang, how did Victor seem to you the last time you saw him?"

Thieu translated. The wait. "He was hopeful. We had a nice dinner. He tries to come over at least once a week, on Sunday, sometimes more. He . . ." She paused and Thieu waited. "It saves him money to come here and eat, I think. He has taken a little while to start making money as a lawyer, and he felt that he was about to make a lot."

"And how was he going to do that?"

"He had a client who was suing the Archdiocese, and he said they—the Archdiocese—had offered to . . ." Thieu listened, turned to Glitsky. "She's apologizing to me," he said. "She doesn't know the jargon."

Glitsky pointedly ignored Thieu. "That's all right, Mrs. Trang, just do your best."

She came back to him, began talking again. Thieu picked it up. ". . . to settle it . . . before going to court. They were not going to go to court and he thought he would make a lot of money."

"He was pretty certain of that?"

"Yes. He seemed very sure, very hopeful. But also worried."

"What about?"

"That it wouldn't happen. That something would go wrong." A pause. "As it has."

"Did he say *what* might go wrong? What he was worried about?"

"That this was a lot of money, and the Church might use . . . connections . . . in the court, perhaps, so that even though Victor was right, even if the law was on his side, they could stop him."

"Did you think he meant violently?"

"No. Now, I don't know. Maybe so."

"How much money was he talking about?"

"He didn't say exactly. Enough to pay off his loans. He thought he would move his office, get a secretary. He wanted to get me a new place." She motioned around their cramped quarters. "Buy me some new clothes."

"Okay, then, how about the next night, when he called? Did he call or did you call him?"

"He called me. The attorney for the Archdiocese . . ."

"Mark Dooher?"

"Yes, I think that was his name. He had called Victor and asked him to stay in the office to wait for a phone call, that they were going to offer more money that night."

"Did he say when he'd gotten that first call, from Dooher?"

"I thought it was just then, just before he called me."

Glitsky made a note on his yellow pad. There would be a phone record of the precise time.

Mrs. Trang said a few more words, which Thieu related. "It's why he stayed late."

"Would he have called anyone else about this, to tell them, perhaps, about the possible settlement?"

"No. I wanted to call my sister and tell her and he told me to wait, that he was going to wait, too. Not to talk to anyone until it was done. He didn't want to . . ." Thieu frowned, trying to find the right word. ". . . to bring it bad luck, to jinx it. He told me this."

"But that doesn't mean the girlfriend or somebody else didn't just happen to drop by." Thieu wanted to talk about it. Still and always.

Glitsky was driving the unmarked Plymouth back to Trang's office, trying to keep from jumping to conclusions, glad he didn't usually work with a partner. He was coming to believe that entirely too much credence was given to the round-table discussion. Sometimes—a radical idea in this bumptious age, he knew—but sometimes solitary contemplation did produce results.

"It had to be somebody he knew, right? It wasn't a robbery—nothing was missing."

"We don't know that. We don't know what was there to be missing."

"I mean his wallet, personal effects . . ."

"It might have just been botched." If Thieu wanted to play these games, Glitsky could at least make them instructive. "Guy's in there and Trang comes back from dinner . . ."

"He didn't leave for dinner." Paul had done his homework. "The autopsy didn't find anything in his stomach."

"So he came back for his keys or something. Or went to mail a letter. *If* he left, though, and came back, discovered the perp burglarizing the place, who killed him, then decided he'd better split . . ."

"That didn't happen."

"No, I don't think so either. But it could have,

which is my point. What I think is what you think—a strong male who knew him killed him."

"Dooher?"

"Maybe, or maybe one of his clients. Maybe one of the people he was hassling for business." A sidelong glance. "That's what they pay us for, to find out."

Trang's office didn't look much better in the daytime, and to Thieu it felt worse. The crime scene tape was still across the door. Inside, the way it had been left by the forensics and homicide teams on Friday night created a sense of abandonment that, to Thieu, was overwhelming.

He noticed that none of whatever weak sunlight there had been outside made it into this cavern. Ever.

Glitsky had zipped up his flight jacket. His breath showed in the chill. He crossed to the one window—the black hole of the other night—and opened it into the brick of the building next door, about four inches away. He stuck his head out and looked up, down, sideways. "If the perp came through here," he said, "he is one skinny dude."

It was the first even remote touch of levity Thieu had heard from the sergeant. Emboldened by it, he dared ask another question. "What are we looking for?"

Glitsky had moved back to the desk, was sitting in the library chair. He motioned to four cardboard boxes lurking in the corner with manila file folders visible in them. "Anything. Why don't you start by looking through those boxes?" Thieu shrugged—the well of Glitsky's humor was proving to be relatively shallow—and went to work.

The files weren't alphabetical, and he'd gone through the first three of them—notes from law school!

—when he heard a click and a hum behind him, and turned to see Glitsky at the computer, legs stretched out, arms crossed, scowling at the monitor. After a minute, the sergeant sat forward and began clicking the mouse.

Thieu left his boxes, straightened up and came around behind him, resolving to ask no questions, though it wasn't his style not to ask. He liked people and believed that the truth emerged from a full and free discussion of ideas and theories. Also, it had been his experience at UCLA that asking professors what they wanted was how you found out what to give them. It wasn't any mystery, just simple communication. And then at the academy it got drilled into them that you *should* just ask questions and senior officers would *always* be happy to help you.

He didn't think anybody had briefed the inspector here on that part.

The monitor was scrolling the pages of a document that was evidently some kind of organizer. Glitsky got to the day of Trang's death, a week ago yesterday now, and leaned forward. "Look at this," he said.

Thieu already was. There were four entries:

10:22–called MD, told him need answer by COB today or filing tomorrow. $3.00 million.

1:40–MD message. I called back. He was at lunch. WCB.

4:50–MD callback. F. out till 6. Extension till midnight tonight okay.

7:25–MD from F's. Settlement possible. Offer $$ still unresolved. Midnight firm.

Thieu couldn't stop himself. "That last one, that's when he called his mother. Who's 'F'?"

Glitsky was scrolling backward now, eyes on the screen. "The Archbishop," he said. "Flaherty."

As expected, it didn't appear that Victor Trang had had a lot of business. The screens reflected few clients, appointments or telephone numbers. At the screen for a couple of weeks earlier, Glitsky stopped: "MD, $600K!!! Declined."

"That's something," Thieu said.

Glitsky nodded. "You betcha."

"He turned it down?"

"Looks like. I guess he thought he could get more."

There was an answering machine with calls from Trang's girlfriend, Lily Martin, and Mrs. Trang and Mark Dooher and Felicia Diep, all wondering if Victor was there, why he'd not called back, would he please call when he got the message.

They also found the folder on the lawsuit, including the amended complaint, predated for Tuesday, the day after Trang's murder. There was a yellow legal pad with pages of notes that were mostly unintelligible to Glitsky, but on the first page Thieu had been able to read enough to learn that Trang had felt "threatened" in his first visit to McCabe & Roth.

"Dooher?" Thieu asked. They were heading back downtown where Glitsky was to talk to Lily Martin, who'd volunteered to come to the Hall of Justice for an interview. "I'd just bring him in and grill him."

"About what?"

"About what? About all this is what!"

"This isn't anything, Paul. This is *squat*. We are

nowhere yet on this." He really didn't want to bite off Thieu's head. After all, what the man was saying could be correct. But there was, as yet, no evidence that it had been Dooher, not even enough to insult him by asking him pointed questions. And Glitsky was still smarting from his fiasco with the *undoubtedly* guilty Levon Copes, where he had just *known* what had happened. He wasn't going to make the same mistake here. But he was really being an unnecessary hardass. He didn't want to burn the kid out before he even got lit.

Although he knew he wouldn't require any translator with Lily Martin, Glitsky decided on the spur of the moment to invite Thieu to remain for the interview with her. Besides, Glitsky knew there was a chance he might need him again. "Let's talk to the girlfriend first, Paul. See what she's got to say."

"One million six hundred thousand dollars was the settlement figure. Which was . . . would have been . . . five hundred and thirty-three thousand for Victor."

Lily Martin was absolutely certain.

She was conservatively and, Glitsky thought, inexpensively well dressed, and she spoke English perfectly, having been in this country since she was four. Her father, Ed Martin, had fought in the war and married her mother over there and brought them all back here. Now she was twenty-five. Working, as she did, as a junior accountant doing her internship with a Big 6 firm, the money angle was no mystery to her.

"Victor's mother said he told her he wasn't going to call anybody to tell them. He didn't want to jinx the deal."

"He didn't call me. I called him. Like a minute

after he got the call." She broke a brittle smile, which cracked almost immediately. "This was going to be the start of our life, of everything. Of course I called him."

"That night? Last Monday?"

"Yes."

"And what did he say?"

"He said that Mr. Dooher had just called from the Archbishop's office, and he wanted . . . before he presented a final number to the Archbishop . . . he wanted to run it by Victor and see if they were going to be in the ballpark."

"And the number was . . ."

"What I just told you, Sergeant, a million six."

"I just want to get this straight, ma'am. Dooher told him they were going to be talking in that range?"

"That's right."

"And if they—Dooher and Flaherty—if they didn't come through . . . ?"

"Then Victor was going to file, but he didn't think . . . no." She folded her arms, too quickly, over her chest. Glitsky recognized the classic body language—she'd decided to clam up about something.

"No, what?"

"Nothing. I'm sorry. Go ahead."

The interrogation room was small and windowless. There was no art on the walls. The furnishings consisted of three folding chairs around a pitted wooden table. This setting could play on the nerves of even the most cooperative witness. The air got stale. People froze, imagined things, got weirded out in any number of ways.

Suddenly Glitsky leaned back, stretching, shook his shoulders, getting loose. He lifted the corners of his mouth, scratched his face. Finally, there was the trick he did with the eyes, letting them go out of focus. He fancied this made people think there was something soft in there. He turned his head to include Paul Thieu. "How about if we all take a break, get a cup of tea or something?"

"So then, after you talked this night . . . ?"

"He was going to come to my place. He asked me not to call again—Dooher might be there. He'd call when he knew, or when it was over."

"And when he didn't . . . ?"

"I just thought it must have gone real late. He just went home. I waited all the next day at work, but no call. I tried his office, his home . . . even Mr. Dooher's office."

"And what did he say?"

"He didn't talk to me." Glitsky and Thieu exchanged glances. Lou the Greek's seemed unusually cavernous, nearly empty here in the midafternoon. It provided a better environment for talking than the tiny interrogation room at the Hall. "So eventually I went by the office and knocked, but there wasn't any answer. Of course." By now she was sniffling occasionally into a napkin. "And then I called the police."

Glitsky kept it casual. "Why wouldn't Dooher talk to you?"

She shook her head. "I don't think it's so much he *wouldn't*, he just didn't. His secretary took my message, which was that I was a friend of Victor's and did he have any idea where Victor was. Had he seen him? Then she called back and said he was concerned, too. Maybe we should both call the police. So that's where I left it."

Glitsky was tearing his own napkin into tiny bits and piling them neatly on the table. "Ms. Martin. Upstairs a while ago there was something you didn't want to talk about, about the settlement with Dooher . . . ?"

She cast her eyes to the ceiling and sighed deeply. "Okay," she said.

That night, at the Glitsky home, it was almost the way it used to be. Isaac, Jacob and O.J. were watching television, perhaps even doing some homework to the mindless background, in the bedroom shared by the two younger boys.

Flo was feeling better today. It went up and down. But tonight it was way up. She was dressed in tight blue jeans, gold sandals and no socks, a maroon blouse. Diamond stud earrings and a brush of makeup, a light touch of lipstick. A maroon scarf artfully curled around her head to hide the hair loss.

The nurse was off at night. And Flo had sent Glitsky's dad back to his home. She told him he needed some time for himself. He should take in a movie, go solve one of the mysteries of the Talmud.

Nat must be sick of taking care of things here and Flo was able to cope today. Who knew how long it was going to last, but for now—maybe a couple of days, maybe more—she craved some semblance of normalcy for them all.

And somehow—she was a genius—she'd done it. Created that feel. Made dinner of stuffed flank steak (everybody's favorite), home fries with onions and peppers, broccoli and cheese sauce, vanilla ice cream over cherry pie. "You know, I just never seem to worry about cholesterol anymore."

Jokes yet.

Now she was rinsing dishes—about a freight car

full—piling them carefully in the dishwasher. Glitsky sat on the counter next to her, telling her about his day, just like old times, about what Lily Martin had suddenly gone quiet about, which was that her boyfriend never really thought he would win the lawsuit if he filed it.

"You mean he was basically trying to extort money from the Church?"

"Lily didn't want to put it so bluntly, but essentially, yeah."

"That is scuzzy."

Glitsky shrugged. "He's a lawyer. *Was* a lawyer."

"You think that's why he got killed?"

"Just because he was a lawyer? I don't know, Flo, that's a tough theory. There's lots of lawyers out there and many of them are alive. You could look it up."

She gave him the eye. "Because of the *deal*, Abraham."

He temporized. "I don't know yet. I think it might be possible."

Another look. "Sergeant goes out on limb. Film at eleven."

He smiled at her, his real smile. "My problem is this: So what? This guy Dooher may have had all this against Victor Trang, but you don't go out and kill somebody who's suing your *client*. And this killing was personal."

"How about if you thought you might lose your client if you lost?"

"But they weren't even playing yet. Nobody was going to lose that big. They were settling."

"Maybe the client wasn't happy about the settlement terms. They'd go with this one because they had to, it had gone too far, whatever—but afterwards they fire the lawyer. Or he thinks they might."

"So he *kills* the guy?" He shook his head. "I just don't see it. It doesn't make any sense. Besides, this lawyer we're talking about, Dooher, he's managing partner of a big firm downtown. He's been at this all of his life. He's not going to kill a professional adversary over a case. Besides, they lose a case, they lose a client, it's not the end of the world. His firm's probably got a hundred clients."

"Only probably? You didn't check?"

Glitsky had to smile. "Yeah, Flo, in my free time I ran a D and B on them. Firms don't usually run on one client."

Flo shrugged. "Okay, so who then, if it's not money . . . ?"

"I know. I just hate to see a money motive go nowhere."

She put in the last dish into the dishwasher, closed it up, and came to stand in front of her husband, between his legs. She put her arms around him. They kissed.

"I remember that," Glitsky said.

Flo nodded toward their bedroom. "Race you."

For a half hour, he'd forgotten all about real life.

Then she was breathing regularly and he was back in it. The clock said 9:45. It was a school night—he had to get the boys down to bed. He had to move, but if he didn't, maybe it would all just stop right here, where he was, where they all were.

She shifted slightly. "Abe?" Not sleeping after all. "Find somebody else. Promise me that."

There was a tremor, a tick, above his eye. The muscle of his jaw tightened. The scar through his lips went white with a surge of anger so sharp, it grabbed his next breath.

"I don't want to talk about it." He stood. "It's time I got those kids to bed."

15

CHRISTINA KNEW IT HAD HAPPENED AT THE DINNER on Saturday at Sam's . . . its aftermath.

On the drive back to her apartment, Joe going on and on. How could Christina think she knew Mark Dooher so well? What was with the two of them? Where did she get off saying he was nothing like a bastard? And while they were at it, what was the real story behind her knowing about these retreats with Dooher and Farrell?

And she'd closed her eyes, too tired to fight him anymore, to explain, to care. The certainty had come in a flash—that Joe wasn't right for her, and all the rationalizing and wishing in the world wasn't going to change that.

He would never be right. She didn't love him.

There had been early admiration, then a desire born of curiosity, followed by a leap of faith. But the fact was that she didn't feel much about him one way or the other. Except when he started talking about *facts*. And even then she didn't hate him—she just found him irritating and boring.

Pleading a headache, she'd gone into her apartment alone, said she'd call him when she felt better.

Which wasn't Sunday. Then on Monday he'd flown to LA and stayed overnight. She'd been out both nights, studying. She'd come home and listened to his petulant messages and it all got clearer.

Now, Wednesday morning, she stood at his office door. He was, as always, hip-deep in work. Ear stuck to his telephone, he was signing something and reading something else, passing paper to his secretary, who hovered beside him with a notepad and an expression of exasperated fear.

Yep, Christina thought, Joe is going to make it.

Fate sealed the decision. At that moment Joe reasonably spoke into the telephone: "I don't think you've got all your ducks lined up, Bill, and that's the plain fact of it."

She came forward into the room. Seeing her, Joe held up one finger, pointed at the phone and smiled as though she were a client he'd been expecting. He mouthed "Be right there."

She sadly shook her head and put the envelope containing the ring and her letter on his desk. Patting it once, she turned and walked out.

"I feel like a coward, just running out like that. I should have faced him."

"And said what."

"I don't know. Told him."

"Would he have listened?"

"Maybe to the fact that I was leaving him. Maybe that." She looked out at the whitecaps pocking the blue bay, sailboats half-keeled in the breeze, San Francisco in the distance, the Golden Gate beyond the Sausalito curve to her right. At Sam's expression, she laughed. "No, you're right. Not even to that. And that look isn't fair."

"What look? And I didn't say anything."

"You know what look. And you didn't have to."

They were at Scoma's, having taken the ferry to Sausalito. Sam had two experienced volunteers working at the Center and decided she could afford a few hours off. For her part, Christina, after leaving her envelope, had been tempted to go to Dooher's office and tell him about it, but thought it would smack of leading him on, which she flatly wasn't going to do.

To what end? He'd made it clear he was married, not interested in her in that way. And what a relief, really, though she did think he was terrific.

She sometimes thought every other man on the planet was incapable of seeing who she was inside. But not Mark. He simply liked her, who she was. It was a joy.

She was aware, however, that her decision to break off with Joe had come about because she'd been unable to avoid contrasting the younger man to Dooher, with his heady mix of physical good looks, substance, experience, power and humor. She decided that her growing friendship with him would be the litmus test for the kind of relationship she would eventually . . . not settle *for*, as she had with Joe. But settle *on*. Someone of Dooher's quality, if one could be found at all. It might take a while.

But that was the other thing, the other wonderful result of this friendship with Mark Dooher—if some other man didn't come along to validate who she was, it didn't have to be the end of the world.

She was trying to explain this to Sam. "I don't know why it took me so long to realize. Sometimes I think about the only man who's ever liked me for me, besides my dad, is Mark."

Sam, mopping up the perfect doré sauce with the perfect piece of fresh sourdough bread, was matter-of-fact. "It's the curse of fabulous beauty." She raised her eyes. "I'm serious."

Christina knew better than to flutter her lids with false modesty. "Well. But now at least I'm getting a glimpse that maybe I'm worth something by myself."

"As opposed to?"

"I don't know. The lesser half of some guy I happen to be with?"

"The trophy?"

Christina nodded. "On some level it's flattering. Or something. So I let it happen—I become the person they want me to be."

"It's tempting, that's why. It *is* flattering. It's also what everybody's always taught you. You want to please. You're hard-wired for it. So it gets internalized." Sam mopped more sauce. "I cannot make a sauce this good at home. How do they do this?" She took the bite, chewed a moment, sighed. "It's one of the hard truths."

"The sauce?"

Sam laughed, shook her head. "What sauce?" Another laugh. "I'm all over the place, aren't I? No, the hard truth about who we are. I went through the same thing about ten years ago."

"I think you've lost me. What same thing?"

"This decision that I wasn't what some man thought I was."

"And you did it, just like that?"

"No." Smiling again, she held up a finger. "But I tried. I *acted* that way for all the world to see. Got my heart broke four or five times. Got bitter and cynical about men. But I did get better about me. I think. Eventually."

Christina nodded. "Well, I'm not going back. Not the same way. Not to another Joe."

"Good. Hold on to that feeling. You're going to need it when it's been six months. You get a little lonesome. Trust me on this."

"I think I can handle lonesome. I've done lonesome before. The difference was that lonely was always clearly the time between one guy and the next guy. Now, I think I'll cultivate some friendships."

"Friendships are good," Sam said. "As long as you don't get confused."

"You mean Mark Dooher?" Christina shook her head. "No. He's not like that."

Sam raised an eyebrow. "He's not a sexual creature?"

"No." She laughed. "He exudes . . . confidence that way, I suppose. But he's married. He's happy. He's got it in balance. He's never come on to me in any way. In fact, more the opposite. Hands off. Be a person first. It's great, actually."

"I've got to meet this guy. Wes thinks he's God, too."

"Speaking of . . ."

"God? or Wes?"

Christina nodded. "Mr. Farrell."

"I'm afraid I let lonesome get the better of me and pursued him a little more, uh, recklessly than I would have liked. Now I like to think we're moving cautiously toward friendship, but we've got a ways to go before we get beyond superficial."

"Which isn't so bad, is it?"

Sam shrugged. "I don't really know. That's the

funny thing. It makes me a little nervous—what we've been talking about all day here. There's no way I'm investing any of this"—she tapped her heart—"until I know him better."

"Until you know it's real."

Sam's face was a kaleidoscope of emotions. She nodded sheepishly. "That's always the question, isn't it?"

Glitsky really hated it when he talked himself out of a plausible murder suspect, and that's exactly what his two talks—the one with his wife and the other with Paul Thieu—had accomplished.

Not only did he lack any physical evidence pointing to Mark Dooher as Victor Trang's killer, but—as he had told Flo—there was no reasonable way that a successful corporate lawyer was going to stab another lawyer to death over the terms of a possible settlement. That solution, much as he would love it if it did, just didn't scan.

So he was going to have to get another approach, and to that end he had dropped in on Paul Thieu in Missing Persons and asked him to call Felicia Diep and set up an appointment for sometime, if possible, before afternoon tea.

In the meanwhile, Glitsky went upstairs to Homicide.

The room looked as it always did—a large open area with twelve desks, no more than three of them occupied at any one time; the doorless corner cubicle "office" of the chief of Homicide, Lieutenant Frank Batiste; two massive drywall columns papered, stuck and tagged with every poster, fax, ammo sale notice, car repo slip, random prostitute's phone number—and so on—

that had crossed some inspector's desk in the past four years or so and which, at the time, had seemed too important, funny or unusual to simply discard in a waste basket.

Glitsky's desk was next to one of these columns. He pulled his chair in, crossed his arms behind his head, and put his feet up. His eyes came to rest on the xeroxed note at his eye level: "Don't let your mouth write a check your ass can't cash."

He let his chair back down, trying to will away the nagging sense that he shouldn't stop concentrating on Mark Dooher, who was, in some ways, the *least* likely probable candidate for the murder. But for just that reason . . .

Instinct counted. That was the problem. Glitsky's instincts were screaming something that he couldn't prove—Trang's murder *had to* have been personal. Someone had hated him passionately.

And that element just didn't seem to be there with his business adversary, Mark Dooher. So Glitsky should stop wasting energy on him. Except if Trang *represented* something Dooher hated passionately. Like Vietnamese people.

No. Forget that. He had a lot of other work, six other pressing homicides.

It might, after all, be the girlfriend, Lily. Girlfriends always had a motive or two. And Lily stood to benefit if Trang accepted Dooher's settlement. Maybe she'd gotten mad at him when he hadn't? Yesterday he'd told himself that no, she was too small; she could never have held Trang up. But—a sudden thought—what if she had another boyfriend? She'd known Victor was alone in the office. He'd overlooked that—if she sent boyfriend number two over . . .

"Abe. Got a minute?"

Frank Batiste stood in the doorway to his cubicle. The lieutenant and Glitsky had come up together through the ranks. Both were nominal minorities—Glitsky half black, Batiste a "Spanish surname"—and both had elected to disregard any advantages, and they were legion, accruing to that status in San Francisco. It had created a bond of sorts. And although Batiste currently outranked Glitsky, they'd been in the department the same number of years and felt like equals.

So Glitsky got up and by the time he reached the doorway, the lieutenant was sitting behind his desk.

"What's up, Frank?"

"Come on in. Sit down. Get the door."

A joke, since there was no door. Glitsky took the folding chair across from the desk. Batiste pulled a pencil from his drawer and began tapping the table. "So you know how to tell the prostitute in the Miss America contest?"

"I'm afraid I don't, Frank."

"She's the one with the banner reading I-da-ho."

The one saving constant in the office, Glitsky thought. Somebody's always got a dumb joke. And Batiste was on a roll. "Okay, another chance for you: You know the difference between Mick Jagger and a Scotsman?"

Glitsky broke a small smile. "I give up."

"Mick Jagger says 'Hey, you, get offa my cloud,' and the Scotsman says, 'Hey, McCloud, get offa my ewe.'"

"You gotta get an agent, Frank. The right agent could make you a star."

"That's true, the downside being that it would leave a vacancy here," Batiste said. He pulled himself up straighter, getting to business. "Which is what this is about. I notice you aren't taking this year's lieutenant's exam. You don't want to make more money?"

"More money would be good."

"Then what?"

"Maybe I don't want to be a lieutenant. Maybe I don't want to leave Homicide." Typically, a promotion to lieutenant meant a transfer out of the detail to which an officer had been assigned. There were exceptions to this rule. Batiste himself had been a homicide inspector before his promotion. That wasn't something to count on, but Batiste was hinting that it could happen again with Abe. But, of course, first he had to take the exam.

Batiste opened the side drawer of his desk and took out a giant handful of peanuts in the shell. He dumped them on the desk between them, then grabbed one and cracked it. The peanuts were another constant in the homicide detail. No one remembered when or how they'd first arrived, but they were always there. "That's fine if that's what you want. I just didn't want it to be an oversight. I know you've had a lot on your mind lately."

Batiste chewed and cracked another peanut, busy with it. This was awkward ground. "You want my opinion, you want to take the test, keep your options open."

Glitsky gave it a minute, then nodded. "Okay, I'll do that. Thanks for mentioning it."

"Good."

The sound of peanuts being cracked. Neither of the men moved. "Hey, Frank . . ."

"Yeah?"

Another long moment. Batiste took another handful of nuts out of his drawer and Glitsky got up, dropped his shells into the wastebasket, looked out through the open entrance of Batiste's office, then sat back down. "Are you sure there isn't anything else? I could handle it, there was."

"Like what?"

"Like I've got so much on my mind that I'm not doing my job?" Glitsky's voice remained matter-of-fact, but his eyes became distant. "That I'd be better off pushing paper as a lieutenant in the Traffic division than as a lowly inspector with a *real* job in Homicide." The eyes rested on his lieutenant. "I'd like to know, Frank, I really would. If I'm an embarrassment . . ."

"Who's saying that?"

His shoulders sagged. "I am, I guess. I'm asking. I couldn't close on Levon Copes. Then I get assigned this clown who shoots up the Tastee Burger when there is no investigation to conduct but it keeps me off the streets? This kind of stuff, it makes me wonder."

Batiste had stopped with the peanuts. He shook his head. "Nobody's saying anything like that, Abe. I don't even *think* it."

Glitsky took a breath. A beat. Another one. Three.

Batiste. "You all right?"

"I'm reading everything wrong, Frank. Sorry. I didn't mean to lay it on you. I'm just getting everything wrong."

Batiste told Abe he didn't have to worry so much about what he might be doing wrong. So what if he wasted a few minutes? They worked in the city's last bastion where results—not hours—were what counted. If Glitsky felt he wasn't on all cylinders, enough were still firing to get the job done. So he should put aside the doubts about why he thought it was Dooher.

Sometimes professionals had hunches. You asked yourself every question you could think of, even if you didn't exactly know why you needed to ask it. Answering them all probably wouldn't take fifteen minutes.

Then he could go talk to Lily Martin again, or Felicia Diep. Or the pope.

Which gave Glitsky an idea.

"By the way, I met your girlfriend again the other night. I think she likes you."

Wes Farrell, leaning against the padded back wall, was sitting on the hardwood floor of the squash court, breathing hard. Dooher wasn't even winded. He was absently whacking the ball into the wall, hitting it back on the short hop. A machine.

"I've got so many, Wes, which one are we talking about."

"The pretty one."

Dooher inclined his racket slightly, the ball bounced, shot straight up off his racket, and arced into his waiting palm. "They're all pretty," he said, smiling.

"They're not all as pretty as she is. The girl from Fior d'Italia? Christina. Your summer clerk. Ring a bell?"

Dooher corrected him. "*One* of my summer clerks, Wes. I think we're bringing on about ten. And I hate to ruin your fantasies, but we've remained platonic."

"I thought I was talking about *your* fantasies."

"I have no fantasies. I live an ordered and disciplined life, which is why I will beat you in this next game. Besides, Sheila and I are enjoying a little renaissance right at the moment." Dooher gave his practiced shrug, minimizing personal complicity in all the good things, such as his wife's sexual favors, that constantly came his way, and bounced the ball off the floor. "Double or nothing? I'm ready. Where'd you see her?"

Farrell slowly pulled himself to his feet. "Actually, I'm having a little renaissance myself."

"With Lydia?"

"Lydia who? Her name's Sam." He was all the way on his feet now, half limping, holding his back. "How did I get so decrepit, anyway? I eat right, I drink right. Am I not at this very moment exercising?"

Dooher was tossing the ball up and down, catching it without looking. "Whose name is Sam?"

"My girlfriend, you fool. And Christina Carrera is a friend of hers. We were at a dinner party."

"And my name came up?"

Wes shrugged. "When we realized half the people there knew you. I said you weren't as bad as you appeared. I'm afraid I told them your Vietnam story."

Dooher's face clouded for a moment. "That story. I don't think it's come up once in the past ten years, and just the other day . . ." Dooher explained about Glitsky. "So I showed him the picture. What was Christina's reaction to all this talk of me?"

"She didn't need your tragic background to think you were a hero. She's one of your fans. Obviously, someone has deluded her into thinking you are a sweet and gentle soul under that craggy exterior."

"She's got a keen insight into human nature," Dooher said. "Maybe I'll give her a raise."

16

IT WASN'T EXACTLY THE POPE, BUT GLITSKY'S POLISH was pretty ragged anyway. He figured the Archbishop was close enough.

Flaherty's appointments secretary was initially inclined to be coldly officious, but after Glitsky had explained that he needed a personal appointment with His Excellency to talk about the murder of one of his flock, the man had first gotten interested, then had thawed. He checked. Flaherty had a two o'clock, but his lunch had broken up early—he was in the office right now. Would Glitsky wait a moment?

Okay, the secretary had told him, if he could get down to the Chancery office, the Archbishop would give him between when he arrived and his appointment, say twenty minutes if he flew.

He flew.

* * *

The windows were open and the sound of children playing down below drifted up to them.

They sat kitty-corner in wing chairs. The spartan office was chilly. Glitsky kept his jacket zipped. The rest of the room reinforced the theme of minimal creature comfort—Berber rug, flattop desk, computer, the chairs, some photos of Flaherty with unknowns and kids and sports figures, a crucifix, a wall of books. With no pretension or sign of earthly power, it was nothing that Glitsky had expected.

Neither was the man himself. In his black pants, scuffed loafers, white socks, green-and-white-striped dress shirt, the Archbishop might have been a high school teacher. The gray eyes, though, were singular. Intelligence there, Glitsky thought, lots of it. The ability to calculate. To see through things.

But in spite of that, he didn't seem to be following Glitsky's line of questioning. "Are you saying that Mark Dooher told you we had a meeting here on Monday a week ago?"

"He didn't say that, no."

"Good. Because that didn't happen."

"There was no meeting to talk about an increase in the settlement you were willing to give Mr. Trang?"

"Yes, we had that meeting. But it was, it must have been three weeks ago. Maybe more. And we decided no. We were sticking with the six hundred thousand."

Clearly, the settlement issue still rankled. But Flaherty wanted to go back. "I'm curious. You said you talked to Mark, Mr. Dooher, is that right? So if he didn't mention this meeting, who did?"

"Victor Trang's girlfriend. And his mother. Independently." Glitsky felt he ought to explain a little further. "I've been talking to people as they've been available, sir. Dooher was first."

"Where did you even get that connection? Dooher to Trang?"

Flaherty might try to present a low profile, but he was used to command. Glitsky sat back, kept his voice low. "Dooher called Missing Persons. Him, the girl-friend, the mother. That's where I started. And Dooher didn't volunteer anything about the meeting, but since that time I've heard about it from two sources. I'm try-ing to find out if it happened."

"Why didn't you go back to Dooher?"

Now Glitsky leaned forward, made some eye con-tact. "Excuse me, sir, but do you mind if I ask a couple of the questions? That's how we usually do this."

The Archbishop let go with a deep-throated laugh, recovered, told Glitsky he was sorry, to go ahead. He'd shut up.

"So there was no meeting?"

"No. Not that Monday night. Not any night. As I said, we discussed the settlement terms at one of our regular daytime business meetings."

Glitsky consulted the notes he'd taken with Lily Martin. "You never discussed the figure of a *million* six hundred thousand."

"No chance. Mark wouldn't even have brought me a figure like that. He knows that would have been insane. Hell, what we did offer—the six hundred—*that* was insane."

"But Trang turned it down?"

The Archbishop shrugged. "People are greedy, Sergeant. It's one of the cardinal sins and I bet you wouldn't be surprised how often it comes up."

"So where was it going from there? The lawsuit?"

"I'd guess Mr. Trang was going to amend the com-plaint and then file it. And lose."

"That's what everybody seems to think. Which makes me wonder why he was going to do it."

Another shrug. "It was a power play, Sergeant, pure and simple. That's all it was. Mr. Trang evidently thinks—thought—that we have infinitely deep pockets. He was, I gather, inexperienced in these matters, and evidently thought he could get more simply by holding out, putting the squeeze on a little tighter. But the suit itself had little merit."

"And yet you were going to settle for six hundred thousand dollars?"

Flaherty broke a cold smile. He hesitated, uncrossed his legs, and leaned in toward Glitsky. "In real life, Sergeant, an untrue accusation can be as damning as a conviction. We were willing to pay something to keep a lid on the accusation."

"But not a million six?"

"No. Not even half that, as I've told you."

"Did Dooher ever mention to you how he felt about Trang? Personally?"

"No."

"Didn't like him or dislike him?"

"He was an adversary. I don't think they saw each other socially, if that's what you mean." Flaherty sat back. "You can't honestly think Mark Dooher could have had a hand in any of this, do you?"

Glitsky pointed a finger, toy gun style, risking a faint smile. "You're asking questions again, but the answer is I don't have a clue. Trang's death seems to have been good for the Archdiocese . . ."

Finally, a degree of frustration peeked through. "Sergeant, we're in constant litigation about one thing or the other. One lawsuit, one scandal, more or less, just isn't going to make too much difference. And that's God's truth."

Not that Glitsky necessarily bought it, but that direction wasn't taking him anywhere. "All right, one last question. Do you have a appointments calendar I might glance at? See what you *were* doing that Monday night?"

This marked the obvious crossing of the Archbishop's threshold into active annoyance. Flaherty nodded curtly, stood up, and went to the door and out. In a moment he returned with a large black book. He carefully placed it open onto Glitsky's lap. "That the day?"

"Yes, sir." He looked down. "Catholic Youth Organization convention. Do you remember that? Did it go on late?"

Flaherty was no longer Glitsky's friend, that was certain. But he answered civilly. "It was at Asilomar, Sergeant, down in Pacific Grove? You know it? It's a hundred miles south of here." He picked the book up and closed it firmly. "And see the line here, to noon the next day. That means I spent the night."

In one of those amazing coincidences, Glitsky thought, just then there was a knock on the door and the appointments secretary opened it, stuck his head in, and told Flaherty that his two o'clock had arrived.

Glitsky looked at his watch, closed his notebook and stood up. The interview was over. He put out his hand and the Archbishop took it. "Thank you, sir. You've been a big help."

Flaherty's grip was a vise and his eyes had gone the color of cold steel. "You know, Sergeant, I try not to stand upon it, but most people address me, at least, as 'Father.' Some even say 'Your Excellency.' "

Glitsky squeezed back. "Thank you. I'll remember next time."

* * *

But what did it mean?

He'd better begin to consider the possibility that there had been no meeting on Monday night. At least not with Flaherty and Dooher. So why did the two women—Lily Martin and Mrs. Trang both—think there had been?

But wait—who said the meeting had been in person in Flaherty's office? Maybe Flaherty hadn't been able to talk to Dooher until later because . . . but no, that meant Flaherty was at the least just plain lying, and at most implicated in the actual murder. And though Glitsky ran into liars every day—murderers too—he did not really believe the Archbishop was involved here. He'd just not been able to resist the urge to jack him up a little. He'd always had a problem with people who thought they spoke directly to God.

He'd picked up a piroshki and a celery soda and sat having a late lunch in his car just off Market Street, his windows down. It was warmer outside than it had been in Flaherty's office and the air smelled sharply of coffee. One of the nearby restaurants must be roasting its own.

He kept coming back to the meeting, or nonmeeting. For now, he was going to believe that the meeting never took place. Further, he *didn't* believe Flaherty had even talked to Dooher on that Monday night.

Which did not mean that Dooher hadn't talked to Trang.

Did it?

Glitsky was wrestling with it, trying to piece together some rationale for Trang to have written up messages on his personal computer, purporting to have come from Dooher, if there had been none. It could have been that he was going to extraordinarily great lengths to run a false story past his mother and girlfriend —"See, I'm just on the cusp of greatness, just about to be rich and successful. It's going to happen any day now. The other side is about to cave in. Look, here are the messages from their attorney to prove it. I'm not a nothing, as you've all believed. I'm going to make it big."

Was that too much of a stretch? Glitsky wasn't sure. He'd known a lot of people—perennial losers—who'd tried to fool themselves and others in similar ways. Maybe that had been Trang, trying to convince himself as well as the women in his life. And then when the settlement didn't come through after all, he'd fall back into victim mode. It hadn't been his fault. The breaks were against him, the power of the Church, the bigger players had ganged up.

But—Glitsky brought himself up short—the truth was that there *had* been a substantial offer. Six hundred thousand dollars had been on the table, and Trang had turned it down. Would he have done that if he wasn't fairly sure he was going to get more?

No. He would have taken it.

Which meant—what?

That the penny-ante psychological profile Glitsky had been drawing of Trang-as-loser was not valid. And if *that* was true, then at the very least, Trang believed something was happening with Dooher and the settlement. He hadn't made it all up. Or possibly any of it.

So Dooher *had* called him. Twice on that Monday. Maybe three times.

He wondered if he'd admit it. It didn't exactly reek of probable cause, but Glitsky knew he could find a judge to give him a warrant for Dooher's phone records based on the inconsistencies. But if Dooher hadn't called Trang from his home or office, any other call would be nearly impossible to verify—the phone company kept track of the calls you made, but didn't keep records of non-toll calls received.

He chewed the last of his piroshki, tipped back the soda. Well, at least now he had a plausible excuse to go back and talk to Dooher, take another look at the Vietnam photograph while he was at it. Maybe casually bring up some other topics. "Say, I was doing the crossword this morning and came across a seven-letter word, starts with 'b,' means infantry knife. What do you think that could be?"

Subtlety was the key.

Dooher was going to be in meetings out of the office for most of the rest of the afternoon, but if he checked in for messages, his secretary would tell him the sergeant had called.

So the rest of Glitsky's Wednesday afternoon was lost in paperwork. He labored over his initial report on the Tastee Burger killing. He checked the transcription of his interviews with three of the witnesses there.

Moving along, he filled out the warrant for Dooher's business and personal phone records. Then there was the application for the lieutenant's exam.

A final homicide issue involved rebooking a burglar who'd killed a seventy-year-old man last week. The elderly resident had had the bad luck to wake up and grab his .38 in the middle of the night when he'd heard the noise.

At five-ten, completely fried with the paperwork, as he was putting on his jacket to go home, his telephone rang. "This is Mark Dooher," he said to himself. And it was.

Dooher was free now, but maybe if the sergeant just had a quick question or two, he could answer it on the phone, save him a trip. Glitsky wondered if he really needed to actually see the Vietnam photograph again. It was quitting time. He wanted to go home and be with his family. He'd worked a long day as it was. He wasn't the same cop he had been. He said some questions should do it.

"Sure, I talked to him that day."

"More than once?"

"I may have. I believe so. Why?"

"When you and I talked last time, you didn't mention it."

"Did you ask about it? I'm sorry. I don't . . ."

"I thought it might have occurred to you as relevant. Talking to a murdered man just before he was killed."

No answer.

"Do you recall what you talked about?"

"Sure. He was asking for my strategic advice on another case he was handling. As I told you, we kind of hit it off. I think he was hoping I'd offer him a job at the firm here."

"You didn't discuss the settlement of your suit?"

Another pause. "No, not that I recall."

"Although he was threatening to file it the next day, ratcheting up the figures?"

"And then we'd duke it out in court. That's how we do it, Sergeant. Those lines had been drawn. There wasn't anything to talk about."

"And he didn't seem concerned, worried, anxious?"

"No, not to me. He seemed normal."

"Do you remember what the other case was about, the one he wanted your advice on?"

"Sure, it was another settlement on a personal injury. Sergeant, am I under some kind of suspicion here?"

"The case is still open," Glitsky said ambiguously. "I've been trying to get a sense of what Mr. Trang did in those last hours." But may as well just come out with it. "Did you have a bayonet as part of your gear in Vietnam?"

So much for the subtle approach.

"It sounds like I should contact *my* lawyer."

"Or just answer the question."

"Yes, I did. Did a bayonet kill Victor?"

"We believe so. Do you still have yours?"

"No. The army takes it from you when they send you home."

"Do you mind telling me where you were last Monday night?"

A sigh, perhaps an angry one. "I believe I went to the driving range, then came back to the office here and worked late. Sergeant Glitsky, why on earth do you think I'd consider killing a man, any man, much less Victor, whom I've told you I liked?"

"I didn't say I did. I'm collecting all the information I can, hoping some of it leads somewhere."

"The implications are pretty damn infuriating."

"I'm sorry about that. Archbishop Flaherty thought so, too."

"You talked to the Archbishop? About this?"

"He's your biggest client, isn't he?"

"By far. So?"

"And Trang's death means the suit gets dropped . . ."

"Trang's death means Mrs. Diep gets another lawyer, Sergeant. And that's all it means."

17

THE EARTHQUAKE THAT ROCKED THE CITY AT FIVE twenty-two the next morning wasn't as destructive as the World Series quake of '89—it didn't collapse any part of the Bay Bridge, for example, or any freeways. However, with a magnitude of 5.8 and an epicenter just a mile into the ocean northwest of the Cliff House, it was by no means a minor temblor. The eventual damage total exceeded $50 million. Seventy-seven people were injured seriously enough to seek medical help, and four people died.

Bart was going insane. He jumped up on Farrell's bed, howling like a coyote rather than the intelligent and sensitive boxer that Farrell knew him to be, so something must be wrong, but Wes had no idea what it could be. He cast a quick glance at the clock next to his bed. 5:19. What the hell! "Bart, Bart! Come on, boy. It's all right. It's all right."

But apparently Bart knew more than his owner on this score. Wes was grabbing for the dog's collar to pull him nearer. It sounded like he was dying, Wes thinking, *I knew I shouldn't have given him that lamb bone. That's what it is—it's cut his stomach to shreds.*

He flicked on the light, holding the dog close now, murmuring to him, petting to try to calm him down. "Please don't die. Come on, hang in there, I'll call—"

Wham!

It was a sharp up-and-down hit, similar to the Northridge quake that had done so much damage to southern California. The experts later estimated that the shock was equal to a vertical drop of five and half feet. It was probably fortunate that Farrell had no art on his walls and very little furniture, so there wasn't much to fall or fly around.

After one terrified bark coupled with a desperate escape maneuver involving claws and fangs that scratched Farrell's face badly, Bart got himself to a corner of the room and set up another howl.

The lights went out. There was a second, smaller jolt, and Farrell rolled from his bed and started crawling, eventually arriving at the bedroom doorway, his hands gripping both sides of it for support should the foundations shake again.

His hands were sticky and wet.

Glitsky hadn't been able to sleep and didn't want to keep Flo up, so at around midnight he'd gone out to read on the couch in the living room. Taking a cue from his father Nat, a Talmud scholar, he had been immersed for weeks in Wilton Barnhardt's epic tome *Gospel*, a story about the missing New Testament book of Matthias. This was about as far from San Francisco crime and politics and his home life as he could get. Which was the point.

Eventually, he'd nodded off.

What got him up wasn't the shock but Flo screaming his name. The lamp next to him crashed to the floor. Sparks and broken pottery. One of the kids—he thought it was Jake, his middle one—was also calling him. God! Why were the other ones quiet?

"Abe!"

"Yo! Coming."

Another shake, knocking him sideways. Bare feet on broken shards. In the short hallway, he turned on the light. Another step, the bedroom, the light. Flo looked at him, eyes wide and tearful, as though he were a ghost.

As well he might have been.

The six- or seven-hundred-pound oaken armoire in which they kept their hanging clothes had jumped four feet across the room and fallen, landing on Glitsky's side of the bed, where he normally would have been lying.

Flo was up and in his arms, and Jake cried out again.

Sheila Dooher nudged her husband. "Earthquake," she said, swinging her feet around, finding the floor. Louder, another push. "Mark! Now!"

People said you never got used to earthquakes, but Sheila had lived in the Bay Area most of her life and had experienced over twenty of them. The great majority of the time, they shook the ground or the building you were in and then stopped. And the other quakes . . . well, by the time you worked yourself up to really scared, they were over, and then you dealt with what they'd done.

Mark opened his eyes, immediately awake in the darkness. He knew that Sheila had moved to her prearranged location in the doorway to the stairs—it was a drill. And he did the same to his, four steps over to the bathroom door.

"You all right?" he heard her say.

There was another, smaller shake. They rode it out —three seconds max—"Fine."

For Sam Duncan, living in a seventy-year-old underground apartment with brick walls, there was no time for any thought. Either Quayle was a sounder sleeper than Bart was, or he wasn't as finely attuned to the tiny movements of the earth by which animals can supposedly predict earthquakes. In any case, Quayle didn't whine, or bark, or howl preceding the event. Sam was sleeping one moment, and the next—feeling something moving, falling around her in the split second she had to react—covering her head as the wall behind her bed gave, collapsing over her.

18

Before Christina was awake, her father, Bill, had gone downtown to the bakery and come back with hot ham-and-Swiss-filled croissants, her favorite. Irene, her mother, left the steaming cup of French roast on the nightstand in her room and brushed a strand of hair back over her daughter's ear.

She stirred.

"Your coffee's here," her mother said.

Having driven down to Ojai in six hours, she'd arrived unannounced at ten-thirty last night and they'd kept the visiting short—she was tired and planning to stay through the weekend, get rested before finals next week—they'd get time to catch up in person. They'd all turned in early, around midnight.

Late April, before noon, and she was sitting out by the pool in her bathing suit, in perfect comfort. She wondered again why she was living in San Francisco, in the wind and fog and bustle. Here it was already warm as midsummer, the pace was slow, life itself seemed to have an element of fluid grace.

Her parents' house was on the side of one of the encircling hills at an elevation of about four hundred feet, and the pool hung out, cantilevered over a deck that seemed to drop off into space.

Far below, the town sparkled in the pristine air, a little terra-cotta jewel nestled in its verdant setting. In the distance, the Topa Topa mountains and the Los Padres National Forest lent some drama to the view. Closer in were the avocado and orange orchards, the golf course, the orange-roofed landmarks of her own childhood—over to the right she could just spy the edge of her high school, Villanova, for good Catholic girls as she had been.

There was the Tower at the post office, and in the peace of the morning she could hear "Some Enchanted Evening" coming up on the thermals—the Tower played show tunes on the hour.

Her eyes continued to roam. There were the trees over Libbey Park, downtown, where she'd gone to dozens of incredible concerts—blues, classical, jazz, rock 'n' roll—all the great LA players loved coming up here. This is where Hollywood came to drop out.

Ojai was the Chumash Indian word for "nest," and she thought it captured the place perfectly. It was her nest, her home. She wondered, again, if she'd ever really have another one.

Her mother was walking down from the house with some iced tea. She normally worked in her husband's brokerage house as his assistant, but decided she'd take the day off to catch up with her daughter.

Irene Carrera had a buffed leather complexion from too much sun, and her body, toned with regular exercise, was still twenty pounds overweight. Nevertheless, in a casual way she believed herself a beautiful woman, and so nearly everyone else thought she was, too. She frosted her hair and wore gold slippers padding about out by the pool, and she appeared to be as shallow as a petri dish. But she'd never fooled Christina.

Now she sat in the wicker chair next to her daughter's chaise longue, put down the tray that held the pitcher and glasses, placed coasters on either side of the table. "You picked the right day to come down. San Francisco's had another earthquake."

Christina sat up straight. "A bad one?"

Her mother handed her a glass. "They're saying moderately serious. Although if you ask me, they're all bad."

"You can ask me, too."

"Do you want to call anybody?"

"No, no. They don't want you to use the phones after emergencies anyway, Mom. Besides"—she took a sip—"there's nobody to call."

Her mother sat back, gestured to her daughter's left hand. "Your father and I noticed there's no ring. We didn't want to press last night. I guess we're not going to be meeting Joe."

"I guess not." A sigh. "It was my decision. It wasn't going to work out."

Irene took a minute stalling with her iced tea—lemon, sugar, mint. "You gave it enough of a chance? You're sure?"

Christina shrugged. "Come on, Mom, you know. Over a year. It just wasn't . . ." She trailed off. "I'm not sad about it, so I don't think you should be."

"I'm not sad about you and Joe, hon. I worry about you, that's all. These relationships that get to . . ." She took a deep breath and plunged ahead. ". . . to intimacy, that go on a year or more, then end. They must be taking their toll."

"I know." Christina was nodding. "They are."

"I just look at you now—and I know this is foolish, don't laugh at me—and I don't see my happy little girl. It just breaks my poor silly heart." Christina started to stop her, but her mother touched her shoulder and continued. "No, I know what you've been through. I do, or a little. With Brian, and the pregnancy, and now this. I do know, hon, how it must hurt, how you're trying. But it just seems to me that every time you give up, when you let it end, then part of you dies. The part that hopes, and you don't want to lose that."

A tear coursed down Christina's cheek. She wiped it with a finger. "The good news is I didn't put much hope in Joe."

"Then why did you say you'd marry him?"

She kept nodding. "I don't know. I was stupid. I wanted to convince myself that I could do just what you said—commit to somebody and make it stick. To *get* there, Mom. You know what I mean? You get so tired of waiting, of things being empty."

Her mother sat back in her chair and looked for a moment out to the horizon. "It has to be right, that's all. The right person to begin with."

"Yeah, well where is he? That's what I want to know, Mom. Where the hell is he?"

"Christina? It's Mark Dooher."

"Mark. Are you all right?"

A refined chuckle. "I'm fine. I was worried about you. We've had a pretty good earthquake up here, you might have heard. Several people didn't make work and you were one of them. So we tried to reach you at home and you never called back . . ."

"Was I scheduled to come in? I've got finals next week. I wasn't starting until after that. I thought I told Joe . . ."

"No, no, it's all right. I was concerned, that's all. I remember you'd told me about Ojai, so I thought I'd see if your parents had heard from you, if you were okay."

"I am. In fact, I thought of you five minutes ago. We're drinking champagne. Remember? The lost art of pouring?"

"I do. How is it down there, by the way?"

She looked out through the French doors. A balmy evening was settling. "It's the pink moment," she said. "The classic pink moment."

She could almost see his grin. "I'm on my car phone, just at the Army Street curve on my way home and it's the classic gray moment here." A moment went by. "I heard about you and Joe. I'm sorry."

"Yes, well . . ."

The pause seemed a little awkward to Christina. She was thinking that Mark didn't want to push. But then he spoke up. "Well . . . good luck on your finals, then. And we'll see you in a couple of weeks?"

"I'll be there."

"I know you will. If it's any help to you, Joe should be down in LA by then. There shouldn't be any awkwardness."

"I know. I guess."

"No guesses. This is a promise. If you have any problems, I want you to come see me, hear?"

"I hear. I will."

"Okay, then." There was a crackle on the line. "Sorry, the call's breaking up. You hang in there, Christina. Things'll turn around, you watch. I'm glad you're okay."

"I am. And Mark?"

"Yes."

"Thanks for checking. It matters."

It might be the pink moment, but it was also the yellow jacket moment. At dusk, the vicious bees seemed to come up like locusts, scouring the foothills for food and making outdoor hors d'oeuvres a challenge at best.

But it was one to which Bill and Irene rose whenever they could. Christina remembered sitting inside a hundred times as a child, afraid to go out. Until one day her father had sat her down: "Look, we can either go outside where the weather's great and we've got the view and the air and things taste better, except we've got the *chance* of being molested by yellow jackets, or we can sit cooped inside wishing there weren't such a thing as yellow jackets, but *definitely* inside, and definitely not having half the fun. I'll take the risk every time."

So tonight they had broken out some pâté, three kinds of cheeses, cornichons, French bread, the works. After she'd hung up with Dooher, she stood a moment at the French doors, looking out at her parents who were sitting in their matching wicker chairs, holding hands, laughing at something.

Okay, she thought. There was her father and there was Mark Dooher. Two good ones. It wasn't impossible. She would simply have to bide her time, do her work, live her life.

The pink shifted, almost imperceptibly, to mother-of-pearl, and she still stood in the door, struck by her third revelation this week. The first had been that she didn't love Joe. Then recognizing something deeper—

something fundamentally different and better—in the way she and Mark Dooher related, something that would be part of her from now on, of any future she had.

Then, watching her parents, the last illumination —that she was still afraid of the yellow jackets, so wary of being bitten that she was afraid to go outside. That was why she had always settled for her lesser men.

It was so clear now, suddenly, and so wrong-headed: there had always been yellow jackets on otherwise perfect evenings, and she'd never gotten stung. And taking that risk of getting stung put you out where you really wanted to be.

It was the only way, with luck, to get you to where her parents had gotten.

To where she wanted to be.

19

"OF *COURSE* NOTHING HAPPENED TO YOU," WES said. "Why did I even feel like I had to ask? In fact, now that I think about it, I'm surprised some fissure didn't open in your backyard revealing a vein of gold."

"I didn't tell you about that?" Dooher put a hand on his friend's shoulder. "Just kidding," he said. "How's the face?"

Farrell had needed seven stitches and a tetanus shot. He had one bandage under his blackened left eye, another on the side of his mouth. "Let's go with unpleasant."

"No, how's it *feel?*"

Farrell gave him a look. "Funny."

It was Friday morning a little before noon, the day after the quake, and they were in Wes's office. Dooher took a seat in the ragged armchair. His friend was putting books back on the shelves. Bart, giving no sign that he'd ever been jumpy in his life, slept under the table.

"So how'd your office make out?" Wes asked. "Don't tell me, it wasn't touched."

"A little. It's a relatively new building with all the codes up-to-date. They don't shake much."

Farrell turned around. "You mean nothing, don't you?"

"Nothing structural. Couple of bookshelves fell over, like here."

"Not like here, Mark! Not like here. *Here* we got cracks in all the walls, maybe you didn't notice, the place has got to get completely repainted, we got plaster in the ducts, the water's out in the bathroom, *every single one* of my books hit the floor running"—he whirled further around, pointing, picking up some steam—"*that* window, check it out, is now plywood . . ." He blew out a long breath. "No! No, decidedly *not* just like here."

Bart came awake, barked once, went back to sleep.

Dooher, sympathetic as a hangman, held up a hand. "*Du calme*, Wesley, *du calme*."

"*Du calme*, my ass. Easy for you to say." His body sagging, Farrell crossed to his desk and edged himself onto the corner of it. "I know there's no justice in the world, and nothing happens for any reason, it's all random—all of that—but what I don't understand is why all this perverse, random shit *happens to me!*"

"It's like Grace," Dooher said.

"And don't give me any of that Catholic stuff, either."

"Not *that* Grace." Dooher crossed a leg, enjoying himself. "This lady, Grace, she's born ugly as sin, half blind, one leg missing, her hair never grows, she gets cancer at thirteen, a mess. Dies horribly and goes up to the pearly gates. God looks at her, says, 'Grace, you're going to hell.'

" 'But why?' she asks, 'why, God? I've tried to be a good person, tried to please you, suffered my whole life . . .'

" 'I don't know, Grace,' God says, 'there's just something about you that pisses me off.' "

Farrell was shaking his head. "I can understand why that joke would appeal to you. *You* are lucky. *I*, on the other hand, am cursed."

"Oh bullshit, Wes. People . . ."

"Stop! Stop! I know what you're going to say. That people make their own luck. *That* is what every lucky person in the world says, and *that* is bullshit!" He pushed himself off the desk, stepping on Bart's tail.

"Ruff!"

"You, dog, shut up! I don't want to hear any more out of you." Back to Dooher. "Look at me here, Mark. Look at me. My apartment is trashed, my office is ruined, my fucking dog—man's best mauling machine—nearly tears my head off . . ." He sank back to his corner of the desk, staring at his shoes.

"Wes . . ."

"I'm sorry. I'm just a whining sack, aren't I? But I have to tell you, sometimes the weight of what appears to be random bad luck just gets a little hard to take. It's not like I want something terrible to happen to you, but don't you sometimes wonder when it *never* does? Does this mean something about me? Jesus."

"Hey, come on." Dooher got out of his chair, walked over to his bud, put his arms around him. "Come on. I love you, Wes, you know that. You need help here, I'll send over some of my associates. You need it at home, some money, whatever, you got it. You want, I'll put a couple of gashes into my own face, bleed a little."

Farrell looked up, shook his head in disgust. "I'm a waste, aren't I?"

Dooher pinched his good cheek. "But cute. Come on, let me buy you some lunch."

It wasn't fancy, but the Chinese food was spicy hot and excellent. There were only six tables in the place, and Farrell took the opportunity to point out that he came here twice a week and *never* got an empty table.

But Mark Dooher walked in the door, and there was one with his name on it, and no, they didn't mind if the dog came in, too. The owner had a dog looked just like Bart. This led Farrell to wonder aloud if there was any part of Dooher's experience untouched by good fortune.

"For the record, I've got some pretty estranged, screwed-up kids, and you don't."

"I never *see* my kids," Farrell said.

"But when you do, they don't hate you, do they?"

"No. At least I don't think so."

"Mine hate me. My failed artist namesake son hates me. My lesbian daughter hates me. My skiboard bum son hates me."

"They don't . . ."

"Trust me, they do. You know it, too. Now I don't know whether that's luck or not, but it's not good. I must have had something to do with it."

"Okay, that's serious. Your life isn't perfect. I apologize."

A macho shrug, Dooher's mini-lesson in handling the pain the way a man should. "It's life," he said. "It hits us all. Which is actually, since we're on the subject, why I wanted to see you this morning. More bad luck for me. But this is business."

"What business?"

"I want to put you on retainer for a while as my personal attorney."

Farrell stopped with his chopsticks halfway to his mouth. "I'm listening."

"Victor Trang."

"Okay, what about him?"

"I think the police think I might have killed him."

"Get out . . . ! You? Are you kidding me?"

"I don't think so."

"Why do they think that?"

"I don't know. I'm not even a hundred percent sure they do, but this cop Glitsky called me the other—"

"Glitsky?"

"Yeah, that's his name. You know him?"

"He was the cop handling my last case, Levon Copes. Screwed it up completely."

"Well, that's a relief, I think. He might be screwing up this one, too."

"He thinks you *killed* Victor Trang? Why?"

"Take it easy, Wes. I'm not sure. But he's called me back a couple of times, zeroing in, asking questions— where was I, did I talk to Trang, that kind of thing."

"And you answered him?"

Dooher shrugged. "Sure. I've got nothing to hide. Why wouldn't I talk to him?"

"That doesn't matter. The first rule is *never* talk to a cop about a crime in your time zone without your lawyer sitting there."

"But I didn't . . ."

"Doesn't matter. What did he ask? What did you tell him?"

"Does this mean you're on retainer?"

Farrell nodded. "Yeah. Of course. What do you think?"

* * *

It was quarter past noon on Friday afternoon. Glitsky was walking the hallway on the fourth floor, heading back to Homicide. He'd spent the morning interviewing witnesses who lived in apartments on either side of his seventy-year-old victim who'd owned a handgun for protection—the man whose last thought had been that his gun was going to help him if a burglar ever broke in. Nope.

The last couple of days had been well over the line into surreal. At home, the earthquake damage had been serious but, miraculously, all cosmetic. They'd straightened up the armoire and rehung the clothes. In the boys' room, Jake had been crying out because it was dark and he'd been tipped out of his bed. Isaac and O.J. had remained so quiet because they'd slept through it all. (As he had, he reminded himself. If Flo hadn't yelled out for him . . .)

Then, all day yesterday, his wife wouldn't stay still. She had been up and around, throwing away the broken dishes, shards of pottery and glass, straightening, vacuuming, rearranging, even washing the windows. Nesting, nesting.

The day of the quake he'd stayed home. (A good day for it, as it turned out. There was not one homicide reported in San Francisco.) Today, day two, he couldn't stand seeing Flo working so hard, singing to herself, reborn. So much energy and sense of purpose—it was going to come crashing down. He couldn't let himself get his hopes up.

This was pure adrenaline—hers.

He wanted no part of it, and she didn't want him moping around, bringing her down. They'd almost had a fight about it—would have if he hadn't left.

So he'd gone to his morning interviews. Now, back at the Hall, his plan was to call around, line up some more witnesses on his other cases, call the phone company and check on the progress of Mark Dooher's records.

There was a package on his desk and he ripped it open. The phone records on Dooher weren't supposed to be delivered for at least another day, maybe two or three, but now here he was holding them in his hands.

Wonders did never cease.

Dooher's home was easy. He'd made no phone calls at all on the Monday that Trang had been killed. His office was a little more interesting. He'd called Trang twice—1:40 and 4:50—precisely the times noted in the dead man's computer.

Which meant that if Trang had been making up a story to impress his mother and girlfriend, major elements of it were close to the truth. His pulse quickening —the thrill of the chase indeed—Glitsky turned to the last little packet of sheets. There, as promised by Trang, was the third call, from Dooher's cell phone, at 7:25.

And even though Glitsky thought the official policy on miscreants in San Francisco was "Three strikes and you're misunderstood," this time he was getting willing to call Dooher out. He sat back in his chair, feet up on his desk, wondering what, if anything, it meant.

Trang's computer notes might have been cryptic, but they also told a consistent story—Mark Dooher was working on the settlement, not acting as an adviser on a personal injury case as he'd claimed. Glitsky could imagine no reason why Trang would lie to himself in his electronic notebook.

And here, looking, was another tantalizing entry —"MD from F.'s." The 7:25 call that Glitsky had interpreted to mean that Dooher had called from Flaherty's office. But, in fact, he'd made it from his car. What did that mean? Was it possible that "F" wasn't Flaherty?

Another thought—did Trang even have any personal injury cases in his files? This, Glitsky thought, was a job for the ever eager Paul Thieu. And the note? "MD message." There might be something the lab could salvage from the tape that had been in Trang's answering machine, even if it had been recorded over. He leaned forward, pulled his yellow pad toward him, and started writing.

He longed to catch Dooher in his lie. In any lie. There had to be one. In a kind of trance, he was lost in his notes. Then staring into the space in front of him. He picked up the telephone and punched some numbers.

"Law offices."

"Hello. This is Sergeant Glitsky, San Francisco homicide. I'd like to talk to Mr. Dooher's secretary, please. And I'm sorry, I don't remember her name."

"Janey."

"That's it. Thanks."

"Mr. Dooher's office."

"Janey?"

"Yes."

Another introduction, a little riff of bureaucratese, then he was saying: "Janey, I need to confirm a couple of things your boss told me. This is just routine . . ."

It turned out Janey did remember the call from Trang on the day he had died. He'd called while Dooher was at lunch, left an urgent message that Dooher get back to him.

"This was about the settlement deadline, isn't that right?"

Janey paused, perhaps wondering if she was saying too much. Glitsky didn't want to lose her. "I'm sorry," he said, "that was the impression I had." Let her think he'd gotten it from Dooher.

It worked. Janey continued. "Mr. Trang reminded me to tell Mr. Dooher that he needed to hear from him before five, no later, or that he'd have to go ahead and file the amended complaint the next day."

So *Trang*'s call to Dooher had been about the settlement. Janey had said as much. And that made Dooher a liar.

And if *that* was true, it dramatically increased the odds that, at the very least, Dooher knew more than he was letting on, and at the most, that he was a killer.

Glitsky was bouncing it off Frank Batiste. The lieutenant was sitting forward in his chair in his office, arms on his desk, pencil in hand, shaking his head. "I believe you, although I'd be a little happier if you had any idea why."

"Wasn't it you who's told us a zillion times that we're not in the motive business, we're in the evidence business?"

"Yep, that was me, and I was right."

"So?"

"So what? Where's your evidence then?" Batiste continued drumming his pencil. "Because we agree you don't have a motive."

But Glitsky didn't want to let the motive go. In his experience, people didn't often get killed—not by someone they knew—for no reason whatever. "Look, the Archdiocese is Dooher's biggest client. If the case gets filed, he gets fired."

"Why would that happen?"

"Because he hasn't done his job, which is keep the lawsuit hush-hush."

"And why would that be?"

Glitsky rolled his eyes. "Because, Frank, it's politically embarrassing to the Archbishop."

"So to keep it from getting filed, Dooher kills Trang? That's a reach, Abe."

"I know. But it's all I can think of."

Batiste straightened up, bopped his pencil a couple more times, stretched out the crick in his neck. "Are you sure you're not just on Dooher because you haven't got any other suspects?"

"Maybe there aren't any other suspects because he did it, Frank."

"Maybe that's it." Batiste didn't want to fight about it. He took a beat. "Well, that was instructive and a hell of a lot of fun. We should do it again sometime. This was where we started, isn't it? No motive? So let's leave motive. You came in here wanting to talk evidence. Evidence is good. What do you got?"

But there wasn't much. Glitsky had gotten his search warrant for Dooher's phone records by trotting out the old probable cause argument to Judge Arenson, who knew him fairly well and was aware that he didn't abuse the privilege.

Now the question was whether the information in the phone records—the three calls that coincided with Trang's notes—moved things along the probable cause trail. Glitsky knew that the judge wasn't about to give him carte blanche on the more invasive search warrants he was going to want to request—Dooher's house, office, car, and so on—unless there was something real—whether or not it was physical evidence—to back up Glitsky's suspicions.

He was hoping the phone calls would be enough, but Batiste wasn't buying that either, and didn't think Arenson would. "So is this just your day to be difficult, Frank, or what?"

The pencil was tap-tapping again. "What do they prove, Abe? The calls."

"Dooher said they were talking about a personal injury case. Trang's notes say it was the settlement." Even as he said it, Glitsky knew the objection, and it was valid.

"So it's 'he said this, but he said that.' "

"But Dooher's secretary, Janey, agrees with Trang."

"She didn't overhear the last two calls."

"Why would Trang have written fictitious notes to himself on the calls? That just doesn't make any sense."

Batiste held up the pencil. "Abe, even if they talked about the settlement, even if Dooher is lying about it, we got nothing. Maybe Dooher was sleeping with Trang's girlfriend."

"Or his mother," Glitsky said. "Maybe his girlfriend *and* his mother."

Batiste liked it. "Now we're on to something."

Glitsky's lips were pressed tightly together in frustration, and the scar stood out in relief. "I need a warrant. I've got to look through the guy's laundry."

Batiste didn't think so. "Arenson won't do it, not with what you've got so far. You're going to need more. What about the bayonet?"

"He never brought it home from Viet—" Stopping short.

Batiste broke a smile. "Says he."

"Lord, I'm stupid! The wife!"

If she invited him in, he would not need a warrant.

He kept a white shirt and regimental tie in the drawer of his desk for the occasional forgotten court date. He changed in the men's room and traded his flight jacket until tomorrow for Frank Batiste's gray sport coat—a little short in the sleeves, but the chest fit. It would do.

He was on the semi-enclosed front porch, his badge out, introducing himself to Sheila Dooher. There had been sun and a cool breeze at the Hall, but out here, a mile from the ocean, the fog clung and a savage wind dug itself into his bones. He didn't mind, though. At this moment, it was to his advantage.

". . . the Victor Trang case. You're familiar with that?"

"Yes. It was really such a tragedy. Mark was very upset about it."

"Yes he was. I'd been planning on coming by a little later, when your husband was home, but I was in the neighborhood, and thought I could save some time. I wanted to ask you a few questions, too."

"Me?"

"Yes, ma'am."

"What about? I didn't even know Victor Trang."

Glitsky shrugged. "But you know where your husband was on the night of the murder."

"Yes. Well, I don't know. You don't think . . . ?"

"I don't think anything at the moment, Mrs. Dooher. But the fact is that your husband was one of the last people we know who talked to Victor Trang. So, far-fetched as it might seem to you, he's a suspect. And you could eliminate that possibility right now. Was he here that night, Monday a week ago?"

He noticed that she was gripping the door handle, her face set, eyes shifting. "I think I should call Mark," she said.

"You could do that, but you understand that anything you say to me now, before talking with him, will have a lot more weight. You could verify his alibi right now and that would be the end of any suspicion." He added conspiratorially, "Really, ma'am. It would be a good thing."

She wrestled with it a moment, then dredged it up. "Monday night. He went to the driving range, I think. I could check."

"That's what your husband said." Glitsky broke his smile. "See, that wasn't so bad."

Behind him, the wind gusted, and Sheila Dooher seemed to notice it for the first time. "I'm sorry, Sergeant. Would you like to come in out of this weather?"

"I wouldn't mind, now that you mention it."

She fixed him a cup of tea. They were sitting on either side of a marble bar in a sky-lit kitchen that was about the size of Glitsky's duplex. Through the French doors, he had a partial view of an expanse of manicured lawn, a patch of early daffodils, stubbly bare roots and trunks marking an ancient rose garden.

He took a slow sip of the tea, swallowed, then plunged in. "Mrs. Dooher, your husband was very upset by Victor Trang's death. He asked me if there was anything he could do to help with our investigation."

Her expression, pleasant concern, teased at the edges of his conscience. But, more importantly, it meant that Dooher hadn't told her that he was under suspicion.

"That's Mark," she said, waiting for Glitsky to continue.

"I really didn't think much about it until we discovered that Trang had been stabbed with a bayonet."

"Oh, God, how horrible!"

He nodded. "Yes, ma'am, it was bad. But the point

is, we weren't able to go much farther than that. The weapon hasn't been found—undoubtedly the murderer's thrown it away. Anyway, I mentioned all this to your husband—he wanted to be kept in the loop—telling him that if we could just identify exactly what *kind* of bayonet it was, from the size of the blade and so on"— he assayed a smile, speaking more quickly now, hoping to keep her riding on the flow of verbiage—"the forensics guys can tell these things, that we might be able to determine where it had been bought, or what war it might have been used in, that kind of thing. And from there maybe get a lead as to where the murderer might have got it."

He hoped.

She was paying attention, still with him.

"I was hoping to compare it with the one your husband brought back from Vietnam. Trang being Vietnamese, it might narrow it down to someone in that community. It's a long shot, but might be worth checking."

She was nodding. "I'm not sure I completely understand, but it sounds like it might be a good idea." She stood up. "I think it's out in the garage, up pretty high. You might have to help me get it. Do you mind?"

20

B Y DUSK, FARRELL STILL HADN'T REACHED SAM.
It worried him enough that he decided to drive by her house, find out what was going on.

Yesterday, the day of the quake, okay, lots of lives had been disrupted, his own more than many others. While he was trying to get his own mess cleaned up, he'd tried to call Sam a few times, but had no luck.

He'd been sure he'd get her today.

But he'd started calling as soon as he woke up, had placed maybe two dozen calls, and nothing. Her machine hadn't even picked up, neither had the phone at the clinic, no one had heard from her. Her brother Larry had an unlisted number.

Farrell eventually even thought to call Dooher back after their surprising lunch, to see if by any chance he had Christina Carrera's number, if she might have heard from Sam. But no, Dooher said Christina was in Ojai, visiting her parents.

Why and how did Mark know that?

The first indication that something might really be wrong was the construction equipment all the way up Ashbury Street, stopping traffic trying to get up over Twin Peaks. Farrell was in his 1978 Datsun, painted by his son six years previously in what Lydia called a "fetching puke yellow." (Lydia was driving the metallic green 1992 BMW—he really hated her.) Bart wasn't enjoying the wait in the fog and fumes any more than he was.

Finally, when divine intervention produced a parking space, he pulled in and decided he and Bart would hoof it. It was time Bart met Quayle anyway, he thought. He attached the dog's leash and they got out.

But drawing up closer, getting to Sam's block, he was struck by the air of disaster, and hurried his steps. There were more than a few police cars, plus other emergency vehicles. A revolving knot of gawkers milled around in the street, quietly taking in the destruction.

Four brick structures in a row on the west side of the street, with Sam's third on the way uphill, had taken the big hit. All of them had lost their chimneys, a majority of their street-facing windows. Though crews were still there and had obviously been at the cleaning awhile, piles of brick rubble and roof slate still littered the area.

Supporting scaffolding had already been erected around the two downhill buildings, but Sam's, from the look of it, might be beyond salvage. The front corner appeared to have caved in completely, and the entire house listed forward as though waiting for one more tiny aftershock to send it toppling.

My God! he thought. That was Sam's room. She was in there!

Farrell walked up to one of the blue-uniformed policemen who were keeping the crowd from getting too close to the unstable structure. "Excuse me. I know somebody who lives in that building. Do you have any news about the tenants?"

The cop turned around, his eyes sympathetic. "Have you tried the hospitals? Maybe I'd start there."

Wes nodded mutely, then stood another minute, struck again by the power of moving earth. "Excuse me," he repeated. "Do you know if anybody died in these buildings?"

The cop shook his head, commiserating, conveying the worst. "I'd check the hospitals," he said again.

Once Sheila Dooher admitted that her husband had owned a bayonet—although it was no longer in the garage—Glitsky thought that getting his search warrant would be easy.

He filled out his new one and brought it down to this week's duty judge, Martin Arenson. But Arenson, like everyone else, was cleaning up from the earthquake. He'd handed off his magistrate assignments to another municipal court judge, Ann Connor, and she hadn't been particularly receptive to Abe's version of probable cause. She'd refused to sign the warrant, which put him in a bind, since once one judge in the Muni court declined to sign a warrant, no one else there would touch it.

Glitsky did have another option—one he'd used in emergencies in the past—he could go to Superior Court and get a sealed warrant from one of the judges on the senior bench. He was fairly well known in Superior Court since most trials he attended were for homicides. And he was anxious to move quickly, before Dooher had a chance to hide or ditch anything else.

* * *

"But the wife can't testify against him." Judge Oscar Thomasino had the search warrant in front of him on his clean desk, awaiting his signature. He'd listened to Glitsky's tale and wasn't close to sold on more probable cause. "And am I wrong? I don't see anything pointing to this man, except your questionably legal search."

"She let me in, Judge."

Thomasino waved a hand. Sixtyish, he wore his gray hair brush cut. He had thick slab of a face, a swarthy, liver-spotted complexion, and a reputation as a judicial hardass.

It was Friday night and he had been going home after a grueling week of earthquake-related delays, but Glitsky had caught him at the back door and tried to guilt him back inside. He'd come, but out of duty, not guilt, and now he wasn't disposed to be cooperative, and he treated Glitsky to his bushy eyebrow trick—up and down over the glare. No words.

"I don't need her testimony, Your Honor," Glitsky repeated. "I just need what might be in the house."

The judge smoothed his hands over the grain of his desk. "Abe, this is a prominent man, not some low-life from the projects, not that as a matter of law that makes any difference, of course. And you're telling me you didn't find out anything incriminating from the phone records?"

Glitsky more or less agreed, but tried to sweeten it by riffing around it for a couple of bars. Thomasino stopped him. "I don't see this one, Abe." The judge straightened up in his chair, considering something, decided to come out with it. "You know, Abe, this business of coming to Superior Court when Muni turns you down is tricky. I know you've got good instincts; you might even be right. But what I see here, I don't have enough. Connor didn't either."

"Judge . . ."

Thomasino held up his hand again. "I understand you can't go back to Muni, not now. But you've got to get me a little more. If you find it, come by the house, I'm around all weekend. I'll sign off. But I need something I can point to. Do you even know where he *was* on the night in question?"

"He was killing Victor Trang."

A face, the eyebrows. "Okay. But what does he say?"

"He says he went to the driving range, then came back to his office and worked late."

"Well, if he did that, maybe somebody saw him. Or didn't."

"That may be."

"Well, good luck," the judge said. "Have a nice weekend."

Glitsky was damned if he was going to find himself a picture of Mark Dooher and go trotting with it out to the city's driving ranges, showing it to employees and asking if they specifically remembered seeing him a week and a half before. If he thought that course of events would produce any results, he might have considered it, but he believed what he'd told Thomasino. Dooher had been killing Trang that night, not hitting golf balls.

But the bottom line was that he didn't have the signed warrant and couldn't go looking where he stood a chance of finding, so what the hell else was he going to do?

Pondering, he was standing in the downstairs

lobby of the Hall, by the elevators, hands in his pockets, oblivious to the passing throngs checking out for the weekend.

"Too much lemon in your tea, Abe?" Amanda Jenkins, the assistant DA who'd shared Levon Copes with him, had moved out of the flow of humanity and, amused, was looking up at him. "That expression—I just sucked on a lemon—it's so *you*."

"It so happens I *did* just suck on a lemon." He held up the unsigned warrant. "But what's really made my day is Thomasino's call on this."

Jenkins snatched it away and scanned it quickly. "This looks good to me. House, car, office, personal effects. What's the problem?"

"You'll notice the good judge didn't sign it. My first choice for perp appears to be a pillar of the community, so he's got a higher probable cause threshold than lesser mortals."

"Ah, democracy . . ."

"Ain't it grand? I don't have any evidence, so I can't get permission to look for evidence."

"It's a beautiful system," Jenkins agreed. "So what *do* you have? You got anything? You must have something."

Glitsky started to tell Amanda what he did have— his hunches, the settlement background, the discrepancy between Trang's women's story and Mark Dooher's, the hazy alibi, the bayonet that had mysteriously—and apparently recently—disappeared, and finally the one search warrant the judge had signed off on, for Dooher's phone records.

"They don't by any chance include a car phone, do they?"

"Yeah. But so what?"

Jenkins's normally stern visage cracked. Her eyes

lit up with excitement. "You got time to take five, get some coffee? All may not be lost."

The downstairs cafeteria was nearly deserted, cavernous and echoing with the cleanup workers' efforts. Glitsky and Jenkins brought their paper cups over from the long stainless steel counter and were sitting down across from one another at one of the fold-up tables, Amanda already rolling with it, explaining the new technological investigating tool breakthrough that had been discovered as a by-product of the cellular phone network. "You never heard of it," she enthused, "because I don't think anybody's ever used it to find out where someone *was*. Normally, they used it to track where somebody *is*, right now."

"Okay?"

But she could see Glitsky still wasn't clear on the concept. "Abe, you remember that big kidnap/ransom thing in Oakland last year? Okay, the kidnapper, he's calling the victim's family every five minutes, making ransom demands, changing the drop point, making sure there's no tail, the usual. So guess what? He's using his car phone, and one of our guys remembers an article in one of those magazines we all throw away. He gets a brainstorm. He calls the phone company, asks if there's any way they can tell, even roughly, where a cell call originates. You know how it works?"

"I'm listening."

"Big metropolitan area like Oakland, there's maybe ten towers around the city—cells, hence the name. Clever, huh? And they work like a combination amplifier/receiver. If you're in your car, you move from one cell to the next and there's a record of it."

"Okay."

"But, and this is the cool part, *within each cell* there are also pie-shaped cones that pick up the signals. So this guy, the kidnapper, he's talking on the phone, calling again, yack, yack, yack. They figure out *exactly which block he's driving around*, and they nail him."

Glitsky was nodding. Amanda was right. This, if true, was cool. "But I don't see how it helps me here," he said.

"I don't either, Abe. But Thomasino said he only needed a little more to get to probable cause, right? So maybe your perp was ten miles away when he said he was at the driving range, that kind of thing. Prove he lied. Hell, you've got the warrant for the phone records already. Might as well use it all up."

Sheila told him what she'd done.

"Are you kidding me? That son of a bitch! He came in here, lied to you, invaded our privacy? I'm calling Farrell, calling somebody. This is pure harassment. I'll have the bastard's badge!"

He threw his leaded crystal bourbon glass with all his might and it smashed into the bottom pane of one of the French doors, shattering glass all over the kitchen. "That son of a bitch!"

Sheila was in a deep couch in her living room, crying. She was of a class and station that had grown up believing in authority. Sergeant Glitsky had represented that to her. And he had betrayed her, tricked her and used her to insult her husband. She had put her husband in jeopardy. She couldn't stop sobbing.

Mark came over and handed her a large glass of white wine and she held it with both hands. He sat down next to her. "It's all right, Sheila. How could you know?"

She shook her head, mumbling through her tears, over and over: "I should have known. I should have just called you."

He put the palm of his hand under her glass and helped her raise it to her lips. She had to admit that it helped. She took another mouthful, the good cool wine.

She'd been getting back to a glass or two regularly lately and it hadn't caused her any ill effects. The doctors nowadays were always so paranoid about alcohol. She should have started out taking their dire warnings with a grain of salt. This wasn't hurting her at all. In fact, it was helping.

She got her breathing back under control. "The whole story didn't make much sense to me, Mark, but I just thought . . ."

"It's all right," he repeated. "There's no harm done. I didn't even have any damn bayonet."

"I know. But I didn't remember . . ."

"I lost the damn thing on a camping trip five ten years ago, maybe longer. You don't remember?"

"But why would he think, the sergeant . . . ?"

Her husband shook his head. "I have no idea. I knew Trang. Maybe I'm the most convenient warm body. I think that's how these guys work." He reached out, laid a hand on her shoulder.

"So what happens now?" she asked timidly.

Mark sat back into the couch. "Now I think he'll probably come back with a warrant and tear the house apart, and maybe my car, and the office. I've got the M-16, after all, and he's seen it, and some judge will probably believe that means something and give him the search warrant. After all, I did steal it from the army, demonstrating my long-standing history of criminal moral character."

"You were twenty-three years old!" she cried. "You haven't broken a law in almost twenty-five years."

"Well, I did cut the tag off a mattress once."

"Don't be funny. Please, not now." She was shaking her head. "God, this is unbelievable. This can't be happening to us."

Farrell kicked himself for being so stupid, but at the moment he hadn't seen any alternative. He had to drive all the way home in the lower Sunset District to leave Bart anyway, and he decided to make his calls to hospitals from there. Ten minutes later, he found himself in his car again, driving the three miles back, nearly an hour at this time on a Friday night, to within five hundred yards of where he'd started—St. Mary's Hospital.

Wes hated almost everything about hospitals—the smells, the light, the sound that somehow always seemed to be simultaneously muted and amplified. As the elevator opened on the fourth floor, he let out a sigh of relief. This wasn't the intensive care unit. He realized he'd been afraid to ask.

He stopped at the door to the room. The bed wasn't visible—the room separators had been pulled halfway around it—but Larry and Sally, Sam's brother and his wife, were sitting next to one another, talking quietly.

"Hey, comrades," he said. "She never calls, she never writes. Is this the party?" Then, seeing Sam, her head wrapped in gauze, one arm above the blanket and one strapped to her body, he came forward, up beside her bed. "Hi."

He found his hand clutched by her free one. There were sickly black and yellow wells under both of her eyes, a bandage over the bridge of her nose. He saw her make the effort, to try to smile to greet him, but it cost her. Her eyes moistened, and he leaned over to her, gently brought his cheek next to hers, left it there. "God," he said. "Thank God."

"She's going to be okay." He heard Larry behind him. "Couple more days and she's out of here."

He straightened up, still holding her hand, looking at her. "I'll ask these guys," he said.

Larry and Sally told him. Sam had, actually, been very lucky, suffering only a concussion, a broken nose, a broken collarbone, multiple bruises and abrasions. She'd been buried by brick and mortar, but the beams in the ceiling had prevented the house from collapsing on her. They'd pulled her out within three hours.

"And how's Quayle? Is he okay?"

Her grip tightened. She shook her head and a tear broke and rolled across her cheek.

Glitsky thought the day might never end, but the trail was getting hot, and this was where you didn't quit.

After he left Amanda, he ran up the outside stairs to Homicide, where he called the cellphone company. Because of the earthquake, a supervisor, Hal Frisque, was actually on duty, working late, pulling a ton of overtime. He would love to help.

So five minutes after faxing a copy of his warrant to Frisque, Glitsky was again on the phone at his desk, a map of San Francisco open in front of him.

"We're talking the seven-forty call, is that right?" Frisque asked.

"That's what I've got here," Glitsky said.

"Okay." A pause. "That's zone SF-43. You got a map there? Looks like he was on the 280 Freeway. Had to be, because a minute later, he got picked up in SF-42, so he was going west."

Glitsky was lost in possibilities, but none of them helped him very much. True, Trang had been killed near the 280 Freeway, south of it, on Geneva Avenue, but to get to the San Francisco Golf Club and Driving Range, or to Dooher's home, for that matter, his car could have taken the same route.

But Frisque was continuing. "Okay, now he moves to DC-3."

"Further west?"

A short moment, then: "No, mostly south. DC, Daly City picked him up. Check your map. I'd say it looks like he left the freeway at Geneva and went south. No way to tell how far, because the call ends. Sergeant Glitsky?"

"I'm here."

Dooher left the freeway and turned south on Geneva at seven forty-one, knowing at that time that Trang was sitting in his office alone.

Got him!

21

ARCHBISHOP FLAHERTY HAD CANCELED HIS OTHER appointments for this Monday morning. This was more important. The entire situation was getting out of hand, as a matter of fact. Over the weekend, the police had torn apart Mark Dooher's world, finding nothing that tied him to Victor Trang in the process. It was unconscionable, irresponsible and appalling.

So his spartan office was crowded with a gaggle of lawyers. His full-time staff corporate counsel, Gabe Stockman, was punching something into his laptop. Dooher and he had been in touch over much of the weekend, and now he and *his* attorney, a man unknown to Flaherty named Wes Farrell, had arrived. They were pouring themselves some coffee from the small table near the window that overlooked the schoolyard.

"What I'd like to know," Flaherty said, "is why they seem to have settled on you, Mark."

Wes Farrell, the new guy, stopped stirring his coffee. "Mark owned a bayonet once. He talked to Trang.

They don't have anybody else. That's what they have. Beyond that, I've got a theory if you'd like to hear it."

"At this point, I'd like to hear anything that makes sense."

"Glitsky. Sergeant Glitsky. I understand you've met him, too. That he also attacked you."

"That might be a little strong," Flaherty said. "He wasn't very sociable, let's say that."

"Well, regardless, Your Excellency, I did a little checking, a couple of people I know at the Hall of Justice. He is having some serious personal problems. His wife is dying. He screwed up his last major investigation —which happened to be another one of my clients. At the same time, he's bucking for promotion and he needs a high-profile success in a bad way. And guess who oversees police promotions? The chief, Dan Rigby, who's a pawn of the mayor, who is, in turn, just a little bit left-wing."

Flaherty interrupted. "You're telling me this is political."

Now Stockman looked up, putting in his own two cents. "*Everything's* political."

Emboldened by the support, Farrell was warming up. "So here's how it breaks. The mayor's support is ninety percent blacks, women's groups and gays, am I right? Hell, he's got two gay supervisors in his pocket. The Catholic Church, represented by my client here, Mark Dooher, is anti-abortion, anti-women priests, anti-gay . . ."

"That's not entirely accurate," Flaherty said. He really didn't like the anti-this and anti-that rhetoric. If Farrell was going to be representing Dooher, he'd have to try to get him to retool his vocabulary. The Church was pro-life, pro-family, pro-marriage. It was not a negative institution.

But Farrell waved off his objection and kept rolling. "So Glitsky is willing to go the extra mile to bring Mark to grief. Even if the evidence is lame, and it's less than that, he puts himself on the side of the people who can promote him, who can watch out for his ass. Pardon the language."

The room went silent.

"Could that really be it?" Flaherty asked. "That's very hard to believe. I mean, this is the police department of a major city."

Farrell sipped his coffee. "It's one man."

Dooher held up a hand. His voice was cool water. "Glitsky's not the issue here, Wes. There is absolutely no evidence tying me to Victor. I was out driving golf balls. I forgot to tell Glitsky that I had stopped on Geneva to get gas on the way out to the range. I foolishly paid with cash. The attendant who took my money had his nose buried in some Asian newspaper and consequently didn't remember me or my car. Or anyone else, I'd wager. So Glitsky thinks I lied, covered up. That's not it. Even if Glitsky's out to get me, somebody out there has got to believe I'm innocent. Maybe the DA himself. Chris Locke."

This, Flaherty realized, was why he valued Dooher so highly. He saw things clearly. Even here at the center of this maelstrom, he was formulating a firm, effective strategy. It was ridiculous to think that Mark Dooher would ever have to resort to violence of any kind. He was too smart. He could destroy without a touch. "Let me try that," Flaherty said. "I'll call Locke, explain the situation. See if he can help clear things up."

Chris Locke was the city's first black district attorney and a consummate political animal, and he was sitting alone in his office thinking about Archbishop James Flaherty, with whom he had just spoken.

Locke knew that Flaherty influenced a lot of votes in San Francisco through parish homilies, position papers, public appearances, pastoral letters. He also knew that conservatives, constituting perhaps thirty percent of the city's voters, played at best only a peripheral role in any election, but that it would be foolish to ignore them completely. Locke, though a prosecutor, was on the mayor's liberal team (as any elected official in San Francisco had to be), but his private support of the Archbishop might in some future election tip the scales in his favor. Locke thought that cooperating with a powerful conservative like Flaherty, behind the scenes, was worth the risk.

But something in Locke knew it wasn't just the votes. It was more visceral, more immediate, and he was addicted to it—having something *on* people who held authority and power. And Flaherty had taken the unusual step of asking Locke for a favor. That was worth looking into.

Though he directed all prosecutions in the city, Locke was rarely current on the progress of investigations being conducted at any given time—they were police business. The DA came later.

But, of course, he had his sources. He could find out.

Art Drysdale sat behind his desk juggling baseballs. Now in his late fifties, he'd played about two weeks of major league ball for the Giants before he'd gone to law school, and the wall behind him still sported some framed and yellowing highlights from college ball and the minors.

For the past dozen years, Drysdale had run the day-to-day work of the DA's office, and Locke depended on him for nearly all administrative decisions. The DA had come down to Drysdale's smaller office, knocked on the door, and let himself in, closing the door behind him.

Drysdale never stopped juggling.

"How do you do that?"

"What? Oh, juggling?"

"No, I wasn't talking about juggling. What makes you think I was talking about juggling?"

The balls came down—plop, plop, plop—in one of Drysdale's hands, and he placed them on his desk blotter. "It's a gift," he said. "What's up?"

"What do you know about Mark Dooher?"

The chief assistant DA knew just about everything there was to date about Mark Dooher. Drysdale believed in a smooth pipeline from the police department, through the DA's office, and on to the courts. He stayed in touch with Chief Rigby, with the calendar judge, with his assistant DAs, such as Amanda Jenkins. He generally knew about things before they officially happened, if not sooner. If asked, he would undoubtedly say that his prescience, too, was a gift.

So he ran the Dooher story down for his boss. It was a tasty mixture: Flaherty's fears, Dooher's mysterious turnoff onto Geneva near the time of the murder, the bayonet question, the interviews with Trang's women, Glitsky's recent overaggressive stand on Levon Copes, the stress he was under because of his wife's illness.

"But not much evidence yet?"

Drysdale shook his head. "Not that I've heard. They searched all weekend."

"Flaherty says this Dooher is a pillar of the community."

"Community pillars have been known to kill people."

"We know this, Art. But His Excellency thinks that maybe Glitsky's harassing Dooher for some reason."

"The famous 'some reason' . . ."

"The point is, Flaherty is really unhappy. *Really* unhappy. He's also worried that Glitsky will arrest Dooher for murdering Trang anyway, even if he's light on evidence."

Drysdale was shaking his head no. "Glitsky's a stone pro, Chris. He's not going to arrest him without a warrant. If there's no evidence, there's no evidence."

"And there is none?"

"Nowhere near enough. So far."

"So I can tell the Archbishop he needn't worry?"

"If things don't change. But"—Drysdale held up a warning finger—"they often do."

"I'll keep that in mind, Art. But in the meanwhile"—he stood up—"if we're hassling this guy, whatever reason, I want the word out it's to stop. We get righteous evidence or we let it go. We in accord here?"

"That's the way we always do it, Chris."

Locke was at the door. "I know that. I don't want to criticize a good cop who's having problems, Art, but Flaherty seems to know that we've got no matching hairs or fibers or fingerprints, no blood, no bayonet. And no motive. Am I right?"

"Yep."

"All right."

Drysdale stared at the door for a moment after it closed behind the DA. Then he picked up his baseballs again. Locke, he thought, had his own gift: The man knew how to deliver a message.

* * *

Glitsky's fears about his wife were well founded. After three days of whirlwind housecleaning following the earthquake, she had faked feeling better on Sunday morning. When Glitsky had left to continue serving his search warrant, she had gone back to bed.

She sent all three boys out to the movies, with instructions not to return until dinnertime. Flo knew that her nurse, and Abe's father, Nat, would be back on Monday. She thought she'd be fine until then. She didn't want to burden anybody, which is all she did anymore.

But this morning she hadn't been able to get out of bed. The nurse was in with her. Abe had put off going to work and now he and Nat sat in the living room armchairs in the same attitude—hunched over, elbows on their knees.

"She's got to do what she's got to do, Abraham. Maybe all the cleaning, it did her some good. For her soul."

Glitsky didn't have it in him to argue anymore. It had been a thoroughly dispiriting weekend. Hours of work and nothing to show for it. There had been no sign of Mark Dooher's bayonet. The lab would be coming in with microscopic results over the next few days, but Glitsky held out little hope of finding anything. Dooher had lots of suits in his closet at home, ten pairs of shoes, and all of them were pristine. It had been basically the same story at his office—less clothes, but everything spotless. His files gave no indication of any meeting with Trang. He kept his golf clubs in the trunk.

And in pursuit of those meager pickings, Abe hadn't been there for Flo, and now his father was talking about her soul. Well, he no longer cared about her soul. He cared about her body—that it wasn't causing her pain, if it could somehow stop betraying her. Even, God forgive him, that it let her rest for good. "Maybe you're right, Dad. Maybe it helped her soul."

"But you don't think so?"

He shrugged. "It doesn't matter. She did it. It wore her out. Now she's worse."

"But for those couple of days, she was better."

There was nothing Glitsky wanted to say. He might feel like howling at the moon, but he didn't want to yell at his dad, who was cursed with the need to find meaning in life, an explanation for the randomness of experience.

The telephone rang and he made some hopeless gesture to Nat, got up, and went to the kitchen to answer it.

It was Frank Batiste. Locke's message had made its way through the system, and he heard it, said "thanks," and hung up.

"Who was that?" His father was standing in the hallway between the kitchen and his bedroom.

Glitsky stared ahead. "Work."

"If it's important, you can go in. I'll be here. Flo . . ."

"No," Glitsky said. "Just a case closing, that's all."

PART THREE

22

On Tuesday, June 7, about six weeks after Abe Glitsky was told to forget about Mark Dooher and Victor Trang, he got a call at his home. It was 11:14 by the clock next to his new bed. He had gotten home an hour before, turned on and off the television, made a cup of tea, opened a book. Finally, he had gone in to his bedroom to lie down.

The house was empty now, except for him. The boys were staying at a friend's until Glitsky could finish the interview process for the nanny/housekeeper he was going to hire.

In the first five days after Flo's death, he'd talked to two pleasant-enough young women, and both interviews had been disasters. Glitsky knew he had been to blame—he probably wouldn't have hired himself under these conditions. He should give himself a week or two to come to grips with his desolation, his anger, his despair.

He was fighting to keep desperation out of the

picture, reminding himself that there really was no hurry, it had only been a few days. He'd find someone.

The new bed was a double. He and Flo had had a queen, but the first night after she was gone he found he couldn't make himself get into it. He knew he would keep turning as he tried to sleep and be newly surprised to find her side empty time after time. So that first night he'd slept, or tried to, on the couch in the living room. The next day he'd called the Salvation Army and they'd come and then the bed was gone. But even the smaller one felt enormous.

He was still in his clothes, one hand over his eyes, squinting at the digital clock. He reached for the telephone.

"Glitsky."

"Abe, this is Frank Batiste. I know you're on leave and you can say no, but they got me at home and asked, and I thought you'd want to decide for yourself. We just got a nine one one from a frantic husband in St. Francis Wood. His wife's been stabbed. She's dead."

"Okay."

"The caller was Mark Dooher. The woman's his wife."

His feet were over the edge of his bed, onto the floor. "Send a squad car by. I'll hitch a ride with it."

Glitsky didn't hear Batiste start to ask if he was sure, he didn't have to . . . he'd already hung up.

He remembered the house more vividly than he would have thought. He saw a lot of homes in his job and they tended to blur together. But this one was distinctive with its tiled front courtyard behind the low stucco fence, the turret in the front, the semi-enclosed entrance, the broad sweeping lawn with its fifty-year-old magnolia tree, which was in bloom, scenting the clear, still-warm air.

Glitsky stood a minute surveying the front of the house, now all lit up. Someone was moving in the turret, but he couldn't see through the blinds.

The coroner's van hadn't yet arrived, but there was an ambulance in the driveway. Three other black-and-white squad cars from the early responding officers were parked on the street. The yellow crime scene tape had been hung over a wide perimeter around the driveway and across the lawn. Within it, a couple of uniforms were standing guard, talking.

Glitsky had to remind himself that this was St. Francis Wood, and that police response time here was measured in minutes, not hours as was often the case in less tony neighborhoods.

He was directed to the driveway and saw three other men standing in front of the ambulance. The two in uniform would be the lieutenant and the sergeant from the district station, which was Taraval. The third saw Glitsky and started walking down toward him. It was Paul Thieu.

On Glitsky's recommendation, Thieu had recently been detailed full time to the death department, and he'd been in the office at the Hall pulling long hours when the eight-oh-two—a coroner's case—had been patched through from Emergency Services. Thieu had called Batiste, which was why Abe was here.

Glitsky met him halfway. Further up the drive, he noticed the pool of light under an open side door. "Where's Dooher?"

"Library downstairs, over in that turret area. Couple of guys are with him." Thieu had quickly improved in the chatter department. He'd also learned how to answer questions.

"Okay. I guess he'll wait."

They approached the Taraval station people—Lieutenant Armanino and Sergeant Dorney—and Thieu introduced Glitsky around. Armanino was taking pains to explain to the downtown homicide inspectors that the guys from his station had secured the place well. The woman upstairs was, in fact, dead. She'd been obviously and thoroughly dead when they got here. So the paramedics hadn't moved the body or touched anything.

Thieu needed to talk. "Stabbed in her bed, Abe. It looks like a burglary gone bad, maybe attempted rape. Sheets and blankets tossed pretty good. Lots of blood—she must have cut the guy."

Hands in his pocket, Glitsky nodded. "Okay, let's go on up."

"Before you do," Armanino interrupted, "there are a couple of other things, Sergeant. The paramedics and responding officers were here when we arrived, but we got here right after. Nobody else has been in the driveway. There was no obvious blood on it, though there might be a drop or two, some spatter. I'll keep it clean till the crime scene guys get here." Armanino was a stickler for details. Glitsky thought it was undoubtedly how he'd made lieutenant. "But in the meanwhile, one of my guys"—he indicated the policemen standing in the driveway—"found this." He showed Glitsky a Ziploc bag containing something white dotted with red.

Glitsky took it. "What is it?"

"It's a surgical glove. It was there in the dirt by the back door, which was evidently the point of exit. Maybe entry, too. The lightbulb, by the way"—again he indicated with gesture—"was dark, unscrewed."

"Unscrewed?"

Armanino nodded. "Dorney here put on his own

gloves and turned it and it came right back on. And this."

Another, larger bag, containing what, at a glance, appeared to be the murder weapon—a high-quality kitchen knife. "The blade's pretty clean, isn't it?"

"It got wiped."

"But a lot upstairs?"

Armanino shrugged. "You'll see." What it meant, if anything, wasn't for him to determine. Neither was Glitsky's definition of "a lot." He was simply reporting what he and his men had found.

"That it?"

Armanino looked at Dorney and the sergeant nodded. A well-oiled machine, these two. Good cops. "For now, I think so."

"Okay, Paul," Glitsky said, "let's go."

At the side door, he turned and added quietly, "Thanks for having Batiste call me."

The side door opened onto a laundry room with black-and-white-checkered tile floors, a washing machine and dryer. They walked through into the beautiful, marble-countered kitchen, where Glitsky had once sat with Sheila Dooher and had tea.

There were voices coming out of the turret room, but Glitsky followed Thieu as he turned into the foyer and they ascended the stairs to a balustraded landing. It seemed that every light in the house must be on.

A large circular rug with a Navajo design covered the floor up here. Two paneled doors on the left were now closed.

The bedroom was huge and well lit. Double French doors led to a balcony. There were two darkwood dressers, and a door through which he could see a makeup area and, beyond that, the bathroom.

The woman lay diagonally across the king-size bed in an awkward position—half turned with one arm under her, the other splayed. Glitsky stood a minute, registering it. Something, though he couldn't say precisely what, struck him as odd. She looked almost as though she'd been dropped.

He remembered the face and looked at it now. In death, there was no sign of fury in Sheila Dooher's last moments—in fact, Glitsky thought, her expression was remarkably peaceful. The hair, mussed from sleeping, still bore the traces of its last brushing and, perhaps tellingly, no visible blood.

Which is not to say there was no blood elsewhere. A blood-spattered white cotton nightie was bunched around her neck, covering her left breast, leaving the right exposed. Only one wound was visible, an inch-long slit out of which seeped a brownish-red ribbon. Her underpants were still on, though they'd been pulled down forcefully, and were ripped.

Glitsky straightened up, backing away a step for a wider angle. Thieu's statement that there was a lot of blood was a relative one. But Glitsky knew that blood was one of those things—if you weren't familiar with it, a little could go a real long way.

Glitsky's first take on the blood in this case was that there wasn't nearly enough of it. Even Victor Trang had bled substantially more than this, and his killer had used the bayonet to plug the flow. If the knife wound here had gone to the heart with the victim on her side, which was what it looked like, there should have been massive quantities of blood. Pints. Not a cupful.

"What?" Thieu asked.

But Glitsky didn't answer. Instead, from his new

vantage point, back a little from the bed, he noticed something he should have seen immediately. He wasn't going to touch or move the body to make sure, but there were four or five other apparent blood marks on the nightie—he leaned in to see more clearly, now that he thought he knew what he was looking at. They were like brush strokes—straight-sided and tapering, the concentration of blood heavy at one end and lighter at the other.

It could only be one thing, something he'd seen only once before—with Victor Trang—in his career.

The killer had wiped the blade off on his victim's clothes.

Farrell didn't look like a lawyer at the moment.

He was in the pair of white painter's overalls that had been next to his bed. He'd finally finished all the repairs, the caulking and the cracks in the walls of his apartment. For the past few weeks, after work, when he wasn't visiting Sam, he had been haphazardly painting a baseboard here, a door there.

Tonight, after the midnight call from Mark, he threw on the paint-stained pants, stepped barefoot into his trashed Top-Siders, threw on a ragged and grubby University of California sweatshirt, and grabbed his Giants hat from the peg by the door.

So he didn't look like a lawyer, but he wasn't here as a lawyer. At least he didn't think so. He was here as a best friend. Mark's voice had been calm, though there was no mistaking the anguish. They'd had a burglar, he said. Sheila was dead.

He pulled his Datsun up behind the police cars. The driveway and the street in front of Mark's house were clogged with the ambulance, the coroner's van, the knot of curious neighbors, two local news trucks.

He went up to the nearest uniform. "Excuse me, I'm a friend of the resident here. He asked me to come over. I'd like to go up to the house."

The cop had his orders, though. His arms remained crossed, and he shook his head. "Afraid not. This is a crime scene. It's closed to the public."

"I'm not the public. I'm an attorney."

The officer looked him over. "Then be an attorney outside. This is still a crime scene."

"Look, why don't you go ask Mr. Dooher if he wants Wes Farrell up there with him?"

"You're Wes Farrell?"

"Yeah."

"Well, Wes, we don't run things the way Mr. Dooher wants them run, especially at a murder scene. You know what I mean? We're investigating a crime here. We don't want people tramping all over the evidence. That's how we do it. Now, when we're done, you can go up. Meanwhile, somebody comes out, I'll send word up *if* I can see some ID."

Wes patted his empty pockets. He could visualize his wallet on the top of the dresser next to his bed at home.

He considered breaking and running up the pavers, but figured he'd get shot or arrested or something for his troubles. No. The only hope was to drive the two miles back home and get his goddamned ID. "Have a nice night," he told the cop.

A polite smile. "You too."

The CSI—Crime Scene Investigation—unit knew the drill, and Glitsky knew them. He didn't want to step on toes, but he wasn't working backward from any theory now. This time he was looking at what he knew was evidence, not wanting it to go away through inadvertence or simple bad luck.

He walked up to Sergeant Jimmy Ash from the photo lab, a gangly, forty-year-old freckled albino who, tonight with the late hour, even had pink eyes, and who'd already "painted the room" in videotape. Ash was standing by the bed, taking stills of the body that had been Sheila Dooher.

"Hey, Jimmy. You got any special technique for splatter stains?"

"The blood?" He swallowed, a prominent Adam's apple bobbing. "No, nothing special. Clear photos—my particular area of expertise, you know—and something to provide perspective in the picture. You see something?"

"I think so."

"Then you got it."

Thieu was standing next to them both. Glitsky could figuratively almost hear him panting there, dying to ask what he'd seen and having no clue. He started to take pity on him, turned to answer, when Alice Carter, the coroner's tech from the other side of the bed, spoke up.

"Abe?" She pointed a finger at him and curled it toward her. Come here. "Anybody move this body?"

"I don't think so. Not since I've been here."

Thieu spoke up. "She was this way when I came in, too."

"I think you want to be sure on this. The responding officers still below?"

Thieu was already moving out the room's door, going to get them if they were still there.

"Why?" Abe asked.

Ms. Carter pointed at Sheila Dooher's bare right shoulder, the exposed back beneath it, a slight darkening, red under the skin. "Because we've got what looks a whole lot like fixed lividity here in the upper right quadrant."

"Which means she was moved . . ."

"Right, and after she'd been dead awhile."

It was well after midnight. Thieu trailing behind him, Glitsky stopped in the doorway to the library and caught Dooher in an unguarded moment, sitting back in his wing chair, legs crossed, talking with another man. He couldn't hear what they were saying, but Dooher's expression was bland, his body language relaxed.

It had been a week now since Abe had lost his wife and he had yet to draw an easy breath. His tired muscles seemed as though their ache would never end and his jangled nerves, strung with fatigue, twitched like a Thoroughbred's.

And here was Dooher, his wife gone less than three hours, all but holding court. The comparison invited conclusions. Glitsky was going to have to concentrate to keep his personal feelings from intruding.

This had to be by the book.

Today's date is Wednesday, June 8th. The time is approximately 0020 hours. This is Sergeant Inspector Abraham Glitsky, star number 1144. I am currently at 4215 Ravenwood Drive, San Francisco. Present and being interviewed is Mark Dooher, Caucasian male, 4/19/47. With me is Sergeant Inspector Paul Thieu, star 2067, and Mr. Dooher's attorney, Wes Farrell.

Q: Mr. Dooher, I'll be tape-recording your statement, as you can see. Do you have any objection to this?

A: No, none.

Q: But, for the record, your attorney did raise some objections to your coming downtown to give your statement.

A: (Farrell) Sergeant, we've been through that. It's after midnight and the man's wife has just been killed. Since Mr. Dooher wasn't home all night, he couldn't possibly be a suspect in this crime. He voluntarily has agreed to give a statement here and now. There's no reason to go downtown.

A: (Dooher) It's all right, Wes. What do you need for the statement, Sergeant?

Q: How about starting by telling what you found here tonight?

A: All right. At about nine forty-five, I got home from hitting a couple of buckets of golf balls at the San Francisco Driving Range. (pause) As you know, I've had some bad luck with driving ranges lately.

Q: You got home at quarter to ten . . .

A: Right. I came inside . . .

Q: What car were you driving and where did you park?

A: I was driving my Lexus. It's light brown with personalized plates reading ESKW. I drove up the driveway and parked in the garage behind the house. I closed the garage door behind me —it's automatic—and walked out the side door of the garage on the path next to my back lawn, to the driveway, and in the side door.

Q: Was the door locked?

A: I don't remember, to tell you the truth. I wouldn't have noticed anyway. I always just put my key in first, give it a turn, it opens. I don't remember specifically.

Q: Do you remember if the overhead light was on?

A: No. I don't believe it was. It must have burned out.

Q: Okay. What did you do then?

A: I went to turn off the alarm system—we have a box next to the doors—and I noticed it hadn't been set.

Q: Was that unusual?

A: Unfortunately, no. Sheila . . . that was one of the things she wasn't . . .

A: (Farrell) Give him a minute, here, would you? You all right, Mark?

A: (Dooher) Yeah, okay. Sorry. Sheila often forgot to set the alarm system. She would go in and out a lot and thought it was silly—unnecessary—while we were home. She thought it was more for when we went on vacation, times like that. She thought I was paranoid.

Q: All right. Then what?

A: Then I went into the kitchen, did the dinner dishes which were still there. Then I had a beer and read the mail.

Q: You thought your wife had gone up to bed?

A: I knew she had gone up to bed, Sergeant. We'd split a bottle of wine for dinner. She hit the wall around seven-thirty and said she wanted to turn in. So I thought I'd go to the range. Anyway, I finished my beer and went upstairs . . .

Q: Did you touch your wife?

A: No. I turned on the lights and it was obvious she was dead. I suppose I froze a minute or two. I don't remember. Then I guess I called nine one one.

Q: And then what?

A: Then I sat on the stairs and waited. No, I checked the other upstairs rooms, too.

Q: You didn't try to resuscitate her, anything like that?

A: (Farrell) Sergeant, he's answered that. She was obviously dead.

Q: Did you touch the body at all?

A: (Dooher) There was blood all over the place! There wasn't any doubt—you can tell when somebody's dead. I didn't know what to do, to tell you the truth. I don't even know exactly what I did. I was afraid. I suddenly thought the guy might still be in the house. I don't know. I just don't know.

Q: I'm sorry, Mr. Dooher, but I need a specific answer to the question. Did you at any time up to right now touch Mrs. Dooher's body?

A: No.

Q: All right, let's go back. Earlier in the day, before—

A: (Farrell) What's that got to do with anything, Sergeant?

A: (Dooher) It's okay, Wes. My attorney here wants to make sure I don't say anything to incriminate myself. But I can't incriminate myself since I didn't do anything. How far back do you want to go, Sergeant? Last week?

Q: Let's start when you got off work.

23

CHRISTINA STOOD BY THE FRENCH DOORS AND watched Dooher move about his backyard, greeting the other mourners.

She was fighting the feeling that she really didn't belong here, guilt that in her heart she didn't mourn Sheila Dooher's passing. It freed Mark—there was no sense denying it. She sighed heavily.

"I'm glad you're here. I don't know anybody."

She turned to see Sam Duncan, her arm still in a cast. "You know me now. But why are you here?"

Sam gestured behind her. "Wes. He's taking over details for Mark for a while. Even without the police stuff, this whole thing is just so horrible."

Christina laid a hand on Sam's arm. "What police stuff?"

"Damn." Sam's face clouded. "I'm not supposed to talk about it. Wes doesn't want any rumors going around." She lowered her voice. "He's worried that they're going to say Mark did it, killed his wife."

Christina mouth dropped. The idea was absurd. "What? He wasn't even here, was he? How could he have . . . ?"

"I know, but Wes is afraid they might. I mean, so soon after the Trang thing and all."

"But they didn't find anything there either."

"No, but apparently our friend Sergeant Glitsky didn't like being proven wrong. And he's the inspector on this case."

"But Mark wasn't even here . . ."

"Evidently the police can make a case that he was." Sam held up a hand. "Wes says if they really want to get you, they can make your life pretty miserable."

"I guess they didn't really want to get Levon Copes."

Sam made a face. "Still a sore subject. But that was Glitsky, too."

"But what does Glitsky have against Mark?"

"No one knows. Wes isn't sure if there's any reason. And nothing's happened yet. He's just worried. He thinks Glitsky might be overworked and guessing wrong. He did screw up on Levon Copes. And you know about his search warrant on Mark. There's two strikes."

"You don't think he'd plant evidence, do you? The police don't really do that, do they?"

Sam shrugged. "I don't know what they'd do."

Farrell was sitting in a corner of the kitchen with a beer, listening to Mark's two youngest children, Jason and Susan, talking to their friends. He'd known the two kids their whole lives, and they looked very much alike, both very thin with slack blondish hair, waiflike features, and piercing green eyes—Mark's eyes. Susan wore black silk—tunic and pants—and Jason had the baggy pants, an outsized brand-new dress shirt buttoned to the collar, a camouflage jacket.

. None of Farrell's own kids had made it home for the funeral, which very much disappointed him, especially since Sheila and Mark had been godparents to Michelle, his youngest. But he consoled himself with the fact that neither had Mark's eldest, Mark, Jr., the wildcatter sculptor.

Wes had tried to help Dooher out with breaking the brutal news, making the call to Mark, Jr., and had been unprepared for the venom he'd heard. His dad never needed him for anything before—he didn't need to see him now. Besides, it was too much of a hassle to come down from Alaska, he said. His mom was already dead anyway. What good was it going to do? And he didn't have the money to spare.

Oh, Dad was offering to pay, to fly him down? No thanks—one way or another, he'd wind up owing him. He'd have to pay. Even for something like this.

The young people were drinking beer.

He was comfortable here in the kitchen with them, especially since Lydia was out in the great room, mingling as she did. So he was avoiding her. And he didn't particularly want to introduce her to Sam, either. That kept him in here, too, not that it had been uninteresting up to now. He was learning a lot, listening. Just edit out the "dudes" and profanity and most of it was English.

Jason, sitting on the counter now, had sat next to his sister in the pew with Mark, but both of them down five feet or more from their father. An eloquent enough statement. The boy cried at the mass, but was over that now.

He was enthusing over the snow in Colorado, the winter he'd spent back there, how he was going down to

Rosarito from here, surf the summer away, like, starting tomorrow. He had to get out of here. This scene here with his dad was just too weird.

His sister leaned up against the sink, holding hands with another young woman. "How Mom took it I don't know," she said.

More dad-trashing coming up, Wes thought— even a child could do it. Suddenly, stoked by the beers, he stood, deciding to butt in. "Hey guys. How about you give the old man a break, would you? He's having a tough enough time."

Susan nearly snorted. "Dad doesn't have tough times."

"I've just been through one with him, dear."

"I'm sure." She dropped her girlfriend's hand and walked the four steps over to him—a bit unsteadily. "You think you know my dad, don't you? You think he's devastated by all this?" She shook her head hopelessly. "You're a good guy, Wes, I really think you are, but dream fuckin' on," she repeated.

"Dream on what, Susan. What are you talking about?"

Jason: "Hey, come on, look around."

"I'm looking around. What am I supposed to see? I see your dad trying to maintain here. I see he's lost his partner . . ."

Susan snorted derisively, nodded over at Jason. "Six months?"

"Tops," he said.

"What are you guys talking about?"

They were both shaking their heads, but it was Susan who said it. "You'll find out."

* * *

Finally summoning the nerve, Christina walked out into the backyard. He was standing now in the dappled sunlight under the budding elm, and she thought she had never seen a more magnificent face.

Not the face per se, but that it so clearly reflected the man beneath, *that* was what was so magnificent. It was all there—the agony he was in, the strength to bear it, the grace, eventually, to rise above it.

He was deep in conversation with a priest who wore a black cassock with a purple lining, but when he saw her, it was as though he bestowed some benediction on her, pulling her forward, to him. Almost physically, she felt her steps grow light. Welcome, even now.

Taking both her hands, he leaned forward and kissed her on the cheek. "Thanks for coming."

"I couldn't not have."

They were still holding hands. Suddenly, realizing it, he gave a brief squeeze and let go. "Well . . ." Remembering, turning back to the priest. "I don't know if you've met the Archbishop of San Francisco, James Flaherty. Christina Carrera. Christina's one of the firm's future stars, Jim."

She shook Flaherty's hand, heard him uttering the usual commonplaces, kept her smile in place. But her eyes and mind stayed on Dooher.

He was holding up, his own eyes elsewhere—within—crushed by the weight of his loss. He caught her watching him, then, and tried to smile, an apologetic turn of the lips for having caused her, even briefly, to glimpse the pain he was feeling within. He did not mean to show it, to wear it on his sleeve. He was a man. He would be all right. It wasn't anyone else's problem. He was alone and he would survive.

She thought her heart would break.

* * *

Seeing her ex with another woman—of course younger, that's what they all did, wasn't it?—had gotten under Lydia's skin. Not that she was romantically interested in Wes anymore—heaven forbid!—but it skewed her vision of her own importance.

How dare he!

So after Wes and Sam had gone, Lydia decided she deserved a couple of drinks. Then, in the kitchen, she'd gotten to talking with the kids—she was godmother to Susan, "Aunt Lyd" to Jason—and they traded Sheila stories—laughing, crying, laughing again. Rituals.

The two children left when their father had finally come in from the backyard, after nearly all the other guests had said their good-byes. The kids' departure wasn't exactly abrupt, but it wasn't leisurely either. After the exodus, Lydia had exchanged one of those "what-can-you-do" glances with Mark, then picked up the bottle of gin on the counter.

"How about one?"

His shoulders sagged. From Lydia's perspective, Mark had held up like a trooper all day, making the required rounds, having to listen again and again to how sorry everybody was, to the advice and the sympathy and the anecdotes. He had been endlessly patient, as he always appeared, under tight control. That was Mark Dooher, after all.

Although, just for a moment, the final abandonment by his children did seem to take the resiliency out of him. Then he bounced back, smiled, nodded. "Hit me a good one," he said.

She was sitting on one of the barstools, and when he came over, she rubbed a hand across his back. He straightened up, leaned into it. "That beats the drink," he said. But then he took the drink, too.

She'd stayed to clean up. She knew the house, was good with the caterers. It was a help having her there. Everybody else had gone by six, and she went back into the kitchen and though they certainly didn't need it, poured two gins on the rocks and brought them out to where he sat in the living room, in his black suit, his hands shading his eyes, at one end of the chamois-soft white leather couch.

They clinked glasses. "Long day," she said. "Why don't you take off your coat and stay awhile?"

"I guess I should."

As though she were his valet, she helped him out of it. On the way over to the closet to hang it up, she caught sight of herself in the large gilt hall mirror.

Stopping there, she had to think again that Wes was an idiot. She was slightly out of focus, but she looked terrific. In her own black tailored suit, her high heels and black hose, she could have been ten years younger, trim, toned, her hair lightened to ash, cut à la Princess Di.

Well, screw Wes *and* his girlfriend.

She hung the coat in the closet. The day was still warm and suddenly the top to her own suit felt binding. She unbuttoned it, shrugged out of it and hung it next to Mark's. Her black blouse, too, was tight at her neck, and when she came back to him, it was undone to the second button.

He handed her her glass, and she stood in front of where he sat as they clinked them again. She felt him looking up at her as she drank.

"God bless gin," she said. "I don't think I've had anything but wine for six months. But sometimes you need a real drink, don't you think?"

"Here's to that." He tipped his own glass back. "To quote the great Dean Martin, that sometime is now."

"Get you another one?"

He drained his drink and handed her up his glass. Back in the kitchen, she grabbed the silver ice bucket and the bottle of Bombay and brought it out with her, setting them on the coffee table, building two fresh ones.

She was standing in front of him again.

"Here we are," he said. "Who would have thought?"

She stepped out of her heels. "How are you, Mark? Really?"

He took a thoughtful sip, rotated his head, brought his hand up behind his neck. "Tell you the truth, I'm tight as a drum."

Putting her glass down, she walked around behind the couch and put her hands on his shoulders. "Close your eyes," she said. "Take a deep breath."

As her thumbs dug into the muscles around his neck, he let out a small groan of relief. "You've got a half hour to cut that out, Lydia." His head fell back against the couch and he slumped down.

She stopped. "Now your angle's all wrong."

"That's what *she* said."

"Down on the floor," she said. "On your stomach."

He was stretched out as she'd directed, arms folded now under his head. She knelt at his waist, reaching up, and began to knead his shoulders, his neck, down his backbone.

Reaching across, then, over the broad back, another bad angle. She straightened up, hitched her skirt up, and straddled him, her hands moving, pushing, rubbing. Pulling the shirt out, then, going under it. Up his backbone with her thumbs.

Another sigh of pleasure.

She reached to her side and undid the button then, unzipped, stood and stepped out of her skirt, her nylons. Dooher still lay on his stomach, unmoving. "Turn over."

His eyes were closed, his hands crossed behind his head. The belt, then, the button. Zipping slowly over the bulge.

He still didn't move.

Sam and Wes were on the roof of his apartment building, sitting barefoot in beach chairs, holding hands, watching the sunset. Bart lounged between them. A small pot barbecue smoked and Sam had tuned Farrell's boom-box radio to a country music station, which he barely knew existed until six weeks before.

Now he was worried that he was getting hooked on the stuff. Something in him rebelled at the idea of a middle-aged urban professional like himself relating to this corn, but dumb as they were, about every fourth song seemed to bring a tear to his eye. A couple of tunes over the past weeks—Tim McGraw's "Don't Take the Girl" and Brooks & Dunn's "Neon Moon"—had made him outright weep.

When he'd been alone, painting.

But all of 'em were about those country things— old-fashioned values, mommy, daddy (sometimes grandpa), true undyin' love, God, beer, dogs and trucks.

But dang, he couldn't deny they hit something in him.

Wynonna was just finishing up "She Is His Only

Need" and Wes was blinking pretty hard. Sam squeezed his hand. "You're just doing that to impress me."

"Doing what?"

She laughed. "That misty eye thing to every mushball lyric you hear."

"It's nothing to do with the lyrics. I happened to look too long at the sun and it made my eyes water. Or else it was the smoke."

She ignored him. "So maybe I'll think that way deep down you've got a tender and gentle soul."

"No, that is not me. I'm not trying to impress you. I'm a cynical big-city attorney and nothing touches me. I am a rock. I am, in fact, an island."

"My understanding is that no man is an island."

"I tell you, I am a fucking island."

"Okay, you're an island. Anyway, I am impressed." She lifted his hand and kissed it, then nudged Bart with her bare toe. "I think he actually feels things, don't you, Bart?"

Bart raised his head, put it back down on his paws.

"See?" she said. "The mute beasts concur."

Wes got up and took the top off the kettle cooker. A couple of T-bone steaks filled the whole grill. He gave them a turn and came back to sit down. "You know why people cry at happy endings in movies? Or at weddings? Or even, some incredibly weak slobs, at country music lyrics?"

"They're crybabies?"

"I'm going to hit your broken arm."

"Crybabies isn't the answer?"

He shook his head. "They want it that way again. Something in them remembers that they used to think it was that way, that things in life could turn out good, and seeing that hope, being reminded of it, it's too much to take. So they cry."

"But you still think things turn out good, don't you?"

"No. I still wish they did just as bad, but I don't think so anymore."

She reached and took his hand. "Seeing your wife today?"

"Lydia?" He let out a long breath. "No, Lydia's over. It was more, I think, the kids. Mark's kids."

"What about them?"

Again, he sighed. "I don't know. All the effort, the hopes, the lessons, the tears, the fights, the sicknesses—and at the end, what do you get? You get some kids who are total strangers, who don't want anything to do with you."

"Your kids?"

"Well, some of that, maybe. But mostly Mark's. They really hate him."

"Maybe he wasn't a good father."

"That's just it. He was a *great* father. I was around. I saw him. Baseball, tennis, soccer, Boy Scouts, Girl Scouts, private schools, great summer camps—you name it, those kids had it."

"But did they have *him?*"

He seemed to deflate. "I guess I don't know that. Did my kids have *me?* I mean, both of us—Mark and I— we worked like dogs so Lydia and Sheila didn't have to. This was, of course, the Middle Ages. Back then this wasn't considered the height of oppression."

The silence, as well as the difference in their ages, hung between them. "I better get the steaks," Wes said, but he didn't get up. He didn't want to let go of Sam's hand. He turned to her. "His kids really hate him, Sam, and I know them. They're not bad. They're fine with me. They call me Uncle Wes even, sometimes. But their dad . . . I just don't get it."

"Maybe he's not the person you think he is. Not with everybody else. He seemed pretty cold to me."

Now he did let go of her hand. "Let's not take my best friend apart four days after his wife was killed, okay."

"I'm not taking him apart, I'm saying he seemed cold. Maybe he was cold to his kids, that's all."

"And maybe he's trying to keep from breaking down, so he's guarded right about now, how's that?" He had raised his voice and Bart sat up, growling.

Sam took a beat, a breath. "You're right, I don't know him at all, I'm sorry. The steaks aren't going to be rare."

Downstairs, in his kitchen, they sat at his table. Sam stared down at her food. Wes couldn't stop the smile that crept up. Sam wasn't going to be able to cut her steak. "Your cast." Standing up, he came around the table and kissed her. "I'm sorry," he said. "I don't want to fight."

Sam lay her head against him. "Don't be mad at me. I'm not attacking your friend."

"I know. With your permission." He pulled another chair out from the table, sat down, picked up a knife and began cutting. "And the fact is, he might have been a terrible father. I don't know. Maybe husband, too. We didn't pride ourselves on that so much in those days. He's just my friend. Some of us white males —even if we're not angry—occasionally feel unfairly attacked here in this modern world. It's tempting to band together. So I suppose I've got a gut reaction to protect him. Especially now."

"I can see that. But I'm not attacking you either, okay?"

"I know, but I wonder if it's just that I didn't see what he might have really been like with his kids, couldn't let myself see because I was doing the same thing."

"And what about now?"

That stopped him again. For a moment. "What about now?"

She only dared meet his eyes.

"No," he said. "Flatly, emphatically no."

"Okay, but since we were talking . . ."

"I don't understand how can you even say that."

"I didn't actually. I looked it. But I was talking to Christina today—her reaction to Mark being under suspicion kind of reminded me of you."

"You told her about it?"

"A little. It's okay, Wes, she won't alert the media."

"So how was her reaction like me?"

"Just very knee-jerk. Not really looking at it. She's in love with him, you know."

"She told you that?"

"No."

He rolled his eyes.

"But a girl can tell."

"So Christina's in love with Mark. And he's my best friend. Now let me get this straight—because of those reasons we both don't believe he killed his wife while he was out driving golf balls. How strange. Do you think he killed her?"

She shook her head. "No. Your steak's getting cold. It's perfect, by the way."

Standing up, he kissed her and went back to his seat.

"All I'm saying," she continued, "is that I have a

hard time believing Sergeant Glitsky goes around planting evidence to convict people for no reason."

"Well, I hope you're right." He cut a piece of meat. "Christina's in love with him?"

" 'Tis the season," she said sweetly. "She may not even know it yet, but you wait. Six months . . ."

Wes stopped chewing. The words were almost exactly those used by Mark's kids when he hadn't known what they were talking about. He did now, and it made him nervous.

Most nights, Sam stayed with her brother Larry. She was apartment hunting in a haphazard fashion, but it was never easy finding the right place. And tonight she was staying at Wes's.

Now she slept peacefully next to him. Unable to do the same, he carefully lifted the blanket from his side of the bed and got out, threw on his old terry cloth robe, and padded into the living salon, sitting on the futon. The streetlights outside painted their designs on his hardwood. He'd left the kitchen window open over the table where he and Sam had eaten, and the breeze coming in through it still felt almost balmy.

Bart climbed up next to him and he petted him absently. His mind wouldn't stop racing. Maybe he ought to write a country song, he thought, 'bout settin' up all night while your girl's asleep, your love is deep but you're feelin' blue, what's a poor country boy to do? It had possibilities.

But that thought didn't hold. He kept returning to Christina Carrera . . . which brought him to Mark. Of course, as he'd told Sam, Mark had an airtight alibi. Hell, it wasn't even that, he reminded himself, it was the truth.

The past twenty-five years of Wes's professional life had been spent in the mud and trenches of criminal law, taking on the causes and cases of a seemingly endless procession of people who'd been careless, negligent, drunk, stoned, or stupid—strangely, rarely malicious—and who found themselves called to answer for their mistakes and misdeeds.

He didn't often torture himself with whether any of his clients had done what they'd been accused of. He generally preferred to ask them about the evidence against them and how they might explain it. Sometimes, if he liked his clients, he'd provide two or three explanations and ask if any one of them had a particularly nice ring.

He *never* asked directly if a client was guilty. That was a conclusion for the jury. Similarly, he tried not to ask any open-ended questions about what someone had or hadn't done because he might get an answer he didn't like, and then be stuck with it. And there was always the very real possibility that his client would lie to him anyway. This was in the very nature of people, he believed, and hence understandable, human, acceptable.

But his adult pragmatism was a far cry from the idealism that had drawn him to the law in the first place. It was a rationalization, as so much of his life had become. You did what you had to. And that was okay.

Most of the time.

He'd been trying to convince himself of all this now for the last decade or so. It was the recurring topic in his "retreats" with Mark Dooher, who would always argue the opposite—you didn't do what you had to do, you did what you *believed* in.

Before these troubles, Farrell thought that had been easy for Dooher to say. He'd never had to struggle in his career, in his life. He could afford the luxury of idealism, of believing he was always on the side of the angels. He was Job before the curses.

But Dooher was right about one thing. The accommodation ate at you. It made you cynical. Sometimes it seemed to Wes that the endless litany of "good enough," "good enough," "good enough" was a prescription for failure. That there really wasn't any such thing as good enough—there was your best, and then there was everything else.

And, in his darkest moments, Wes sometimes believed that his marriage had failed, his business had never really prospered, he'd never achieved all he'd set out to do—in law school, he'd dreamed of being appointed to the Supreme Court!—because he'd burned himself, his best self, out on the altar of "good enough." Lord knew, it had been *hard* enough, raising the kids, getting and keeping clients, making time for Lydia. He'd put in all the energy he thought he could spare, instead of all he had, on just about everything he put his mind to. *What had he been saving the rest for?*

Was this the source of his mediocrity? The secret of the nonentity he'd become?

He knew the reason for his nervousness after dinner. Because for once, now, he'd committed. He had a potential client and best friend that he totally believed in.

And now there was Christina Carrera, his own albatross. Why couldn't she just go away?

Farrell, too, had caught a glimpse of them together for a moment on Mark's lawn this afternoon. Witnessing firsthand the almost embarrassing connection between them, he kept coming back to the one salient fact that he wished he could forget. Or—better—never have known.

Which was that Mark had wanted her from the first moment he laid his eyes upon her.

But what did that mean? Nothing, he told himself. It was merely one of those late-night chimeras that tantalize or frighten, and then in the morning turn out to have been a shadow falling on an uneven surface, a wisp of white fabric blowing lonely in a faraway tree.

"Wes?"

Sam's quiet whisper from the bedroom. Worried, obviously caring. Was he all right? Did he need her?

Petting Bart a last time, he pushed himself up. The doubt, the ghost, the mirage—whatever it was—would be gone in the morning.

He was sure of it.

24

THE NEXT DAY, GLITSKY WAS AT MARINE WORLD with Nat and the three boys.

He still hadn't found a nanny, and had decided that what they all needed was some time together, a change of scene, a nice day outside, away from the city. So he'd picked them up at the friend's house where they were staying, and they'd made the drive across the bay and north to Vallejo.

At the amusement park, the sun was out and although there was a steady breeze, it didn't have that arctic intensity you got off the ocean out in the Avenues where they lived.

Now he was sitting high in the grandstands, watching the killer whale show. Isaac and Jacob had gone down to the seats by the water with their grandfather, all of them, including Nat, deciding that they really needed to get soaked. But O.J., ten years old, didn't want to do that and didn't want to leave his dad, either.

In fact, after the older boys had gone down, O.J. asked Abe if he minded if he sat in his lap. Which was where he was now.

The huge mammals entered the pool, but O.J. couldn't have cared less. "Dad," he said, "can I ask you something?"

Ever since Flo had first gotten sick, O.J. had preceded nearly every remark with this question. Glitsky thought it was because he was such a sensitive little kid, so aware of the pressure everybody was under. He didn't want to add to it by asking any question that someone would have to answer. He didn't want to be a bother.

This sometimes translated to Glitsky as though his youngest son didn't want to exist, and that drove him crazy. But he kept his voice modulated and answered the way he always did.

"You can always ask me about anything, O.J. You don't have to ask permission to ask."

O.J., as always, then said, "But can I ask you something?"

Patience, Glitsky told himself. Patience. "Yes, you can ask me something."

"Okay. What if all the sudden, you know Merlin?"

"Merlin?"

"Yeah, Merlin, King Arthur's musician . . ."

"Magician. But yeah, okay, I know. Merlin."

"Right. So what if Merlin came back to life and he decided all the unicorns were going to be down on earth from now on?"

O.J. had also been playing with variations on the coming-back-to-life idea for the past few months. What if Robin Hood came back to life and got disguised as one of the Power Rangers? What if George Washington really didn't die, but was just waiting to see if he could live to be three hundred and then he could be president again? What if Bambi's mother . . . ?

"Things don't come back to life," Abe said, gently but firmly as he could. "Dead means you're gone forever. That's what dead is."

"I know *that*, Dad, but Merlin was a musician and *he* could come back if he wanted to, and then he could decide the unicorns could live on the earth."

He wanted to tell him there were no unicorns, either. The boy was ten years old, closing in on puberty, and he really ought to stop seeking comfort in these fantasies.

But somehow his energy failed him. He let out a long breath. "Instead of where? Where do they live now?"

O.J. couldn't believe his father's ignorance. "Well, now they live in the clouds, in Unicorn Land."

"Okay."

"And then they could come down and be here on the earth and we could ride them, and maybe even have one as a pet. What if that happened?"

Glitsky tightened his arms around his gangly son, came up with the answer he always wound up with. "If that happened, O.J., that'd be really neat."

Isaac was still very wet. He exceeded by several years the twelve-year-old age limit for the playground, but dripping as he was, he didn't look it. And even though he was a cop, pledged to enforcing the laws, Abe wasn't going to call him on it.

He and Nat had left their food—french fries and corn dogs—on one of the picnic tables behind them, where the ravenous seagulls had spirited it away and scarfed it all down.

Now the two men stood at the fence that kept the adults in their place. All three of the boys were clustered together, up high in a corner of a climbing structure made of rigging rope. Hanging together.

The killer whales had dumped a couple of swimming pools' worth of water into the lower gallery. By now, Nat's hair was recombed, but his clothes stuck to him. He was marching in place, his tennis shoes making squishing noises. "This is a good place, Abraham, but I wish someone had told me about this getting splashed. They don't mean a little damp, let me tell you."

"I didn't know."

"But I noticed you didn't go down yourself, am I right?"

"O.J. didn't want to get so close to the water. That's why I didn't go down."

"I wish I believed this completely. I don't want to think you sandbagged your old man."

"I would never do that. You didn't raise that kind of boy."

A sideways glance. "That's a good answer." He pulled his shirt away from his body, did a little dance with his pants. "And O.J., I happened to see, he was on your lap."

Glitsky nodded. "He's having a hard time. He's trying to figure it out."

"And you are back to work?"

"I've got to work, Dad. It's what I do." But he realized that his father needed more of an explanation. "Look. The Hardys are great people, Frannie's taking better care of them than I can right now. And the boys are in school anyway most of the day. I'm there for them. I see them. I go over some nights. We go out on weekends. Like now, Dad, like right now. I've got a lot to get set up."

"I understand this."

"So?"

"So nothing."

"But what?"

Nat shrugged. "Just to think about, that's all."

He knew what his father was getting at, but there wasn't anything he could do about it. He should have taken some more days off, he supposed, gone over every single night to be with the kids, but when he'd gotten the call about Sheila Dooher, his priorities found themselves rearranged.

Or maybe it was just an opportunity to dwell on something other than the emptiness. His father had implied that, to some degree, he was running away, denying what he needed to confront, shunting off his responsibility to his children. And maybe there was an element of that. He had something to do, something that needed to be done, and it was consuming. The simple doing of it—regardless of the outcome—could save him, could pull him through this time.

He didn't know, but he had to try.

This was why on Sunday night, the boys were back at his friend's house and he was at his desk downtown on the fourth floor, reading the autopsy report on Sheila Dooher that had finally come in. He had done legwork all week long—interviewing neighbors and driving range employees and Dooher's co-workers and anybody else he could think of. Going over the initial lab reports, studying the room-painting videotape, combing the Dooher house (again, with another warrant, while Dooher was downtown working) for fibers and hairs and fluids.

But without the autopsy he was whistling in the

wind and he knew it, and there had been some bottle-neck on paper coming out of the coroner's. Autopsies normally took almost six weeks to get typed, but he'd asked for a rush on this one.

He had the report in front of him now, and he scanned it once, trying to make sense of it, wondering if it might be the wrong one. For a different body.

Because the autopsy report he was looking at listed the cause of death as poisoning.

And what the hell was *that* about?

25

THE WOMAN WAS WAITING AT THE DOOR TO THE Rape Crisis Counseling Center when Sam arrived at nine on Monday morning. Slightly matronly though not unattractive, she wore jeans, hiking boots, a brightly colored sweater jacket and a purple beret. She held a designer purse, out of the top of which peeked an Amy Tan paperback. Sam stopped in front of her.

"Hi."

"Hello." A cultured voice.

"Are you waiting to get in here?"

Behind the self-conscious expression, not all that unusual in this setting, she projected a strong attitude of resolve. Even as she nodded, her eyes surveyed the street in both directions. "I thought this would be a good place to start."

"It often is," Sam said. "Let me get the door."

* * *

Diane Price had removed her sweater and beret and sat easily in one of the wing backs in the tiny room behind the reception desk. Thick gray hair fell over her shoulders. The natural woman, Sam thought, she wore no makeup and, with a generous mouth and gray-green eyes, really didn't need any. Her nails looked professionally manicured, but they were clear.

She'd waited while Sam put on the pots of water and coffee—told herself that she'd waited long enough, a few more minutes wasn't going to hurt. The bell over the front door tinkled again as Terri, the first of the day's volunteers, came in to work.

Sam brought the mugs—black coffees for them both—back into the room where Diane was waiting and sat across from her.

"I feel a little awkward about this, but I didn't know where else I should go."

Sam waited. It would come out.

Diane sipped her coffee and took another moment. Exhaling then, as though satisfied with something, she began. "I imagine you know why I've come here?"

Sam inclined her head. "You've been raped."

"Yes." Diane took another sip of her coffee, repeating it. "Yes," she said, "I've been raped."

Sam leaned forward. "It's difficult to say the words, isn't it?"

"Yes." The monosyllable hung between them. "It's been a long time now. I didn't know if I'd *ever* say it."

"How long?"

Again, Diane's eyes raked the small room. Sam had the feeling she was trying to decide whether or not she should continue with this, whether it was too late to back out. All the staring around, putting off bringing the rape into focus.

She put her mug down and crossed her hands on her lap. "A long time ago. Twenty-seven years ago."

"And you've been silent about it?"

Diane folded her arms, self-protective. "Now it's called a date rape. I knew him. He seemed so nice. I've been living with it all this time. I don't think I've denied that it happened. I suppose mostly just feeling that it happened so long ago, what difference can it possibly make, you know?"

"But it has, of course."

A nod. "I don't really know how I feel about it all anymore. Not clearly. All the parts of it."

"That's all right. Why don't—as you said—why don't you just start somewhere. What do you feel the most, right now?"

"It changes. That's what's funny. I guess now, today, it's all resentment because I've been thinking about it so much. First, though, when it came up again, it was just this overwhelming anger, this rage. But for such a long time before that, you know, living my life with my husband and being the school mom and doing soccer leagues and just *living*—I didn't see what good it would do to bring it all up again."

"Does your husband know about it?"

"Don. He does now, but . . ." A lapse into silence. "He's a great guy, but I'm not sure he understands. Not completely." The cultured voice was flattening by degrees, losing what had appeared to be a natural animation. "What I'm trying to deal with now is, I guess, my anger over this sense of loss, of having lost so much of my life over this one . . . this one episode." A wistful smile. "It's funny, you know. You don't really believe that one day can change everything, I mean if you'd just done one little thing differently . . ."

"Everybody feels that, Diane. If it's any consolation, it's one of the mechanisms we use to blame ourselves. Somehow, at least a little bit, it's our fault."

This didn't seem to help. "But I really wonder if it *was* my fault—I don't mean just the rape, where okay, no doubt I led him on, but I really believed . . . I didn't know anything then. I mean, I was a virgin. You said 'no' and it stopped, right?"

"That was the theory," Sam said.

Diane sat back in the chair, put her head all the way back and closed her eyes briefly. Opening them, she abruptly reached for her mug of coffee. Something to do that wasn't this recitation of history. She forgot to drink from it. "Even now," she said, "even now I wonder how much of it was my fault."

"Diane, if he forced you . . ."

"He said he'd kill me."

"Well, then, you . . ."

But she was shaking her head. "No, not just that. Not just the rape itself. Everything after that. My whole life." Another silence, another shake of the head. "No, not my whole life, that's an exaggeration. Only most of a decade. Only." Suddenly, she slapped the arm of the chair. "God, I *hate* this victim thing! I'm not a victim. I don't want to be a victim."

Sam waited.

"Before, I was going to be a doctor." The brittle laugh shook her. "It wasn't ridiculous—you don't get into Stanford if you're dumb, and I'd never gotten a B in my life. I was fun, smart, pretty. And now I tell myself—have for years—I've had to tell myself that it was this . . . this *thing* that made it all change. That it wasn't my fault."

"That wouldn't be so unusual, Diane. In fact, it would be more normal if it was."

"I know that. I'm still not stupid. But don't you

see, it makes me sick, that victim excuse. I should have just risen above it, put it behind me. Instead, it just ate me up, and I let it. I just let it." Her fists were clenched on the chair's arms, and one of her eyes overflowed. "I'm sorry." She reached into her purse, pulled out a handerchief, dabbed. "There's no reason to cry about it. This is stupid."

"No it isn't."

She managed a condescending smile. "Well, of course you're trained to say that."

Sam wasn't going to fight her about it. Yes, she was trained to say that, and that was because it was the truth. It wasn't stupid to cry about it. Almost everyone did. "So what happened, Diane? What do you blame yourself for?"

"Everything! Don't you understand? I'm mad that it *happened*! I'm mad that I *do* blame myself, I don't care what the proper modern response is supposed to be. I could have been . . . I don't know, *more* somehow. Who I was really meant to be. And instead"—she visibly deflated—"instead I'm who I am."

"And is that so bad?"

"I don't know. That's what I'm trying to figure out, I suppose. That's why I'm here. I can't believe . . . it seems so small a thing, somehow."

"The rape? A small thing."

She nodded. "I know that sounds crazy, but it's what I tell myself when I'm just so full of loathing. It was one small thing, and I let it change the whole direction of my life. I mean, one day I'm in pre-med pulling A's, I go to football games, I'm kind of rah-rah and carefree, and the next day, the next time I turn around, I'm a mess. I'm taking every drug in America. And this was the sixties, remember, there were a lot to choose from. I survive another year or so before dropping out of school. And sleeping with anybody, not caring. Losing touch with my mom and dad and family and not caring at all."

"So what happened finally?"

She brought the handkerchief back to her eyes, left it there a minute, pressing. "Finally, I woke up. I don't know how else to put it. I just woke up. I guess I didn't want to die. And I never thought about that until my mother did. That's the thing I regret the most, I think. I mean, if she could see me now, it'd be all right. But I was still that other way, that other person, when she died. So she never knew."

Sam nodded. There was nothing to say. Sometimes, she knew, closing that circle could be the toughest pull of a person's life, and it seemed to her that Diane Price was well on her way to doing it.

Diane was going on. "And by now it seems behind me. I married Don, went back to school and at least got my degree. I've got two great teenagers, and I'm actually working in a lab where my brains count. And I got there —I got all of that—by finally not being a victim anymore, just pulling myself up by the bootstraps and *deciding*, that was it, deciding I wasn't going to have this cancer in my life. I wasn't going to talk about it, think about it, refer to it. It was the past, over, done."

"But you're here?"

"I'm here."

Sam hesitated. "Did something else happen?"

Diane shook her head. "Not to me, thank God. But then, suddenly, last week, I was reading the paper and I started shaking at the breakfast table. I couldn't stop shaking."

"What was it?"

"The story about this woman who'd been murdered, Sheila Dooher her name was."

Sam felt the hair begin to stand up on her arms.

"So the name caught my attention, and I looked down the article, and then opened to the inside page and there was the picture of her and her husband at some charity thing last year. Her husband Mark."

Sam knew what was coming.

"The man who raped me."

Father Gorman knew why he'd been summoned to the Archbishop's office. Not only had he been absent at the rosary when Sheila's body had been laid out, he'd not attended the wake afterward, then begged off officiating even peripherally at the funeral mass. He hadn't gone to the gathering at Dooher's home afterward.

Now they'd kept him waiting nearly twenty-five minutes at the end of the day. Not a good sign. He was more exhausted than he'd ever been in his life. For weeks, he'd slept no more than four hours a night, plagued by nightmares about his own long-gone parents, of all things.

And then, finally, he was inside the austere office. James Flaherty stood up behind his desk, but didn't come around it, didn't offer the kiss of peace as he sometimes did. Instead, his lips moved into a perfunctory smile, but his eyes did not change in any way at all, and he sat back down immediately.

"Gene, I'll get right to it," he said. "Mark Dooher is one of my most trusted advisers. He is also, not incidentally, a substantial contributor to the Church and to your parish. He's been president of your Holy Name Society, president of your parish council, president . . ."

Gorman didn't need the glowing litany. "Yes, Your Excellency. I know who he is."

The Archbishop was not used to being interrupted and his eyes flared briefly. After a long silence, Flaherty continued. "He has also lost his wife to murder, as you well know. The police have been hounding him on another matter because of some kind of political vendetta. This is not a time to abandon those people who need us most. The man is going through some kind of hell right now, and I found it incredibly unchristian, not to say callous as a human response, that you didn't see fit to assist at his wife's funeral or visit with us afterward." He changed the tone of his voice, making it more personal. "Mark was incredibly hurt by it, Gene. Incredibly."

"I'm sorry," Gorman said. "I . . ." He didn't know what else he could say, and left the sentence unfinished, hanging in the room.

Flaherty waited for more, but it didn't come. "You're sorry?"

"Yes."

"Sorry doesn't seem like quite enough, Gene."

"I'm sorry about that, too, Your Excellency."

Flaherty cocked his head. "What's going on here? You two have a disagreement, a fight?"

"No."

"Do you want to talk to me about anything else? I checked your most recent reports, and things at the parish seem to be going along smoothly. Am I wrong about that?"

"No, Your Excellency . . ."

Flaherty tapped the table. "Let's drop the Excellency. I'm Jim Flaherty. We've known each other a long time. Is there something going on in your parish?"

Gorman knew what he was asking—was he having an affair, was there a scandal brewing? He shifted his burning eyes to the ceiling, to the sides of the room. "I do feel like I'm under a lot of stress lately. I'm not getting much sleep. I . . ."

Again, the rogue syllable, and again it hung there.

"What would you like me to do, Gene? Would you like some time off? A short retreat?"

"Maybe so, Jim. Maybe that would help."

The Archbishop sat still a minute, lips pursed, eyes unwavering. "All right," he said at last, "let's give that a try."

Farrell knew he was fouling the air. The Upmann Special tasted delicious, and normally he made it a point not to smoke cigars in small offices, but he didn't much like Craig Ising, and it gave him some pleasure to realize that Ising was going to have to get his suit cleaned to get the smell out. Farrell thought it was a fair trade—he felt dirty near him, but he was a client and your clients were not always people you admired.

"But I didn't do anything wrong. This isn't even a crime in Nevada!"

Farrell coughed, then blew a vapor trail into the air above them. "We've been through that, Craig. You should've been in Nevada when you committed it."

Thirty-six years old, physically fit, nicely tanned, Ising had told Farrell all about the suit that he would soon have to clean. It had set him back $450 in Hong Kong. A silk blend that supposedly felt even better than it looked. If you could get it in America, it would go for more than a grand.

Farrell had spent most of the day in this tiny conference room in Ising's plush Embarcadero office, the two men discussing a plea so Ising wouldn't have to go to jail. That was the hope, anyway. And Farrell was ready to go home.

Ising's position, early on in the day, was that he was a businessman and all he'd done was take advantage of an investment opportunity. He'd been making some pretty serious money at this particular endeavor for the past couple of years. The investment was straightforward enough—Ising had been buying the insurance policies of people infected with AIDS, in effect becoming their beneficiary when they died.

In Ising's view, everyone benefited by this arrangement. The AIDS patients sold their discounted policies for cash that they needed for their medical bills—normally sixty percent of the value of the policy—and their policies were then sold by middlemen to investors like Ising, who paid between $6,000 and $200,000 for the policies based on the patient's life expectancy.

Ising had gotten lucky with his first couple—the patients had died almost immediately and he'd cleared nearly half a million dollars in less than a year. Unfortunately for him, the State of California regulated this particular investment (by outlawing it) and Ising was looking at two to five years in state prison and a six-figure fine.

"This doesn't bother you at all, does it, Craig?"

"What bothers me is they're trying to take me down for it. That's what bothers me. Other guys have done a lot worse."

This was inarguable, so Farrell didn't push it. Instead, he got down to tacks. "You're lucky, you know. The DA's taking heat for the court's dragging along on violent crimes, so he gets the idea he wants to clear some massive backlog on these white-collar cases, get 'em processed out without taking up court time. You fall in the crack. Otherwise, you'd be looking at hard time. This is actually a sweet offer."

Ising rolled his eyes. "It's so sweet, why don't you

put up the money?" The deal was a fine of half a million dollars earmarked for AIDS research and two hundred hours of community service for Ising. "And the time. Where am I supposed to get two hundred hours?"

Farrell shook his head. "Two hundred hours is five weeks full time, Craig. You get the minimum prison time and it's two years. Five weeks. Two years. Think about it." He sucked on his cigar, keeping it lit. The air in the room was getting as opaque as fog. "But hey, it's your decision."

"It's robbery is what it is. We ought to sue them."

"Sue who?"

"Whoever passed this law. It's criminal. No wonder this state's down the tubes. A man can't make any kind of living."

Farrell didn't know exactly what Ising had made last year, but the rent here in the Embarcadero high-rise was not close to cheap, and Ising had personally ponied up nearly $30,000 for Farrell's legal fees in the past year, so it was a little hard for Farrell to work up much sympathy for how difficult it was for an entrepreneur without morals to make a living in California. "What's the matter, Craig? You afraid this community service is going to put you in contact with the riffraff?"

"Yeah, among other things. You got a problem with that? You get your commoners out there rubbing shoulders with me and they find out who I am and next you know I'm getting hit up for money. You wait, you'll see. It'll happen."

"Does that mean you're going with the plea?"

Ising pulled at his upper lip, drummed his fingers on the table in front of him. "Damn," he said.

* * *

"I didn't know if I should call. I was worried about you."

"You've always been able to call, Christina. I appreciate it. But there isn't anything to worry about. I'm a big boy. I'll be all right."

"I'm not trying to argue with you, but you don't sound all right. And Saturday . . ."

"I thought Saturday I was pretty good."

"But it was an act. I could see that."

"Well, yes. But what was I going to do with everybody there? I couldn't very well sit in a corner and cry, could I?"

"No. I'm sorry. I didn't mean . . ."

"I know what you meant, Christina, and I thank you. You're right. You're saying it's okay if I show it a little. People aren't judging me so hard right now. Is that it?"

"Of course you see it. You see things."

"Still, it's good to remember. And I'm very glad you called. A time like this, you don't want to . . . you don't want to push yourself on your friends. The house has seemed to get pretty big . . ."

"Mark?"

"I'm still here. I'm thinking maybe I should just sell the damn thing."

"I don't think I'd make any decisions like that for a while. Give yourself a little time."

"For what, though?"

"For things to become clearer."

"Oh, they seem clear enough now. That's almost the problem. Everything's crystal clear. This is just the way things will be from now on."

"Time will make it better, Mark. Eventually, it will. It does."

"Okay."

"I'm sorry. I'm not saying it's not horrible now."

"No, I know, that's all right. Well, listen, I'm not much for conversation right now. And I do thank you for calling me. Really. I'll be back in the office in a couple more days. I'll see you there?"

"Sure."

"Okay then. Take care."

She put the phone down gently, stood looking out at the traffic passing by her front window, then picked it up and hit the redial button.

"It's me again."

A surprised chuckle, wonderful to hear. "How've you been?"

"I've been insensitive."

"Not at all."

"More than I want to be. I don't know what you're feeling, other than the pain, Mark. It's stupid to say time will make it better. Maybe it won't. I just wanted you to know that if you need to talk sometimes, it wouldn't be a burden. That's all I wanted to say."

He didn't respond right away, and when he did, the voice was husky with suppressed emotion. "You're great," he said. "Thank you."

When he realized that the AIDS-insurance matter involving Craig Ising was going to take up most of the day, Farrell had called and left a message with Sam's brother that he'd pick her up on his way home and they could go out to dinner someplace.

Larry and Sally lived over Twin Peaks from Sam's old place in a gingerbread Victorian, and Farrell wasn't halfway up the dozen stairs leading to the front porch when the door opened. Sam was coming out to him, slamming the door behind her, moving fast. "We've got to talk," she said. "Where have you been?"

"So let me get this straight," he said. "Some lady . . ."

"Some *woman*, Wes."

Uh oh, he thought.

"Okay, some woman comes in to where you work and tells you this story . . ."

"It wasn't a story. It was the truth."

He stopped. She walked a couple more steps. "Here we go, now," he said. "I'm going to try to finish one sentence. Then you can have one. How about that?"

"You don't need to get snippy."

"I'm not being snippy. I'm trying to respond in whole sentences to the topic we are trying to discuss. Now. This woman tells you that twenty-some-odd-years ago, she went on a date with Mark Dooher and she took him back to her apartment and got him drunk and then he raped her."

"And threatened to kill her."

"Sure, why not? That, too. And because of that, if it is true . . ."

"It is true."

"*If* it is true, I should abandon my lifelong best friend, whom you now seem to believe is a murderer. That's where we are?"

"That's right."

"He killed his wife because he allegedly raped this woman?"

"Wes, don't go all lawyer on me. He didn't *allegedly* rape this woman. He raped her."

"No, wait a minute. She invited him up to her apartment, plied him with drink, started making out with him . . ."

"And then told him to stop, that's right. And he didn't." She was giving him that look—eyes hard and challenging. "That's rape."

"Ex post facto."

"What does that mean?"

"It means now it's considered rape. Then it wasn't considered rape. It's like people who say Lincoln was a racist; when they didn't have the same concept back then. By today's standards, everybody was a racist a hundred years ago. Same with date rape. It's all semantics."

"It's not semantics at all. He raped her."

"I'm not saying date rape isn't rape. I'm saying thirty years ago, a lot of girls said no and didn't really mean no."

"I'm not going to get into how Neanderthal that sounds, Wes, but this particular *woman* didn't just say no. She tried to fight him off and he told her he'd kill her."

"No he didn't."

"What? How can you possibly . . . ?"

"Because I know Mark Dooher. He's not going to kill somebody in college over a piece of ass. Come on, Sam. You're a rape counselor, for Christ sake. You know how this goes. She invites him up . . ."

"She asked for it, right? Don't give me that one, please."

"I don't know if she asked for it. I wasn't there, but it sure wasn't the same thing as lurking in the bushes and assaulting her as she walked by."

"Yes it was, Wes. That's the point."

They were still standing where they'd stopped, in the middle of a fogbound street in the gauzy glow of one of Church Street's lights. Wes had his hands in his pockets. He hadn't thought they were going hiking, and in his business suit, he wasn't dressed for the chill.

He forced himself to slow down, take a breath, not let this escalate. They'd work it out. It was just that right now they were both charging at one another. He thought he'd pull back a little, lower the voltage.

"Look, Sam. How about we go someplace? Sit down. Maybe have some food. Calm down a little."

She crossed her arms. "I am calm. And I don't need that condescending take-the-little-lady-someplace-she-can't-make-a-scene bullshit either."

"I am not doing that. I thought we might be able to have a reasonable adult discussion in a more comfortable environment."

"This environment seemed to be comfortable enough until we got on this."

"On rape, or what you're calling rape, you mean?"

"What I'm *calling* rape! Goddamn it, Wes, I expected a lot more from you."

"Well, yelling is a big help."

"There!" Now she *was* yelling. "Put me down again. Don't discuss the real subject, whatever you do. Jesus Christ!"

"I'd like to discuss the real subject, Sam, but first I can't get out a whole sentence, and then I'm getting screamed at while I'm freezing my ass off, getting all kinds of motives laid on me for the truly ominous, condescending idea of finding someplace warm to sit down. Give me a break, would you? I didn't rape anybody. I'm not the enemy here."

"My enemy's friend is my enemy."

He brought a hand up to his forehead. "That's good. What's that, Kahlil Gibran or the PLO Handbook?"

"It's common sense is what it is. It's survival."

"I didn't think we were in survival mode."

"All women live every day in survival mode."

"Jeez, that's good, too. What are you doing, writing a book of feminist slogans?"

"Fuck you."

She turned and was walking off.

He followed after her, his own volume way up. "You've been working at that Center too long, you know that?"

She whirled on him. "Yeah, that's right. I've been working, of course that's the problem. Women shouldn't work, should they, Wes? They shouldn't have their own lives."

"Sure, that's what I'm saying, Sam. That's what I think. I wonder if you could twist it any more."

"I'm sure I could. I'm a woman, after all, I don't get things right."

"I'll tell you something. You didn't get at least this one thing right. My friend Mark Dooher didn't kill his wife and I'd be goddamned surprised if he raped this lady, either. She saw his name in the paper, she wants her twenty minutes of fame. You ever think of that?"

"Oh no, Wes, that never crossed my mind. You asshole." She started walking away again. Stopped, turned back. "I *heard* her. I saw her face. This *happened*, God damn it, whether or not you believe it."

"*What* happened? She *maybe* said 'no' thirty years ago, and just forgot about it until now? I'm sure."

Sam said nothing.

"Did she seek counseling? Did she tell anybody? Did she report it to the police back then? *Did she do a fucking thing?* No."

"It ruined her life. It changed everything in her life."

"How sad for her. And now, damn, look at this, what a surprise! Mark Dooher's in the news and it all comes back. *And*—this is the great part—this means my best friend, who I've known only a hundred times longer than I've known you, this means he *killed* the wife he loved and raised a family with? Please. I mean it, Sam, you got to get a life here. This is ridiculous."

This time, she started walking away and didn't turn back.

"Hey, Bart. Daddy's home."

It was ten o'clock.

The dog got up, yawned and walked slowly over to where his master stood. Wes petted him distractedly, then schlumped into the kitchen, turning on the light, checking for dog shit. He paid a young woman who ran a small graphics business out of her apartment in the building to take Bart out two or three times a day, but sometimes that wasn't quite enough. Today it had been.

The refrigerator held a couple of six-packs of Rolling Rock, and he took out two bottles and opened them both, drank one half down, pulled out the kitchen chair and sat heavily at the table.

He felt a hundred years old.

He ached to simply pick up the phone right there on the wall and apologize until dawn. But he didn't move. The phone didn't, either. Eventually, he lifted the bottle of beer again, staring out at the night.

This was not supposed to happen. Everything had been going better than it ever had in his life, even better—he thought—than it ever had with Lydia when they'd been young and believed they must be in love.

In the first heady rush of physical pleasure, and then in the next weeks of growing intimacy, he'd put

Sam's occasional penchant for volatility out of his mind. That first night, when she'd thrown him out after learning that he was defending Levon Copes—he'd chosen to believe that that had been an aberration born of insecurity and alcohol.

But evidently it wasn't.

It was better he find out now rather than later, he supposed, but he wasn't in the mood to put much of an optimistic spin on anything just now.

He'd wracked his brain all the way home, playing devil's advocate with himself, conjuring all the negative images of Mark that he could remember. But there were so few of them and that was the truth.

Once, in college, when they were engaged, Mark had cheated on Sheila. But he'd been riddled with guilt because of it—told Wes all about it on one of their "retreats," wondered if he should call off their impending marriage because he was such a bad person.

He'd backhanded his son, Mark, Jr., across the face for throwing his bat in a Babe Ruth League game. That, West thought, was Mark's worst moment. But at the time Mark had been working eighty hours a week trying single-handedly to save his ailing firm. And he'd tried to turn even that incident, bad as it was, into something positive—treating it as a type of wake-up call. He was working too hard, ignoring what was really important. His family, his spiritual values.

In some way, these peccadilloes reassured Wes about his friend's character. Mark would be the last to say he was perfect. Of course he had sinned—he was human. He'd done things he was ashamed of. But these were why, to Wes's mind, he was balanced. He wasn't wound so tightly holding in every tiny impulse to evil that he would one day need to explode.

So he tried to figure out what it was, why the

sudden rush from so many quarters to slander and vilify Mark Dooher.

Jealousy was one thing. Mark was wealthy, powerful, and up until a couple of months ago, lucky. He was exactly the kind of person that lesser people loved to see destroyed.

Then the Trang business, politically motivated and unfounded as it was, had put a hole in Mark's bubble of invincibility. And Wes knew that an enduring truism of life was that accusations bred more accusations.

And now—finally—the dominant bull was injured, limping. This was the time to take him down, when it could be done. Everybody was abandoning Mark. People were lining up to take shots at him when he was least able to defend himself.

Well, Wes wasn't anybody's hero, and he couldn't stop anybody from taking aim and firing, but he could stand in front of his friend and try to defend him until he was strong again.

Trang's murder. This woman's rape story. The enemies were assembling and he didn't have to think too hard to figure out what was coming next. They were going to charge him with Sheila's murder.

And Wes knew he would be the last line of defense. And for once—whatever they might dig up and however it spun—he knew it wouldn't be true.

Wes was going to defend him.

26

A WEEK LATER, PAUL THIEU GOT HIS FIRST REAL
break in the case.

It was not without some trepidation that he guided
his city-issue Plymouth off the freeway at the Menlo
Park exit, forty miles down the peninsula south of the
city, and negotiated the narrow entrance to the parking
lot by the Veterans Administration building. The short
drive between the freeway and the VA reminded him of
6th Street between Mission and Bryant in San Francisco, the most dangerous walking blocks on the map.

Though the climate down here was infinitely more
benign, the small-town thoroughfare itself was a no-
man's-land of Reagan's enduring legacy, the mentally
impaired homeless. The cops called these people "eight
hundreds" and their social workers called them "fifty-
one fifties" after the Welfare and Institutions Code sections that defined them, but by any name, they were
tragic. Derelicts, drug addicts, bag people.

Thieu saw them every day in the city, but here

within a long spit of Silicon Valley, where the sun always shone and the real estate glittered, he found all this evidence of poverty and despair especially dispiriting.

He was also keenly aware of his Vietnamese nationality. Men in old army uniforms—singly or in small groups—loitered here and there on the main street and under the trees that provided the shade for the parking lot. Thieu didn't have to guess which war they were veterans of.

And time might have passed, he knew, but in the brains of some of these guys, it still might be 1968.

He opened the car door into what was, by San Francisco standards, blazing heat. It was not yet noon and already in the mid-eighties. Thieu was wearing an ivory linen suit and decided he could leave his raincoat on the passenger seat where he'd thrown it. It was misting heavily in San Francisco, forty miles away. The temperature was in the fifties.

A couple of guys in old fatigues nudged each other as he passed them on the way to the imposing doors, but he smiled and said hello and was past them and through the doors before they had moved two steps.

The place had that old institutional building feel and smell. A wide entryway with linoleum floors made every sound inside echo. To his left, a waist-high counter separated the government workers from the veterans, who were for the most part queued up waiting for their numbers to be called. Across from the counter, a shiny, light green wall sported wood-framed photographs of all the presidents since Eisenhower, as well as a decent assortment of admirals and generals (including another one of Eisenhower in uniform). At the end of the entryway, a large paned window let in a lot of light.

Thieu stood a minute, getting his bearings, reading

from the building directory in its glass bulletin board. Gradually, he became aware that the noise had ceased behind him.

Deciding to ignore it, he found the room number for his appointment and moved out directly.

"Hey!"

Somebody was calling after him, but he came to the big window, hung a left, and took the stairs two at a time.

They had been lucky, locating Chas Brown here at the south peninsula VA detox. Neither Thieu nor Glitsky had really known where Brown might lead them, but Glitsky was directing this investigation and he'd sent Thieu down to conduct the interview.

Last Thursday and Friday, he'd run around trying to get a handle on either a Chas Brown or a Michael Lindley, the two other survivors of Mark Dooher's platoon in Vietnam. Their names had been provided, during the Trang investigation, by Dooher himself.

Now, Glitsky smelled blood. He told Thieu that they simply had to find out everything they could about Dooher, from whatever source. Glitsky was working St. Francis Wood, talking to the neighbors, working the pawnshops in the adjoining neighborhoods, still looking against hope for the bayonet, the clothes Dooher was wearing, *something*.

And Thieu, with his background, started out to find yet another missing person.

Chas Brown wasn't a total burnout case. True, in his faded jeans and flannel shirt, with his long, un-washed graying hair and beard, he didn't look like anyone who worked for a living, blue or white collar. But his eyes were clear, his handshake firm.

He showed up at his counselor's office on time, promptly at noon, exhibiting no signs of prejudice toward Thieu. After a couple of minutes, Thieu offered to take him to lunch. There was a terrific pizza place not far away named Frankie, Johnny & Luigi Too.

Brown looked like he wouldn't turn food down— he weighed about a hundred fifty pounds. He was nearly six feet tall.

Thieu also thought he'd get franker answers if he was away from his counselor.

So now they were sitting at a table outside under the green and white umbrellas, sharing a large pizza, of which Thieu wouldn't be able to eat more than one enormous piece. Fully loaded with pepperoni, sausage, olives, mushrooms, peppers, double cheese and anchovies, one slice weighed in at nearly a pound.

Judging from how he started it, Thieu guessed Chas would finish the entire large pitcher of Budweiser he'd ordered. He was already on his third glass. Thieu was having iced tea.

The two men weren't yet friends, but the beer wasn't exactly making Chas taciturn. The pocket tape recorder was rolling and they'd already covered *Thieu*'s background, verifying that he was too young to have fought in Vietnam. His father hadn't been in uniform, either, though he'd been anticommunist all the way. A capitalist in the silk trade in Saigon, the elder Mr. Thieu had to leave when the city was abandoned by the U.S. So Thieu and Chas were on the same side.

"That's when my name changed." Brown had a lot of nervous energy. Tics and scratches, eyes moving all the time. But he was talking clearly, if a little rushed. Maybe the beer would eventually mellow him out. "Before I got in country I was Charles, Charlie Brown. When I was a kid, I would have done *anything* not to be named Charlie Brown, so of course it stuck like glue. Then I get to Nam and Dooher says there's no Charlie in his platoon, I'm Chas. So I'm Chas. I thought it was a good omen at the time. I thought Dooher was a good guy. Shows you what I knew."

Thieu didn't want to stop him, and remained silent as Brown downed another deep slug of beer, the eyes going blank a moment. Another drink, more emptiness. Blink, the lights went back on, led to the abrupt segue. "Tried to be my friend, y'know, after."

"After what?"

The eyes came back, then darted away. "You know."

"I don't know."

"About the dope, all that. I thought that was what you came down here for."

In fact, Thieu's main avenue of inquiry was going to be about the ease of smuggling bayonets and rifles out of the country when your hitch was up. Instead, a bonus, Chas Brown was heading in a different direction.

"What dope?" Suddenly, Brown's expression closed up. Was Thieu trying to sandbag him in some way? The open camaraderie—the ruse of drinking together, having lunch—faded. The change in Brown was palpable. Suddenly Thieu was the heat and that wouldn't help his investigation, so he moved into damage control mode. "I'm not interested in dope, Chas. I'm interested in a murder."

"Well, yeah." Meaningless, unforthcoming.

Thieu pressed it. "Look, Chas, it's none of my business what drugs you're taking, or took. I want you to understand that. Here"—he pointed at the tape recorder on the table between them—"I'm saying it on this tape. It's on the record. This has nothing to do with you except insofar as you know something about Mark Dooher. Did he take drugs, was that it?"

Brown moved out of the blazing sun, into the shadow of the table's umbrella. He wiped his high forehead and took a long pull of beer. "Everybody took drugs," he said. "Everybody." He scratched at his neck. "Dooher *bought* our drugs. He was the connection."

"Mark Dooher was selling marijuana?"

Brown laughed. "Marijuana? Look at me, you think I'm strung out on marijuana? You think thirty years down the line, my brain's fried on some doob?" He shook his head, amazed at Thieu's worldview. "We're talking shit here, china white, skag." Thieu digested this. "Horse, man. Heroin."

"You're saying Mark Dooher sold you heroin?"

A continual nod. "That's what I'm saying. That's what I'm saying. Not just me. The whole platoon. Got his own stash free and sold to his guys. Did us a favor, lowest price in the Nam."

Thieu sat back, rocked by this information.

But Brown was going on unbidden. "And you know, if you look at it the way it really was, Dooher's the one who let it all happen. It was his job to keep us straight. Instead, he kept us wired."

Thieu leaned forward. "Let what happen?"

Brown wasn't good with direct questions. They seemed to spook him. He leaned back, found himself out of the umbrella's shadow, his face in the sun, and that moved him forward again. "You don't know about this, why did you want to see me?"

"I wanted to see if the guys in your platoon—Dooher specifically—smuggled out your weapons. If you knew if Dooher had."

"Why?"

Though it had nothing to do with Sheila Dooher, which was his case, Thieu ran with what he had. "We think Dooher used a bayonet to kill somebody, that's why."

Brown's face cracked—a broken smile. Thieu had just verified something for him. "Yeah," he said.

"Yeah what?"

"That's how he did Nguyen, too."

Thieu was learning about the art of interrogation with this man—don't ask directly. Just keep him talking. "Nguyen?"

"His source. Andre Nguyen. Had a little shop just outside Saigon, pretended to sell groceries." Thieu must have looked confused. Brown put his beer mug down, brought his face in close, eye to eye. "Come *on*, man! The guy he killed."

The story came out. There had been no ambush with a platoon of stoned soldiers. Nguyen had sold Dooher a load of bad heroin, or maybe it was extra-good heroin. In any event, Dooher sold it to his troops and it overdosed all but two of them.

"And this never got reported?"

Again, an expression that told Thieu that his world and Brown's operated on different planes. "Dooher covered it. He wasn't part of it. We—me and Lindley—we weren't part of it. We all alibied each other. We were out on patrol, the guys left back at camp had this bad load of shit, and it killed them."

"And the authorities believed you?"

Brown nodded. "Enough, but that wasn't really the end of it." A slug of beer. "Problem is, Dooher knows it's his fault. And *we* know it's his fault. So now he like wants to be friends, afterwards. Make sure Lindley and me, we got no hard feelings."

"How'd he try to be your friend?"

"You know, pulled us—me and Lindley—some cherry R and R in Hawaii. He had a knack getting what he wanted. He thought he'd show us a good time, make up for the other, some bullshit like that. Lindley wouldn't do it."

"Why not?" It was a direct question and Brown hesitated again, but Thieu couldn't stop himself. "Chas, why didn't Lindley want to go out with Dooher?"

"He thought he was going to kill us."

"Why?"

"Why? 'Cause he knew he'd fucked up, that's why. We could ruin him if we told. We were the only witnesses left and we were pretty bitter."

"At Dooher?"

Brown shrugged. "At the whole thing, man. You get tight over there with your guys. You're like twenty years old and then, wham, they're all dead but you. It makes you bitter."

Thieu believed it. "But you went out with Dooher? In Hawaii?"

Chas nodded. "I just didn't see it. He wasn't going to kill nobody. Lindley was just paranoid. I thought."

"Now you don't think he was?"

"Well, he didn't try to kill me. There's the proof of that."

The eyes seemed to go empty again, but Thieu saw something in them that Chas Brown was trying to keep hidden. Chas grabbed for the crutch of his beer glass, but Thieu surprised himself, reaching out, grabbing his wrist, stopping him.

"What?" he asked.

"I always thought, later, that if Lindley had come along, he might have. Killed us both, I mean. When I showed up at his hotel alone, it was like he freaked out, goes all quiet on me, like 'What the fuck? I ask my guys out for a good time, on me, and they stand me up. What kind of bullshit is that?' "

"So what did happen? That night?"

"Nothing. We got drunk. Well, tell the truth, first time in my life, somebody got drunker than me. I was, I guess, still a little scared what he might do." Brown's ravaged face creased into a little-boy smile. "I poured out a lot of good rum that night. Still breaks my heart to think about it."

"I bet it does." Thieu found the thread again. "And so, after that, you became friends?"

"Not hardly."

"Why not?"

" 'Cause he was an officer." This time he got the beer to his mouth. "No, not that. I thought he was pathetic, I guess. That's why?"

"Pathetic?"

A nod. "You ever have somebody push on you too hard they want to be friends so bad?"

"And Dooher wanted to be your friend?"

It was all coming back now, and Brown's head swung from side to side. "No, no, no. He wanted to be *forgiven*, that's all he wanted. I mean as long as we were alive, and he wasn't going to kill us, then he wanted us to *understand* how bad he felt, how he had proved it, how he'd made fucking amends."

"How did he do that?"

"Shit, I shouldn't be telling you this. You're a cop."

"I am a cop. So what?"

Thieu's hand was still locked around his wrist, and suddenly Brown became aware of it, moved it, raised the beer to his mouth and tilted the mug. Drained it. Took a deep breath. "So he killed Nguyen, the guy who sold us the shag. Went to his store and gutted him with his bayonet, wiped the fucking blade clean on his pajamas. Told me all about it, man to man, how he'd taken this great risk and all to get the guy who'd been responsible for everybody's o.d. So I'd forgive him, see what a hero he was. Can you believe that?"

"My Lord." Glitsky, sitting on the table in one of the interrogation rooms on the fourth floor, the door closed behind him, flicked off the tape recorder.

"That's what I thought," Thieu said, "except I didn't use exactly those words."

"He wiped his bayonet on the guy's pajamas!"

"That was my favorite part, too. Do you think this is enough to play for Drysdale?"

"I think we're getting there. You know, you came barging in with this, you didn't hear the other news."

"What's that?"

"We got the blood lab report in today. You know what EDTA is?" Glitsky consulted his notes.

"Sure. Ethylenediaminetetraacetic acid." Glitsky's mouth hung open. "My sister's a nurse," Thieu explained. "I used to test her on stuff. But what about it, the EDTA?"

Glitsky was still shaking his head. "You think— well, most people think—when you give blood, they take it out, put it in a vial, spin it down or whatever, do their tests, right?"

"Right."

"Right. But often they need to add an anticoagulant to the blood to keep it from clotting, and that, my son, is EDTA. Actually, that's not precisely right. They don't add it to the blood. It comes in the vials. They've got purple stoppers on the top."

"All right?"

"So the blood all over Sheila Dooher's bed? Supposedly left there by the perp when he was cut in the struggle? It's not Dooher's blood type. But guess what?"

"This is going to have something to do with the EDTA, isn't it?"

Glitsky almost smiled. "You're going to have a future here, Paul, I can tell. The blood on Mrs. Dooher's bed was loaded with EDTA."

"Which means?"

"Which means that Dooher got his hands on some blood—maybe at his doctor's, maybe the same place he got the surgical glove, I don't know. He thought he'd leave a bunch on the bed, send our slow-witted selves off in search of a man with A-positive blood, which could not be him. But, sadly for him, the vial he picked up wasn't pure."

Thieu tsked. "And how could he have known?"

Glitsky stood up. "Of such questions are tragedies made."

27

At ten-fifteen on Tuesday morning, Glitsky, Thieu, Amanda Jenkins and Frank Batiste were all jammed in front of Art Drysdale's desk. The door was closed behind them.

Art was sitting back in his chair, getting an angle on them. "It's awful swell having you all stop by at once. If I'd a' known you was comin', I'd 'ave baked a cake. Any of you know that song? No?"

Glitsky was thinking that he bet Thieu knew it, but didn't want to draw attention to himself. The other guests looked around at each other, and it was Amanda Jenkins who spoke up. "We want to talk about Mark Dooher, Art."

"Okay. What about him?"

"He killed his wife," Glitsky said.

"All right. What's the problem? I don't need a committee to tell me that."

Since Glitsky had the ball, he decided to keep rolling it. "The problem," he said, "is that he also killed

Victor Trang, and Frank here tells me that Mr. Locke may have had a hand in shutting down that investigation. And if he's got some kind of political tie with Dooher . . ."

Drysdale held up a palm. "Whoa. Stop right there. Chris Locke didn't stop any investigation, period. Chris Locke does not obstruct justice, and we're not going to talk about that here. Everybody understand that?"

Everyone nodded.

Drysdale pointed at the head of Homicide. "Frank, did I tell you to drop the Trang investigation?"

Batiste swallowed. "You did say that unless we got some real evidence pretty soon, we ought to move along."

"And did we get some real evidence? Physical evidence that would withstand the rigors of a jury trial?"

"No."

"Okay. So much for the old news. Now what's this about his wife. Sheila, right?"

Glitsky took over again. "I'd like to just run the whole thing down—it's a little complicated—and you tell me how you think it looks."

"Excuse me, Abe." Drysdale's gaze went to Jenkins. "Amanda, you've heard this already?"

"Yes, sir. But you remember I heard Levon Copes, too, and you and I came to different conclusions."

"This is like Copes?"

Glitsky butted in. "It's one of those times—like Copes—where we know the perp, yeah. We know that first."

Drysdale was shaking his head, his lips tight. "And you know how uncomfortable that makes me?"

"Which is why we're here seeking your counsel and advice."

Drysdale laughed out loud in the small room.

"Beautiful," he said. "Let the record reflect that I am duly snowed by this display of sincerity and trust." He leaned forward, elbows on his desk. "All right, tell me all about it. If I like it, we'll ask my wife. If *she* likes it, we'll go to the Grand Jury. I promise."

Later, around eleven-thirty, Drysdale poked his head into Homicide on the fourth floor, saw Glitsky at his desk and walked over.

"I just called Lou's," he said, referring to Lou the Greek's, "and today's special is Kung Pao Chicken Greek Pizza." Lou's wife was Chinese and the menu at the place often featured interesting culinary marriages such as this. "I ordered a medium, enough for two, and it's going to be ready in"—Drysdale checked his watch—"precisely seven minutes."

"Sounds delicious," Glitsky said, getting up, "but I'm really only going because I want to see how they do it. I make that stuff at home, it almost never turns out."

They were in a booth along a wall in the back of the darkened restaurant. The table was below street level. The wood-slatted windows began at their eyes, and outside the view of the alley included two garbage Dumpsters, the barred back door of a bail bondsman's office, rainbows of graffiti on every surface.

At the big meeting in his small office, Drysdale had listened attentively and said he wanted to review the reports, but tentatively wasn't going to object to proceeding with the Grand Jury indictment on Mark Dooher.

But he and Glitsky had a bit of a longer personal history, which was why they were having lunch now.

Lou the Greek himself was hovering at the table, wondering how today's masterpiece was being received. "It's good," Drysdale was saying, "but—you want my honest opinion, Lou?—I'd leave off the goat cheese."

Lou was in his fifties and he'd lived underground in a cop bar for twenty-five years, so he looked closer to a hundred. But his eyes still sparkled in a long, lugubrious face. "But the goat cheese is what makes it Greek."

"Why does it have to be Greek?" Glitsky asked. "How about just plain old Kung Pao Chicken pizza like everybody else makes?"

"You've had this before?" Lou asked. It bothered him. This was San Francisco, a major restaurant town, and Lou featured his wife's cuisine as cutting-edge, which, in fact, it was. Not particularly good, but nobody else made anything like it.

"Lou, they got this at the Round Table, just without the goat cheese."

The Greek turned to Drysdale. "He's putting me on."

"It's possible," Art agreed. "But here's an idea. The chicken. Why don't you just serve it over rice—forget the pizza altogether. Call it Kung Pao Chicken?"

"But then it's Chinese food." The idea clearly distressed Lou. "Everybody makes Kung Pao Chicken. People come here to eat, they expect Lou the Greek's, something Greek, am I right? I let my wife take over completely and pretty soon I'm Lou's Dragon Moon, a Chinese place. I'm fighting for my ethnic identity here."

Glitsky took a bite of the pizza. "On second thought, leave the goat cheese, maybe sprinkle on some grape leaves."

Lou straightened up, struck by some merit in Glitsky's suggestion. "Kung Pao Dolmas," he said. "You think?"

Drysdale nodded. "Worth a try. Abe?"

Glitsky's attention had suddenly wavered. He was staring blankly out the window at the alley.

"Abe?" Drysdale repeated. "You with us?"

"Yeah, sure."

"I was telling Lou. Kung Pao Dolmas? Good idea?"

Coming back from far away, Glitsky nodded. "Yeah, good idea. Definitely."

But the real purpose of the lunch.

"I'm just going to pretend to be a meddling, picky defense attorney here now for a couple of minutes," Drysdale was saying. "I can see you and Amanda want to run with this and my instinct tells me it's going to go high profile in about ten seconds, so I'd like to have answers for some questions that I predict will be asked by our ever-vigilant media, to say nothing of my boss."

The pizza was done, the tray cleared away. Glitsky had his hands folded around a fresh steaming mug of green tea on the table in front of him. "Okay, shoot."

"All right. Dooher comes home from work, brings some champagne, into which he intends to put some chloral hydrate, thereby to knock his wife out so that he can come back later and kill her. But when he gets home, she is already dead. This is the theory?"

"Right." This was, of course, the nub of the problem. "But he doesn't know she is dead. He's got his plan all worked out and he's moving fast, all nerves. He comes in, says thank God she's not awake, not moving, and he sticks her, rearranges the body to make it look like a_struggle, gets back to the driving range before anybody notices he's gone."

"But he *was* gone, Abe. He's been gone at least a half hour. And nobody noticed? You talked to people there at the driving range, right? Anyway, forget that. Let's go back. You're saying he poisoned her with chloral hydrate, is that it? How do we know she just didn't take the stuff? What if she was committing suicide?"

Glitsky spun his tea slowly. "So your argument is that Dooher waits until his wife commits suicide and then comes in and stabs the body with a knife and makes it look like a burglary?" He shook his head. "No, Art. The knife wound is why it's not suicide. The drugs is why it's not a burglary. Besides, there wasn't enough chloral hydrate to kill her."

Drysdale spread his palms. "I thought she was poisoned. Didn't you just say the chloral hydrate . . . ?"

"The chloral hydrate is the drug Dooher gave her to knock her out, make her go to sleep. But what he didn't know was that she was evidently having a tough time with menopause and was already taking a drug called Nardil for depression. Also, just that day had evidently dosed herself up with Benadryl. She had an allergy shot that morning. So she was already drugged to the gills. Then she drank the champagne. Add alcohol, mix and pour. The chloral hydrate pushed her over. It did her in."

"Okay." Drysdale sighed. "So what, exactly, does that leave us with? The stabbing is a crime, okay, but it's not murder one. Hell, it's not murder anything to stab a dead body."

"It *is* murder one to poison somebody to death."

Drysdale sat back in the booth, contemplating it.

A quiet edge crept into Glitsky's voice. He leaned in over the table. "This works, Art, listen—Amanda's argument isn't going to be that he meant to kill her with chloral hydrate, even though that was the result. He didn't intend to kill her until he stabbed her later, *but he did intend to give her poison*, and she died from that. And the beauty is that stabbing her is what proves it."

"And, of course, we can *prove* that?"

"We know he stabbed her."

"Not exactly my question."

"Okay. This is what we've got. You tell me." Glitsky outlined it all. It was Dooher's knife and contained only his fingerprints. He had left his house alarm system off and his next-door neighbor had seen him unscrewing his side-door light on the way out to the driving range. Another neighbor saw his car parked on the street around the corner from his house during the time he was supposedly hitting golf balls. Then there was wiping the blade on the victim's clothes, which Glitsky had never encountered before in all his years in Homicide—and now it had happened twice in cases implicating Mark Dooher, three times if you included Chas Brown's Vietnam story. Finally, there was the blood that had been contaminated with EDTA. "And who else would have stabbed a dead woman and then faked a burglary?"

When Glitsky finished, Drysdale sat still for a moment. "You've got an eyewitness for the car?"

Glitsky nodded. "Emil Balian. Swears it was Dooher's car, swears it was that night, that time. Rock solid."

Drysdale appeared satisfied. "There's your case," he said. "Don't let that guy die." A beat. "But now, just for me, Abe, one more thing. You want to tell me why he did it?"

"Frank's always telling me we don't need motives. We just need evidence."

"And Frank's right, Abe, he's right. But Chris Locke is going to be curious as to why a model citizen suddenly decides to kill his wife . . ."

"Don't forget Victor Trang."

"Okay. Him, too, maybe—two of them for no apparent reason. Why did he do this?"

"Maybe Sheila and Trang were having an affair." Glitsky held up a hand. "Just kidding. The real answer is we don't know. Not yet."

"Well, Chris Locke is going to ask, Abe, and I'd be a whole lot more comfortable if I had something to tell him."

"Amanda's got two possible theories."

"Which are?"

"This thing with Sheila's drinking. We've heard some talk—both from neighbors and from some of Dooher's partners, that she got silly when she was out in public. She might have pushed it too far, become an embarrassment."

"I don't think so," Drysdale said flatly.

"The other one is money."

"Money is always good. What kind of money?"

"A million six. Insurance."

"The *wife* had a million six. Now we're talking."

"Well, they both had it."

"The same amount on each other? Why?"

"I gather when Dooher reorganized his firm a couple of years ago, things got pretty lean. They were living on their savings, deferring his salary, the whole thing. Dooher thought he'd turn it around eventually, and he did, but if he died halfway through, Sheila was pretty exposed, so they started to buy some term on him just in case, and then she evidently wanted to protect him if *she* died in the middle of it."

"So, bottom line, Dooher's getting it?"

"Yep."

Drysdale stretched his neck, looked around the now near-empty bar. "All right," he said, slipping out of the booth. "It could be tighter, but I think we've got enough. I'll tell Amanda that if we need it we're going to go with the insurance."

Drysdale waited until the end of the day. He was going to be reporting to Chris Locke anyway on a host of other matters, and while he didn't for a moment dream that he'd simply slip this one through, he thought he would package it to appear within the realm of normal business.

Hah.

"As you might imagine, Art, I've already gotten a call on this, warning me to expect just such a moment. The Archbishop is not going to be pleased. He is convinced there is some kind of vendetta going on against Dooher."

"I don't think so, Chris. I think he killed his wife for a million six in insurance money."

"And why did he kill Trang? Jesus Christ, Art, people don't just become homicidal maniacs one morning out of the blue for no reason at all."

Drysdale was suddenly happy—in the midst of this reaming—that he'd earlier decided not to mention as part of his argument the Chas Brown story. Instead, he stuck to the question at hand. "He killed Trang because Trang pissed him off—hey, I'm not saying it's the best reason I've ever heard—but it worked. He got away with that so he got cocky, decided he could do the same with his wife and collect big time."

"Why does he want to collect big time? Does he need the money? Is his business failing?"

Since Drysdale knew that, if anything, the contrary was true, he thought it would be wiser to shift gears, get onto the evidence. "The point is, this time we've got witnesses, we got fingerprints on the murder weapon. We have one good citizen who saw Dooher's car near his house when he said he was at the driving range. Chris, we've got a case. We've got a righteous murder one."

But Locke was still frowning, his head swinging slowly back and forth, side to side. "And Glitsky's the investigator again? How'd he get on this?"

"I don't know, Chris. But he's—"

"He's got a damn conflict of interest if I'd ever heard of one, you ask my opinion. Even if he's not out to get this guy, for whatever reason, it *looks like* he is, which is just as bad." Locke didn't want to add, although they both understood, that Glitsky, who for statistical purposes within the bureaucracy was considered black, was someone Locke couldn't afford politically to alienate or even, to a great degree, to criticize. As a show of solidarity, Locke had even attended Flo's funeral a few weeks before.

"Well, I'm afraid that's water under the bridge now, Chris. Glitsky's the inspector of record."

Locke stood still for a moment, then swore and slammed his hand down on his desk. He walked over the windows and stood staring out, his hands clasped behind his back. Without turning, he spoke conversationally. "I really, *really* don't want to charge anybody, much less an influential lawyer, with a murder he didn't commit."

"No sir. Neither do I."

Now Locke did turn. "What do you think, Art?"

Commitment time. Drysdale spoke right up. "I think Glitsky's right, though it may be a bitch to prove."

"You don't think there's anything to him being out to get Dooher, planting evidence, anything like that? Or his wife's death has . . . ?"

But Drysdale was emphatic. "Not a chance."

Back out to the window. "All right, I'm going to give you my decision and you're not going to like it, but here it is. We go for the indictment on killing his wife, but *not* on Victor Trang. From what you say, we're not going to prove Trang."

"Well, sir, there is the consistent M.O., with wiping the blade . . ."

"Forget it. It's not going to happen. So we go with one count, murder one, no specials . . ." This meant special circumstances murder—killing a police officer, multiple murders, murder for profit, and other especially heinous crimes.

"But we've got specials at least two ways."

"No." Locke was emphatic. "I am supporting my staff on the one charge that it has any chance of proving. But personally—I must tell you, Art—I am not convinced. It smells funny to me, but I can't *not* charge it, can I?"

"I don't think so, no."

"All right. Then go get the indictment, but I want you to ride this case like white on rice—it starts to go sideways, I want to know about it yesterday, all right?"

"Yes, sir."

"And one other thing. I want you to ask for a quarter-million dollars bail."

"What?" Drysdale was stunned. This was unheard of. Murder suspects did not get out on bail, or if they did, it was for millions. A quarter-million dollars bail meant that Mark Dooher could put up his ten percent bond on one of his credit cards and be out of jail before he was in. In effect, he would never be arrested.

"You heard me, Art. This particular man is innocent until he's proven guilty, and I want him *treated* innocent. Do you understand?"

"But this bail, sir. The precedent alone . . ."

"This is an unprecedented case. If Amanda Jenkins wants it and you think it's a winner, I'll go along because I respect you, Art. But we'll do it my way. And that's the end of it."

"But . . ."

He held up a warning hand. "No buts! That's the end of it!"

28

GLITSKY LIKED THIS WOMAN. THE APPOINTMENT WAS scheduled for his home at seven-thirty and that was the exact moment she rang the doorbell. Glitsky generally believed that cleanliness was next to godliness, but punctuality was next. Rita was starting off on the right foot.

He'd been surprised, at first, by her nationality, since he'd expected Rita Schultz to be somehow vaguely Germanic. But she was a hefty and healthy-looking Hispanic woman. Her great-grandfather, she explained, had come over to Mexico with the Emperor Maximilian's troops, then stayed. She was thirty-three years old and her English was accented but at least as grammatical as most of what Glitsky heard on television.

She had been working for six years for the same couple—the references were glowing. The couple were having their third child, and the woman had decided that she was going to take an extended leave from her job in advertising and stay home with her new baby and the other two, so they wouldn't need a nanny anymore. But it did mean that Rita could not start for Glitsky until after the baby was born. It was due any day.

He thought that for Rita Schultz it would be worth the wait.

The light had faded long ago and Christina was sitting alone in her office at McCabe & Roth. The room was small, stark and utilitarian, with a desk, a computer terminal, a bookshelf, a gunmetal legal file. With her door open, she could look out across the open reception area and catch a glimpse of the Oakland Bay Bridge, but she had no windows of her own. The walls in her office had been bare when she'd moved in, but she'd tacked up a couple of posters to lessen the claustrophobic feel. On her desk she had a picture of her parents smiling at her from the pool deck in Ojai.

She heard a noise somewhere on the floor and glanced up from the brief she was writing. Seeing her parents in the picture, smiling and carefree in the bright sunlight, she felt a pang and looked at her watch.

9:35.

What the hell was she doing with her life?

She stretched and stood, thinking she'd go see what other lunatic was burning the oil the way she was. At her door, she paused—it was Mark's office, the light on now. He hadn't been back in to work yet. She crossed the reception area.

The sense of disappointment when it wasn't Mark brought her up short. She hadn't really been consciously aware that she was waiting to see him, wanting to see him again. She'd been biding her time, waiting until he could face coming back in to work, and then, thinking it must be him in his office this late at night, her heart had quickened.

But it wasn't him. Another man was standing by the wraparound windows, looking out at the mesmerizing view. She knocked on the open door. "Wes?"

Farrell turned, smiled weakly. She couldn't help but notice how drawn and tired he seemed. "*C'est moi.* I thought everybody would have gone home by now."

She took a step into the room. "Can I help you?"

"I don't think so." He held up a key by way of explanation. "Mark asked if I'd stop by on my way home and pick up his in-box. He must be thinking about coming back to work." Wes moved over to Dooher's desk, picked up his briefcase and opened it. "What are you still doing here?"

Christina shrugged. "Brownie points, I guess. I wanted to finish my brief by the morning. How is Mark doing?"

Farrell raised his eyes. "He's lying pretty low. I haven't seen him since the funeral. We've done some phone." He finished stowing Dooher's papers in his briefcase, snapped shut the lid. "He'll be all right, Christina. He's pretty tough."

"I don't know if tough helps at a time like this."

"Well"—he smiled ruefully—"it doesn't hurt." Lifting the briefcase, he came around the desk, over next to Christina. He gestured her out, turned off the lights in Dooher's office, closed the door and locked it.

"Wes? Are you worried?"

"About what?"

"Mark. The police. Sam said . . ."

He turned to her and his shoulders sagged. "I don't want to talk about Sam. And I don't know what's going on with the police, to tell you the truth. I don't think

Mark does either. So far they've left him alone. Maybe that's a good sign."

"You don't sound very confident."

"I don't think I am."

"But if he wasn't there . . ."

"I know. But if you're predisposed to see something, you'd be amazed how often you'll see it. I think the police got stuck on the Trang murder and suddenly Mark went from being an upstanding businessman to potential suspect. And once you're a potential suspect, well, you know this. It's a lot easier to accuse somebody a second time."

"But not if he wasn't even there!"

"Maybe. But all they've got to do is have somebody at the driving range say they couldn't swear he *stayed* there all night, and then they walk around the neighborhood asking everybody if they saw Mark Dooher or somebody who looked like him, or his car, or a car that looked like his car. And somebody will have seen something, or thought they did, and that's all they'll need. Even Sam . . . no. I've got to get going."

He started toward the elevator.

"What about Sam? Wes!"

He made it another couple of steps before the spring gave out and he stopped.

"What happened with Sam?"

He turned around. "Actually, Sam is a perfect example of what I'm talking about."

After he hired Rita and she left, Glitsky was back in his kitchen, rattling around, when his beeper went off. He called the number and learned that Paul Thieu was still working, had beeped him from a pay phone not ten blocks away.

Glitsky had sent him out on what appeared to be another wild-goose chase, and for the second time in two days Thieu had discovered something. Glitsky gave him his home address and told him to come on up.

No sooner had he opened the door when Thieu enthused: "Dr. Peter Harris. I realized going over to his place that I couldn't ask—he wouldn't know—about any missing surgical gloves, they're not any kind of a controlled item. But the blood, he's sure of. He even thinks he knows precisely whose blood it was, though we'll never be able to prove it."

"And why is that, Paul?"

"Because the man is dead and cremated. He's gone."

It had been Glitsky's idea to question Dooher's physician to see whether any vials of blood had gone missing in the past month or so. He reasoned that Dooher had to have gotten it somewhere, and his own doctor's office seemed the most likely spot. So he'd told Thieu that the place to start would be Sheila's female doctor, whom they already knew. It might not be much of a stretch to suppose that the family physician— Mark's doctor—would be somewhere on Sheila's documentation or records.

"Did you have to mention Dooher?" The police were keeping the EDTA angle out of the news for the time being, so it would be better if no names were used.

Thieu's face, already animated, lit up even further. "No. He didn't even ask. I showed him my ID and told him we were talking to a lot of doctors, doing a kind of informal survey on how often blood got lost from their offices or labs."

"You made this up?"

"Yeah. I told him that with our new DNA tracking and all, we were seeing more and more criminals contaminating crime scenes with—we thought—stolen blood, to throw us off. So we were trying to track the sources of it."

"And he bought this?"

Thieu broke a grin. "I have an honest face. Anyway, he said it almost never happens, especially since AIDS. Blood is a high-security item. But it turns out his lab did lose this one vial last month. The doc was really upset because the patient was an old guy with bad veins who pitched a fit over having his blood taken at all, and then they had to do it again."

"And he is Mark's doctor, Harris?"

"I couldn't help but notice Dooher's name in the Rolodex on his receptionist's desk. So unless it's a coincidence . . ."

Glitsky still hadn't closed the door or invited Thieu in, but neither of them seemed to notice. "Okay, let's get a subpoena tomorrow for Harris's records and find out the last time Dooher saw him."

"Do we need to do that? If we're letting the cat out of the bag about the EDTA, why don't I just call him back and ask him? If you want to invite me in?"

In ten minutes they knew. Dooher had gone for his yearly physical a couple of weeks ago. Dr. Harris would double-check on the exact date in the morning, and also when the blood was reported missing. But he thought the two dates were in the same general time span.

Wes Farrell delivered Dooher's in-box and his friend asked if he'd like to come in and talk about things. Now, in the turreted library, Wes crossed one leg over the other, sinking back into the soft leather. "I've got to ask you, Mark. I've been wrestling with it all day.

Sam and I broke up over it, and I'd kind of like that to have not been for nothing."

"You two broke up over whether or not *I* slept with somebody in college?"

"Not slept with, Mark. Raped."

"I don't believe this." He began pacing, fingers to his temples. "What's next? Where are they digging this up? What did Sam say the woman's name was?"

"Price, I think."

He stopped pacing and took a breath. "I have never heard of anybody named Price. I never dated anybody named Price. I swear on Sheila's grave. And p.s., old buddy, I've never raped anybody either. It's not my style. Jesus Christ. Sam believes I did this? Where did this Price woman come from?"

"I don't know. She walked into the Center and said you'd raped her."

"When, exactly, did I rape her?"

"In college sometime. You were out drinking and she brought you back to her room? I don't know."

Suddenly Dooher snapped his fingers. "*Diane?* Lord, Diane Taylor. Of course, of course."

"You do know her?"

"No, I'm not sure." An ottoman was handy and Dooher sat heavily on it. "I don't know any Diane Price, Wes, but I did go out a couple of times with a Diane Taylor. If it's Diane Taylor . . . let's hope it's not Diane Taylor."

"Why not?"

"Because Diane Taylor is an unbalanced person, Wes. She's done every drug in America twenty times over. She slept with every single other guy I knew at Stanford."

"Including you?"

"Including me, before I even met Sheila. And

with her full consent, I assure you." He moved the ottoman forward, lowered his voice. "Wes, *you* know more than anybody. The couple of times I screwed up on Sheila, didn't I come crying to you? But this wasn't a screwup. This—if it was Diane Taylor—was getting laid a couple of times before I developed any taste in women. Jesus, she's now saying I *raped* her?"

"Evidently. And ruined her life in the bargain."

Dooher hung his head and shook it. Raising his eyes, he met his friend's gaze. "It's just a black lie, Wes. I don't know what I can tell you. I didn't do anything like that. I wouldn't."

"I know," Farrell said. "I didn't think so, but I had to ask, all right?"

A long, frustrated sigh. "Okay. But this gets old, especially at this particular juncture in my life, you know what I'm saying? I'm not having my best week."

"No. I'd imagine not. Me, neither, actually."

Dooher's voice softened. "I am sorry about your girlfriend. I feel if it hadn't been for me . . ."

"No, it's not you, Mark. It was her. It was me."

"So go back and tell her you're sorry. Leave me out of it. I can get another lawyer whose life I won't ruin."

"You're not ruining my life, and I *am* your lawyer."

"Just so you're sure."

"I'm sure. I'm sure you didn't do any of this."

"That's good to hear, because I didn't."

"Well, then, here's to the old-fashioned idea of friends standing by each other. And to hell with the rest of 'em."

"Amen to that," Dooher said, "and thank you."

29

THE CONFERENCE ROOM AT McCABE & ROTH HAD seen more somber moments, but not since the downsizing layoffs. And this may have been worse than any of those.

It was five o'clock on this Monday evening, one day shy of two weeks from the day of Sheila's death. Mark Dooher waited until the room was full before having Janey page him and tell him it was time.

Dooher lingered one last moment outside the room, aware of the muted tones within. These people were worried. He had returned to work the previous Wednesday, enduring the sympathy of his partners and staff, taking individual meetings with key people for the rest of the week, reassuring one and all that life would go on, he was fine, the firm's client base was solid.

And then Sunday's *Chronicle* broke the story with the front-page headline—LOCAL LAWYER SUSPECTED IN WIFE'S MURDER.

"Sources at the Hall of Justice have confirmed that

the Grand Jury is considering an indictment on a prominent San Francisco attorney, Mark Dooher, for the murder of his wife, Sheila." The long article went on to
include all the other details that the unnamed "sources"
provided, the other allegations—from the rape of Diane
Price to the murders of Victor Trang ten weeks earlier
and Andre Nguyen in Vietnam.

Dooher and Farrell had spent all of the morning
denying everything. They had held a press conference in
Wes's office. Yes, they were planning on suing the
Chronicle and the police department. No, he had never
raped anybody. He'd never killed anyone in Vietnam or
anywhere else. This was a carefully orchestrated character assassination . . . political overtones . . . despondent, desperate police inspector . . . blah blah blah.

They'd hit all the high notes, and the media had
gone into their fandango. All the local stations were
carrying it by the noon broadcasts, radio talk shows
picked it up. The office had gotten calls from *Newsweek*
and *Time* and *USA Today*. Clearly, it was going to turn
into a circus.

He opened the conference room door and all noise
ceased. He went to the chair at the head of the table
and stood a moment, meeting the eyes of his people one
by one. He came to Christina and gave her an almost
imperceptible extra nod. Finally, he cleared his throat.

At his earlier request, Janey had placed a copy of
the Sunday *Chronicle* in a folder at his place. Dooher
picked up the folder, opened it, and withdrew the paper,
holding it up so that the headline fairly screamed. He,
by contrast, spoke with great control, quietly. "I did not
do any of this," he said. "I will fight these charges until
the day I die."

No one said a word.

He scanned the room again, the sea of faces staring back at him, rapt. The current of tension was palpable, underscored by the barely audible sibilance of heavy breathing. Janey and three of the other women in the room were crying.

He continued. "I wanted to meet with all of you, face-to-face, and tell you this. I want to sit here and answer any questions you might have. We're a room full of lawyers and you'll notice I don't have my lawyer present in here—he's sitting in my office, waiting until we're finished. I don't have anything to hide." He glanced a last time at the newspaper, then put it back in its folder. Sitting down, he clasped his hands in front of him on the table. "I am at your complete disposal."

Glitsky and Thieu, armed with their warrant, stood in the empty reception area for a couple of seconds, wondering where everyone was. That odd, red evening light seemed to shimmer in the moted air and the place appeared absolutely deserted.

"This is spooky," Thieu whispered.

"Dooher's office," Glitsky said. "I know where it is."

They walked the long hallway through the center of the building, offices to either side, all of them empty, the light blessedly shaded in the interstices between them.

The area opened up again in front of Dooher's office—Janey's area, the view again, the light. Glitsky knocked on Dooher's door and sensed the movement inside. He put his hand on his gun and the door opened on Wes Farrell.

"We've been expecting you," he said.

* * *

Still with his staff in the conference room, Dooher looked over and stood when the door opened. "Excuse me," he said to the silent table in front of him. He came outside to meet them, closing the door behind him. "You're making a terrible mistake, Sergeant," he said.

"You have the right to remain silent," Glitsky began, while Thieu—more or less gently—took Dooher's arm and placed a handcuff over one wrist, turning it behind his back.

"Is that necessary?"

The door opened again and Thieu put out a hand against it. "Just a minute, please. Police."

But the door got pushed open anyway. Roughly.

"Sergeant Glitsky!"

Glitsky stopped his recital. He remembered her now, no problem. Stunning in the sepia light, her color high, eyes flashing. "Ms. Carrera," he said. "I'm sorry, can I ask you to please wait back inside?"

"No, you can't! This is outrageous!"

Farrell stepped forward. "Christina . . ."

She jerked her arm away, faced off on them all. "What's the matter with you, Sergeant? Can't you see what you're putting this good man through? Look at him. He didn't do anything. Goddammit, *look at him*, would you?"

But Glitsky was looking at her.

"Christina, it's all right," Dooher said.

Thieu had snicked the other cuff on Dooher and now he was advancing on Christina. "I'm afraid I'm going to have to ask you to get back in there, ma'am. Right now."

Glitsky said, "Paul, it's okay."

"It's *not* okay!" Christina's hands were clenched. Tears of anger were beginning to gleam in her eyes. "This isn't right. Why are you doing this?"

"Christina," Dooher repeated. Softly, almost like a lover. "They can't prove it. It's all right." Then, to Wes, gently, "Take care of her, would you?"

Christina looked pleadingly at Dooher. He met her eyes. She started to reach a hand up, but Wes Farrell took it. Some profound energy, unmistakable, flowed between them.

Glitsky saw it, and suddenly knew that the very slim chance that he might in fact be wrong had disappeared. They had inadvertently given him the last piece, the elusive key to the whole puzzle—a motive.

PART FOUR

30

THE DOOHER CASE HAD ENTHRALLED MUCH OF THE public and captivated the media not only because of the bizarre set of facts in the case itself but because it had so deeply polarized the already Balkan-like factions that made up San Francisco.

Wes Farrell had carefully manipulated the coverage, accusing Glitsky of using Dooher as a pawn in his own campaign for advancement within the police department. There was simply no case against Dooher. It was all political.

Glitsky, abetted by activist feminist prosecutor Amanda Jenkins, was simply trying to make his bones by pushing a high-profile case in front of police chief Dan Rigby, who was a rubber stamp for the liberal mayor Conrad Aiken. At the same time, Glitsky was counting on the support of District Attorney Chris Locke, a black liberal supported by two gay supervisors.

On Dooher's side, he had the Archbishop of San Francisco, most of the city's legal community, a host of independent angry white males, including some very vo-cal radio personalities.

Dooher was white and male. Stories appeared where people who had known him (whom he'd fired) recounted his insensitive remarks about his own lesbian daughter. There were no gay attorneys in the firm he ran. He *must* be homophobic. No women had made partner in his firm, either. He was on record as being anti-abortion.

In short, Mark Dooher's public defense was that he was a modern-day Dreyfus—*exactly* the kind of scape-goat an ambitious liberal zealot like Glitsky would need to bolster his reputation and advance his career. The sergeant had taken the lieutenant's exam and, in what was widely viewed (and roundly criticized in certain cir-cles) as another liberal end run to enhance his prestige as a prosecution witness, he had been promoted to head of Homicide.

Outside Oscar Thomasino's courtroom on the third floor of the Hall of Justice, things were heating up.

Building security had erected a makeshift sawhorse chute through which spectators at the trial would have to pass before they entered the courtroom. At the double doors, a metal detector further slowed ingress. (The metal detector at the front entrance to the Hall had been known to miss the occasional weapon—Thomasino didn't want to take chances in his court-room.)

So on this cold and clear Monday morning, the ninth day of December, the hallway outside Department 26 was a microcosm of the city, and it was all but unbri-dled bedlam.

There had already been a mini-riot between the

Veterans of Foreign Wars, who supported Dooher, and the Vietnam Veterans of America, who believed Chas Brown. Seven people had to be restrained by the building cops, and two were removed from the hallway and arrested.

But that hadn't ended it. Their blood up, a couple of hippies from the VVA group waded into a contingent of Vietnamese activists who were there protesting the fact that Dooher wasn't being charged with the Trang or Nguyen murders, both of which had received enormous media attention.

It didn't help that the chute was funneling everyone into the same place.

Inside the courtroom, it wasn't much calmer. The hard wooden theater-style fold-up seats, and all the standing room area in and around them, were crammed with print and network reporters jockeying for space. Women's rights activists wanted Diane Price's story to be heard. Pro-choice and pro-life advocates sniped at each other across the central aisle. The veterans who'd made it inside weren't getting along much better than they had in the hallway.

And this was merely for the pretrial motion phase, before jury selection had even begun. Attorneys for both sides went before the judge and talked about the evidence they would be presenting, about what would be allowed, what barred.

Normally, this was not a public, "sexy" part of a trial. It was often a lot of legalese and mumbo jumbo. But if any of the political and social issues that surrounded this trial were going to be part of it, today was when everyone was going to find out.

The judge hadn't yet entered the courtroom, but the court reporter was at her machine in front of the bench, the clerk sat with his computer printouts off to the side, and the three bailiffs stood at ease in their uniforms.

At the defense table, Mark Dooher was a study in careful control. He and his attorneys had come into the Hall of Justice and then into the courtroom through the back door to avoid having to confront either the reporters or the crowds demonstrating in the hallways outside. Now Dooher sat, somber and subdued, his hands folded in front of him on the table.

On his right was Wes Farrell, who'd lost his ten extra pounds and abandoned his former air of slovenliness—with his maroon tie and charcoal gray Brooks Brothers, he was every inch the successful lawyer.

On the other side of the defendant sat Christina Carrera, by some accounts the "other woman" for whom Dooher had killed his wife. This theory seemed to suffer under the burden of inspection—the two had been hounded by reporters nearly constantly for months now and they had spent little or no personal time alone together. They'd never been caught out at any private tryst. They denied any personal involvement with each other beyond a mutual friendship, respect and commitment to proving Dooher not guilty.

Christina had passed her bar exam only two weeks before, but at Dooher's request, had been on his defense team from the beginning. Over Farrell's strenuous objections.

Dooher had sprung the idea on him as they were leaving the Hall of Justice after posting bail. Farrell had laid a hand on his friend's sleeve. "Let me get this straight. You want Christina Carrera, who hasn't even passed the bar, to be my second chair in your *murder* trial?"

"She'll have passed the bar by the time we go to trial."

"Okay, so even then, that's your plan?"

"That's it."

Farrell nodded, appearing to give it serious thought. "How can I phrase my response so that it's both powerful and unambiguous and yet subtle and sensitive? Ahh, the words are coming to me: Are you out of your fucking mind?"

"Not at all, Wes. It's a terrific idea."

"It's the worst idea I've ever heard. The very worst."

Dooher started walking, forcing Wes to tag along down off the steps of the Hall, along Bryant. "No, listen . . ."

"I can't listen, Mark. It doesn't bear discussion."

But Dooher was going on. "We both agree we've got political issues on our hands here, right? Here we are, two old white guys, the very image of what San Francisco hates, what any representative jury is going to hate . . ."

"It doesn't hate—"

"No, hear me out. And at the prosecution table, we've got a woman DA and a black cop, representing the forces of justice. We need, to steal their own thunder, diversity."

"Okay, so we'll get a second who doesn't look like us, but not her. I've already heard talk about the two of you . . ."

Dooher stopped walking. "There is *nothing* to that. Nothing."

"I didn't say there was, Mark. I'm telling you what I've heard, what other people are saying."

"Well, then, all the better. Get the rumors out of the closet. Put her on the team and we'll all be under a microscope for months, and they won't find a damn thing 'cause there isn't anything. She is very bright, you know. Law review, top of her class."

"Bright, schmight, Mark, she's not even a *lawyer!*"

"We've covered that. She will be. She's got passion and brains and she'll work her ass off for you at a fraction of what you'd have to pay somebody else."

"You mean what *you'd* have to pay someone else. You're telling me money's the issue?"

"No. That's incidental. I'll save a few bucks, but I want her with us. She's pretty as hell, men on the jury are going to want to be on her side."

Farrell was shaking his head. "Men on the jury will be jealous of you and women will be intimidated by her."

"Not true."

"You want to risk your life on that?"

Dooher seemed to consider that notion. "I'm a risk taker, Wes. My gut tells me I'm right in this case. I've lived my life believing what my gut tells me. So yeah, I guess I'd risk my life on this. That's who I am, and I've done pretty well with it, don't you think?"

Wes caught the unspoken message: Better than you have, old buddy old pal.

But this was a terrible idea. Wes couldn't make himself just roll over and accept it, though he could see where this discussion was going to lead. "What if I can't work with her? What if we don't get along?"

"Why wouldn't you get along? Two professionals, one cause you both believe in? What's not to get along?" Then a sop to Farrell's ego. "You'll be the man, Wes. She takes orders from you. And she'll jump at the opportunity, then through hoops if you ask her to."

They were walking again. It was a blustery midafternoon and cars packed all of Bryant's four lanes—traffic lined up for the five o'clock commute across the Bay Bridge, stopped. Horns and swearing.

"Why do you want her, Mark? Really?"

"I just told you."

Farrell shook his head. "No, I mean personally. I'm asking this as your friend, not your attorney, okay? You've *got* to see how badly this could play. Don't you?"

"Yeah," he finally admitted. "We've said there's a risk. I think it's worth taking."

"But why?"

Dooher walked on for a few more steps, then put an arm around Farrell's shoulder. "I guess the same reason I want you. I just don't feel comfortable with a hired gun." He pulled Farrell closer to him. "She's got faith, Wes. She believes in me."

On the prosecution side of the courtroom, Amanda Jenkins had abandoned her trademark mini-skirt for a conservative dark blue suit. She'd let the frost grow out of her hair and now wore it shoulder length, curled under. Next to her, helping her arrange her papers at this moment, was Lieutenant Abe Glitsky.

Glitsky had tried to put the madness of all of this out of his life over the past months—he'd had enough on his mind with his children and his new job. Batiste's prediction had come true and Glitsky had been promoted within his unit, and now he was running Homicide. The paper could say whatever it wanted about the politics of his promotion, but he knew he'd been Batiste's first choice as his successor, and he'd scored second highest among applicants for lieutenant. He'd earned it.

The way he saw it, Mark Dooher was unfinished business from his days as a sergeant. He had investigated the case, assembled the evidence, and delivered it to the district attorney. It was his case until Dooher got sentenced.

So as the DA had requested, as the investigating officer, Glitsky sat inside the rail, at the prosecution table next to Amanda Jenkins, wearing the dark suit he'd bought for Flo's funeral and hadn't worn since.

Almost seven months ago.

He was going to be there every day for the duration of the Dooher trial. California Evidence Code Section 777(c) provided that the DA could appoint an "officer or employee" to be present at the trial, and prosecutors liked the investigating officer to be there for any number of reasons—to prepare other witnesses for what they might expect, to bounce theories and strategies off another professional, to have someone to talk to during recesses, to watch the judge and the jury. If a juror fell asleep during testimony, for example, he'd tell Jenkins that perhaps she should go over it a second time.

But mostly he was there as a second set of ears, to hear what a witness actually said, as opposed to what everyone—except the jury—expected and therefore heard. There was a huge difference, and that's what Abe was listening for.

"All rise. Department Twenty-six of the Superior Court of the City and County of San Francisco is now in session, Judge Oscar Thomasino presiding."

Farrell stood, pulled at his tie and cleared his throat—his nerves were frayed nearly to breaking. He had been in courtrooms hundreds of times, but nothing came close to the electricity surrounding this case. And now, finally, after all the preparation, it was beginning.

Thomasino, in his black robe, ascended to the

bench. Sitting, he adjusted his robe, arranged some papers, took a sip of water, whispered something to his court reporter, who smiled. Knowing that it was undoubtedly a ritual pleasantry, Farrell still wondered what the judge had said—if it was about any of them. Thomasino raised his bushy eyebrows to include the courtroom. Everyone was getting seated again, shuffling around, and the "Good morning" Thomasino perfunctorily uttered went largely unheeded.

It didn't seem to bother the judge. He turned to the court clerk, tapped his gavel once as though checking to see that it still worked, and nodded to the clerk. "Call the case."

The clerk stood. "Superior Court number one five nine three one seven, *The People of the State of California* versus *Mark Francis Dooher*. Counsel state their appearances for the record."

Farrell looked at his client to his left, farther down the table to Christina, his second chair. A thumbs-up, a practiced smile for her confidence, for his client's. He felt little of that confidence himself, concerned that the weakness of his nature, his reluctant acceptance of Christina as second chair would fatally harm the defense.

Christina looked good—hell, she always looked good—and she certainly was game to fight this battle for as long as it took. Farrell even had to admit she was a substantial and resourceful person with a damn good legal mind.

But so what? In spite of that, in spite of her gung-ho attitude and good humor, he wished she could simply disappear.

Because she was in love with their client, goddamn it.

Wes believed that there was nothing yet between

them, but he never doubted that there would be, and privately that shook him.

This was the unspoken motive. Farrell had no indication that Amanda Jenkins was planning to bring it up during the trial—but it was the only argument for Dooher's guilt that Farrell couldn't refute.

This one question lay buried under the rational arguments in the very pit of his being. There had been nights when it rose ghoulish and woke him in a sweat.

But the time for reflection had passed.

Thomasino, all business, ostentatiously opened his folder, read for a nanosecond, and was now skewering both attorneys' tables. "Ms. Jenkins," he began, "Mr. Farrell. Before we call the first jury panel, we've got a four-oh-two to rule on."

Jenkins stood up at her table. "Yes, Your Honor."

The judge was reading again. "You've got two motions here and both of them have to do with character evidence, which you know can only be used in rebuttal by the prosecution."

Thomasino was clarifying this technical point, but that was what 402 motions were about. As a matter of law, evidence of bad character could not serve as proof that a defendant had committed any particular crime. One couldn't say, for example, that because Joe Smith beat his dog, it followed he'd killed his wife.

The law further recognized the perhaps natural, human inclination for the prosecution to want to tarnish a defendant's reputation by bringing up every bad thing that person had ever done, so that it would seem more likely that that person had done the particular thing of which they were accused. So it created a check to keep this from happening.

Unless the defense brought up evidence of a defendant's good character *first*, the evidence code forbade the prosecution from introducing evidence of bad character.

Farrell had filed his motion because Amanda Jenkins's witness list had included some of Dooher's past co-workers, not all of whom had the fondest memories of him. But most of all, the accusations of both Chas Brown and Diane Price had become joined at the hip to the actual murder charges against Dooher.

Jenkins clearly thought that these were critical to an understanding of who Mark Dooher *was*. The thrust of her prosecution strategy, obviously, was that Dooher was not the man he appeared to be, and without character evidence, that was going to be a tough nut. She may have thought she had enough physical evidence and a provable *theory* that stood a chance of convicting him, but she wanted more if she could get it.

On the other hand, if Farrell stuck only to refuting the physical evidence that Jenkins presented, the issue of Dooher's character would never come up. The defense had to be first to bring up character or it would remain inadmissible. So it was tempting to simply forget it. Farrell wasn't sure he was going to need it, anyway.

On the other hand, Farrell knew that sometimes you could refute all the evidence and still the jury would not see it your way. Innocent until proven guilty was a wonderful concept, the prosecution had the burden of proof, all right, but the day-to-day reality of human beings was to assume that people didn't get arrested and brought to trial unless they were *probably* guilty. So Farrell—like Jenkins in this regard—knew it never hurt to have *more*.

And he had the best possible character witness he could have dreamed of—James Flaherty, the Archbishop of San Francisco. Whether or not any of the jury members turned out to be Catholic, Farrell believed that the moral authority Flaherty would bring to the witness stand would be unassailable.

He was torn.

To be safe, he'd put the Archbishop on his witness list. His 402 motion asked for a ruling—once he'd called the Archbishop and thus put character at issue, would Jenkins be allowed to call Price and Brown? Farrell obviously did not want the jury to hear from either of them.

Jenkins was responding to this. "Your Honor," she was saying, "Archbishop Flaherty will not be testifying that he was with the defendant on the night of the murder. He doesn't corroborate Mr. Dooher's alibi for the time of the murder. Therefore, his only possible connection to this case is to serve as a character witness. And once he does that . . ."

Thomasino's eyebrows lifted slightly and he spoke right up. "I know the law, Counselor. But I still question the relevance of the proposed testimony of either of *your* two witnesses."

"Your Honor, if the court please." Farrell was on his feet. "Mark Dooher has lived most of the last year under the shadow of these ridiculous accusations, unsubstantiated slander without any shred of evidence to support them. Even if the prosecution had dug up some witnesses to bolster these baseless charges, they will be talking about alleged crimes from thirty years ago. This is very remote in time."

These remarks brought the first unanimity from the disparate factions in the gallery, and it was negative. Everyone except the reporters was here with some kind of agenda, and Farrell was trying to nip in the bud any discussion of the social issues represented by the testimonies of Diane Price and Chas Brown.

"Remote in time, my ass!" one of the gallery women yelled. "He still raped her." She was ejected from the courtroom for her pains.

When Thomasino had restored order, Farrell stood again and found himself making a speech. "Your Honor, any examination of these charges will involve a substantial waste of court time, litigating ancient history. This whole trial—and we see proof of this already in this courtroom—will end up being about an alleged rape and alleged homicide that happened years ago and thousands of miles from here. It's going to confuse and prejudice the jury and it's just plain not fair to introduce this flimsy stuff. How are we supposed to defend against allegations from a couple of substance abusers who say nothing for thirty years, then come out of the woodwork at the first sign of a TV camera?"

At the explosion following this question, which Farrell expected, Thomasino slammed his gavel five times, glared, did it again. He ordered three more people out. After the bailiffs had gotten them removed, a deathly silence ensued. "I want everyone to understand this." Thomasino's voice was barely audible, forcing everyone to listen. He pointed a finger at the back of the courtroom, waving it back and forth to include everybody. "You people watching these proceedings are not a part of it, and any attempt to make yourselves part of it will force my hand. Any more outbursts, I will clear this courtroom." He pointed his gavel at Farrell. "You may proceed, Mr. Farrell. Carefully."

Farrell got the message. The judge understood that he had purposely provoked the gallery. This wasn't going to be tolerated. He deemed it prudent to wrap it up. "Ms. Jenkins hasn't got any real evidence in this case, so she's thrown in these baseless charges in the hope of convicting my client through attrition. She would have us believe these witnesses will testify about Mr. Dooher's character, but that's precisely *not* what they're going to be doing. They're going to be accusing him of other crimes for which the prosecution has no evidence. They have no place in this courtroom."

Jenkins had heard enough. "We *do* have evidence . . ."

"Then formally charge him," Farrell shot back.

The gallery didn't exactly rumble behind them, but Thomasino held up his gavel and whatever noise was starting came to an abrupt end. "I would ask counsel to address their remarks to the court, not to one another." He was silent a moment, then continued. "The defendant is on trial here for killing his wife. That is all he has been charged with, and that is what this trial is going to be about."

Farrell nodded with satisfaction. If this was the judge's decision—that the jury wasn't going to hear from either Chas Brown or Diane Price—it was a good sign for them.

"Therefore," Thomasino was going on, "it is this court's ruling under Section 352 of the Evidence Code that the proposed testimony of Chas Brown regarding the alleged murder of an unnamed person committed by the defendant in Vietnam some twenty-five years ago is inadmissible. It is much more prejudicial than probative. Not only is the alleged event remote in time, any discussion of it would be unduly consumptive of court time. Especially, Ms. Jenkins, in light of the fact that Mr. Brown did not see this alleged murder, and therefore cannot testify that this murder happened at all."

There was a muffled chorus of "right-ons" and "Yeahs" from the gallery, but Thomasino's glare put a quick stop to it. "However," the judge continued, "although equally remote in time, the character testimony of Diane Price regarding her alleged rape is that of a firsthand witness . . ."

"Your Honor!" Farrell could see the way this might go, and he had to object. "This alleged rape never took place, and even if it did, it has nothing to do with the crime Mr. Dooher is charged with. You can't allow—"

"Mr. Farrell! The issue is only going to arise if you bring up character in the first place. If you do, then as you know, the prosecution can bring rebuttal witnesses. If you, in turn, wish to attack the credibility of those witnesses, you may."

"Yes, Your Honor, but—"

Thomasino cut him off by addressing Jenkins. "Ms. Jenkins, it is the court's ruling that you may call Diane Price as a character witness once that issue has been tendered by the defense."

"Thank you, Your Honor."

"But I must tell you that I will instruct the jury as to how to consider this proposed testimony. This is not going to turn into a rape trial."

There was another buzz in the gallery, and this time the judge did bring his gavel down. He looked at his watch. "Mr. Farrell, Ms. Jenkins, any other last-minute motions you'd like the court to consider before we begin jury selection? No? All right, then, we'll take a twenty-minute recess while the first panel gets settled in."

The tedium of jury selection consumed the rest of the morning, and judging from Thomasino's thoroughness as he directed the voir dire, it was going to continue to be a slow process. Sixteen prospective jurors out of the first panel of sixty had already been dismissed because of their familiarity with the case. This was an enormous percentage, indicative of the intense media coverage to date, and the trial was only beginning. It was going to get much worse.

The defense team had rented a small room next to a bail bondsman's office across the street from the Hall of Justice, and Wes went out to get sandwiches, which inadvertently left Christina and Mark alone. They entered the room together and closed the solid wooden door.

Christina put her briefcase on the desk and turned around. Mark had been a couple of steps behind her, and the room was cramped in any event. They stood, a foot apart.

Christina had been—figuratively—backing away for months. Suddenly now, the physical being that had been Sheila Dooher no longer stood as a barrier between them. The opening volleys in the trial signaled a new phase.

Mark had to recognize it now, too. He had to know that Christina would be there for him. She met his eyes. "I don't know about you," she said, "but I could use a hug."

Farrell could feel it as soon as he came into the room with the sandwiches. Something had transpired in here. There was an uneasy tension, a palpable sense that he'd interrupted. "Hey, cowboys," he said.

Christina was leaning against the windowsill, combing her hair with her fingers. Mark was sitting on the desk, swinging his feet like a schoolboy. Wes decided he'd unpack the bags and keep on talking, give whatever it was a chance to dissipate. "So I was thinking we just wouldn't call Flaherty. That'll avoid the whole can of worms."

Dooher jumped right on it. "We've got to call him," he said. "We get one good Catholic on the jury— and I think we can guarantee that—and the Archbishop tells that person I couldn't have done anything they said I did—which we know is the truth—at the very least the jury's hung. And besides, we want Diane Price to testify against me."

Christina moved from the window. "No, Mark, we . . ."

But, emboldened, Dooher stood, grabbed his soft drink and popped the top on it. "I know originally we said no, but did you hear Thomasino in there? Even the judge thinks it's bullshit. It will make Jenkins look like she's grasping at straws. It's a question of credibility. So then you, Christina, cross-examine her."

"I do? Why not Wes?"

But Wes knew the answer to that. "Because you're a woman. It'll be much more effective if you start talking about the drugs Mrs. Price has taken and how many men she slept with in college and whether or not she ever reported this alleged rape and why it kind of slipped her mind for the intervening decades. In short, you eat her for lunch."

Shaking her head, Christina was staring at the floor.

"What?" Wes asked.

"I don't want to do that. I don't want to eat anybody for lunch. I feel sorry for her. Don't you guys understand that?"

"I do," Mark said.

"Excuse me, but fuck that! I'm glad you two are so sensitive. It gives me a warm feeling deep down inside." Farrell spun himself, a little circle in the tiny room.

"Here's lesson one—a trial is a war. You don't take prisoners. You destroy everything in your path because if you don't, make no mistake, it will destroy you. Sympathy does not belong here." Farrell reined himself in, slightly. "Listen, Christina, this Diane Price is trying to send our client to jail for most of the rest of his life, and that makes her my enemy. And she's *lying*! That makes her your enemy."

"I'm just not used to thinking that way."

Dooher to the rescue. "Wes, you could do it. It doesn't have to be Christina."

Farrell got to escape velocity in record time. "*Of course* I could do it! Mister goddamn Rogers could do it! We could phone it in and get it done. But Christina here, being a woman, could do it *best*, and that's what we've got to go with. Our best shot every time out. That's how you win. It's the *only* way you win." Farrell glared at them both.

"All right, Wes, all right. You're cute when you're mad. Anybody ever tell you that?"

"No," he said. "Nobody ever has. Christina, how about you?"

Farrell was gratified to see that she'd gone a little pale. Maybe she was finally beginning to understand what she'd gotten herself into. But she put up a brave front. "No," she said, "I think you're cuter when you're *not* mad."

When Thomasino called the lunch recess, Glitsky made his way out through the tide of humanity in the gallery and then no-commented his way past the reporters in the hallway. He took the stairs, rather than the crowded elevator, up to Homicide, to his hundred and twenty square feet partially enclosed by drywall. He intended to eat his bagel and apple in peace and maybe get in some administrative work before court reconvened at one-thirty.

But there was Paul Thieu, up out of his own desk before Glitsky was a step into the room. And another person—long hair, eyes burning, pumped up, unhappy and unkempt. At a glance Glitsky recognized the symptoms—this guy was cranked up, high on methamphetamines.

"You remember Chas Brown?" Thieu asked.

Glitsky was about to nod, shake his hand, be polite, but Brown didn't give him the chance. "What's this I don't get to be a witness? All the time I spend with you guys and what do I get out of it for me, huh?"

Thieu popped in. "Chas heard about Thomasino's ruling from his friends in the courtroom. He'd been kind of hoping he'd get a couple more days at the Marriott." The city put its witnesses in various hotels, and Chas had evidently been looking forward to a bit of a longer vacation.

Abe was low affect. "It wasn't our decision, Chas. We wanted you there. The judge ruled against us. We lose."

"Why? The guy kills one guy, then another guy, then his wife. You're telling me they're not related?"

"No, I think they're related."

"Then why, man?"

"No proof. No proof there was even a murder."

"Me saying it? That's not proof?"

Glitsky kept it cool. "You didn't see it, Chas. You weren't a witness. All the Saigon records, if any, were destroyed." He shrugged, repeated it. "We lose."

"We've been over this," Thieu said. "What do you want us to do, Chas? You want another night at the Marriott?" He threw a hopeful glance at Glitsky.

"No, I want . . . I mean I told everybody I was going to be in this trial . . ."

And now, Glitsky thought, even that tiny drop of limelight had evaporated. He imagined it was probably disappointing, but mostly he just wanted Chas to go away. He wasn't needed anymore, and cranked-up eight hundreds in the Hall of Justice were something he could do without.

"And Dooher's going to get off, isn't he?"

"We hope not, Chas. That's why we're having a trial."

"But they can't hear about the guy he killed over there?"

"No, I'm afraid not."

"That son of a bitch," he repeated. "He never pays for anything, does he?"

In that moment, something shifted for Glitsky. He'd met Brown before, and always he'd been less than completely sober, but never particularly hostile to Dooher. Now, granted, he was cranked up and that could do it, but suddenly there seemed to be a different edge. "I thought you didn't really have any personal gripe with Dooher," Glitsky said.

Defiant. "I don't. Who said I did?"

"You're acting like it, Chas. Nobody said it."

"I'm not acting like anything. I haven't seen the dude in like ten years."

This straightened Thieu up. He had interviewed Brown at least five times and had never heard this. "I thought it had been more like twenty-five, Chas."

Brown's eyes shone, flashed from Glitsky to Thieu. He backed up a step, put his hands into his jeans pockets. "Ten, twenty-five, what's the difference?"

"Fifteen years," Glitsky said.

Brown shrugged. "So?"

"So which one is it, Chas?" Thieu picked it up. "Did you see Dooher ten years ago?"

"Maybe. Maybe eleven, I don't know."

Glitsky. "What about?"

"I don't know. This same thing."

The two inspectors looked at each other. Glitsky nodded and Thieu talked. "You talked to Mark Dooher about this Saigon murder ten years ago? What about it?"

Brown scratched at his beard, rolled his eyes around, let out a long breath. "I was having, you know . . . like I couldn't find much work. I was looking through the paper and saw Dooher at this like charity thing, and it said he did a lot of that, so I figured, hey, he's doin' pretty good, maybe he could help out an old buddy."

"You tried to blackmail him," Glitsky said.

"First I just asked him if he could spare a little, you know. It wasn't like strong-arm."

"And what'd he do? Did he pay you?"

Chas was shaking his head. "He threw me out, the son of a bitch. Said nobody'd believe a lowlife like me anyway. He just laughed at me. Didn't give a shit my life was in the toilet."

"Why didn't you ever mention this before, Chas?" Thieu asked.

"I thought it would make me look bad. I don't know."

"And you wanted to testify to get back at him?" It made perfect sense to Glitsky. It was all about macho posturing—power and payback.

"Yeah. Show the bastard." He looked at the faces of the two inspectors. "Hey, it don't mean he didn't kill the guy."

31

I DON'T KNOW ABOUT YOU, BUT I COULD USE A HUG. Dooher kept reliving the moment, savoring the sweetness of it, the smell of her, the press of her breasts up against him, her arms around him inside the coat of his suit.

They'd stood there, holding fast to one another for a long time—perhaps thirty seconds, forty. He'd started to become aroused, and she felt it, making a small noise deep in her throat, leaning into him. Then pulling back, looking up, inviting the kiss that came—tentative and gentle at first, then openmouthed, consuming.

Then Wes was outside, saying something to someone in the hall. She crossed over to the window and he sat on the desk.

That night—the defense team was all but living together—they'd all had dinner at a French restaurant on Clement Street. As was their routine, Farrell drove Dooher home. Both of them were beat after the long day in the courtroom. There would be plenty of time to second-guess jury selection.

Christina hadn't called him, and he hadn't called her.

Then, all day today, the sexual tension, and Farrell seemed to take extra care that Mark and Christina were never alone.

At home after another late dinner and another day of jury selection, Dooher changed into a pair of khakis and a black cotton sweater. Then, barefoot, he wandered downstairs into his library and stood at the window.

Christina was coming up the walk, through the gate into the patio. Except for the kitchen lights, the house was dark. Snooping media types might believe that the house was empty. He opened the door. "Can you see?"

"Fine."

They got to the kitchen. She wore the hood up on a heavy ski parka. Flipping the parka back, she blew a strand of hair away from her mouth. "Okay, I'm nervous."

He stepped forward and gathered her in. When he released her, there was no kiss. He gave her a wistful half smile, then retreated to the counters. "Can I get you a cup of coffee? Some wine? You want to take off your coat?"

She said wine would be good and shrugged out of the parka, draping it over one of the stools. Mark busied himself in the refrigerator, getting out the bottle, opening it, taking down the glasses. Coming over to her, he slid a glass before her and pulled up another stool. He held up his glass and she touched it, a ringing chime.

"Just so you understand, Christina," he began, "I didn't plan on this. On yesterday."

"I didn't either. It's not the kind of thing you plan."

Mark sipped his wine. "And now I don't know what to do with it. I don't know how you feel. I don't know anything."

"Do you know how *you* feel?"

"Not really. Confused, I suppose. Guilty as hell, though in this context that's a poor choice of words. I mean . . ."

She reached over and covered his hand. "I know what you mean. You think it's still too soon."

"I don't know what 'too soon' is. But I know what this is, what yesterday was."

"Me too."

He smiled at her. "I'm not talking about the feeling."

She squeezed his hand. "I am."

He moved his hand away. "No. It's more than that, and I don't think I can trust it. I don't trust it."

"What?"

"You and I being thrown together like this, the stress of this situation. You helping to defend me, me dependent on you. It's a false environment."

"Driving us together through no fault of our own?"

He put his glass down and broke a lopsided grin. "You're making fun of me."

She leaned toward him. "A bit."

"Okay, but I'm being serious. I think we deserve a better chance than that. Especially, that *you* do." He sighed. "I never thought I would love anybody again, and now here it is and the timing's all wrong. Everything's all wrong."

"Not everything," she said.

"Almost."

She was shaking her head. "You feel like you love me. And I love you. That's not almost everything wrong—that's almost everything right."

He twirled his wineglass, tiny circles on the counter. "And if they find me guilty of murder, I don't get out of prison until you're older than I am now."

"They won't find you guilty. You didn't do it."

"I would have said they'd never have gotten me to trial because I didn't do it. But guess what?"

She sipped her wine. "So what are you saying?"

He looked down, sighed again, raised his eyes. "I'm trying to tell you I love you," he said, "and I've got two temptations. The first is to take you upstairs and not think about what any of it means or where it might go."

"I choose door one," she said.

He reached over and touched her face. "And the second is to pretend it isn't here, none of this, to pretend that yesterday was a moment of weakness. But I don't think it was. I think it was real, so real I'm terrified we're going to threaten it."

"And how would we do that, threaten it?"

He closed his eyes briefly and took a last deep breath. "By doing anything about it." He went on. "Right now we're in a pressure cooker. I think we ought to wait until we're out of it, until we can see where we are."

"I know where I'll be. I'll be right here."

"If you are, so will I. So maybe we should acknowledge this—what we have, this connection—and then put it on a shelf until the time is right."

"And when will that be, Mark?"

"When this is over. When they find me not guilty. It shouldn't be long now, a couple more weeks, a month. After the drama and the prying eyes, then we'll see where we are. But this . . . I don't trust it. It would be too easy for both of us to get caught up in the romance of it . . ."

"I don't think so."

"It's not a matter of thinking, Christina. The reality is persuasive enough. Here I am, the classic tragic figure—innocent man unfairly accused—and you are my savior." He softened things, covering her hand with his. "I'm not saying the feeling isn't real. I'm saying maybe it's not *us*—the real people we are—feeling them. It's the roles we're in, and they're temporary. And I can't have us be temporary. I couldn't live with that."

Her eyes held steadily on him, and suddenly a spark of humor flared. "The last noble man in America, and I had to go and find him." She came forward and pressed her lips to his cheek, holding them there. "You don't trust the *rush*, do you?"

"The rush isn't going away, Christina. If the real stuff is here, the rush will find its way back."

She kissed him again. "Okay." Searching his face. "In the meantime, I'll be a professional, I won't feed the gossip mills, I won't give them any ammunition. But when this is over, this is fair warning. I'm going to be here. For you."

The *Chronicle* photographer with the night vision camera caught them kissing at the front door—nothing passionate, although they did stand together, embracing, for nearly two minutes, saying good night.

It was plenty.

32

THE GALLERY WASN'T A PRESENCE FOR GLITSKY anymore.

Mark Dooher's fate was going to be determined inside the bar rail and Glitsky glanced across the courtroom at the defense table and felt his blood quicken with hate. It was a reaction he rarely felt. He had dealt with many despicable people, many of whom had committed heinous crimes, but his own feelings for them had almost never gotten personal.

Dooher was different. Not only had he attacked Glitsky on a variety of grounds, threatening his career and reputation—the reverberations were still echoing—but killing his wife, that struck at the heart of things.

The defendant sat, his expression serene, while on either side of him, his acolytes tried not to appear nervous and angry, though to Glitsky's practiced eye, they were failing. This, he knew, was probably in reaction to the *Chronicle*'s story and accompanying picture—

Dooher and Christina kissing on his darkened front porch.

Christina's mouth was set, her eyes cast downward. She was pretending to read from a folder in front of her, but she looked up too often to be reading.

Wes Farrell seemed somewhat cooler. He was a pro and knew you didn't show your feelings to the jurors, but Glitsky had heard him answering one of Dooher's questions at the defense table. The two men didn't seem to be best friends anymore.

In spite of Thomasino's detailed approach to questioning prospective jurors, once he had winnowed out the people who'd known about the case and the other obvious exclusions—victims of other crimes, family members of law enforcement people—jury selection had gone rapidly. Now it was Thursday of the first week, the lunch recess was behind them, and the show was getting under way.

Amanda had told Glitsky that she didn't subscribe to the belief that there was a fine art to picking members of the jury. In spite of all the fancy theories people had, it was more or less a crapshoot. Evidently Wes Farrell felt the same way. Amanda basically preferred married women to single men for this type of case, and Asians if she could get them, but those seemed to be her only criteria. Farrell liked men who had jobs. But both attorneys seemed inclined, mostly, to keep things moving.

And now the new and improved Amanda Jenkins was facing the panel of twelve. Glitsky tried to take some clues from the jurors' faces, but he didn't know what he might be looking for. None of them particularly avoided his gaze, although none held it either. They were focused on Amanda, not him.

There were seven women and five men. Five of the jurors—two of the men and three of the women—

were what Glitsky would call well dressed. Another five had thrown on something at least marginally respectful. Of the remaining two, a younger white man with a half-grown beard and long hair wore a faded army fatigue shirt, untucked and unbuttoned over a T-shirt. Amanda had let him stay because she guessed he'd be prejudiced against lawyers such as Dooher. It was a surprise when Farrell left him unchallenged.

Another, a middle-aged, very heavyset Hispanic man, wore jeans and a blue denim shirt that he evidently had gone to work in many times. Farrell had apparently wanted him because he was Catholic, and Amanda told Abe she hadn't objected because she thought he was pretending to be dumber than he was.

There were four Asians (three women and a man), two Hispanics (one and one), three African-Americans (two and one), and three whites (one and two). Glitsky had no idea what the demographics meant, and Amanda, in her no-nonsense style, had set him straight over lunch. "Nobody has a clue."

Now she was about to address them, and Glitsky thought that, her softer image notwithstanding, her body language put her at a slight disadvantage. She was holding a yellow legal pad for a prop, standing slightly hip-shot before the jury box.

Amanda made no bones about the fact that she did not like juries, about having to explain every fact or nuance so a moron could understand it, about the cutthroat legal world in which she found herself. Glitsky thought she wore all these feelings on her tailored sleeves, her forced smile betraying all of it. At least it did to Abe. He hoped he was wrong.

Nevertheless, no one was in this room to make friends. He supposed a serious demeanor wasn't the worst handicap a lawyer could have, although all the *successful* trial attorneys he knew allowed a great deal more personality to peek through when they got in front of a jury.

"Ladies and gentlemen of the jury. Good afternoon."

She checked her notes—maybe the pad wasn't a prop after all—took a deep breath, and began.

"As Judge Thomasino told you, the prosecution's opening statement is to acquaint you with the evidence in the case, the evidence that the People of the State of California will use to demonstrate the *facts* that we will then assemble to prove, and prove beyond a reasonable doubt, the *truth*: that on June seventh of this year, Mark Dooher"—she turned and pointed for effect—"the defendant here, willfully and with malice aforethought, murdered his wife, Sheila.

"I'm going to be presenting evidence about what happened on that day, a Tuesday. The weather was exceptionally pleasant, sunny with temperature in the low seventies, and at about four-thirty, the defendant"—throughout the trial, Jenkins would try to depersonalize Dooher by avoiding his name whenever possible—"called his wife, Sheila Dooher, and suggested that he take off work early and they have a romantic evening together. Sounds nice, doesn't it?"

Glitsky wasn't surprised to hear Farrell's first objection—nearly guttural with some suppressed emotion, but clear enough. His focus, missing this morning, was coming back. Glitsky knew that though the alleged idyll between Dooher and his wife might have sounded nice, it wasn't up to Jenkins to portray it as such.

Thomasino's eyebrows lifted up and down. "Sustained."

It didn't slow Jenkins. She took her eyes off the jury to consult her pad, then went right back to it. "In his own statement to the police, the defendant admitted what happened next. He left his office downtown and, on his way home, made a stop at Dellaroma's Liquor and Delicatessen on Ocean Avenue for a bottle of Dom Pérignon champagne and an assortment of meats and vegetables. He went home and he and his wife shared the champagne and the hors d'oeuvres. Then, because she was tired, Mrs. Dooher went upstairs for a nap. The defendant went to the driving range."

Listening to it, Glitsky was confronted again—it happened to varying degrees every time he came to court in other cases—with the chasm of difference between his essentially freewheeling job of gathering evidence and the court's job of objectively analyzing it. But Jenkins evidently realized how benign it all sounded because she stopped a minute, walked to the prosecution table to break her own rhythm, and took a sip of water.

She turned back to the jury. "That's what the defendant told the police. What the defendant did not tell police was that even then, he was planning to kill his wife.

"The plan was a simple one.

"The defendant had long ago obtained—for his own use—a prescription for chloral hydrate, a strong sedative he said he needed because he had trouble sleeping. Chloral hydrate is often commonly referred to as 'knockout drops,' and that's how the defendant intended to use it. He would puncture some of the gel tabs and slip some of the drug into his wife's champagne. He would help put her to bed. He would go to a nearby driving range to establish an alibi. Then he would return, stab his wife to death in her sleep and make it look like a burglary. He almost got away with it.

"What the defendant did not know was that his wife was already taking two other powerful drugs—

Benadryl for her allergies, and Nardil for depression. When the defendant gave his wife the chloral hydrate, the dose, combined with the alcohol and these other drugs in her system, was enough to kill her."

There was an audible stir in the courtroom. This was evidently a surprise to people who'd only read the articles as far as the grisly stabbing. Thomasino gently tapped his gavel and quiet returned.

Jenkins continued. "If Mrs. Dooher had been allowed to remain unmolested as she lay dead in her bed, Mark Dooher would probably not be in this courtroom today, charged with her murder. But Mr. Dooher is a lawyer. He is a clever man and—"

Farrell was up out of his seat. "Your Honor . . ."

Thomasino sustained him again. And this time Jenkins turned to the judge and apologized to him, then to the jury. She didn't mean to characterize the defendant.

Jenkins was playing well for the jury—friendly, courteous, professional. "Intending to stab his wife to death, the defendant instead poisoned her to death. Legally, it makes no difference—either killing is murder in the first degree.

"Factually, it makes all the difference in the world. Defendant's miscalculation got him caught. That's because much of the evidence deliberately planted by the defendant to suggest a burglary, much of the evidence designed to explain Sheila Dooher's violent death at the hands of a knife-wielding attacker, takes on a very different light once we know Sheila Dooher was poisoned to death. It shows the calculated and methodical attempt of a cold-blooded murderer to conceal guilt.

"We're going to show you a knife—a classic 'murder weapon,' complete with Mark Dooher's fingerprints. You're going to hear from witnesses who help to piece together the real story of what happened on that evening of June seventh. And that is this: that the defendant, having made sure his wife would be sleeping soundly—drugged with chloral hydrate—left his house by the side door, without activating the alarm system, and reached above the door, unscrewing the porch light so the driveway would be dark upon his return.

"Then he drove to the San Francisco Golf Club, *not* to the Olympic Club which is closer to his house and where he is a member, and bought two large buckets of golf balls. After hitting a few balls, he walked through a break in the fence, went to his car, and drove home.

"We know he drove home because one of his neighbors, Emil Balian, recognized his car with its personalized plates parked on the street down from his house at between eight and nine p.m."

Yes, Glitsky knew Balian had said that, but he thought that if ever a witness were born to be broken, it was the neighborhood busybody, who'd already changed details in his identification story three times. Glitsky thought that Farrell would destroy him on cross-examination. But, as Drysdale had said, Balian was very nearly the key to the case. Sometimes you had to take what you could get.

"By now it was dark out, and the defendant entered his darkened house. Upstairs, in his bedroom, he plunged a knife into his wife's heart as, he thought, she lay sleeping. He tore her bedclothes and threw blankets around, simulating a struggle. He poured a vial of blood that he had stolen from his doctor's lab around the body. He tore the wedding and engagement rings from Sheila Dooher's hand, and then rifled the bureau in the room, taking other jewelry, including his own Rolex watch. Then he went back to the driving range, climbed back through the fence—"

"It's all a goddamn lie!"

Glitsky was startled nearly out of his seat. Dooher was suddenly on his feet, pointing at Jenkins, who stood openmouthed, stunned at the outburst. And it wasn't over. "And you're a goddamn liar!"

Thomasino, who'd been listening intently to Jenkins, reacted as if he'd been jolted by electricity. He reached for his gavel, missed it, and it fell behind the desk, so he had to stand himself. "Mr. Dooher, you sit down! Mr. Farrell! You control your client, you hear me? Sit down, I said!"

Glitsky was up and the two bailiffs were moving across to Farrell's table, but Wes held up his hands, motioning them back. "Come on, Mark, easy . . ." Christina, too, was up, an arm around Dooher's back, whispering to him.

But Dooher glared at one and all. "I cannot believe I am hearing so much bull-*shit*!"

Everybody in the courtroom heard him.

Dooher turned to the jury and suddenly his voice was in the normal conversational range. "None of this happened this way," he said. "Not any of it."

Thomasino had found his gavel and slammed it down again. "Mr. Farrell, I'll gag your client if you don't . . ."

"Yes, Your Honor." A hand on Dooher's arm, pulling him down. Whispering through clenched teeth. "Mark, sit down. Get a grip, would you?"

Then, Farrell to Thomasino again. "Your Honor, if I could ask for a short recess . . ."

But Thomasino was shaking his head. "Not during an opening statement, Mr. Farrell. You control your client and let Ms. Jenkins finish up, and if there are any more interruptions, I'll hold *you* in contempt. How's that? Clear?"

* * *

"What the hell was that? What are you trying to do, kill yourself out there?"

Farrell, in their tiny room across the street, was himself now nearly out of control. There was spittle on his lips and he seemed almost struck with palsy—now pacing, now hovering in front of his client. Dooher, again, had hoisted himself up onto the desk. He was swinging his feet, relaxed. Christina stood at the window, arms crossed over her chest.

Thomasino was going to allow Jenkins all the time she needed to wrap up her opening statement, but it turned out that she only made it another ten minutes before *she* asked for a recess. Dooher's interruption had poleaxed her, and what had begun as a reasonably compelling recital of events had degenerated into a disjointed shopping list of purported evidence whose relevance and connection seemed to elude Jenkins herself. She kept referring to her notes, stumbling over her words, until she finally gave it up.

"Wes, relax," Dooher said, "it's all right. You're going to have a heart attack."

"You're goddamn right I'm going to have a heart attack. I deserve a heart attack. What were you doing in there? What was that all about? How could you lose your temper like that?"

Dooher actually broke a grin. "I didn't."

"This is funny? There's a joke here maybe I'm missing?"

"I didn't lose my temper, Wes."

"Well, damn, Mark, that was one hell of an imitation."

Christina came forward, daring to speak for the first time since Wes had dressed down both Mark and herself for their incredible stupidity and duplicity and every other negativity he could think of over the kiss. She talked to Dooher. "What do you mean, you didn't lose your temper?"

He turned to her, palms up. The grin faded. "It was an act. I thought it would humanize me for the jury."

Farrell seemed to sag and let out a chuckle without a trace of humor in it. His eyes went to Christina, back to the client. "This is what, in the trade, we call a bad idea. What it did for the jury, Mark, was made you look like guy with no respect for the law, some kind of hot-head . . ."

"Wait wait wait! Don't you see?"

"I don't see. Christina, do you see?"

She didn't answer.

Dooher included them both. "All right. I'll spell it out. Jenkins is up there painting this picture. I'm cold. I plan things to the nth degree. And here I am, sitting at the defense table trying to keep some kind of impassive face while Jenkins just goes on and on, lie after outrageous lie. So I react. Who wouldn't react? It's natural. What's unnatural is just *sitting* there, cold and unfeeling, playing right into their hands. I wanted to show them who I was."

"Well, you did that."

"You're damn straight, Wes. I looked 'em right in the eye and told them none of it was true. You don't think that's going to have an effect?"

"Oh, I'm sure it is. I just don't think it's going to be the one you wanted. Here you are, supposedly a good, practicing lawyer, and you're not showing respect for the system . . ."

"Because they got it wrong! Don't you see that? I've been falsely accused of something I didn't do and it's gotten all the way to this fiasco of a trial. How can I have respect for that? How can I even pretend to?'"

"But to yell at the jury . . . ?"

"No. I didn't yell at the jury. I very carefully avoided doing that. I looked at them as *people*, and that's how they are going to see me."

Farrell glanced at Christina as though he would ask for her help, but simply shook his head.

There was a knock on the door and Dooher slid off the desk and opened it. The cop from the Hall said that Judge Thomasino wanted to see Mr. Farrell in his chambers, right now.

Farrell stood. "Why don't you two try to keep your hands off each other while I'm gone," he said, and quit the room.

Which left the two of them alone.

Dooher turned. "He's mad at us."

"There's a good call."

"I suppose I should have told him before I disrupted the sacred order of the court, but the moment just came and I took it. If I'd've warned Wes, he'd have counseled me not to do it anyway. What did you think?"

"I don't know, Mark. I haven't done any other trials. I don't know how they play out. It shocked me when it happened, but now, hearing you explain it, it might work."

"It won't hurt me, I'm sure of that. That's not what Wes is mad about anyway."

She let herself down onto one of the wooden chairs. "I know," she said, "it's us. But we told him we weren't going behind his back. It wasn't about the trial."

"He didn't believe us."

"You're the master of insight today, aren't you? First Wes is mad at us, and then Wes doesn't believe us."

"Maybe we should mend a few fences?"

"I don't think that's a bad idea."

Mark went over to the window and separated the blinds, looking out over Bryant Street and downtown beyond. "I'm just not willing to concede," he said, "that there's a telescopic-sight camera set up on Nob Hill, trained on this window."

He crossed back over to her and took her in his arms.

Judge Thomasino's chambers were neither large nor imposing, furnished as they were in functional Danish. Three tall teak bookshelves closed in the walls, and various diplomas, honors and commendations in wooden frames seemed to have been stuck randomly on the green drywall. A robust ficus sprawled in the corner by a large window. One of Remington's brass cowboys graced a broad teak coffee table, but that was the extent of the decorative touches. The rug was faded brown Berber over the Hall's linoleum.

Jenkins and Glitsky were seated in low leather chairs in front of the judge's desk and they both turned at the bailiff's knock. It was Farrell, and Glitsky stood, ceding pride of place to the attorneys. He was here because Amanda had asked him to be.

Farrell didn't sit, but walked to the front of Thomasino's desk. "I'm glad you're here, Amanda," he began. "I wanted to apologize for my client. And to you, Judge. I'm sorry."

Thomasino barely acknowledged the words with an ambiguous gesture, then got right to it. "I asked you down here, Mr. Farrell, to see if you can give me any reason why I shouldn't yank your client's bail. You should know that I already told Ms. Jenkins that if she asked, I'd do it. I'm thinking of doing it in any event. If you want a mistrial, your client can do sixty days next door"—meaning in jail—"while he waits for his new court date to contemplate whether he wants to interrupt the proceedings again."

Glitsky wouldn't have thought Farrell could sag any further than he had when he walked in, but he did. Visibly.

Jenkins took it up. "I'll be honest with you, Wes," she said. "You and I know this is the first murder I've gotten to trial. My colleagues in the DA's office are starting to wonder why I'm on the payroll if I'm never actually in trial. I don't want to wait another sixty days."

"*Minimum,*" Thomasino intoned.

"Minimum," she repeated. "And I think the argument can be made that the outburst was potentially as prejudicial to your client as it might have been self-serving."

A rueful nod. "We were just discussing that," Farrell said.

"So it's a wash," Jenkins concluded.

Glitsky admired the way Jenkins delivered it. It sounded genuine enough, although he knew the truth was quite different. As the recess had been called, Jenkins had sent Glitsky upstairs to get Art Drysdale and tell him she was asking to get Dooher's bail revoked.

Drysdale had made a quick phone call—cryptic enough, but it must have been to Chris Locke—and then accompanied Abe back to Department 26, where Jenkins sat, still fuming, at the prosecution table.

From Glitsky's perspective, there was no question that Locke had some personal—political—connection to this case. The DA didn't want to see it postponed, to let it remain unresolved, much as he had asked for the unreasonably low bail. He was doing the Archbishop a favor.

As Drysdale had been explaining that the DA did not want to ask for bail to be revoked, Thomasino had sent word that he wanted to see Jenkins in his chambers and discuss that very thing, and Drysdale had supplied her with the reason she was to give for *not* wanting it.

Farrell, for his part, was a drowning man who'd just gone down for the third time, opened his eyes underwater, and saw the lifebuoy. He reached for it. "Your Honor, I will not let this kind of thing happen again."

The glare. Thomasino growled once, settled into his chair. "All right, now there's one other thing." The two opposing attorneys looked at each other, wondering. "I don't know how much control you have over your client's behavior, Mr. Farrell—I'd gather not very much. But perhaps you could exert some influence over your second chair. I don't want to sequester this jury, but if we get too many more stories about Mr. Dooher and Ms. Carrera, I'm not going to have any choice. A man's accused of killing his wife, it's the better part of valor to keep his dick in his pants—excuse me, Amanda —at least until a jury's had a chance to make up its mind.

"Now I've told the jury not to watch television or read newspapers, but we all know what will happen if the defendant keeps getting on the front page. That's not in anyone's interest. Are we in agreement here?"

"Yes, Your Honor."

"Good." Thomasino paused for a couple of seconds. He looked at his watch. "I'm going to adjourn for today, giving you, Mr. Farrell, a lot of time to make these points to your client and your associate. I'd use as much of it as you need."

Farrell could only nod. Whatever the judge wanted, that's what he wanted, too.

33

So Glitsky was off early.

It wasn't yet three o'clock on a Thursday afternoon and no one expected him upstairs, so he signed out a car from the city lot and drove himself home, found a parking spot directly in front of his duplex, and let himself in.

Rita was sleeping on the couch, which was okay. She'd awaken with them all at six-thirty, and she kept the place spotless. She got up with Abe when any of the boys called out in the night, and if she needed to take a nap to catch up, Glitsky was all for it.

In the kitchen, a pot of thick black sauce—mole, he now knew—simmered on the stove, steaming the windows, filling the room with its heady smell. A couple of disjointed chickens were thawing on the counter.

He opened the kitchen window a crack and heard Isaac down in the trees. He was lucky with his backyard. Though he shared it with his downstairs neighbors, there was plenty of room. And along its border, a bicycle path traced the edge of the Presidio.

Back when there had been money for such amenities, the city had built a small playground—a set of swings, parallel bars, a slide—thirty yards down the path.

Glitsky let himself out the back door and down the steps, across the yard through the lengthening shadows, onto the bike path. He'd pushed pretty hard at the idea of the boys playing together, sticking together—the family—and this was one of those miraculous days when it was working.

They were seeing who could sail farthest out of the swing set—one of the activities Glitsky felt better hearing about than actually witnessing. And today they'd added a new wrinkle, a stick that two of them held while the third one sailed, going for height *and* distance.

And broken legs, he thought. Chipped teeth. Ruined knees.

But he watched from a small distance. Life is risk, he told himself. They're enjoying the moment. Let it happen.

And then Jacob landed sprawled in the tanbark and, rolling over, saw his father. He let out a whoop— "Dad!"—and came running over, stopping himself a split second before what would have been an embarrassing hug. But he did let his father put his arm around him.

"What are you doing home?"

"Yeah, it's still light out." Isaac, sauntering up, put in the barb. Glitsky knew he was working all the time, but didn't see a way to change it. And he was home now, wasn't he?

"I thought we'd go get a Christmas tree."

O.J. stabbed a fist into the air and screamed

"Yeah!" and was already running back toward the house and the other two tore off after him.

Even Abe broke into a trot.

At night, Rita put down the fold-a-bed and slept behind a screen in the living room in the front of the duplex. That fact wasn't in the front of Glitsky's mind when he bought the largest tree he could find, and now the never spacious living room was all but impassable.

His own overstuffed easy chair and ottoman had been relegated to the kitchen to make space for the tree, which made the kitchen tight as well. Rita had lost more than half of her precious counter space.

The scent of the new Christmas tree permeated the house and Rita had made hot spiced apple juice. They had Lou Rawls doing Christmas out of the speakers, the lights were strung up, the old bulbs, and now the boys were hanging tinsel.

Glitsky sat hunched on his ottoman in the open doorway between the kitchen and living room, drinking his mulled cider, taking it all in as though from a great distance. Rita was on the couch, directing the boys to any open spaces on the tree.

He had come home early. He'd taken the boys out for the tree, and now he was home in the midst of his family, wishing he was anywhere else, wishing he could try harder not to show it.

Flo wasn't here. Everything else was here, and not his wife. So what, exactly, was the point?

When the telephone rang, Glitsky knew it was work—it was always work—and Isaac yelled that he shouldn't answer it, let the machine get it. But he was already up, at the wall phone in the kitchen.

It was Amanda Jenkins. "I'm working on motive," she said, "and tomorrow it's fish or cut bait."

No "got a minute, Abe?" No "hello," even. But there was no fighting it. Like it or not, he was in trial time, and simple politeness suffered as a matter of course.

He took a sip of his juice—the tang of cinnamon. She was breezing right on. "I want your take on his second chair, Carrera. I know we've been trying to decide between insurance and whether his wife was a drunk, an embarrassment, but I'm just watching the tube and this picture of the two of them kissing, it's turned up the heat."

"I saw the picture, Amanda. We talked about it, remember? It wasn't exactly X-rated. I wouldn't even give it an 'R.' It's a good-night kiss."

"At his house. They're alone, in the dark," she countered.

"So what?"

"So in spite of all the tabloid speculation, it's really the first actual proof that these two have something going, and if they do, it's a lot stronger than anything else we've got."

"That picture doesn't prove anything. They're not upstairs in his bedroom, half dressed, anything like that. This is a kiss like you give your mother. Besides, even if you had major groping, how are you going to prove they had something seven eight months ago, which is when it would have had to be?"

"I don't have to prove it," she said. "We can assert it, show this picture, let the jury draw the inference."

Glitsky moved some dirty dishes to one side and seated himself on the crowded counter. He, of course, had wrestled with this issue himself, so he decided to give Jenkins the argument that had stopped him. "That assumes she was in on it, too."

"She might have helped him plan it, Abe. Now she's defending him for it. It's not that far-fetched."

"Then you'll have to explain why we didn't charge her, too."

"Because there was no proof of *conspiracy*. We just couldn't arrest her without . . ."

Glitsky sipped his juice, giving her time to hear herself, to wind down. This was the last-minute panic to bolster a case that he'd seen dozens of times.

"It sucks, doesn't it," she asked.

"Insurance," he said. "Juries tend to understand money."

"You think?"

"It's your decision."

Jenkins sighed. "Something tells me it's her, Abe."

"You don't need motive, Amanda. You might just want to let it go, prove the facts."

A long pause, then "okay" and then a click and a dial tone.

No hello, no good-bye. Trial time.

Across town in his apartment, Wes Farrell sat at his Formica kitchen table, which was littered with yellow legal pads, manila folders, three days' worth of newspapers, a manual typewriter, four coffee mugs, and a thick three-ring binder that he'd divided into sections labeled "Evidence," "Argument," "Witnesses," and so on.

Each of these sections was further divided into subsections, and each subsection contained color-coded tabs in a particular order. Farrell had been living with this binder for the past six months and by now felt he could wake up and put his finger on anything he wanted in pitch darkness.

Bart was under the table and the clock radio, which had been keeping him company with old rock 'n' roll, suddenly broke into "Jingle Bells." Immediately, he reached over and turned the dial and thought he'd found another soft rock station when he realized it was Mary-Chapin Carpenter telling her lover that everything they got, they got the hard way.

Somehow, he couldn't find the will to turn it off. He'd been consciously avoiding country music since he and Sam split, but this song, intelligently invoking passion and spark and inspiration, was ripping him up. Sitting back, he ran his hands through his thinning hair, then reached for one of the mugs of tepid coffee. He forced down a swallow.

His eyes roamed the empty apartment—the same blank walls, thrift store furniture, the same *space*.

He'd called Sam twice after the first big fight and they'd had a couple of bigger ones after. And now Thomasino had ruled that Diane Price *was* going to be allowed to testify after all, and Christina was going to take her apart, and Sam would probably be in the courtroom, counseling her.

Shaking his head to clear it—this was going nowhere—he flipped off the radio. He and Sam were finished. Pulling his typewriter through the debris, he thought he'd put this negative energy to some good use by working on some notes for his opening statement, but as he reached for his legal pad, he had to move the morning *Chronicle*, and The Picture hit him again.

Jesus, he thought, could it be?

Aside from the strategic disaster the photo represented, he was having trouble overcoming his own sense of personal betrayal. Though Mark and Christina had both denied that anything untoward had taken place between them, the fact that they'd met at Mark's house, at night, alone, without telling him about it, was more than unsettling.

It had thrown him back on his own demons.

This was the real reason for the tantrum he'd thrown at them this morning before they went to court. This wasn't just another trial for him, where he'd have to pump himself up with some secondhand, third-rate rationalization that his actions were *relatively* important.

It was far more personal—a last opportunity, dropped into his lap by a benevolent fate, finally to do something meaningful with his life. With the responsibility and the commitment to Mark's defense, something had already changed inside himself, motivating him to summon the discipline he needed to lose the extra weight he'd carried for years, giving him confidence to try a new face-softening mustache, a crisp and stylish haircut. He'd present the new, improved Wes Farrell to the world, and to that end had bought five new suits (one for each day of the work week), ten shirts, ten ties, two pairs of shoes. Perhaps these changes weren't fundamental, but they indicated that his image of himself, of who he could be, was changing. He even started vacuuming his apartment, cleaning up his dinner dishes on the same day that he ate off them. Unprecedented.

This trial was going to be his last chance. It was life itself, a test of all he was and could be.

He had to believe.

And then this morning he'd opened the newspaper, and in a twinkling the foundation seemed to give— psychically it shook him as the earthquake had. And, following that, he'd sat at this table trying and failing to ignore the other signposts on the trail that had led them all to here—the party at Dooher's, Mark's decision to bring Christina on as a summer clerk, Joe Avery's transfer to Los Angeles, which had preordained Joe and Christina's breakup, Sheila's death, and now, finally, the two of them—Mark and Christina—nearly united.

Viewed from Farrell's perspective, the progression was linear and ominous.

He tried to tell himself that it didn't necessarily mean what it *could* mean.

Wes *knew* Mark, who he was, what he was. And Mark could never have done what he was accused of. It was impossible.

Wes wasn't religious, but Dooher's innocence was an article of faith for him. If he didn't know Mark, he knew nothing. This was why, as the preparation for trial had uncovered enough unpleasant assertions about Mark to make even Farrell feel uncomfortable, he had never truly doubted.

Assertions were just that, he had told himself time and again. They weren't proven. People, often with axes to grind, would say things.

Farrell had tried to look objectively at all this alleged wrongdoing, and came away convincing himself that it was all smoke and mirrors. There was *absolutely no evidence* tying Mark Dooher to any other murders or rapes or anything else.

But now there was Christina. She was a fact, as was her connection to Mark. And worse, because of her the seed of Wes's own doubt had germinated. He closed his eyes, picturing her in his mind. A beautiful woman, no question about it. He himself was not immune to the power of beauty—what man was? But that did not mean his friend had killed to have her.

Farrell kept trying to tell himself that Mark's life-long luck had delivered Christina to him at the moment he needed her most, after his wife was gone, for whatever comfort and hope she could give him.

But suddenly, after last night, this was a hard sell.

"Christina, this is Sam. Please don't hang up."

"I won't."

"I argued with myself all day about calling you."

"I kissed him good night, Sam. That's all there was to it. This whole media frenzy is insane."

"But you know you're . . . with him."

"I represent him. I'm his lawyer."

"That's not what I mean. I know. I knew back . . . when we were still friends."

"I'm sorry, I have no comment."

"Okay, that's all right. I don't need a comment. But I just had to try to tell you—because we were friends, because you do know so much about the psychology of rape—that you and Wes are both wrong about Mark Dooher. I can prove—"

"Sam, stop! You'll get a chance to prove everything you want to at the trial."

"That won't prove what I'm talking about. I'm telling you—sit and talk to her, you'll be convinced. She's telling the truth, she's . . ."

"I'm going to hang up now, Sam. Mark didn't do that. He couldn't have done that."

"Why are you so blind? Why won't you even consider it?"

"Good-bye, Sam."

34

FARRELL WAS RUNNING ON PURE ADRENALINE. HE'D slept less than five hours but this was precisely the moment that all the nights of insomnia had been in service of.

He reminded himself that the trial was simpler than life—all he had to do here was refute the prosecution's arguments, and Mark Dooher was going to walk. He could do that in his sleep.

In California, the defense has the option of delivering its opening statement directly following the prosecution's, where it has the general effect of a rebuttal; or it can choose to wait and use its opening statement to introduce its own version of events, its case-in-chief. Farrell chose the former.

He didn't believe he was going to get surprised by any prosecution witness. He knew the direction he was going to take—deny, deny, deny. And he wanted to prime the jury, at the outset, that there was reason to question every single point Jenkins had raised.

He'd thought it out in detail. He would begin casually, standing beside Dooher at the defense table. He would not consult any notes—his defense was from his heart. He wouldn't use a prepared speech. His body language would scream that the truth was so obvious, and he believed it so passionately, that it spoke for itself. By contrast, Jenkins had stood delivering the rest of her opening statement for the better part of the morning, consulting her legal pad over and over, laboriously spelling out her case-in-chief.

Farrell sipped from his water glass and stood up.

"You've all heard Ms. Jenkins's opening statement. She's given you a version of the events of June seventh that she says she's going to prove beyond a reasonable doubt. There is no way she can do that because those actions of Mr. Dooher that she got right did not happen for the reasons she contends, and the rest of them she simply got wrong.

"I'm going to strip this story of Ms. Jenkins's sinister interpretation, and give you the facts. On that Tuesday, Mark Dooher purchased champagne and brought it home because he was a loving husband. He made a phone call from his office to his home on the afternoon of June seventh, and asked his wife if she would like him to come home early. He made a date with her, ladies and gentlemen of the jury. After nearly thirty years of marriage, Mark and Sheila Dooher were having a romantic interlude. A date.

"Before he got home, *his wife* took a dose of Benadryl because she suffered from allergies. She *helped herself* to a glass or two of champagne. Sheila Dooher was forty-seven years old and she was neither senile nor dim-witted. She could make her own decisions, and did, on matters of what she ate and drank. She had been taking the menopause drug, Nardil, for over a year.

Many times, in front of many witnesses, she drank alcohol within this time frame. Several witnesses will testify that Sheila Dooher was skeptical of her doctor's recommendations to avoid certain foods and alcohol. Tragically, it looks like Mrs. Dooher was equally careless about mixing drugs."

Farrell sipped again from his water glass, slowing himself down. Jenkins hadn't objected once, all eyes were glued to him. He was rolling.

"What happened next? The Doohers had a late lunch. Nothing more sinister than that. Sheila Dooher went up to her bedroom to take a nap. She was tired, and she took a sedative, her husband's chloral hydrate.

"Ms. Jenkins has told you that Mark Dooher gave her the chloral hydrate. Rubbish, absolute rubbish. There is not one witness, not one shred of evidence that even suggests that this is the case. Ms. Jenkins says it is so because she needs it to be so to convict Mark Dooher. She cannot prove it because it never happened."

Jenkins now did get up, objecting that Farrell was being argumentative.

Farrell supposed he was, but knew Jenkins had made the objection, as much as anything, to throw off his rhythm. It wasn't going to work. She was sustained by Thomasino and Farrell moved out from the desk now and went on, a smile tugging at the corners of his mouth so the jury could see what a good guy he was—magnanimous at this silly interruption.

It also gave him his third opportunity to repeat the sequence that had led to Sheila's death.

After which. "And what were Mr. Dooher's actions after his wife had gone upstairs? Well, he did not set the burglar alarm in his house. A prosecution witness, Mr. Dooher's next-door neighbor Frances Matsun, will tell you he then reached up and appeared to be doing something with the lightbulb over the side door. Mr. Dooher does not remember this. Perhaps there was a cobweb on it—he doesn't know.

"Next he drove to the San Francisco Golf Club. Now you'll remember that Ms. Jenkins made rather a big issue out of the fact that Mr. Dooher belongs to the Olympic Club and on this night chose not to go to his own club's driving range, but rather to a public range. It is going to be for you to decide how big an issue this was. But I will tell you that Mr. Dooher is a personable man . . ."

"Objection."

"Sustained."

"I'm sorry. Mr. Dooher has many business contacts at his club, and he didn't want to have to be . . ." He paused, smiling now at the jury, including them in the humor, "personally interactive. He wanted to spend the time working on his golf swing without interruption.

"The golf pro at the driving range shop will testify that Mr. Dooher bought two buckets of balls and sometime later returned with two empty buckets. He will also testify that Mr. Dooher and he discussed golf clubs and corrections to his swing and exchanged other pleasantries—in short, that Mr. Dooher's actions appeared completely normal."

Farrell shrugged in tacit apology to the jury for the time this was taking. He was on *their* side and all must agree that this was clearly a waste of everyone's time.

"When he got home, Mr. Dooher did the dishes and drank a beer, after which he went upstairs and discovered his wife's body. Horrified, he punched up nine one one. We will play the recording of this call for you and again, you can decide if the voice you hear is believable or not.

"But we are not finished yet. After the police came to begin their investigation, Mr. Dooher cooperated fully with Inspector Glitsky"—and here Farrell stopped and theatrically gestured across the courtroom—"who is the gentleman sitting there at the prosecution table. He gave a full and voluntary statement and answered every question until Inspector Glitsky had no more to ask."

Farrell deemed this a reasonable moment to pause. Going back to his table, he took another drink of water, glanced at Dooher and Christina, and turned back to the jury box.

"Now, as to some of the other allegations and alleged evidence the prosecution has put in front of you—the tainted blood sample, the knife with Mr. Dooher's fingerprints on it, the surgical glove found at the scene, and so on—we are at a disadvantage. We can't explain everything. That's one of the problems with being innocent—you don't know *what* happened. You don't know what someone else did."

"Your Honor," Jenkins said. "Counsel is arguing again."

Thomasino scowled, which Farrell took to be a good sign. He had been arguing, no doubt, but Thomasino had allowed himself to get caught up in it, and resented being reminded of his lapse. Still, he sustained Jenkins's objection and told Farrell to stick to the evidence.

Farrell met some eyes in the panel. "I'm going to say a few words now about motive. The prosecution has told you that Mr. Dooher killed his wife to collect an insurance policy worth one point six million dollars. This is their stated motive—I urge you to remember it."

Farrell went on to explain that the defense would disclose all financial records of Mr. Dooher personally and those of his eminently solvent firm. He was nearly debt-free, his 401K money, fully vested, amounted to over $800,000, savings accounts held another $100,000. He owned his home nearly outright and it had most recently been appraised for over a million dollars. In short, while one point six million dollars was not chump change, so long as Mr. Dooher continued with his regular lifestyle and did not plan to take up cruising the Aegean in luxury yachts with full staffs, he didn't need any more money.

Farrell spread his hands, "Ladies and gentlemen, the prosecution cannot prove that Mark Dooher had a motive to kill his wife because he had no motive. The prosecution cannot prove he poisoned his wife because he did not. They will not prove he is guilty because he is innocent. It's as simple as that.

"At the end of this trial, when you see that the prosecution has not proven these baseless accusations, I will ask for the verdict of not guilty to which my client is entitled."

For lunch, Dooher—mending fences—took them all to Fringale, a tiny bistro a couple of blocks from the courtroom. They were at a table in the back corner and Wes, desultorily picking at a dish of white beans with duck, didn't seem to be responding positively to the gesture.

By contrast, Dooher was in a celebratory mood, enjoying a double order of foie gras with a half bottle of pinot noir all for himself. Hell, he wasn't working—he was spectating.

Christina, oblivious to the attention she was receiving from the other patrons and their waiter (her water glass had been refilled four times), had forgotten Sam's call and the kiss and was enthusing over Farrell's performance. "You know, Wes, I believe you could make a living at this."

"It was a great statement," Dooher agreed. "You put all that in your nine nine five." This was a motion that Farrell had earlier filed under California Penal Code Section 995 that there wasn't sufficient evidence to convict Dooher. "I can't believe Thomasino let this turkey go on."

Farrell kept his head bowed over his food, his shoulders slumped. Anyone seeing him would have trouble identifying him as the showman who'd worked such wonders in the court less than an hour before. "It's a long way from over, Mark. You'll notice I did gloss over a few of what, from our perspective, are non-highlights."

Christina put her fork down. "What do you mean?"

"I mean the hole in the fence at the driving range, blood missing from Mark's doctor's office, Mark's fingerprints on the murder weapon . . ."

Dooher was concentrating on his little toast points, spreading his foie gras with perfect evenness. "You hit all that." He took a bite, savoring it. "You said we couldn't know, that was the problem with being innocent. It could have been your finest moment."

But Christina was staring at Wes, something else eating at her. She'd never heard him use this tone before, and it worried her. He was still upset about the kiss.

She knew that Wes had been angry yesterday, but Christina had assumed that his fury would blow itself out. But now she wondered if it went deeper. She reached over and touched his hand. "I want to tell you something," she said quietly.

He raised his bloodhound's eyes.

"You're still mad at us and you think we've lied to you, but me going over to Mark's, that was an honest mistake. I would not lie to you. Mark wouldn't lie to you."

Dooher had stopped chewing, listening intently. And now he eyed Farrell levelly. "If you've got doubts on that, Wes, I want to hear them."

Gradually, Farrell shook his head. "I'm just tired," he said. "I'm going to sleep all weekend."

"What the hell is *he* doing here?" Mark asked.

Christina and Wes were having coffee and Dooher was enjoying a snifter of calvados when Abe Glitsky entered the restaurant and made his way over to their table.

Nodding all around, friendly as you please, he leaned over Farrell's shoulder. "Ms. Carrera, I'd like to ask you a few questions before court reconvenes. I wonder if you'd stop by my office on the fourth floor after you've finished your lunch."

"How'd you know we were here?" Dooher asked.

Glitsky favored him with the scar-split smile. "Spies," he said. "They're everywhere."

Farrell was torn between the impulse to tell Glitsky to shit in his hat and curiosity over what he wanted to talk about with Christina.

He insisted he be present and Glitsky said no.

He then reminded the lieutenant that he was entitled to all discovery in the case. This didn't rate an answer.

Glitsky simply asked again if Christina would talk to him or not. She told Farrell she wanted to go, she could take care of herself. It would be best to find out what Glitsky had on his mind.

* * *

"What's this about, Sergeant?"

"Actually, it's Lieutenant now. I've been promoted."

"Oh, that's right, I remember. Congratulations."

Guarded, but curious, she sat kitty-corner from Glitsky at a scarred oak table in one of the interview rooms adjoining the homicide detail. He left the door open, and let her have the power position at the far end of the table. He took his mini-recorder from his jacket pocket and sat it on the table in front of them.

"This is Lieutenant Abe Glitsky, star number 1144," he began, "and I'm speaking with . . ."

Christina reached over and grabbed the recorder, flicking it off.

"Wait a minute, what are you doing?" Life was a constant surprise, Glitsky was thinking. Never before had anyone—hardened criminal or antisocial cretin— ever taken his tape recorder and turned it off. He was sure this should be instructive, but didn't know what it meant.

"I thought you invited me up here to have a discussion."

"That's correct."

"So what's this?"

"The tape is how we do interrogations."

"You're interrogating me?"

"You got it right the first time, Ms. Carrera. We're having a discussion. But it's pursuant to my investigation of Mark Dooher . . ."

"Well, I'm not going to answer! I represent the man, Lieutenant. He's my client. Anything between me and Mark is privileged and you ought to know that."

"Actually, not. You only became a lawyer a couple

of weeks ago, isn't that true?" He knew it was true; he didn't have to wait for her reply. "And even if a case could be made that you had an attorney–client relationship before that—not saying it could—that relationship certainly didn't exist before Mr. Dooher got charged with his wife's murder, and that's the time I want to talk about."

It rocked her. She sat back in her chair and took a breath, studying him. "What for?"

"Can I have the tape recorder back?"

"I'm not going to talk to you. Are you accusing me of something?"

"No, ma'am. If we come close to that and you'd like to have your own lawyer present, we can do this some other time, but one way or another, we're going to do it."

Her eyes narrowed. "No we're not. Not now, not ever if I don't choose to. Nobody ever has to talk to the police, Lieutenant—not me, not my client, not anybody. And you know it."

Glitsky backpedaled. He didn't want to lose her. "I thought this would be the most pleasant way. You know what the newspapers are saying. I'm the investigator in this case. When questions come up, it's my job to get an answer for them, even if it happens to be in the middle of the trial."

"You're trying to get me to become a witness against my client." She was getting angry herself now. "This is the most unprofessional thing I've ever heard of, Lieutenant, and I really resent it. I met Mark Dooher on Mardi Gras of last year, say ten months ago. There was absolutely nothing between us until after his wife was dead. Does that answer your question?"

"Yes it does," he said.

She looked at him for a long moment. "Lieutenant

Glitsky, do you remember when I came up here to talk about Tania Willows and Levon Copes, and you sat in that chair out there"—she pointed through the open doorway—"and laughed until tears came to your eyes? Do you remember that?"

"Sure."

"And there was a moment right after that, after your lieutenant came out and asked if you were okay, when you and I looked at each other and something went 'click'—I don't mean sexually—where we just *got* something together. You remember?"

Glitsky nodded.

"So were we intimate then?"

"That's not the kind of intimacy we're talking about."

"Well, then, Mark and I were not intimate. *Are* not intimate. I care about him a great deal. And while *we're* speaking so frankly, I don't know why you're persecuting him so horribly."

"The evidence says he killed his wife, Ms. Carrera."

"I don't think it does. That's what you want to see."

Glitsky held himself in check, his voice flat. "Because of my abiding hatred of the Church of Rome and my single-handed campaign to bring it to its knees?" He gestured to the empty walls of the room they were in, the external office with all the glamour of a train wreck. "Or perhaps it's my ambition to rise to the top of this dung heap? You pick. One of the above."

He had gotten to her. Lowering his voice, Glitsky leaned in toward her. "I'm trying to figure out *why.*"

She put her elbows on the table. Their heads were inches apart. "Lieutenant, there's no *why.* He didn't do it. That's why you can't find a reason for it."

"How about *you?*"

"I've told you. I don't think he did it."

Glitsky was shaking his head. "No. How about if you're the reason, if he killed Sheila so he'd be free to have you?"

Her eyes went dull. She seemed to stare through him. Finally. "You know, I'm sorry, Lieutenant. You must live in the bleakest world there is. You're telling me you've got Mark killing his wife, risking a murder trial and life in prison, all on the remote chance that he'll be *free* to have me, who has made no commitment to him? You flatter me, but please."

"It's not impossible."

"It is impossible," she said. "It's insane. The only way that's even remotely feasible is if I . . ." She stopped. "If we did it together."

Glitsky had his arms crossed. He didn't respond except to reach over and turn the tape back on.

After a few seconds, Christina stood up. Leaning over, she turned it off. "If you want to pursue this further, Lieutenant, next time I'll bring an attorney."

He was watching her, her face a shifting kaleidoscope of emotions and reactions. "I just want to say one last thing."

He nodded. "All right."

"I am so sorry about your wife. I never had a chance to tell you that."

Then she was gone.

Glitsky remained in his chair, legs stretched out, arms crossed. He had a couple of minutes before the lunch recess was over and he had to be back in court. Reaching under the table for the second tape recorder that was hidden there, he pulled it out, stopped the tape, and rewound to the last seconds.

"I am so sorry about your wife. I never had a chance to tell you that."

He played it back again. A third time. It had struck him as genuine when she said it. Now it sounded sincere on the tape.

Paul Thieu poked his head in through the door. "How'd it go?" he asked. "She looked rattled. She had to stop at the door and take a few deep breaths, then . . . what's the matter?"

"Nothing. She didn't have anything to do with it. Dooher did it alone."

"How do you know?" Thieu asked.

Glitsky sat still another minute. "I just know," he said.

35

FARRELL'S PLANS MIGHT HAVE INCLUDED SLEEPING ALL weekend, but the weekend was a long afternoon away.

Jenkins called John Strout, the coroner, as her first witness. The lanky southern gentleman was at home on the witness stand, and gave a dispassionate and complete account of the medical issues surrounding Sheila's death.

Most, if not all, of these could have been stipulated by both parties—that is, they could have had the judge read to the jury the undisputed facts about the details of Sheila's death—but prosecutors always wanted to have the coroner make a murder seem *real* to the jury, and in this case, Farrell had a small but, he thought, important point to make himself.

"Dr. Strout." Farrell's fatigue had dissipated. He was standing in the center of the courtroom, listing slightly toward the jury. "In your testimony, you often referred to the drug overdose that was the cause of

Sheila Dooher's death. Did you list this on the coroner's report, People's One?"

"I sure did."

"Could we look at that page of People's One a minute, your honor? Let the jury pass it around?"

Thomasino hated this kind of theatrics. Of course the jury *could* review People's One, although there were all kinds of information in the coroner's report that had little or nothing to do with anything the jury needed to know. But Farrell wanted to keep them involved. As they were passing it back and forth, he said, "Paying particular attention to the cause of death, which, you will notice, does list drug overdose along with a significant amount of medical jargon," and moved over directly in front of Strout.

"Now, Doctor, we had a talk—you and I—a couple of days ago, and you gave me several other coroner's reports from different cases that you've handled over the past months, isn't that correct?"

"Yes."

Jenkins was on her feet. "Irrelevant. Your Honor, what's the possible relevancy of the causes of death in unrelated cases?"

Thomasino leaned toward agreement. "Mr. Farrell, I'll give you about one minute to make your point."

Farrell had the other coroner's reports entered as Defense Exhibits A through D, and then came back to the witness. "Let's start with manner of death here in Defense A, Dr. Strout. What does it say here, for the jury's benefit, please, under 'cause of death'?"

"It says 'drug overdose.' "

Farrell did his imitation of Thomasino raising his eyebrows. "In fact, Doctor, in each of Defense A through D, the cause of death is listed as 'drug overdose,' isn't that true?"

"It is."

Satisfied, Farrell nodded and moved a step closer to the witness. "All right." He'd primed the pump, and now Farrell was ready to strike oil. "Dr. Strout, do a lot of people die of drug overdose every year?"

"Yes, hundreds."

Thomasino leaned forward over the bench. "Your minute's about up, Counselor."

"My next question brings in Sheila Dooher, Your Honor."

The judge nodded impatiently. "All right, go ahead."

"And what about the overdoses that these hundreds of people die of every year? Except for the specific drugs involved, are these drug overdoses particularly different from that suffered by Sheila Dooher?"

Farrell darted a quick glance at Thomasino. At least he'd brought his questioning back to people involved in this case.

But Strout was frowning. "I don't understand the question. *Every* case is different, though there are similarities if the same drugs cause the death." He waited for Farrell to clarify what he wanted.

"In the hundreds of drug overdose deaths every year, is there a common feature that might point to a murder rather than, say, an accident or a suicide?"

Strout considered a minute. "Generally, I'd say no."

"And in Mrs. Dooher's case, specifically, was there any *medical* indication that she'd been murdered?"

"No."

"So, Doctor, it's your testimony—it sounds to me —and correct me if I'm wrong—as you sit here now, based on your autopsy, you don't know whether Sheila Dooher was murdered or not, do you?"

"Well, the introduction of so many different drugs within such a limited time just shut down the respiratory apparatus. It's likely she had a malignant hypertensive response, potential cardiac arrhythmias, and then subsequently, severe hypotension."

"Excuse me, Doctor, but in your opinion, was this a crime or an article in the *New England Journal of Medicine?*"

"Objection!" Jenkins, he knew, was out of her seat. He didn't have to turn around.

Thomasino grunted. "Sustained."

Farrell shot a glance at the jury. He knew it never hurt to put in a dig when things got pedantic. Farrell was just a regular guy, a layperson, like these long-suffering jurors. There were traces of smiles on a few faces. He turned back to Strout. "I'll repeat the question, Doctor. You don't know whether Sheila Dooher was murdered or not, do you?"

"It's somewhat unusual to see so many different drugs . . ."

"Excuse me again, Doctor, but it's a yes-or-no question: You don't know whether Sheila Dooher was murdered or not, do you?"

Strout had to admit it. "I don't know."

"You don't know whether Sheila Dooher was murdered? Is that your testimony?"

"Yes."

"Thank you."

It didn't take Amanda Jenkins long to realize that Wes Farrell wasn't the modest-intellect, low-rung attorney he pretended to be. He'd hurt her on his opening statement and then again with Strout. She thought it was time she put some of her own points on the board, and she stood and told the court that the people would call Sergeant George Crandall.

Crandall had been a marine and—though today he wore a business suit—still looked and acted like a marine. He stood up in the gallery and walked, a ramrod, up to the witness stand, where he preempted the clerk, raising his hand and swearing to tell the truth, the whole truth, and nothing but the truth so help him God without any prompting. Obviously, Crandall had been here before.

Controlling his own show, he sat down and nodded at Jenkins.

Crandall sat up straight, but completely at home in the witness box. Knowing it was going to be a while, he unbuttoned his suit jacket, though he did not lean back in the chair, did not cross his legs.

Jenkins spent a moment or two establishing that Crandall was an expert homicide investigator with fifteen years of experience and was now, in fact, head of the police department's Crime Scene Investigation unit. He had arrived at the murder scene within an hour of the 911 call.

"Were you the first policeman on the scene?"

"No. Sergeants Glitsky and Thieu of homicide were already there as well as the lieutenant and sergeant from Taraval station and some patrolmen."

"And had these people found anything relating to the murder by the time you arrived?"

Farrell knew Amanda would be using the word "murder" a lot that day—trying to condition the jury to accept what she couldn't prove. He couldn't do anything about it, and let it go.

"Would you tell us, Sergeant, what you found at the scene of the murder?"

"One of the first things we found is what we did *not* find."

"And what was that, Sergeant?"

"We found there was no sign of a forced entry at the side door. Or anywhere else for that matter."

"No sign of forced entry?"

"No. We believe that egress was through the side door, by the driveway, because we found a surgical glove and a knife near that door."

Jenkins produced these and they were entered as People's Exhibits 2 and 3. "The knife matches other knives found in the defendant's kitchen, is that right?"

Before Crandall could even think about answering, Glitsky noticed some quick back-and-forth at the defense table. For the first time, Christina stood up. "Your Honor, we've stipulated that the knife belonged to the Doohers."

Glitsky moved uncomfortably in his seat. Jenkins hadn't gotten her sea legs yet and he felt for her. Her first murder case had gone high profile and sideways, and she wasn't doing well. She appeared to be groping for another direction, a specific question, but she couldn't seem to frame it except in a general way.

"Was there anything else about this side door?"

Fortunately, Crandall was on her side, inclined to help. He nodded. "The sergeant from Taraval reported that the light over the door had been out when they arrived, but he turned it and it went back on." This was technically hearsay, but nobody objected. "The alarm system also was not turned on. Upstairs, in the master bedroom, Mrs. Dooher was in the bed."

"And how was she lying?"

"On her side."

"On her side? Not on her back?"

"No, on her left side."

Jenkins moved back to Glitsky's table and he gave her a surreptitious thumbs up as she gathered some material. "Sergeant Crandall, would you look at these crime scene photographs and tell us if you recognize them?"

Jenkins handed them over and Crandall agreed that they were accurate. The jury got to look at them. Crandall continued—the tossed blanket and sheets, the missing jewelry, the blood. He described the lividity that had been on Mrs. Dooher's shoulder.

"And, Sergeant, based on your training and experience, does this lividity help you reconstruct the crime scene?"

"Yes it does." Glitsky had known Crandall for a long time, and knew he could be personable and even funny in a cop sort of way. But here on the stand, the man was a machine. "As the coroner has said, when a person dies, the blood settles into the down side of the skin due to gravity."

"But didn't you just say that this lividity was on Mrs. Dooher's upper shoulder?"

"Yes I did."

"And what does that mean?"

"It means that she was moved after she was dead. Rolled half over."

"And why was that?"

Farrell stood this time, quickly, on top of it. "Objection, Your Honor. Speculation."

The objection was sustained, but Jenkins was finally beginning to roll. "Sergeant, when you first entered the room, did you have an impression of what had occurred there?"

Crandall nodded. "Yes."

"And what was that?"

"It looked like a burglary that had been interrupted when the victim woke up, that there'd been a struggle, and in that struggle the burglar had killed Mrs. Dooher."

"But don't we know that Mrs. Dooher was already dead when she was stabbed?"

"That's right. Because of the lividity, that was my assumption at the time—she was dead when she was stabbed."

"And had the nightclothes had been ripped or partially ripped from the victim?"

"Yes."

"And had the bedding been thrown about?"

"That's right."

"And was there blood splattered on the bed and on the floor under the bed and so on?"

"Yes."

"Even though Mrs. Dooher could not have struggled at all because she was already dead?"

Crandall said yes again, and Glitsky thought he didn't have to provide any speculation after this testimony. What had happened ought to be clear enough.

Jenkins came back to the table for her pad. Consulting it, she faced Crandall once more. "Now Sergeant Crandall, let's change directions for a moment. What did you do with the blood samples you found at the scene of the murder?"

"I sent them for analysis to the crime lab."

Farrell knew he had a hostile witness in Crandall, but it wasn't his style to pussyfoot. He got up from the defense table, crossed the floor of the courtroom, and positioned himself about two feet in front of the witness. He smiled warmly.

"Sergeant Crandall, I'd like to begin by talking

about the side door, where you've testified that there was no sign of forced entry. No sign at all?"

Crandall nodded. "That's right."

"In your thorough investigation of the premises, did you discover anyplace else where somebody might have broken into the house?"

"No. Whoever came in appeared to just open the door."

"So there was no sign that anyone broke in." Farrell brought in the jury with a look. "None. And no one had tried to make it *look* like a break-in either, had they?"

Crandall paused a second before answering. "I don't know whether anyone had tried."

Farrell appreciated this answer and he told Crandall as much. "That is what I asked, isn't it, Sergeant?"

A nod.

"But whether or not anyone had tried, it didn't *look* like anyone had tried to make it look like a burglary, did it?"

"No."

"All right, thank you. Let's leave that for a moment." Farrell took a few steps over to the exhibit table and lifted something from it. "I call your attention to People's Exhibit Number Two, the kitchen knife which we all agree belonged to the defendant and his wife. Did you have this knife tested for fingerprints?"

"Yes."

"And what did you find?"

"We found the defendant's fingerprints on the knife, as well as those of his wife."

"Anybody else's?"

"No. Just those two."

"All right. Now did you discover anything about the defendant's fingerprints that would indicate that he held this knife during or after it was plunged into his wife's chest? For example, were there fingerprints over blood on the knife, or fingerprints in blood?"

"No."

"Nothing at all to indicate that *the defendant* had ever used this knife as anything other than an ordinary kitchen implement?"

"No."

"Nothing at all?"

Jenkins spoke from behind Farrell. "Asked and answered?"

Thomasino agreed, sustaining her.

Farrell nodded genially, glanced over at the jury and included them in his good humor. "All right, Sergeant, I think we're getting somewhere here on all this evidence that was found at the murder scene. I'd like to ask you now about the surgical glove, People's Three, that was found outside the house, by the side door that showed no sign of forced entry. Did you submit this glove to rigorous lab analysis?"

"Yes, of course."

"Of course. And what did you find on it? Any fingerprints?"

"No. No fingerprints. The rubber does not hold fingerprints. We did find some spots of Mrs. Dooher's blood."

"Only Mrs. Dooher's blood?"

"Yes. Only Mrs. Dooher's."

"A lot of blood."

Crandall shook his head. "I wouldn't say a lot. A few drops, splattered and smudged."

"But again, *nothing* at all that ties this piece of evidence to the defendant. Nothing at all, is that right?"

"Yes. That's right."

"Good!" Farrell brought his hands together histrionically, delighted with the results of his questions so far. "Now, Sergeant, don't the police routinely wear surgical gloves, just like this one, when they are investigating crime scenes?"

Jenkins stood up, objecting, but Thomasino let the question stand, and Crandall had to answer it. "Yes, sometimes."

"Just like this one?"

"Sometimes, yes."

"Sometimes, hmm. So you, personally, have access to gloves just like this one?"

"Objection! Your Honor, Sergeant Crandall isn't on trial here."

But Farrell spoke right up. "Your Honor, I'm trying to establish that the glove could just as easily have come from the police presence at the scene. Absolutely *nothing* has been offered to connect this glove with the defendant."

Thomasino nodded and sighed. "It seems to me you've done that already, Mr. Farrell. Let's move on to the next point."

Farrell bowed, acquiescent. "Sergeant, you've told us that your initial impression upstairs—before you knew about the lividity in Mrs. Dooher's shoulder—was that a burglary had occurred and she'd woken up and the burglar had stabbed her after a struggle. Do I have that right?"

"Yes." Crandall shifted in his seat. Farrell, keeping him to short answers on simple factual questions, had succeeded in making him appear restless, edgy. And he wasn't finished yet.

"In other words, the room *looked*, to your practiced eye, as though a burglary had been in progress, isn't that correct?"

"That's the way it looked to me. Until I looked more carefully at the body."

"It was made to look like a burglary?"

"Your Honor." Jenkins stood at her table. "How many times do we have to hear the same question?"

Thomasino nodded. "Let's move it along, Mr. Farrell. You've established that the scene looked to Sergeant Crandall like a burglary had been interrupted."

"I'm sorry, Your Honor. I just wanted it to be clear." Farrell turned to the jury and bowed slightly, an apology. Turning back, facing the judge and the witness box, his voice was mild. "So, Sergeant, based on your training and experience, you reached the conclusion that Mr. Dooher had been the person in the room who had faked this burglary?"

Crandall did not respond quickly. "Yes, I'd say that's right."

"He wanted it to look like a burglary, and so he left the side door open so there'd be no sign of a burglar's forced entrance? Is that your contention?"

"I don't know why he left the door open. Or even if he did. He might have let himself in with a key."

"Indeed, he might have, Sergeant. So, what evidence did you uncover that shows that Mr. Dooher, as opposed to someone else, did any of this?"

"Objection. Argumentative."

This had been Farrell's intention, so it didn't surprise him when Thomasino sustained her. Moving a step or two closer to the witness box, he had his hands in his jacket pockets. "Just to recount for the jury, Sergeant, so far we've established that none of the evidence found at the scene in any way places Mr. Dooher there at the time of the stabbing of his wife, isn't that the case?"

"Not directly, but . . ."

Farrell held up a finger, stopping him. "Not only not directly, Sergeant. You've testified that there was *nothing at all*. These were your own words: nothing at all. Then you concluded that Mr. Dooher attempted to make it look as though a burglary had taken place when in fact he returned to his home to kill his wife, and yet he apparently took no great pains to create a false impression of illegal entry, which surely would have aided his deception. Then he left no evidence behind, *none at all*, that would implicate another person?"

"No, that's not true. There was the blood."

Farrell gave every impression of relief that Crandall had reminded him of that thorny problem. "Ah yes, the blood, the blood. The tainted blood. But, of course, that's not your area, is it?"

"No, it's not."

Farrell had wounded Crandall and had him in his sights again. He was going to bring him down.

"Sergeant, in your thorough investigation of the crime scene, you must have found a great deal of evidence that Mark Dooher, in fact, lived in this house, isn't that right?"

"Yes. Of course."

"Did you find his fingerprints, fibers from his clothing, hairs and so forth?"

"Yes we did."

"And would you have expected to find those things?"

"Of course."

Farrell gave him another smile. "A simple 'yes' is fine, Sergeant, thank you. Now, did you find anything you would not have expected to find relating to Mark Dooher?"

"Like what?"

"I don't know, sir. I'm asking you, but I'll rephrase

it for you. Did you find anything specific—either at the crime scene itself, or in Mr. Dooher's car, or his office, or in your subsequent analysis of lab results and blood tests and so forth that, based on your training and experience, led you to suspect that Mark Dooher had killed his wife?"

Crandall didn't reply. Farrell pressed his advantage.

"And isn't it true that you found no physical evidence, either in the bedroom itself or on the person of Mrs. Dooher that linked Mark Dooher with this crime?"

Crandall hated it. His face had flushed with suppressed anger. "I suppose if you—"

"Sergeant! Isn't it true that you found no evidence linking Mark Dooher with this crime. Isn't that true?"

He spit it out. "Yes."

Another smile. "Thank you." He beamed up at Thomasino. "That's all for this witness, Your Honor."

36

HAD GLITSKY NOT ENCOUNTERED SIMILAR SITUA-
tions dozens of times before, he wouldn't
have believed it. It still amazed him. Amanda's next
witness, who'd been sitting out here in the hallway
forty-five minutes ago, had disappeared.

So Glitsky was out in the echoing, linoleum corri-
dor, chatting with a severely displeased George Crandall. Crandall had vented his pique about Farrell's
cross-examination for a couple of minutes, and now was
telling Glitsky about a book he was going to write, based
on his true-life experiences as a big-city cop.

"Really, though, I don't have much more than a
title at this stage. I got friends who say that's the important part, anyway. You get a good title, you sell a lot of
books."

"What's the title?" Glitsky asked him.

"Wait. First, here's the idea. You know all these
celebrities who grow up and remember that somebody
abused them when they were seven and that's why

they've been married eight times and they've got sub-stance abuse problems and if all of us normal people just tried to understand them they'd be happier?"

"Sure. I worry about them all the time."

"Exactly. So I'll call it, 'Who Gives a Shit?' What do you think?"

Glitsky liked it a lot, but didn't think it would sell very many books. He was starting to tell that to Crandall, but had to cut the discussion short. Amanda Jenkins was ascending the stairs holding the arm of a tall, disheveled young man with horn-rimmed glasses—the crime lab specialist, the "blood guy," Ray Drumm.

Mr. Drumm, exquisite boredom oozing from every pore, endured a two-minute lecture from Judge Thomasino on the relative merits of wandering off, leaving the Hall of Justice to smoke a cigarette outside when you were due to testify in a murder trial. Contempt of court was mentioned, but didn't seem to make much of an impact. Finally, Drumm was sworn in and took his seat in the witness chair.

Like most of the professional lawpersons in the building, Glitsky had no use for Drumm. A career bureaucrat who wasn't yet thirty-five years old, Drumm was taciturn when he wasn't being simply obstinate. Perhaps he was truly brain-dead, but Glitsky didn't think it was that. He had the attitude—I got my job, I can't get fired, bite me.

But Jenkins couldn't let her feelings show, though Abe knew she shared his own. Getting information from Drumm was pulling teeth under the best of circumstances. God forbid you did something to put his back up—and Jenkins had already interrupted his precious cigarette.

He sat slumped on his elbow, and she greeted him cordially, then began leading him through the blood issues, bringing him around to the samples found in the room. "And what did you find in analyzing these samples?"

A roll of the eyes. Drumm had much more important things to do at this moment. Clearly. He sighed. "There were two different blood types, Mrs. Dooher's and another one."

"Was the second one Mr. Dooher's?"

"No."

"Do you know whose blood it was?"

"We know it was A-positive. We ran DNA tests and—"

Farrell was up, shot out of a cannon. "Your Honor! This is the first the defense has heard about DNA testing. The prosecution has said they couldn't . . ."

"Just a minute just a minute." This was Jenkins, voice raised.

Thomasino gaveled the room quiet. Jenkins turned to the witness. "Mr. Drumm, you did *not*, in fact, run DNA on this blood, did you? Perhaps you were thinking of Mrs. Dooher's blood."

He shrugged. "Maybe that was it. I thought you were talking about her."

Jenkins looked around at Farrell—what could she do about this idiot?—and then turned back to Drumm. "No, I was asking about the other blood sample from the murder scene, the blood type of that second sample. What was that?"

"I just said. A-positive."

Jenkins shook her head. "No, Mr. Drumm, you just said Mrs. Dooher's blood type was A-positive. Were they both A-positive?"

Drumm couldn't have cared less. "Did I say that?"

They wasted another minute or two while the reporter read back what he'd said, and then Drumm asked to see his lab results again and Jenkins got them from her table and brought them to him. He turned a page, turned a page, turned back a page.

"Mr. Drumm, have you found the blood type . . . ?"

Glitsky wanted to take out his gun and shoot off the guy's kneecap. Wake him up. Or maybe shoot him in the head, put him to sleep.

"I'm looking," Drumm said. "Yeah, here it is. A-positive for the second blood."

"And while we're here, what was Mrs. Dooher's blood type?"

As though he hadn't just a second before reviewed the report, Drumm scanned it again. "She was O-positive."

"Did you run DNA testing on the second sample?"

"No."

"And why not?"

"I don't know. Nobody asked me to." Jenkins was hoping against hope that Drumm would supply the useful information that they hadn't run DNA because they had nothing to compare it to—the blood had belonged to a man who was dead and cremated. But then, certainly without meaning to, Drumm gave her something. "The DNA didn't matter anyway."

This brought an audible reaction from the gallery —nothing approaching an outburst, more a sustained hum. Thomasino tapped his gavel and it disappeared.

"Why didn't it matter whose blood was mixed with Mrs. Dooher's at the murder scene?"

"Because the blood did not come directly from a body. It came from a vial." Jenkins questioned him to bring out the EDTA and the picture gradually began to emerge.

"In other words, Mr. Drumm, the second blood discovered at the murder scene was brought there?"

"Looks like it."

Farrell's direction was becoming clear. He wasn't going to take up much of Mr. Drumm's incredibly valuable time. His cross-examination consisted of two questions.

"Mr. Drumm, did you find any of Mr. Dooher's blood in either of the two samples you analyzed?"

"Mr. Drumm, did you find any of Mr. Dooher's blood on either the knife or surgical glove that were found at the scene?"

The answer to both was no.

Dr. Peter Harris didn't like testifying for the prosecution against one of his patients. From the witness box, he raised a hand, greeting Dooher. The jury certainly noticed.

But Jenkins needed him to put the tainted blood in Dooher's hands. "Dr. Harris, are you the defendant's personal physician?"

"I am."

"And on what date did the defendant have his last appointment with you?"

Harris by now knew the date by heart, but he pulled out a pocket notebook and appeared to be reading from it. "It was a routine physical, Friday, May thirty-first, at two-thirty."

"Friday, May thirty-first, at two-thirty. Thank you.

Now, Doctor, do you draw blood from patients in your office?"

"Yes, certainly."

"Often?"

A shrug. "Ten times a day, sometimes more. It's a routine procedure."

Jenkins nodded. "Yes. And when you draw blood, what do you do with it?"

"Well, that depends on the reason we drew the blood in the first place."

Glitsky saw Jenkins straighten her back, take a deep breath. He was glad she was slowing herself down. Her questions weren't precise enough. She wasn't getting what she wanted. She tried again. "What I meant, Doctor, is when you draw this blood, you put it in vials, don't you?"

"Yes."

"And what happens to these vials?"

"We send them to the lab."

"Good. Before you send them to the lab, do you lock them up?"

"No."

"Are they within anyone's reasonable reach?"

Harris was uncomfortable with this, but was trying his best to be cooperative. Again, he looked over at Dooher, gave him a nervous, apologetic smile. "Sometimes."

"On a counter, or a tray, or by a nurse's station, something like that. Is that what you mean?"

"Yes."

"Before you can take these vials to the lab, they are often left sitting out in your office, accessible to anyone who wanted to take one, is that right?"

A wry expression. "Not so much anymore, but yes."

"Do you lose a lot of these vials, Doctor?"

"No."

"Have you ever lost a vial?"

"Yes. A couple of times."

"Did you lose a vial on Friday, May thirty-first?"

"Yes we did."

"And whose blood was that, the blood missing from your office on May thirty-first?"

"The patient was Leo Banderas."

"And what blood type does Mr. Banderas have?"

"A-positive."

Glitsky shifted his gaze over to the defense table. This testimony was going to be Dooher's darkest hour. The defense team seemed to know it, too, and the three of them sat, rapt, waiting for what was going to come next.

"Do you happen to know, Doctor, what time Mr. Banderas's appointment was for on that Friday, May thirty-first?"

Slowly, though he knew the answer, Harris reached for his little book and checked it one last time. "One forty-five."

"Or forty-five minutes before the defendant's appointment?"

For the third time, Harris made eye contact with Mark Dooher. Then he nodded to Jenkins. "That's right."

Jenkins glanced up at the wall clock. It was late enough that Thomasino would adjourn for the weekend the minute she let Harris go, and the jury would have a couple of days to live with this most unlikely of coincidences. "Thank you, Doctor. That's all." She turned sweetly to Farrell. "Your witness."

But Farrell had barely moved to get up when Thomasino interrupted. "Ladies and gentlemen, it's a quarter to five and I think we've all had a long week. We'll adjourn now until—"

"Your Honor!" There was a shrillness now to Farrell's voice, an edge of panic. "Your Honor, if the court please, I just have a few quick questions for this witness and then we can start out fresh on Monday morning. And the doctor won't have to come back downtown to court," he added helpfully.

The judge looked again at the clock, shook his head no, and whacked his gavel. He told Farrell and the rest of the room that court was adjourned until Monday morning at nine-thirty.

37

GLITSKY, THIEU AND JENKINS WERE AT A SUBTERRA-
nean table in Lou the Greek's, savoring their
moment of glory. Glitsky and Thieu were nursing iced
teas, but Jenkins had a double martini half gone and
another full one in front of her. It was Friday, by God,
and she'd earned it.

"I love this blood thing," Jenkins said. "Even
without the DNA on Banderas, it's pretty strong."

Glitsky finished chewing some ice. "It could always be stronger," he said, "but this is good."

Thieu hadn't been in court, and as usual wanted to
know everything. Glitsky thought if he kept up the way
he'd been going, soon he would. He already knew everything about everything else.

When Thieu had been filled in, he said, "It's a
shame old Leo died and got cremated before we knew
what was up. A sample of his blood to compare to what
we found at Dooher's would sink our boy, wouldn't it?"

Jenkins wasn't going to cry over that spilled milk.

"The story the jury just heard—the missing vial—that's all we needed. Juries don't believe DNA, anyway. They don't understand it."

"Paul does," Glitsky said. "I think he invented it, in fact."

"What's to understand?" Thieu, in fact, had no problem with it. "It's a fingerprint. It's there, it's you. It's not, not. Am I wrong here?"

"Nope," Glitsky answered. "That's the theory, and a fine one it is, too." He started to slide out of the booth, then stopped. "Oh, Amanda? In the rush I forgot. The second chair, Christina? I talked to her at lunch. She didn't know about it. She's not the motive."

Thieu leaned forward. "I was thinking about that this afternoon, Abe, and she still could be the motive, even if she didn't know about it."

Glitsky was shaking his head. "Not if the two of them didn't have anything sexual going into it. How's Dooher going to know he can get her, sure enough to kill his wife for it, risk a trial, all of this? It's too much."

Thieu shrugged. "The guy loves games. Look at Trang, look at Nguyen, the Price woman. This is who this guy *is*. I could see him doing it just for the challenge, not even knowing how it's going to come out."

With anyone else, Glitsky would have been tempted to laugh off this idea as too far-fetched, but Thieu hadn't been wrong very often so far.

"I hope you're wrong," he said.

"Why?"

" 'Cause if you're right, it's only a matter of time before she's next."

In the defense room, when the door closed behind them, Christina hung the coat of her suit over a folding chair and walked to her window as she always did. The winter night was closing in, and over the Hall across the street, Christmas lights were coming on in some of the downtown towers.

Now Mark spoke quietly. "You're thinking I might have done it after all, aren't you?"

Still facing the night, she was silent. He slid off the desk and she felt him begin to come up behind her before she saw his reflection in the window. "Please," she said, "don't."

He stopped. "I have no explanation for the blood, Christina. I don't know anything about it." A pause. "We joked about it at lunch, about it being Wes's finest hour, but in fact what he said was the truth—the problem with being innocent is you don't know what happened."

"Yes. I've heard that a couple of times now. It's got a nice rhythm to it, as though it's a universal law, as though it's *got* to be true."

"It *is* true."

Crossing her hands over her chest, she barely trusted herself to breathe. Mark stood behind her. "Christina, we've known about this blood all along. *You've* known about it."

Finally, she turned around. "All right, I've known about it, Mark. It's been there all along, no doubt. I guess I just figured there had to be *some* explanation, and eventually it would come out. Well, eventually just happened and nothing came out."

He just looked at her.

"What I'd like to know is how a vial of blood from *your* doctor's office came to find its way into *your* wife's bed."

"*I don't know.*"

"You don't know?" With an edge of despair.

"Don't you think I wish I knew? Wouldn't it be great if I could make something up, something you'd believe, that we could tell the jury?"

She didn't trust herself to answer, to say anything. The silence roared around her.

"I'm going to say a few things, Christina." His voice, when it finally came, was strangely beaten down. She didn't remember ever hearing that tone before. "I know you'll probably have thought of most of them, but I'm going to go over them again, then we'll see where we are."

He was sitting now, behind her. She hadn't noticed when he'd moved. She held herself, cold, wrapped in her own arms.

"The first question," he began. "How the vial from my doctor's office got in Sheila's bed. Well, listen, how do we know that happened? How do we even know blood is missing? How do we know that, if it is, it ended up at the scene?"

She whirled. "Don't patronize me, Mark."

He shook his head. "You think that's it? You think I'm condescending to you? That's the last thing I'd do, Christina."

She waited, arms crossed.

"I'll tell you what we don't know, and the first thing is that we don't know any blood is missing. How do we know some lab technician at Dr. Harris's didn't just drop a test tube and not want to admit it? Maybe he's done it before and if it happens again, he's fired. Maybe Mr. Banderas's blood is still sitting at the lab with the wrong label on it."

He held up a hand, his voice low. "I'm not saying it is, Christina. I don't have a clue what *is* anymore, but let's go on down with what else could have happened, okay? Look at what they say they have—a vial of

A-positive blood. They don't know it's Banderas. They didn't run DNA, for Christ sake, did they?

"Why isn't it just as likely that the police lab here made a mistake? Did you see that guy Drumm? This is the guy whose testimony's gonna put me away? I don't think so.

"Maybe there was some of this EDTA left on the last slide they looked at. Maybe the guy who killed Sheila had A-positive blood and bled all over the place and the lab screwed it up. Are you saying people don't make mistakes on blood tests? And if they did that to begin with, you think they'll admit it now?"

She was leaning now, half sitting against the windowsill.

"So what's easier to believe? That the guy who killed my wife got ahold of a vial of A-positive blood and poured it all over the room? Or that the killer just bled?

"And why—I don't really get this part at all—why in the world would I—assuming I did all this—why would I dream up this blood idea at all? What does it accomplish? You've known me now for almost a year. Am I a moron? If I'm trying to make it look like somebody else did it, why do I use my own knife, why do I leave my fingerprints all over it?"

At last he ventured a step toward her. "All right," he said levelly. "I'll admit at this point it's a matter of faith. You can't know. But why do you assume that everybody else has done their job, that nobody made a mistake, that everybody is telling the truth except me?"

She raised her eyes. "I don't assume that, Mark. I'm trying. I'm listening."

His shoulders slumped. His face, for the very first time, looked old to her. Diminished. This was not arrogance, she was sure, but nakedness. She was looking into the core of him.

"I didn't do this," he whispered. He was not even pleading, which would have made him suspect. "I swear to you. I don't know what happened."

When the doorbell rang, Wes assumed it was the pizza delivery and buzzed the downstairs entrance. Opening his door, he stepped out into the hallway to wait. Bart came up around him, sniffed, and walked to the head of the steps, where his tail began to wag and he started making little whimpering noises.

"Bart!" Farrell moving forward, raising his voice. Delivery people got nervous around big dogs. "It's okay," he called out, "he's friendly. He won't bite."

The dog started down the steps, which he'd been trained against. "Bart!"

"It's okay. He's missed me." Sam stopped where she stood, three steps from the top, one hand absently petting Bart. The other hand clutched a leather satchel that hung over her shoulder. "Hi," she said.

"Hi." His gut went hollow.

She was wearing a green jacket with the hood still up, hair tucked into it. Jeans and hiking boots. Her face was half hidden, unreadable, looking up at him, and then she was fumbling with the satchel.

"I wanted to bring you something."

"We shouldn't be talking, Sam."

"I'm not here to talk." She pulled a red accordion file out of the satchel. "You need to see something."

He knew what he needed to see. He needed to see her. To have things be back the way they'd started. But that couldn't happen. They'd come to here, and he was in the middle of a trial and she was with the enemy. He couldn't forget that, or he would lose.

"I'm pretty busy right now. I don't have time to read anything else. I've got about all I can handle, unless your friend Diane's changing her story."

Holding the file against her, she threw back the jacket's hood. Her eyes glistened with rage or regret. "Wes, please?"

"Please what?"

"This is important. This is critical. Not just for the trial. For you."

But she didn't move, and neither did he. Finally, she nodded, gave Bart another pat, laid the folder down on the steps, and turned. When she got to the door, she didn't pause—as he thought she might. He would have a chance then to call out, to see if . . . but there was no hesitation at all.

The door closed behind her.

His intention was to leave it on the stairs. But he didn't do that.

Then, once it was inside, he decided he would just throw the damn thing in the trash, but he didn't.

He'd read all of the newspaper and magazine articles about Diane Price, and he'd about had it up to his earlobes with them. Clearly, the woman was some kind of publicity hound who'd struck gold with the touching story of the brutal rape that had cut short her promising future and forced her to a life of drugs and promiscuity.

Right.

He'd read somewhere that she'd optioned her life story to some Hollywood outfit, and he thought that was just perfect. She was a charlatan and a liar and had parlayed a couple of weeks with his famous client into a cottage industry among the politically correct. He had nothing but contempt for her and what she stood for.

But now the accordion folder was on the milk crate in the other room while he sat at his kitchen table pretending to go over Emil Balian's testimony about Mark's car as he chewed on his pizza and drank his second and third beers of the evening.

He kept the radio on low—Christmas carols. He didn't want to hear any random country music. None of Emil Balian's story made any more sense than it had the fifth and sixth times he'd reviewed it. The nosy neighbor didn't know what car he'd seen on the night of the murder.

The last quarter of the Warriors game was like the last quarter of all basketball games. Farrell was coming to the opinion that they should change the rules of pro basketball—give each team a hundred points and shorten the game to two minutes. You'd wind up with the same scores and save everybody a lot of wear and tear.

In the end, he swore to himself, flicked off the tube, then the radio, opened another beer, and sat on his futon with the folder in his lap, still hesitating.

What did Sam mean, this was for him, not the trial?

There were a lot of pages. The first was from a high school yearbook—Diane Taylor with a beaming smile, the mortarboard graduation photo, under it the list of organizations she'd belonged to and awards she'd won—rally committee, debate society, chess club, varsity cheerleader, biology club, swim team, Bank of America Science Award, lifetime member California Scholarship Federation, National Merit semifinalist.

Wes flipped to the next pages. More yearbook, the

individual photos that showed her as she'd been back then—vivacious, pretty, popular.

But so what? The newspapers were filled with file photos of mass murderers who'd looked like this and done this much in high school. You just couldn't tell. Wes had no trouble recalling his own high school yearbook photo—with his Beatle haircut, he'd been voted "Best Hair." Now he was forty-seven percent bald by actual count. And that alone, he thought, pretty much said it all about the relevance of high school pictures.

But he kept going, turning the pages within the folder, sipping his beer. A change in focus now—from photographs to xeroxes of report cards and transcripts. Senior year—all A's. First semester at Stanford: A's. Second and third semester: A's. Fourth semester: a B, two C's and an incomplete.

So something happened during the spring semester of her sophomore year. Wes had seen this, too, a million times. This was—he double-checked the date on the transcript—1968. Drugs happened was what. Martin Luther King got killed. Bobby Kennedy. The Chicago Democratic Convention and Humphrey and then Richard Nixon. America fell apart. Wes wouldn't be surprised if 1968 set a record for grades going to hell, somebody ought to do a study, get a government grant. But what did it mean?

It meant nothing. It was yet another example of a person—Sam in this case—seeing what she was already disposed to see. He finished his beer and went to get another one. He should go to sleep.

But something tugged him back to the futon, to the folder. He owed Sam something, didn't he?

No he didn't. She was wrong here and he was right. She had caused him all the pain, not the other way around. She was still hurting him.

The next stapled group of pages, forty-two of them, contained xeroxes of diary entries in a confident female hand—two to a page, the first eighty-three days of the year, ending March 23.

He read it all. Diane was a chatty and charming diarist. She was still swimming competitively. She was taking German, chemistry, biology and Western civ, and she was worried that they were too easy, that she wouldn't be prepared when she got to med school. She had two close female friends—Maxine and Sharon—and on March 14, she'd met Mark Dooher, the first male mentioned in a romantic context within the pages.

No drugs, no sex. No innuendos of either.

On March 17, she went to an afternoon college baseball game with Mark Dooher. Burgers. A kiss good night.

The last line on March 22. "Mark and I m.o. a little. First boyfriend this year. Whew! Thought it was my breath."

The last line on March 23. "Tomorrow date with Mark. Can't wait."

Wes turned the last page of this section and frowned. The next stapled section seemed to be more xeroxes of diary pages, again two to a page, beginning March 24, but these pages had no writing. He flipped through, page by page.

Nothing for seventeen days, where before March 23, Diane had never skipped more than a day. Then, on April 10, the handwriting had changed—subtly, but recognizable even to Wes. It was more cramped somehow, less confident.

"Didn't get out of bed. Too scared. Seeing everything different now, what people are capable of now. Since Mark. From *that*? I'm afraid I'll see him and then what? I've got to tell somebody. But he said he'd kill me.

I want to go home, but I can't leave school without saying why, but I can't think. I can't talk to anybody. God, my mom . . . how can I tell them?"

And then another sheaf of blank pages until June 5, when, presumably, school got out.

Wes was asking himself why hadn't he seen this before. Why hadn't Sam given it to Amanda Jenkins? If she'd done that, Wes would have read it in the discovery documents. But it hadn't been there.

But what did it mean anyway?

Legally, it was worthless. Purportedly, this was nothing but copies of pages, *maybe* from a diary, of twenty-some years before. The entire package could have been reconstructed, or originally created, in the past month. In no way was it evidence.

But, as Sam had said, it wasn't meant to be evidence. The pages weren't for the trial, they were for Wes.

38

ON MONDAY MORNING AT NINE THIRTY-FIVE, WES Farrell stood before the witness box in Department 26 and said good morning to Dr. Harris. The two men had had a long talk on Sunday afternoon, discussing what they would say this morning. Harris had always liked Mark Dooher—had liked Sheila, too. The police had more or less set him up to make Mark look bad, and he was more than willing to try to work some damage control.

"Doctor," Farrell began. "On Friday, you testified that you lost a vial of blood from your office on May thirty-first. Have you ever located that vial of blood?"

"No."

"In other words, it's lost."

"That's right."

"How did you discover it was lost?"

"It didn't come back from the lab when it was supposed to."

"Oh!" Farrell was intrigued. "This blood then, was it supposed to go to a lab from your office?"

"Yes. We send our blood work out to the Pacheco Clinic where they've got a lab facility."

"Is the Pacheco Clinic far from your office?"

"No. A mile, maybe a little more."

"All right, then. Now, Doctor, how do they keep track of the blood they work on in this lab?"

"We have a requisition slip that we attach to the vials with tape. Then they fill in a report form for results."

"Let's back up a minute, shall we? You attach your requisition slip to these vials with tape?"

"Yes."

"What kind of tape?"

"Regular Scotch tape."

"Scotch tape on glass vials. Hmm. Is that sticky enough, doctor? Does the tape ever come off?"

"If the vial gets wet, sometimes, yes."

"All right. Did you discover that this missing vial of blood—Leo Banderas's blood—never got to Pacheco lab because it wasn't logged in? Was that it?"

"No, not exactly. They're not logged in as such."

"So you don't know whether this vial of blood ever got to the Pacheco lab?"

"No, I don't know."

"It could have been delivered there and lost there, isn't that true?"

Jenkins objected to the question as speculation, and she was sustained, but Farrell thought he'd made his point anyway. He decided to move along. He turned to the jury and gave them a relaxed smile.

"Dr. Harris, you testified that you'd lost other vials of blood from your office, is that true?"

"Yes."

"Many of them?"

Harris thought a minute. "Over the years, say three or four."

"Three or four? Has it ever happened, to your knowledge, that someone has dropped a vial of blood?"

"Yes."

"Is this something—dropping a vial of blood—that could get someone fired if it happened a lot?"

"Possibly."

"Your Honor, objection! Speculation."

Again Thomasino sustained Jenkins, and again Farrell didn't care. He was putting points on the board.

"Dr. Harris, did you have the opportunity to review the lab report that Mr. Drumm signed?"

"Yes I did."

"And the blood in the second vial, was it the blood of your patient, Leo Banderas?"

"I don't know. There was no way to tell."

"But the blood in the vial was A-positive, was it not?"

"Yes. But there was nothing to compare it with. Mr. Banderas died several months ago and was cremated. There's no trace of his DNA left."

"So you're saying, Doctor, that there's no way to tell if the blood in the second vial belonged to Mr. Banderas or not, is that right?"

"Yes, that's right."

"Then there is no particular reason to believe that the blood in the second vial, the blood found at the crime scene, had ever been in your office, is there?"

"No."

In his free time over the weekend, when he wasn't chatting with Dr. Harris—and amid all different kinds of soul-searching regarding Diane Price—Farrell had tried intermittently to focus on Abe Glitsky. He wished he'd had better luck formulating a plan, because the lieutenant was in the witness box now and Farrell was approaching him and didn't know what he was going to say.

Glitsky's testimony, easily delivered over two hours with Amanda Jenkins leading him every step of the way, had done some damage. This was in large part due to Glitsky's air of authority on the stand—if he had come to suspect Mark Dooher, there had to be some reason. He was a professional cop with no particular ax to grind. In fact, he was the head of Homicide. It looked to him as though the defendant was guilty. That's why he had delivered Dooher's case to the DA, and why the Grand Jury had indicted him.

"Lieutenant, you've given us Mark Dooher's version of the events of June seventh, and then your own interpretation of those events, which led you to arrest him for the murder of his wife. For the benefit of the jury, can you tell us a specific instance of an untruth you uncovered in Mr. Dooher's statement to you on the night of the murder?"

"A great deal of it was untrue. That's what all these other witnesses are here to talk about."

"Yes. But do you have any proof you can show us that Mr. Dooher lied? Say a credit card receipt that proves he was really buying clothes downtown when he said he went to Dellaroma's Deli? Anything like that?"

"I have statements of other witnesses," Glitsky repeated.

"And the jury will get to decide who they believe among those witnesses, Lieutenant. But to get back to my question—now for the third time—do you, personally, have something you can show us, or describe for us, that *proves* anything about Mark Dooher's actions on the night of the murder?"

Glitsky kept his composure, wishing that Jenkins would object about something. The testimony of the other prosecution witnesses—taken together—would constitute proof, he hoped. But he didn't have a smoking gun, and Farrell was nailing him for it. "I don't have a credit card receipt, no."

"Isn't it true, Lieutenant, that you don't have *anything* that proves Mark Dooher told even one small lie?"

"Not by itself, no."

"Not by itself or not at all? Do you have something specific, or don't you?"

Farrell was going to squeeze it out of him. He glanced at Jenkins. Couldn't she call this speculation or leading the witness or something? Evidently not.

"No."

But Farrell wasn't going to gloat over this minor victory. He simply nodded, satisfied, and took aim at his next target. "Now, Lieutenant Glitsky, as the investigator in charge of this case, did you analyze the reports of the crime scene investigator, Sergeant Crandall, and the lab reports on blood submitted by Mr. Drumm?"

"Yes I did."

"And yet didn't you hear both of those gentlemen testify that they found no evidence tying Mark Dooher to the scene?"

"No."

A look of surprise. There was some whispering in the gallery. A few of the jurors frowned and leaned forward in their seats. Farrell took a step toward him. "You did not hear them say that?"

"No, sir. That was a conclusion you drew."

This stopped Farrell cold. Glitsky had maneuvered him into a trap. Crandall's testimony—the knife, the fingerprints—did not *preclude* Dooher from being on the scene. Neither did Drumm's tainted blood.

But two could play this game. They were going to do a little dance. "Your Honor," Farrell said, "would you please instruct the witness to answer only the questions I ask him?"

The judge did just that—a rebuke for the jury's benefit. See? Farrell was telling them, Lieutenant Glitsky doesn't play by the rules.

Farrell inclined his head an inch. "Lieutenant, did you hear Dr. Strout identify the kitchen knife, People's Three, as the murder weapon?"

"Yes."

"And did you hear Sergeant Crandall testify that the only fingerprints on the knife belonged to Mr. and Mrs. Dooher, and were entirely consistent with normal household use?"

"Yes."

"And did you also hear Sergeant Crandall's testimony about the surgical glove found at the scene?"

"Yes, I did."

"Well, then, Lieutenant, I must ask you. In your professional opinion, why did Mr. Dooher wear this surgical glove if he knew—as he must have known—that his fingerprints were already all over the murder weapon?"

"To point to a burglar."

"To point to a burglar?"

As soon as he'd repeated Glitsky's answer, Farrell realized it was a critical mistake. Glitsky jumped on it before he could stop him. "Without the glove there's no evidence of a burglar."

Farrell kept his poker face on, but these, suddenly, were bad cards. He couldn't let it rest here. "And yet,

Lieutenant, didn't Sergeant Crandall testify there were no fingerprints on the glove?"

"Yes."

"There was absolutely nothing connecting this glove to Mr. Dooher?"

Glitsky had to concede it. "That's right."

Farrell decided that wisdom dictated a shift of emphasis. This was where, Farrell knew, it was going to get serious in a hurry, and he took in a breath, slowing down, coming to a stop in the center of the courtroom. In the jury's eyes, here was a man wrestling with a moral dilemma.

Finally, he turned back to Glitsky, having come to his difficult decision. "Lieutenant, do you ever wear surgical gloves when you investigate a bloody crime scene?"

Jenkins stood and objected, but Thomasino overruled her.

The Lieutenant nodded. "Yes."

Farrell saw no need to say more. He had larger prey in his sights. "In the early portion of this year, and especially in the latter half of April, did you have occasion to spend a great deal of time in St. Mary's Hospital?"

Jenkins slammed a palm on the table and was up out of her chair. "Your Honor! I object. What does that question have to do with the death of Sheila Dooher?"

But this time, Farrell wasn't going to wait meekly for a ruling. "I'm afraid it has everything to do with it, Your Honor. Its relevance will become clear during my case. Either I make the point now or I'd like permission to re-call Lieutenant Glitsky at that time."

The judge's eyes were invisible under his brows. He called a recess to see the attorneys in his chambers.

* * *

Glitsky stayed in the witness box. There was no place else he wanted to go, anyway. No one he wanted to talk to.

Across the courtroom, Dooher and Christina had their heads together, conferring in whispers, their body language so intimate, it was embarrassing. He tried to imagine Dooher objectively in that moment—a middle-aged white male in the prime of his life. He kept himself fit. He looked good. And clearly, he could attract a beautiful younger woman.

Studying him, Glitsky tried to imagine the moments of rage. Or had it been calm deliberation? How was it possible that none of it showed? And yet there was no visible sign, no way to see what Dooher had done except in what he'd inadvertently left behind.

And yet Glitsky *knew*.

Dooher looked up, perhaps feeling the long gaze on him. His eyes came to Glitsky for a fraction of an instant—flat, completely without reaction, as though Glitsky didn't exist—and then he was back in his conversation with Christina Carrera.

In the gallery, the huge crowds from the pretrial had slimmed somewhat with the judicial rulings on what issues were going to be allowed, but still, every seat appeared to be taken, although just at the moment a knot of reporters had congealed around the bar rail. They smelled a fresh kill coming, and Glitsky was afraid it was going to be him.

"All right, Lieutenant. Do you remember the question I asked you, if you'd had occasion to spend a lot of time in St. Mary's Hospital in the spring of this year, around the time of Sheila Dooher's murder."

A wary look. "Yes."

"How many days?"

"I don't know exactly. Thirty or forty."

Farrell was damned if he was going to ask why and get the sympathy flowing for what Glitsky had gone through. His wife had been dying of cancer. The jury didn't need to know that. For Farrell, this was a tough moment—personally he felt for Glitsky's grief. But so be it. He had to have the testimony.

"Were you a patient or a visitor there, Lieutenant?"

"A visitor."

"And during those thirty or forty days, were you ever near a nurses' station?"

"Yes."

"Did you ever witness blood being drawn?"

Glitsky knew where this was going, and cast a cold eye on Jenkins. But the attorneys must have slugged this one out in chambers. The cavalry was not on the way.

"Yes."

"Do you remember ever seeing any vials of blood, sitting out on a tray, or a table, or at a nurses' station?"

"Yes."

"And were these vials guarded in any way? Or under lock and key?"

"No."

"All right. Thank you, Lieutenant. That's all."

Lunch was a somber affair.

A fierce, cold, wet storm had blown in off the Pacific while Glitsky had been on the stand during the morning, and Christina was standing at her window, watching the rain slanting down while her two companions sullenly finished their takeout Chinese.

She'd flown down to Ojai on Saturday morning, back again last night. She'd needed to get some perspective, get out of the glare of all of this. To a degree, it had worked.

But now the heaters had come on and smelled musty in the tiny room, and Mark and Wes still hadn't gotten back to the people they'd been before she'd kissed Mark on his doorstep.

That kiss had changed Wes profoundly. In spite of his skills in the courtroom, he appeared more distracted with every passing day, more upset with her and, especially, with Mark.

She wanted to shake Wes out of his doubts. She'd had her round of them on Friday, all about the blood. Glitsky's testimony had opened up another whole universe of possible explanations. Doubts had to be part of it—if the prosecution didn't have some decent facts, it wouldn't get cases past the Grand Jury. And hadn't Wes been the one who'd drilled into her the notion that the facts aren't as important as how you interpret them? Why couldn't he see that now?

She knew what was bothering Wes. This case wasn't about the facts to him. It was about his confidence in Mark. And the kiss had undermined that.

She turned from the window, about to say something, try to lighten things up, but just then the cop from the Hall knocked and said they were reconvening.

Emil Balian had dressed well, in a conservative dark suit with a white shirt and rep tie. Amanda Jenkins had paid for his haircut, which eliminated the unruly shocks of white hair that normally emanated, Einstein-like, from the sides of his scalp. Most importantly, Glitsky thought, he'd shaved, or someone had shaved him. Abe thought, all in all, he looked pretty good—respectable, grave, old.

Abe had met Balian on the day after the murder. With Paul Thieu, he'd gone back to the scene early in the afternoon and there was an elderly man in plaid shorts and Hawaiian shirt standing in the driveway. "Saw all about it on the television," he'd said without preamble as they'd gotten out of their car. "You guys the cops?"

Balian introduced himself, saying he lived a couple of blocks over on Casitas. So this was the place, huh? Too bad about the lady. He'd known her a little. He knew just about everybody, which was what happened when you walked as much as he did. You got to know people, stopping to chat while they worked on their gardens or brought in groceries or whatever.

Emil worked for forty years as a mail carrier and just got in the habit of walking, plus he had a touch of phlebitis and he was supposed to stroll three or four miles a day, keep his circulation up.

Balian wasn't shy. He talked incessantly, telling Glitsky and Thieu all about his life in the neighborhood. He bought into St. Francis Wood back when a working man could afford a nice house. Eleanor, his wife, had a job, too—and this was in the days before women worked like they do now. They hadn't had any children, so pretty much had their pick of neighborhoods. Money wasn't much of a problem back then, not like it is now being on a fixed income.

During this extended recital, Glitsky kept trying to back away, get to the house. He knew they were going to have to canvass the area sometime for witnesses anyway. He was reasonably certain that this old man was talking for the sheer pleasure of hearing himself talk.

But it turned out better than that.

Jenkins crossed the floor and came to rest a couple of feet in front of the witness box. "Mr. Balian," she began, "would you tell us what you did on the evening of June seventh of this year?"

"I sure will. I had supper with my wife, Eleanor, at our home on Casitas Avenue, and after supper, like I always do, I went out for a walk."

"And what time was this?"

"It was just dusk, maybe a little before, say eight o'clock, thereabouts. We always eat at seven sharp, used to be six, but about ten years ago we went to seven. I don't know why, really, it just seemed more civilized or something. So it was seven."

"So to get the timing right, was it seven o'clock when you began dinner, but near eight when you started your walk?"

"That's right."

"Was there any other way you could mark the time? Did you check your watch, anything like that?"

"No, I don't usually wear a watch. In fact, I don't *ever* wear a watch. After I retired, I said what do I need a watch for anymore and threw the old thing in my drawer . . ."

"Yes, well, was there any other . . . ?"

"The time. Sure. As I said, it was near dusk. When I left it was still light out and when I got back home, maybe an hour later, it was dark. While I was out the street lights came up, so that ought to pinpoint it."

"Yes, it would, thank you."

Jenkins turned back to where Glitsky sat at the

prosecution table and he gave her a reassuring nod. The way Balian answered questions drove Amanda crazy, and she didn't want to lose patience with him. After all, he was her witness, the backbone of her case. She took a breath, turned and faced him again.

"All right, Mr. Balian. Now on this walk, did you happen to notice anything unusual?"

"Yes I did. There was a different car parked out in front of the Murrays'."

"A different car. What do you mean?"

"I mean the Murrays don't own that car, or else they just bought it, so I wondered who it was might be visiting them, was how I come to notice it."

"Can you describe the car, Mr. Balian?"

"It was a late model light brown Lexus with a personalized license plate that read ESKW."

Jenkins entered a photograph of Dooher's car into evidence. The vanity plate was meant to be sort of a humorous rendering of ESQ, for "Esquire"—Dooher's advertisement that he was a lawyer.

"And what street was this car parked on?"

"Down the end of my own street, Casitas."

"Which is how far from Ravenwood?"

"Two blocks."

"And did you ever see this car again?"

"I sure did. The very next day, which was how I remember it so clear." Balian was getting caught up in his story, enthusiasm all over him. Glitsky knew that this was where he tended to embellish, and hoped Jenkins would be able to keep him reined in. "And where did you see this car?"

"It was parked in the driveway at 4215 Ravenwood Drive. That's why I was still standing out front when the police got there the next day. I thought I'd go by and see the house where there'd been the murder—it was all on the TV—and there was this same car the next day in the driveway, so I was looking at it, wondering what the connection was."

Farrell got his blood up when it was time to perform. Leaning over to both Dooher and Christina as Jenkins handed him the witness, he whispered, "It's almost unfair."

He rose slowly and made a little show of pretending to be reading something from a file in front of him, getting his questions down. From the table, finally, he raised his head and smiled at the witness. "Mr. Balian. On the night we've been talking about, June seventh, before you took your walk, you had dinner with your wife at your home. Do you remember what you had for dinner that night?"

At the opposition table, Christina saw Glitsky and Jenkins exchange a look. They must have known what would be coming, but that didn't make it any easier to sit through.

On the witness stand, Emil Balian crossed his arms and frowned. "I don't know," he said.

Farrell looked down at the file before him again and creased his own brow. "You don't know? And yet in your second interview with the police, didn't you tell Lieutenant Glitsky that you'd had corned beef and cabbage for dinner on that night?"

"I think I said that, yes, but . . ."

"I've got the transcript of that interview right here, Mr. Balian. Would you like to see it?"

"No, that's all right, I know I said it."

"But in a later interview, were you as sure of what you had for dinner?"

Balian nodded. "Not really. But that was a week or

so after I first talked to the police, and Eleanor reminded me she thought we'd had pork chops and applesauce that night, Tuesday, if it was going to be important. The night before was corned beef. It doesn't have anything to do with the car," he added petulantly.

"Do you remember *now* which dinner it was, the corned beef or the pork chops?"

"No. I'm not sure."

Farrell put his pad down and walked around the table, out into the center of the courtroom. "Mr. Balian, would you have had a drink with either of these dinners? Let's say the corned beef?"

"Usually with corned beef, I'd have a beer."

"One beer? A couple of beers?"

"Sometimes a couple of beers."

"And how about pork chops? Would you have a drink with pork chops?"

"Sometimes. White wine."

"A glass or two?"

"Yes."

"But on this night, you don't remember what you ate or if you had anything to drink exactly, do you?"

"Not exactly, no."

"You do admit, however, that you probably had a couple of drinks—that was your habit with meals—regardless whether it was corned beef or pork chops."

"That's the first thing I said, wasn't it? That I didn't know?"

"Yes, it was, Mr. Balian. That was the first thing you said, that you didn't remember what you'd eaten. But now, let's get on with what you say you *do* remember, the car with the ESKW license plates. You saw this car parked on your street on Tuesday night, June seventh?"

On more solid ground for a moment, Balian settled himself in the witness chair. He loosened his collar at the knot of his tie. "I did. It was in front of the Murrays' house."

"And where were you? Did you walk right by it?"

A pause. "I was across the street."

"Across the street? Did you cross over to look at this car more carefully?"

"No. I could see it fine. I didn't study it or anything. I just noticed it, the way you notice things. It wasn't a car from our street."

"Okay, fair enough. Is Casitas a wide street, by the way?"

The petulance was returning. "It's a normal street, I don't know wide."

Farrell went back to his table and turned with a document in his hand. He moved forward to the witness box. The questions may have been barbed, but his tone was neutral, even friendly. "I have here a notarized survey of Casitas Avenue"—he had it marked Defense E—"and it shows that the street is sixty-two feet from side to side. Does that sound right, Mr. Balian?"

"If you say so."

"But you had to be more than sixty-two feet away when you saw the license plate that read ESKW, isn't that true?"

"I don't know. Why?"

"Because you couldn't read the plate from directly across the street, could you?" Balian didn't answer directly, and Farrell believed the question might have struck him ambiguously. So he helped him out. "From directly across the street, you'd only see the side of the car, wouldn't you. You would have had to have been diagonal to it to see the license plate, isn't that so?"

"Oh, I see what you're saying. I guess so. Yes."

"Maybe another ten, twenty, thirty feet away?"

"Maybe. I don't know. I saw the car . . ." Balian paused.

"So how far were you from the car, Mr. Balian? More than sixty feet, correct?"

"I guess."

"More than eighty feet?"

"Maybe."

"More than a hundred feet?"

"Maybe not that much."

"So perhaps a hundred feet, is that fair?" Farrell smiled at him, man-to-man. There was nothing personal here. "Now, when you saw this car from perhaps a hundred feet away . . ."

"Objection." Jenkins had to try, but she must have known the objection wasn't so much for substance as it was for solidarity. Her witness was beginning to shrivel.

Farrell rephrased. "When you saw this car from across the street, was it at the beginning of your walk or more toward the end of it?"

"The end of it. I was coming around back to my street."

"And so the streetlights were on, were they not?"

After another hesitation, Balian responded about the streetlights. "They had just come on."

"They had just come on. So it was still somewhat light out?"

"Yes. I could see clearly."

"I'm sure you could, but I'm a little confused. Haven't you just testified that you walked for an hour, and when you got back to your house, it was dark? Didn't you tell that to Ms. Jenkins?"

"Yes. I said that."

"And this street you live on—Casitas—is it a long way from the Murrays' house, where you saw this car, to your own home?"

"No. Seven or eight houses."

"And did you continue your walk home after you saw this car in front of the Murrays'? You didn't stop for anything, chat with anybody?"

"No."

"And you've said it was dark when you got home?"

"Yes."

"Well, then, I'm simply confused here, maybe you could explain it to us all—how could it have been light, or as you say, just dark, when you were seven or eight houses up the street?"

"I said the lights were on."

"Yes you did say that, Mr. Balian. But you said they were 'just' on, implying it was still light out, isn't that the case? But it wasn't light out, was it? It was, in fact, dark?"

"I said the streetlights were on, didn't I?" he repeated, his voice now querulous, shaking. "I didn't tell a lie. I saw that car! I saw the license plates. It was the same car I saw the next day."

Warfare, Farrell was thinking. No other word for it. He advanced relentlessly. "And it was a brown car, you said, didn't you? You knew for sure that the car you saw the previous night had been brown because it had the same license plates."

"Yes."

"When you first saw the car that night, could you tell it was brown in the dark?"

"What kind of question is that? Of course it was brown. It was the same car."

"Couldn't it have been dark blue, or black, or another dark color?"

"No. It was brown!"

Farrell took a moment regrouping. He walked back

to the defense table, consulted some notes, turned. Then. "Do you wear glasses, Mr. Balian?"

The witness had his elbows planted on the arms of the chair, his head sunken between his shoulders, swallowed in the suit. "I wear reading glasses."

"And you see perfectly clearly for normal activities?"

"Yes."

"Twenty-twenty vision?"

Another agonizing pause. "Almost. I don't need glasses to drive a car. I've got fine vision, young man."

"For a man of your age, I'm sure you do. How old are you, by the way, Mr. Balian?"

Chin thrust out, Balian was proud of it. "I'm seventy-nine years old, and I see just as good as you do."

Farrell paused and took a deep breath. He didn't want Balian to explode at him, make him into the heavy, but he had to keep going. A couple more hits and it would be over. "And then the next day, at what you knew was a murder scene, you saw a similar car in a driveway to the one you'd seen the previous night, in the dark, after you'd had a couple of drinks, and Lieutenant Glitsky showed up and suddenly it seemed it might have been the *exact* same car, didn't it?"

"It *was* the same car!"

A subtle shake of the head, Farrell indicating to the jury that no, it wasn't. And here's why. "When was the first time you talked to police, Mr. Balian?"

"I told you, the next day."

"And Lieutenant Glitsky asked if you'd seen anything unusual in the neighborhood, right?"

"Right."

"And you told him about the car, and Lieutenant Glitsky pointed to the brown Lexus parked in Mr.

Dooher's driveway, and asked you if that was the car, didn't he?"

"Yes."

"And it looked like the car, didn't it?"

Balian sat forward, tired of all this. "I'm pretty sure it was the same car."

Farrell nodded. "You're pretty sure. Thank you."

39

One of Archbishop Flaherty's predecessors had organized the Corporate Santa Claus Party to give a year-end tax incentive for businesses to help provide toys, games, clothes and various other Christmas presents for the underprivileged children in the city and county of San Francisco. This year the St. Francis Yacht Club was hosting the event, which was the society set's unofficial kickoff to the season's hectic party schedule. Over three hundred guests—the cream of the city's business community—had gathered for an evening of dining and dancing to big band music.

Mark Dooher, in his tuxedo, was in his element, among friends. The room, like the people in it, was elegantly turned out. Dessert and coffee had been cleared away and the band had kicked into what some guests had decided was a danceable version of "Joy to the World."

Christina had been amazed and gratified by the volume and apparent sincerity of expressions of support and sympathy for Mark. Now they were alone at their table. She held his hand under it.

"Look at Wes," she said to Mark. "It looks like he's finally having some fun."

The bark of Wes Farrell's laughter carried across the room, even over the band. Everybody who wanted to buy Wes a drink had succeeded, and he wasn't feeling much pain.

Dooher looked over benevolently. "He deserves it. He's been doing a hell of a job, but the guy's been killing himself. I didn't realize—even knowing him my whole life—that he had all that fight in him. I think he's going to have himself a career after this."

Christina squeezed his hand, was silent a moment, then said, "I don't know if I am."

Surprised, he looked at her. "What do you mean?"

She shrugged. "I don't think this is the kind of law I want to do."

"Why not? You're getting an innocent man off. Don't you feel good about that?"

"Sure, I feel great about that. But how it has to be done." Her free hand reached for the salt shaker and poured a small pile of it onto the linen, then traced circles with what she'd poured. "Last night I couldn't get my mind off poor Mr. Balian, how he looked when Wes got finished with him. And bringing up that stuff with Lieutenant Glitsky . . . I know it has to be done. They got it wrong, but . . ."

"I can't tell you how much good it does me to hear you say that again. I thought you'd given up faith in me."

Again, she squeezed his hand. "You were right," she said. "It is faith. There are unanswered questions about almost everything else in life. It's just here they seem so ominous."

"I know. Sometimes, the past couple of months, they almost had *me* thinking I did it after all. I mean, I remembered being at the driving range. I remember coming home and finding Sheila. But when I first heard about Balian, or the blood, I wondered where those things could have come from. Maybe I blanked, went sleepwalking, something. Maybe I did it." He squeezed her hand. "But I didn't. I can't blame you for having your doubts."

"It's just so hard to see these other people—Glitsky and Mr. Balian and Amanda Jenkins—doing what they do. I have to think they really believe they're right."

Dooher was silent for a moment, wrestling with it. "People get committed to their positions. Glitsky got himself committed, and he sold it to Jenkins. I think that's what's got us to here. But we can't let them ruin our lives. We've got to fight back. That's the world, Christina. Misunderstandings. I don't know if people are malicious—I don't like to think so. But sometimes they're just wrong, and what are we supposed to do about that?"

"I know," she said. "But seeing Wes take them apart, that's hard for me. And if we do get to this Diane Price as one of their witnesses, it'll be me up there, and it will feel personal, and I don't know if that *is* me."

"You'll do fine."

But she was shaking her head. "No, not that. I'm not worried whether or not I *can* do it. I know what I'm going to be asking her—I've rehearsed it a hundred times. As you guys say, I'll eat her for lunch. But I have to tell you, I'm not comfortable with it. This isn't what I feel I was born to do."

He covered her hand with both of his, leaned in

toward her. "What do you think you were born to do, Christina?"

"I don't know really. Something less confrontational, I guess. There must be something in the law—"

"No," he interrupted, "I don't mean with the law. I'm not talking about your professional life. You'll do fine there, whatever you decide. I mean you personally. What were you born to do?"

Her finger went back to spreading the salt around. The band finished one song and started another. "I don't know anymore, Mark. I don't think about that."

"But you used to know?"

She shrugged. "I used to have dreams. Now . . ." She trailed off, biting down on her lip. "It's stupid. You grow up and all the variables have changed and what you thought you wanted isn't really an option anymore." She met his eyes.

He raised her hand and turned her palm to him, kissing it gently. "You're thinking an old man like me— hell, nearly fifty, there's no way I'd want what you used to think you were born for . . ."

"I don't . . ."

He touched her lips with his index finger. "Which is babies, a family, a normal life like your parents have, is that it? Is that what you used to think you were born for?"

She pressed her lips together. Her eyes were liquid with tears, and she nodded.

"Because," he said, "we could do that. We could have all the kids you want. I didn't do so well the first time around, maybe we could both start over. Together."

She leaned her head in against his. He brought his arms up around her and felt her shoulders give. Holding her there against him, he whispered, "Whatever you want, it's do-able, Christina. We can do it. Whatever you want. Anything."

Nat Glitsky left a message for his son at Homicide, then braved the new storm that had just arrived air mail from Alaska. He got to Abe's duplex, where he told Rita she could take the night off. He was driving his three grandsons downtown where they were going to meet their father at the Imperial Palace in Chinatown for dim sum, Nat's treat.

It had been a tough enough year for the family, and after Abe's testimony at the trial, Nat's personal seismograph—sensitive to these things—had picked up rumblings with the boys that made him uncomfortable. Now they were all on the first round of pot stickers. Their father hadn't shown up yet, and the rumblings were continuing. "What I don't get," Jacob was grousing, "is no matter what time we plan something, Dad's late, even if it's like five minutes from where he works."

. "Your old man's busy, Jake, he's in the middle of a trial on top of his regular job." But it bothered Nat, too, and checking his watch every five minutes, he wasn't entirely successful at hiding it. "He'll be here. He's coming."

"So's Christmas." Isaac really wasn't saying much lately. His mother's death had carved out a hole in his personality where the kid used to be, and now a sullen, gangly, hurt teenager glared across the table at his grandfather. Isaac was the oldest and having the worst time of it, but in Nat's view none of the boys were doing very well.

A waitress came by, as one of them did every couple of minutes, with a new selection of foods—all kinds of sticky buns, chicken, beef and pork dishes, various seafoods (Nat didn't keep kosher all the time), vegetables and noodles, each served on a small white plate, a pile of which were accumulating quickly at the side of the table. At the end of the meal, the waiters would count the plates and compute the cost—simple and efficient.

"So you been reading about your father in the newspapers?" Nat wasn't going to sidestep into it. He knew what the undercurrent was about and knew there wasn't any solution except to talk about it. But none of the boys answered, so he persisted. "You taking grief at school?"

O.J., sitting next to Nat, was the youngest and looked across the table to his older brothers for cues, but they were pretending to be busy peeling aluminum foil from some chicken wings, so he piped up. "I don't think Dad's a liar. I don't think he cheated."

"Shut up, O.J.," Jacob said. "He's doing what he's got to do, that's all. He's a cop. It's not the same."

"What's not, Jake?"

"The rules."

Nat didn't like hearing that. "You're dad's not breaking any rules, Jake. He's got the same rules as everybody else."

Isaac snorted. "You read the newspaper, Grandpa? You watch any television?"

"Yeah, I've seen it."

"Well?"

"Well, what?"

"Well, what do *you* think?"

"I think this man Dooher killed his wife and he's got a smart attorney. Your dad arrested him because he thought he did that. You know he didn't take any blood from the hospital."

Isaac looked down, unconvinced. Jacob spoke up.

"It doesn't really matter, Grandpa. Everybody thinks he did."

"Not everybody," Nat said. "I don't. You boys shouldn't. Anybody starts telling that stuff to you, you tell them they're full of baloney."

"But why do they keep saying it?" O.J. wanted to know.

"Because people don't know your father. And people do know, or they like to believe, that there are cops out there who do bad things, who cheat and lie and plant evidence so they'll win their cases. But that's not your father. You guys gotta believe in your old man. He's going through a hard time right now, just like you all are. You got to help him get through it."

But Isaac was shaking his head, disagreeing. "Why? He doesn't help us with anything. He's gone in the morning, gone at nights, gone on the weekends. Work work work, and he dumps us off on Rita. He just doesn't want to be with us. It's obvious. We remind him of Mom."

"If he did," Jake added, "he'd be here."

O.J. was having a hard time holding back tears. "I just wish Mom would come back. Then we wouldn't even need Dad. Then it would be all right."

Nat reached out a hand and put it over his youngest grandson's. "You do need your dad, O.J. Your mom really isn't coming back."

"I know," he said. "Everybody always says that." His voice was breaking. "I just wish she would, though."

"I don't think we do need Dad, Grandpa," Isaac said. "I mean, look right here. Where's Dad now? Who cares? We're taking care of each other. Quit crying, O.J."

"I'm not crying."

"Leave him alone, Isaac." Jacob pushed at his older brother. "He can cry if he wants to."

"I'm *not* crying, you guys!"

"Shh! Shh! It's okay." Nat smiled at the customers around them who were looking over at the disturbance. "Let's try to keep restaurant voices, all right. Oh, and look, here comes your dad now."

Eleven o'clock, Glitsky's kitchen.

"Abraham, they need you."

"Everybody needs me, Dad. I'm sick to death of people needing me. I don't have anything to give them."

"Just some time. That's all they need. Some of your time."

"I don't have any time. Don't you understand that? Every minute of my days and nights . . ."

"But this is your own blood. You signed on for this."

"Not this way I didn't!"

"Any way, Abraham. They didn't ask to be here either, not like this."

Glitsky stopped pacing and lowered himself onto the ottoman that filled the center of the small room. His dad leaned against the refrigerator. The two men's voices were low and harsh. They didn't want to wake Rita, sleeping in the dim light of the Christmas tree in the next room.

"You know what went on in this trial today, Dad? To me? You have any idea?"

"Of course." Nat touched his brow. "You think I've got Swiss cheese up here? But you know what's going to happen in the next couple of months *here*,

Abraham, you don't start paying attention? You're going to lose these boys. Now which is more important?"

"I'm not going to lose them."

Nat shook his head. "Were you listening about tonight? They're losing sight of you, son. They read about you in the newspaper, they hear bad stories on the tube. How do they know what to think?"

"They know," Glitsky said. "They've got level heads. They know me."

"This, Abraham, is malarkey. They don't know anymore, not for sure. Jacob tonight said you don't have the same rules as everybody else. Is that your message? Is that what you want to teach them?"

"He doesn't think that."

"He said it. You gonna say he didn't mean it? It sounded like he meant it. He needed some answer for his friends saying you broke the rules, so that's what he came up with. You're allowed to—because you're a cop."

Glitsky hung his heavy head. After a minute, he raised it again. "Lord, Dad, I'm tired. When's this Dooher madness going to end? I keep thinking if I could just find more evidence, something that's not ambiguous. Because otherwise, he's gonna walk. We're going to lose."

Nat pulled a kitchen chair up in front of his son. "So then he walks, Abraham. It's not the end of the world. It's one bad man, that's all."

"But it will look like me, don't you see? It will look like all the accusations against me are true."

"Which they're not. The people you work with, they know that."

Glitsky barked a short, humorless laugh. "That's a beautiful theory, Dad, it really is. But the truth is this could be the end of my credibility."

"First, you won't lose your job, Abraham. Even if you do, you'll do something else."

"But I'm a cop, Dad. That's what I do, it's what I *am*."

Nat shook his head. "Before you're a cop, you're a father. After you stop being a cop, you're a father. Your boys, especially now, they need a father. This is your main job. The rest"—he shrugged—"nobody knows the rest."

There was a rush to winning, no doubt about it.

Wes was still at the bar at the yacht club, pounding some more Yuletide cheer. Mark had prodded him into coming along. The public appearance would be important, he'd said, especially for after the trial.

Yesterday, after Wes had continued his onslaught against the prosecution, taking apart Emil Balian on the stand, the television news had picked up on him, on the "brilliant" defense he was conducting. This morning's *Chronicle* headline had read: KEY PROSECUTION WITNESS FOUNDERS IN DOOHER CASE. The pundits were unanimously calling for a quick verdict of not guilty, and Wes was enjoying the celebrity.

Suddenly the world seemed to understand that Wes Farrell was in fact the champion of the underdog and a tiger of a defense lawyer. After five months of tedious trial preparation, hours upon days spent studying transcripts and analyzing evidence in his dingy office or his dirty apartment, after the breakup with Sam and the doubts about his friend, now at last he was getting some recognition for who he was, for what he did—the sweet, sweet, sweet nectar of success that had eluded him for so long.

It was nearly one o'clock and the party was basically over. The staff was folding up tables behind him. The band was breaking down. Wes was alone at the bar just enjoying the living hell out of his sixth or seventh drink, thinking that maybe it had all been worth it, after all.

Christina and Mark had taken the limo home, and he'd need to get a cab later, but that was all right. He wasn't quite ready to call it quits yet.

Mark—his old pal—had been right about coming down for this party. Mark and Christina might have opened a few eyes when they walked in, but it was he, Wes Farrell, who'd been the sensation. Everybody had read the paper today, watched the news over the past nights. Front page, thank you. Yes, it appeared he was winning, winning, winning. Kicking ass, taking names.

Jocko, behind the bar, had become his close personal friend. Imagine, Wes Farrell the working-class guy here all buddy buddy with the bartender at the St. Francis Yacht Club. In his wallet, Farrell had at least half a dozen business cards of people he should call, who might know some people who'd need his services. Where had he been hiding? they'd all wanted to know.

He felt a hand on his shoulder and the Archbishop of San Francisco was asking Wes if they could have a nightcap together. Wes was finally, after a lifetime of mediocrity, moving into Dooher's circle. God, it was intoxicating!

And certainly one more drink, with Jim Flaherty, wouldn't hurt—a little more of that Oban single malt. They touched their glasses together. "Great party, Your Excellency. I hope you raised a million dollars."

"Three hundred and ten thousand in pledges," he said. "A new record. This is such a generous city." Flaherty savored his drink. "It looks like you had a pretty fair night yourself. I saw you holding court in here most of the evening. You're going to get Mark off, aren't you?"

"It looks like it. I don't want to jinx it, but we've certainly got them on the run."

The Archbishop sighed. "How did it even get to this?"

Farrell looked sideways at him. "It's bad luck to make enemies in the police department. Glitsky's a bad cop."

"Who just got promoted."

Again, a sidelong glance. What was Flaherty getting at? He couldn't figure it exactly, so he shrugged. "He's black. It's his turn." Then, on a hunch, the new Farrell blurted it right out. "You having doubts?"

"About Mark? Never. It's just the accusations. You can't help but have them affect your view a little, can you?"

"No, I don't think so. I've had a few myself—doubts—tell the truth. You wonder how many other cases, witnesses show up out of the woodwork who say they saw something, or heard it, or smelled it. What is it, power of suggestion?"

"I think it must be." The Archbishop sipped his drink.

"Your Excellency," Farrell said quietly, "you're not getting cold feet about testifying for us, are you?"

"No, of course not."

"Good, because I don't know if we're going to need you, but if we do, I wouldn't like to open the door and then have it close on us."

"No, I understand."

They both stared out through the rain-pocked glass. Faintly, they heard the wind as it pushed the cypresses nearly to the ground. "Lousy night out there, isn't it?" Flaherty said. Then, "You know, when this is over and Mark is found not guilty, we ought to try to make this up to him somehow. First he loses his wife, which is horrible enough, then the burden of this trial. He's been through the wringer. I don't know how he's surviving."

"Well, Mark's a survivor."

"Plus, he's in love again, I think."

Farrell sipped his drink and nodded. "You noticed," he said laconically. "Though I suppose if you've got to be in love with somebody, she'd do."

"Although the timing could be better, couldn't it?"

Farrell agreed that it could. Sitting together at the bar, each harboring his thoughts, the two men sipped at their drinks. The ship's bell behind the bar chimed once, and Jocko said it was last call.

"No, I'm good," Farrell said, and asked the bartender to call him a taxi.

Bill Carrera wasn't sleeping. His daughter's visit the previous weekend had brought to a head the fear that he had been living with since finding out she'd joined up with Dooher's defense team.

So now, downstairs, looking out over the few lights that remained on at this hour in Ojai, he sat in his deep wing chair, the one he called his Thinking Chair. In spite of the fact that Bill was the kind of man who named things—his Bronco was Trigger, for example; his tennis racket was Slam—he was not without intelligence or insight.

And he was worried sick about Christina.

The light came on in the hallway and after a minute he felt a hand on his shoulder, Irene saying, "You should have just got me up. How long have you been down here?" She came around and sat on the arm of the chair.

"Forty-five minutes, an hour."

He was suddenly aware of the ticking of the grandfather clock, and then his wife said, "She wouldn't be with him if she thought he did it, Bill."

"I'm not worried about whether *she thinks* he did it. I'm worried about if he did it."

"I think we have to trust her judgment on this."

"Like with Brian? With Joe Avery?"

"Come on, Bill, don't start that. They were different."

"But not so very different, were they? I wonder if we've failed her somehow, that she can't . . ." He stopped.

"It's not her. She hasn't met the right man."

"And Mark Dooher's the right man? God help us."

"Bill! We haven't even met him . . ."

"But he's on trial for killing his wife, hon. I'm sorry, they don't usually get to there unless . . ."

"Usually."

He took a breath and let it out. "Jesus. So what are we supposed to do?"

Irene draped her arm over his head. "Stand by her, I think, don't you? Hope she finally gets happy. Hope he's found not guilty."

"But that's just the law. How do you ever really believe it after all this?"

"I don't know if you do. But if he's found not guilty, we've got to support them. Don't you think that?"

"I don't know. I don't understand why her life changed, how it got so complicated and sad. It just breaks my heart."

"Mine too." She sighed. "Which is why we've got

to be with her, Bill. If it's right, if finally this Mark Dooher can make her happy."

But he was shaking his head. "People don't make other people happy. People make themselves happy. That's what I'm worried about."

She tugged at his hair gently. "You make me happy."

"No, you were happy when I met you, and we get along. We're lucky. Christina's got to decide that it's up to her, herself. She's still thinking it's all centered, one way or another, around some man. And it's not."

"It is for me," Irene said. "It really is. Maybe I'm not a highly evolved life form, but I believe choice of mate is relatively important in the scheme of things. And that's why I'm going to embrace them if it all works out, and do everything I can to see that it does. And you should, too."

40

On Wednesday afternoon, Amanda Jenkins rested for the prosecution, having never really recovered—or established—her momentum. She had called all of her witnesses.

The maintenance man at the San Francisco Golf Club had shown the jury the Cyclone fence by the end of the parking lot. It had a large hole in it.

Jenkins had trotted out Paul Thieu and the Taraval cops and the next-door neighbor, Frances Matsun, who (it turned out) had never gotten along with Mark Dooher very well, and who hadn't actually seen him screw the lightbulb from on to off at all.

On cross, Farrell clarified it—Dooher had reached up, fooled with it, done *something*. It looked like he might have unscrewed it.

Jenkins tried not to show it, but it was clear to Glitsky that she'd been beaten down by the relentless barrages that Farrell had launched against her witnesses. She was still trying to believe that the blood alone would be enough to convict and, further, that Emil Balian had convincingly put Dooher near the scene. It was a brave front: Jenkins pretending that the jury would come back with a guilty verdict, especially if they got to call Diane Price on rebuttal, if they could get her to paint the picture of a very different Mark Dooher. Glitsky admired Jenkins for not crumbling in public, but she was getting killed and everybody knew it.

Certainly, the newspapers and television had reached their verdict. This morning, driving to work, Glitsky had heard his name on the radio while he'd been channel surfing, and had forced himself to listen to his friendly local conservative radio talk jock who opined that the decision to bring Mark Dooher to trial at all on such shoddy evidence was an example of affirmative action's failure in the halls of the city. Glitsky, a black, and Jenkins, a woman, had been promoted beyond their levels of competency, and let's hear from you callers out there who think we ought to put an end to this nonsense and get back to hiring and promoting on merit alone.

The current had shifted.

Nevertheless, the morning began with a setback for the defense. As soon as Jenkins had finished her case-in-chief, Wes Farrell had filed a motion for directed verdict of acquittal, which asked the judge to find that no reasonable juror could convict on the evidence presented by the prosecution.

This motion was routinely filed by the defense when the prosecution rested, and was almost never granted. If the judge did rule favorably on this motion, he would dismiss the case, and Mark Dooher would be free. Thomasino opened by denying the motion, and Jenkins whispered to Glitsky, "The blood."

He nodded, noncommittal.

* * *

Farrell, having elected to give an opening statement in rebuttal to Jenkins's at the outset of the trial, stood and told Thomasino that the defense was ready to present its case and would like to start by calling the defendant, Mark Dooher.

This was a calculated gamble, but it showed the level of Farrell's confidence. The defendant had the absolute right not to testify, but a sympathetic demeanor and good story could go a long way toward humanizing a defendant, and this was to the good.

Also, after Dooher's outburst on the first day, he'd worn a mask, careful to show no emotion. Quietly paying attention to every word and nuance, he would occasionally confer with his two attorneys when some point struck him. He was interested and unbowed, though not yet a *person* to the jurors.

Dooher leaned over to Christina and whispered, "Wish me luck," then placed a fraternal hand on Farrell's shoulder, gave it a squeeze, and walked around his attorney. He approached the witness box in long strides. To all appearances, he was confident, even eager—finally—to tell his story.

Farrell came forward to the center of the courtroom and walked him through the familiar territory of the early afternoon, the hors d'oeuvres, the champagne, and so on.

"And after Sheila said she was going upstairs for a nap, what did you do then?"

Dooher looked toward the jury for a minute. He didn't want to include them too often—it would appear insincere, as though he was playing for them. But he knew it wouldn't hurt—it was only natural—to acknowledge their presence. "I moped around the house for a while, then I decided to go to the driving range. So I went out to my car . . ."

"Just a minute, Mark. You went out to your car. But before that, at the back door, do you remember what you did?"

"I don't remember anything specific, no."

"And yet we've heard Mrs. Matsun testify that you stopped and did something with the electric light above the door. Do you remember doing that?"

"No. There may have been cobwebs up in the light. Sometimes they gather there, I might have cleared them away, but I don't specifically remember doing anything." A quick look toward the jury, explaining. "I may have."

This, of course, had been rehearsed. Dooher wasn't denying anything that Frances Matsun had testified to. He was being reasonable, telling his own truth without attacking hers. It played, as they knew it would, very well.

"Mark, your house has an alarm system, doesn't it?"

A wry shake of the head. "Yes, it does."

"Did you turn it on when you left the house on this day?"

These carefully prepared questions would defuse Jenkins's contentions before she could even make them. "No. I just walked out of the house."

"Didn't you lock the door behind you, either?"

"No."

"Was this unusual? Why didn't you do either of these things?"

Dooher sat back a minute, phrasing his response. "I guess the real reason is that neither of them even occurred to me."

"Why not?"

"Well, first, it was light out. I wasn't thinking about somebody breaking in. We'd never been broken into before."

"But you didn't lock the door?"

"I go out to work every morning and don't lock the door behind me. It wasn't like I was leaving an empty house. Sheila was there. It never occurred to me she couldn't take care of herself. We live in a safe neighborhood, or I thought we did. When I do check the locks, it's usually before turning in at night, you know, like people do."

"What about the house alarm?"

"Sheila doesn't—didn't—like the alarm."

"Why not?"

"Because when we first got it installed, three or four times she opened a door to walk outside to take out the garbage or whatever, and it went off, and she had some trouble overriding the turn-off switch or something—anyway, it was a hassle for her. We didn't tend to use it unless we went on vacation, or away for the weekend, something like that. I wasn't about to turn it on when she was just taking a nap upstairs. If she woke up and went out for some reason and it went off, she'd have killed me."

Then to the driving range, where Dooher bought two buckets of balls. Yes, he remembered specifically which mat he'd hit from. He wore his most self-deprecating expression. "I'm afraid that before all this"—an inclusive gesture indicating the world they were in—"I used to be vain about my . . . about how I looked. I didn't like to appear to flounder. And this included my golf game. I didn't want people—anybody—to see me when I was working on my swing, maybe overcorrecting to find out what I was doing wrong . . ."

"Your Honor." Jenkins was showing her own impatience. "This is all very fascinating, but it doesn't answer the question of what mat he hit his golf balls from."

Thomasino leaned over the bench. "Just answer the question, Mr. Dooher."

"It was the last mat, at the very end, to the left as you go out the door of the clubhouse."

Farrell kept up the rhythm. "And you stayed, hitting golf balls off that mat, until when?"

"I think around nine-thirty, twenty to ten."

"Did you leave the mat at any time?"

"I went to the bathroom after the first bucket, bought a Coke in the office. Then went back out and finished hitting."

"All right." Farrell led them all, again, through the gruesome discovery, the emergency call, waiting for the police. It all came out, compelling and believable as he told it.

Now Farrell shifted gears. "Mark, Lieutenant Glitsky has testified that I was present at your house when he interrogated you on the night of the murder. Why was I there?"

"I called you and you came."

"Did I come as your lawyer, because you wanted to protect yourself from police questions? Because you knew you'd be suspected of murdering your wife?"

"No. None of that. I called you as a friend."

"Why did you call me, who happens to be your lawyer, out of all of your friends?"

"I have known you for thirty-five years. You are my best friend. That's why I called you."

Farrell glanced at the jury, then back to his client. "On another topic, during your last visit to Dr. Peter Harris's office, did you remove a vial of blood and take it with you?"

Dooher, still obviously amazed at the ridiculousness of the question, shook his head, looked directly at the jury for the last time. "No. No I did not."

"And finally, once and for all, and remembering that you are testifying under solemn oath, would you answer this question for the jury: Did you kill your wife?"

This time there were no histrionics. He sat forward, took a breath, let it out, and answered in an even, clear voice that rang through the courtroom. "As God is my judge, I did not."

Farrell nodded, said "Thank you," and turned on his heel. "Your witness."

Before Jenkins got to the blow-by-blow cross-examination of Dooher's movements throughout the afternoon and evening of June 7, she wanted to clear up one specific point.

She moved to the exhibit table and pulled two poster-size exhibits that she'd introduced as evidence during the questioning of the driving range's maintenance man. The first was a blown-up photograph of the hitting area taken from out in the middle of the range, and the other was a schematic rendering of the placement of the mats. She put both of these next to one another on an easel next to the witness chair.

"As you can see," she said, "these exhibits represent the layout of the driving range. Just so we're clear on where you hit your balls from, would you please point out to the jury the mat that you stood on?"

Cooperative and relaxed, Dooher did so.

"The very last mat, you're sure of that?"

"I am, yes."

"This is the mat nearest the hole in the fence leading to the parking lot, is it not?"

"I don't know about that. I'd never noticed the hole in the fence. Although if your witness says so, I guess it's there."

Jenkins stood unmoving in the center of the courtroom. After twenty or thirty seconds, the judge spoke to her. "Ms. Jenkins?"

She blinked and brought her attention back from where it had been.

Her cross-examination lasted three and a half hours.

She got nothing.

"What was that all about?" Christina sat at the table in their anteroom eating from a pile of carrot and celery sticks on a paper plate while the men busied themselves with salami sandwiches on sourdough rolls. "The exact mat you hit the balls from?"

Dooher shook his head. "I don't have any idea."

Farrell was chewing, staring out the window. "I don't like it. She's got something else she's not showing us."

"You mean new evidence?" Christina couldn't envision it. "How could that be, Wes? We've seen her discovery. We know all her witnesses. She'd have had to tell us before this."

"Well, that would be in the rules, that's true."

But Dooher was looking carefully at his friend. "Anyway, Wes, what could she have?"

"I don't know. But it worries me. It's my job to worry."

"Don't worry," Dooher said. "I was there at the last mat hitting golf balls and that's all there is to it."

Farrell nodded again. "Let's hope so."

Glitsky thought that Richie Browne believed Dooher's story in all its detail. He was the golf pro at the range and could have been sent from central casting—a well-formed man, mid-thirties, in slacks and a polo shirt. He had gotten to know Dooher in the three or four months prior to the murder when the defendant started frequenting his range instead of the Olympic's.

"Sure, he was there the whole time."

"You're sure?"

"I'm positive."

Farrell turned and faced the jury, including them in his certainty, asking back over his shoulder. "Were you aware of him the whole night?"

Browne took his time. "I remember him coming in. We talked about some new clubs he was considering —he'd been working with some new graphite shafts on his woods and thought he was going to go with them, buy a whole set, so you know I was interested. We're talking a thousand bucks here, so I was paying attention."

"And was that when he came in?"

"Yeah."

"And did he seem anxious, nervous, keyed up . . . ?"

"Objection! Calls for a conclusion."

Glitsky noticed that Jenkins was forward on the last three inches of her chair, elbows on the table, fingers templed at her lips. He didn't know what had galvanized her at this late date, when to him the conclusion was all but foreordained, but something clearly had.

Thomasino overruled her, though.

Farrell repeated the question, and Browne told him that Dooher had been relaxed and genial. "He talked about golf clubs. He didn't act any way."

"And then when he went out to hit some balls. When did you see him next?"

"I don't know exactly. Fifteen, twenty minutes later. I walked out to the door with a lady customer and saw him down at the end, head down, lost in it. Whack whack whack."

"Now, Mr. Browne, Mr. Dooher has testified that he came in and got a Coke about halfway through . . ."

"Your Honor, please!" Jenkins shot up from her seat. "Leading the witness."

Thomasino was paying close attention. To Glitsky's surprise, he didn't rule right away, spending a moment mulling. Then, simply. "Overruled."

Farrell couldn't lose. He kept right at it. "When did you see Mr. Dooher next?"

"Again, I didn't notice the exact time. He came in for a Coke." Jenkins slapped her hand on her table in frustration. "Maybe after his first bucket."

"Your Honor, my God!" Jenkins—up again.

Farrell spread his palms. "I didn't ask anything, Your Honor. The witness has volunteered this information."

"It's speculation—move to strike."

Thomasino raised a calming hand. "Yes it is, yes it is." He told the jury to disregard this last information, and Glitsky thought they could collectively do that about as easily as they could levitate on cue.

But the moment passed, and Farrell was finishing up. "And did you see Mr. Dooher at any other time during the course of this evening?"

"Sure. When he left."

"When he'd finished hitting two buckets of golf balls?"

"Objection! Speculation."

Thomasino sustained her again, but Farrell didn't care. He had gotten in nearly everything he wanted, and was finishing up. "Did you see Mr. Dooher when he left?"

"Yes."

"And how was he acting then?"

"Like he usually did. Normal. He came in, we talked a couple of minutes about his game. He told me a joke."

"He told you a joke?"

"Yeah, we talked a couple of minutes and then he asked me how you get a dog to stop humping your leg. That's how I remember I saw him when he was leaving. I was laughing."

"You were laughing together?"

"It was a good joke." Browne paused, looked over to the jury, gave them the punch line. "You give him a blow job."

The courtroom went silent for a second, then erupted into nervous laughter. Thomasino hit his gavel a few times, order was restored, and Farrell gave Richie Browne to Amanda Jenkins for cross-examination.

"Mr. Browne, I'm particularly interested in this Coke you saw Mr. Dooher get in the middle of his round of hitting golf balls. In your interview with Lieutenant Glitsky regarding this night, did you mention this trip to the Coke machine?"

"I guess not. I didn't remember at the time. It came back to me later, that it was that night."

"And do you remember it now?"

"Yes."

"So—to be absolutely clear, Mr. Browne—is it your testimony now, under oath, that Mr. Dooher bought a Coke in the middle of hitting his round of golf balls that night?"

Browne squirmed. "I think he came and got a Coke."

"You *think* Mr. Dooher came and got a Coke? You're not sure."

"I'm pretty sure."

"But not certain?"

Browne was physically reacting to the questioning, sitting back in the witness chair, arms crossed over his chest. "No, not certain. But I think it was that night."

"Mr. Browne, you're not certain you saw the defendant come in midway through the evening and get a Coke, is that your testimony?"

Farrell took the opening. "Asked and answered, Your Honor."

Thomasino agreed with him.

It was beginning to move quickly with Farrell's defense witnesses. No sooner had Richie Browne passed out into the gallery area than Farrell called Marcela Mendoza, a forty-two-year-old former supervisor of medical technicians at St. Mary's Hospital. After establishing her credentials and job duties during the twelve years she'd worked at the hospital, Farrell asked: "Ms. Mendoza, working in the blood unit of the laboratory at the hospital, did you ever experience a situation where blood that had been taken from a patient for tests got lost somehow?"

"Yes."

"Commonly? Wait, please, before you answer that, how many blood tests did you do?"

"Well, we did, I guess, six or seven hundred blood tests every week or so."

"A hundred a day?"

"Roughly. That's about right."

"And how often did a sample of blood get mislabeled, or misplaced, or lost, on average, in the twelve years you worked at the hospital?"

"Objection, Your Honor. The defendant's doctor didn't work at this hospital."

Glitsky had the impression that Farrell had been hoping that Jenkins would say this very thing. "Well, Your Honor, that's exactly the point. We intend to show that the blood could have come from any one of a number of places."

Thomasino's brows went up and down. "Overruled. Proceed."

The question clearly made Ms. Mendoza uncomfortable. It wasn't a piece of information the public would feel very good about. In fact, while she'd been working at the hospital, she would not have answered any questions about lost blood—both because she would not have wanted to, and because she would have been ordered not to.

But Farrell's investigator had found her in August and convinced her that her expertise in this area could save the life of an innocent man. "I'd say we'd lose one or two a week."

"A *week?*" Farrell, who of course already knew the answer, feigned shock. "One or two a week?"

"Sometimes more, sometimes less."

"And this lost blood, where does it go?"

Mendoza allowed herself a small smile. "If we

knew that, Mr. Farrell, it wouldn't be lost now, would it?"

All agreement, Farrell stepped closer to her. "Now in your own personal experience, Ms. Mendoza, did you ever have a lab technician drop a vial of blood and not report it?"

"Yes."

"And why was that?"

"They didn't want to get in trouble, so they said they just never got the blood to do the tests on it in the first place."

"And are you personally familiar with a case like this?"

"Yes."

"Could you explain it a little more fully?"

"One of my people did exactly what I just described, and I didn't report it, which was why I was let go."

This wasn't a point to press, and Farrell moved along. "Ms. Mendoza, about how many blood labs are there in the city?"

"Big labs, there's about eight or nine. Smaller labs, doctor's offices, mobile units, blood banks—there are probably hundreds, I don't know exactly."

"Certainly more than fifty?"

"Yes."

"And in your experience, was there ever a problem with lost blood at any of these facilities? In transit, to and from doctor's offices, something like that?"

Ms. Mendoza didn't like it, but she knew what she knew. "Most of the blood, there's never a problem," she said.

"I realize that. But sometimes . . . ?"

"Of course. Sure."

* * *

The blood testimony continued to build relent-lessly, doubly damning, Glitsky thought, because there really wasn't much Amanda Jenkins could do on cross-examination. Doctors and technicians from County General, St. Luke's, the Masonic Blood Bank and sev-eral other locations all came to the stand and testified for ten minutes each, all essentially saying the same thing: Blood got lost all the time. It was possible—maybe not probable, and perhaps difficult, but certainly possible—for a person to pick up a vial of blood and walk out of a facility with it.

The worst moment from Glitsky's perspective came at the very end of the day when Farrell called a Sergeant Eames from Park station. It was always un-nerving when the *defense* called a law enforcement per-son to testify. For the past six years, Eames had worked on cases involving voodoo, Santeria and satanic wor-ship, all of which used blood from a variety of sources in their rituals. Eames was of the opinion that any cop in the city who wanted to get his hands on samples of human blood would have to look no further than the evidence locker of any district station on a typical Sat-urday night.

41

JIM FLAHERTY WAS ALONE IN HIS SPARTAN BEDROOM. He sat at his desk, intending to put the finishing touches on his yearly Christmas sermon and then—on this blessedly unbooked Thursday evening—he was going to get to sleep before midnight.

But first he'd tune in to the ten o'clock news, where he was heartened by the analysis of the events of the trial. Wes Farrell's parade of defense witnesses had demolished any lingering doubt about its outcome. Mark wasn't going to get convicted—the prosecution's case was in rags.

Flaherty told himself that he'd never really entertained the notion that Mark had killed Sheila, but the blood had come close to shaking his faith. Now, though, it looked as if Farrell had put his finger into that potential hole in the dike, and what Mark had contended all along was true. The blood could have come from anywhere and the missing blood from his own doctor's office had been a terrible coincidence.

It was critical that Flaherty be clear on this score. Farrell had asked him to be ready to testify about Mark's character beginning as early as tomorrow.

He opened his desk drawer and pulled out the sheaf of looseleaf papers.

And there was a knock on his door.

He loathed interruptions in his bedroom—it was the only truly private place he had, the only personal time he ever got. But everyone on the staff here at the rectory knew that and protected his privacy, so this must be important.

Father Herman, his majordomo, stood in the hallway in the at-ease position, and behind him, hands clasped in front of him, was Eugene Gorman, pastor of St. Emygdius. Seeing him, Flaherty's stomach tightened, and he put his hand over it.

Herman was trying to explain that he had asked Father Gorman to wait downstairs and he'd send the Archbishop down to see him in the study, but . . .

"That's all right, Father. This is an old friend. You want to come in here, Gene. I don't have anything but hard chairs to sit on."

When the door closed behind them, Flaherty walked across the room and sat on his desk. Gorman stood awkwardly and finally, looking behind him, sat down on the Archbishop's bed. "I'm sorry to bother you. I wouldn't have if this weren't an emergency."

"It's all right," Flaherty began, "we're—"

But Gorman cut him off. "I have been examining my conscience now for months, and I don't know what else to do. I need for you to hear my confession."

Flaherty cocked his head at the man across from him. He seemed to have aged five years since they'd last spoken in May or June.

The light was dim. A crucifix, the only ornament in the room, hung over Flaherty's bed.

Gorman's eyes were tortured, pleading.

The Archbishop nodded once, boosted himself off the desk, and crossed to the bed. He put his hand behind Gorman's head and stood like that for a moment.

Then he went over to his dresser and picked up his stole—the sacramental cloth. Draping it over his shoulders, he returned to the bed, and sat down next to Gorman, making the sign of the cross.

Gorman began. "Bless me Father, for I have sinned. I am living in a state of mortal sin, in despair."

"God will give you grace, Gene. He won't abandon you."

But Gorman didn't seem to hear. He continued. "I am tormented by guilty knowledge and bound by the seal of the confessional. It's destroying me, Jim . . . I can't function."

Flaherty began to offer his counsel to Gorman— this was one of the heaviest burdens of the priesthood, penitents had terrible secrets they needed to confess . . .

Gorman couldn't hold it in any longer. "This was murder, Jim. Literal murder."

Entering his apartment after another night on the town, Wes Farrell was confronting another of the deadly sins, pride. The headiness of his success had not obliterated his doubts about his friend or any moral qualms concerning his strategies at the trial, but he would be damned if he would let any of that nonsense stand in his way now.

Winning was what mattered. Winners had to learn to ignore those small voices of discontent, the traces of timidity, that hampered lesser souls, that were, indeed, the hallmark of lesser souls.

Wasn't it De Gaulle who had said that to govern was to choose? Well, Wes thought that the sentiment translated well into his own situation—he would no longer consider other paths he might have taken, could have taken, that were perhaps more righteous and less ambiguous. No, he had *chosen* to believe Mark Dooher, *chosen* to defend him. And those decisions had elevated him in his community. And that was what mattered.

After a point, you just didn't have to think about certain things anymore.

He had been reading about his exploits every day, hearing himself described in the various media as brilliant, dogged, ruthless, even charismatic. He wasn't about to give any of this up by worrying too much about the vehicle that had propelled him to here. It was Faustian, perhaps, but he'd often said he'd sell his soul for this chance.

It might have disappointed him when he'd been younger and more idealistic, but right now all he could think was . . . I'll take it, I'll take it, I'll take it, and while we're at it, give me more.

The time was eleven-fifteen. He was entering his apartment, filled with these thoughts. A dinner at John's Grill had turned into a testimonial from some of the other diners who had recognized him. He was resolving to change his residence in the next couple of months, get himself another house and a housecleaner to go with it, a new car, fix up the office as befitted his station.

The telephone was ringing and he crossed the room, petting an ecstatic Bart, and picked it up.

"Wes. This is Jim Flaherty."

The usually husky, confident tone was missing. "Your Excellency, how are you?"

"Well, I'm not too good, to tell you the truth." A long breath. "I might as well come right out with it, Wes. I'm afraid I've decided I'm not going to be able to testify for you, for Mark, about his character."

Farrell pulled out a kitchen chair and sat heavily upon it. He had been expecting to call the Archbishop tomorrow and wrap up his defense.

"But just two nights ago . . . ?"

"I realize that. I know. But something has come up . . ."

"What?"

Another pause. "I'm not at liberty to say."

"Archbishop, Father, wait a minute. You can't just—"

"Excuse me, Wes. This is a very difficult decision, one of the hardest of my life, but I've made it, and that's all there is to say about it. I'm sorry."

The line went dead. Farrell lifted the receiver away from his ear and looked at it as though it were alive. "*You're* sorry?"

He put the phone down and stared at his wavy image, reflected in the kitchen window.

Flaherty sat, alone again, on the side of his hard bed. He'd wrestled with it for an hour or more, trying to find some other interpretation for Father Gorman's words. He grudgingly admired Gorman's decision, the way he'd come to him for confession—the strategy was, Flaherty thought, positively Jesuitical. Gorman never said Dooher's name, never even implied whether it was a male or a female who had committed the murder or, for that matter, whether it was one of his parishioners.

He didn't, technically, break the seal of the confessional.

But there was small doubt about what he was saying, and none at all about whether it was true.

42

A WAR HAD BROKEN OUT IN THOMASINO'S chambers.

The lead attorneys, the judge and Glitsky had originally gathered to discuss logistics. Farrell had decided that, after all, he wasn't going to call character witnesses—he didn't need them. The defense was going to rest.

And then Jenkins had dropped her bomb, saying she would like to call a rebuttal witness, someone who wasn't on her original witness list, a man who had been at the driving range during the time Dooher claimed he was, and who hadn't seen him.

Glitsky was sitting in his chair off to the side, and Farrell, looking again more as he'd appeared earlier in the trial—the King of Insomnia—was screaming.

"She's known about this witness all along, Your Honor! If I'd known about this witness or his testimony, I never would have asked Mr. Dooher to take the stand. And this witness is nowhere on any of her lists. This is an incredible, unbelievable, *egregious* breach of professional ethics."

"Oh get a grip, Wes," Jenkins retorted, "it's nothing of the sort. It's Prop One Fifteen." She was referring to California Proposition 115, which eased the prosecution's obligations regarding discovery to the defense. "The law changes every once in a while, Wes, you'll be surprised to hear. Maybe you ought to try to keep up on it."

"I keep up on the goddamn law as well as a goddamn rookie homicide prosecutor on her first case that she's blown all to hell because she doesn't know how . . ."

Thomasino, atypically wearing his robes in chambers, had heard all he would tolerate—Glitsky was surprised he'd let it go as far as it had—and now he was slapping his hand down on his desk, hard. "All right, all right, enough! I said enough!"

Both attorneys sat, breathing hard, in front of the judge's desk. Thomasino, not jolly on his best day, was a study in controlled rage, his eyebrows pulled together until they met, a muscle in his jaw vibrating under the pressure of holding it so tight.

Gradually, he gathered himself. The face relaxed by small degrees. "This is a matter of law," he said, almost whispering, "not a matter of personality. Although, Ms. Jenkins, I must admit to some discomfort about it. Surely you knew about this witness before this and if that was the case, surely the name should have appeared in discovery."

The name they were discussing was Michael Ross. In the early days of the investigation, Glitsky had gone out to the San Francisco Golf Club and reviewed the credit card receipts for the night of June 7. Michael Ross had paid for a bucket of golf balls by Visa card, and the transaction had been rung up at 8:17 p.m. Glitsky had brought the receipt in to Jenkins and they'd had a discussion about it in her cramped and airless office.

The moment was etched clearly in Glitsky's memory. Jenkins's eyes took on a faraway look as she'd sat at her desk, fingering the receipt. He had figuratively seen the lightbulb go on over her head.

"Why don't you go out and interview this fellow Ross by yourself, Abe? You don't even need to bring your tape recorder. It's probably nothing anyway. And don't write it up until we've had a chance to talk about what he's told you."

Glitsky had been a cop long enough, he didn't need a road map. Jenkins wasn't suggesting anything illegal—it could be said that she was trying to save Abe the trouble of writing up lots of meaningless paperwork. It wasn't even procedurally suspect. He interviewed lots of people in the course of any investigation, and often these interviews were casual, limited, irrelevant to the case. There was no need to tape anything.

Of course, in this case, Glitsky knew what Jenkins was really telling him—she wanted to limit what she had to give to Farrell as discovery. She knew early on that their evidence case was weak, and she was going to sandbag the defense if she got the chance, which was what she was doing in Thomasino's chambers early on this Friday morning.

Perry Mason notwithstanding, real trials were not supposed to deal in surprises. The discovery process—where the prosecution must turn over to the defendant all evidence it possesses relating to the case—is supposed to guarantee that the defendant sees all the cards before the game. It's how those cards are played that determines the winner.

Jenkins was supposed to provide Farrell with a list of the prospective witnesses she might call during the course of the trial. She didn't *have to* call every witness on the list, or any of them, but in theory she couldn't call anyone who wasn't on the list.

And Michael Ross hadn't been.

Back in the war zone, the soldiers continued to scuffle. Jenkins was holding up the faded yellow tissue with Michael Ross's name and Visa number on it, and pointing out that she had xeroxed it, both sides, and it had been turned over to Wes Farrell when he'd requested discovery documents.

"Is that true, Mr. Farrell? Do you have a copy of this document?"

"So what, Your Honor? What's the document mean? I even ask her back last June, July sometime, and she says it means what it means. So I look on her witness list, there's no Michael Ross, she's not allowed to call him, am I right?"

"I'm calling him in rebuttal."

Farrell brought his own hand down on the edge of the armchair. "You knew all along you were going to call him. Don't give me that crap."

"Mr. Farrell." Thomasino, too, was heating up. "If I hear any more profanity out of you in these chambers, or out of your witnesses or defendants in the courtroom, I'm going to hold you in contempt. We're not street fighting here, and we're not gangsta rappers, and if you say so much as 'darn' in my presence, you'd better have an unassailable reason for doing so."

Farrell sat back in his chair. "Sorry, Your Honor. I mean no disrespect."

"Well, intention or no, it *is* disrespectful and I'm not going to have it." Thomasino's eyes strafed the room, came to rest on Jenkins. No one, it seemed, was going to get off easy here. "Now, as to this witness, Ms. Jenkins, do you care to explain to me how you saw fit to include this credit card slip in your discovery documents and yet at the same time omit the man's name from your witness list?"

"Your Honor, he's a rebuttal witness. I didn't know I was going to call him until Mr. Dooher testified."

Glitsky was kind of enjoying seeing Farrell sputter, sitting forward now, seeking nonprofanities. "I believe that is not the truth, Your Honor," he finally said. "When did she interview this witness?"

"Lieutenant Glitsky interviewed him."

Finally in on the action, Glitsky took the chance to goad Farrell further. "About two weeks after your client killed his wife, give or take."

But the attorney ignored the challenge. "Two weeks?" He turned to the judge. "Your Honor, two weeks. She knew she was going to call him. Where were Glitsky's notes on the interview, the transcription, anything?"

Abe was glad to see Jenkins cover for him for a change. "I didn't ask for a tape. It was a preliminary interview."

"Ms. Jenkins," Thomasino said, "I'm not liking what I'm hearing here. It sounds to me like you deliberately tried to circumvent the discovery process."

"Damn . . . darn straight she did!"

The judge pointed a finger across the room. "And you, Lieutenant, I find this hard to believe of you."

Glitsky shrugged. "I just build 'em, Your Honor. I don't fly 'em."

"Judge." Jenkins wasn't having it. "How could I have put this man on my witness list? He was no part of my case-in-chief. What was he going to say? That he didn't see Mark Dooher at the driving range? What am I supposed to do, provide a list of everybody who didn't see Mark Dooher at the driving range? That's pretty much the whole city, isn't it? And, in fact, the prosecution rested its case against Mr. Dooher without using Mr. Ross. If Mr. Farrell here hadn't opened this whole can of worms by having his client testify, we wouldn't be having this discussion right now. It would never have come up."

"All right, all right." Again, the warning hand, palm up. "I'm going to let him testify."

Farrell went ballistic. "Your Honor, please . . . !"

But finally, Thomasino's fuse blew. "Mr. Farrell, if *you* please. We're going outside now into the courtroom and Mr. Ross is going to testify. That's my ruling and I don't want to hear another word about it."

Michael Ross was a twenty-one-year-old student at San Francisco State University—clean-cut, well-spoken, well dressed. From Glitsky's perspective, he was the last hope, if in fact it wasn't already way too late. But Jenkins, no denying it, had played this card masterfully.

"Mr. Ross," she began, "on the evening of June seventh of this year, would you tell us what you did between the hours of seven and ten p.m.?"

Ross had a fresh and open face and he sat forward in his chair, enthusiastic yet serious. "Well, my wife and I put our daughter to bed"—he looked over at the jury—"she was just a year old and we put her down to bed at seven o'clock. Then we had dinner together. We barbecued hamburgers. It was a really nice night, and after dinner, about eight, I asked my wife if she'd mind if I went and drove a few golf balls."

He seemed to think this might need some more explanation, but hesitated, then continued. "Anyway, I went to the San Francisco Golf Club's range and hit a large bucket of balls, and then came back home."

"And what time did you leave the range?"

Ross thought a moment. "I was home by nine-thirty, so I must have left at about ten after nine, quarter after, something like that."

Jenkins produced the credit card slip, showing that Ross had picked up his bucket of balls at eight-seventeen, and entered it into evidence as People's 14. "So, Mr. Ross, while you were out in the driving range area, did you go to a particular station to hit your bucket of balls?"

"I did."

"And where was that?"

"I turned left out of the clubhouse and walked down to the third mat from the end."

"The third from the end on the left side as you left the clubhouse?"

"Yes."

Again, show-and-tell, and Jenkins produced the posters she'd first used with the maintenance man and then during her cross-examination of Mark Dooher. She mounted them onto the easel next to the witness box, side by side. "Could you point out to the jury, Mr. Ross, just where you stood, according to both of these visual aids?"

He did.

"And how far, then, were you from the first mat, the one Mr. Dooher has testified he used on this night?"

Ross stole a neutral glance at Dooher. "I don't know exactly. Twenty or thirty feet, I'd guess."

"So Mr. Ross, to reiterate: You went out with your bucket of golf balls at around eight twenty-five and you stood hitting shots from a mat and a tee three spots from the end on the left side, finishing up at around nine-fifteen. Is this an accurate rendition of the facts you've presented?"

"Yes."

"All right, then. During this period of time, nearly an hour, while you stood two mats away from the last mat on the left, did you at any time see the defendant, Mark Dooher, at the last tee?"

"No. I didn't see anybody. There was nobody at the last tee."

A buzz coursed through the room. Glitsky noticed Dooher leaning over, whispering to Christina. Farrell was sitting, face set, eyes forward, his hands crossed on the desk in front of him.

Jenkins pressed on. "Did you see Mr. Dooher anywhere there at the range, at any time that night?"

Ross again spent some a minute studying the defendant, then said he'd never seen him before in his life.

"Mr. Ross, was there anybody on the second tee? In other words, on the tee next to you, between you and the last tee?"

"No. I was the last one down that way."

"There was no one either at the first or second tee the whole time you were there hitting golf balls, between eight twenty-five and nine-fifteen p.m. on June seventh of this year?"

"That's right. Nobody."

* * *

Farrell tried to smile, to convey the impression that this wasn't a problem. Glitsky didn't think he succeeded—he looked a couple of days older than God.

"Mr. Ross," he began. "You've testified that you hit a large bucket of golf balls on the night in question, is that correct?"

"Yes."

"And how many balls are in a large bucket?"

The witness seemed to be trying to visualize a bucket. He smiled, helpful. "I'd say eighty or a hundred."

"A hundred golf balls. And is it true that you were at your mat, hitting these hundred golf balls for fifty minutes—eight twenty-five until about nine-fifteen?"

Ross did the math and nodded. "That's about right."

"Would that be about one ball every thirty seconds?"

"About, yes."

Farrell glanced over at the jury, including them. "Perhaps some members of the jury aren't familiar with how things work at a driving range. Would you please describe in detail your actions to hit each golf ball?"

This seemed to strike Ross as mildly amusing, but he remained cooperative and friendly. "I lean over, pick a ball out of the bucket, then either put it on a tee—they have a built-up rubber tee you can use—or lay it on the mat. Then I line up my shot, check my position, take a breath, relax, swing."

Farrell seemed happy with this. "And then you do this again, is that right? Do you do this every time you hit a ball?"

"Pretty close, I'd say. Yeah."

"And would you say hitting a golf ball is a fairly intense activity? Does it take a lot of concentration?"

Ross laughed. "It's like nothing else."

"You're saying it *is* intense, then, aren't you?"

"Yes."

"Would you say you get yourself into almost a trancelike state?"

"Objection. The witness is not an expert in trances, Your Honor."

Jenkins was sustained, but Farrell was doing a good job drawing the picture. If Ross had hit a ball every thirty seconds, going through his routine on each ball, and he was concentrating deeply on every swing . . . "Is it possible, Mr. Ross, that someone could have been hitting balls a couple of mats away and, concentrating as you were, you might not have noticed?"

"No. It's not like you're not aware of what's around you."

"It's not? Then you recall how many other people were at the driving range that night, don't you?"

Ross shrugged, discomfort beginning to show. "It was a quiet night. Tuesday. Less than average."

"Were there twenty people there?"

"I don't know exactly. Something like that."

"Were they all men?"

"I don't know."

"Could you give us a rough breakdown as to the races of the people hitting golf balls? Blacks, whites, Hispanics?"

"No."

"Was there someone on the other side of you? Behind you, back toward the office?"

"A couple of mats over, yes."

"Was this person a man or a woman."

"A man, I think."

"You think. How tall was he?"

Ross was shaking his head. "Come on, give me a break, I don't know."

Farrell came closer to him. "I can't give you a break, Mr. Ross. Hitting one golf ball every thirty seconds, is it your testimony that you are positive, without a doubt, that for the entire time you hit your large bucket of golf balls there was no one on the last mat at the end?"

Ross didn't crack. He knew what he knew. "That's right."

Farrell went and got a drink of water, giving himself time to think of his next line of questioning. By the time he was back at the witness box, he had it. With the bonus of a chance to put in a dig at Jenkins.

"Mr. Ross, since we have just this morning learned that you would be a witness in this trial, you have not spoken to anyone from the defense before, have you?"

"No."

"Have you spoken before to anyone from the prosecution or the police?"

"Yes."

"Did you give a sworn statement to them about the testimony you're giving today that they asked you to sign?"

"No."

This was about as far as Farrell could go in attacking Ross's credibility. He had to go fishing again. "What do you study at college, Mr. Ross?"

A welcome change for Ross. He brightened right up. "I'm a criminal justice major."

This surprised Farrell, but it didn't make him unhappy. "Indeed. By any chance do you plan to pursue a career in law enforcement?"

"Yes I do. I'd like to go to the San Francisco Police Academy."

A pause, Farrell formulating it. "Have you been following this case in the newspapers, Mr. Ross. On television?"

"Sure."

"You know, then, don't you, that your testimony is helpful to the prosecution here?"

"Yes."

This was the best Farrell was going to do. He decided to quit while he was ahead. "Thank you. No further questions."

43

DIANE PRICE WAS LESS NERVOUS THAN SAM Duncan, which was why she was driving. In the six months since she'd first come to Sam with her story, her life had changed.

At first, Diane had been opposed to any public admission of what had happened between her and Mark Dooher—it had been her own personal tragedy, tawdry and shameful. She'd testify at the trial if she got the chance, but until then she'd keep a low profile, live her normal life with her husband and kids.

She did not factor in the insatiable maw of the media, the hot-button buzz of her story, the fact that she was attractive, articulate and intelligent. Sam Duncan asked her permission to go to then-Sergeant Abe Glitsky and tell him about the rape—surely it was relevant to the murder charge Dooher was facing. He'd agreed and called in Amanda Jenkins, and within two weeks Diane had been identified and the notoriety had begun.

The story in the *Chronicle* had been followed by an

interview in *People*. *Mother Jones* put her on the cover and devoted half of their September issue to "Life After Rape." Diane had been contacted by a movie producer and signed an option agreement on her life story. She'd been invited to speak at least a dozen times, at first to small groups around San Francisco, but later to larger gatherings—a NOW convention in Atlanta, a gender issues conference in Chicago, a sexual harassment seminar in Phoenix.

And it was ironic, she thought, that all of this public discourse had been what had finally healed her private heart. Her husband, Don, stood by her through the fifteen minutes of her fame, and when the first flush had died down, they were left with their home and their family. And the bitterness that she'd carried all the years, which had finally prodded her to go to Sam Duncan's Rape Crisis Center in the first place, had been replaced by a calm sense of empowerment.

She didn't need to talk about it anymore. She'd learned from the experience, albeit the hard, slow way, but she'd come to the belief that this was the only way people really benefited from pain or loss or hardship anyway—first by acknowledging it and then, over time, to see how it had changed you and fit those changes into how you lived.

She became a regular volunteer at the Rape Crisis Counseling Center, working alongside Sam Duncan, helping other women, perhaps keeping them from going where she'd been. It was fulfilling, immediate, therapeutic.

So today, what she thought would be her one last public appearance didn't worry her. Amanda Jenkins had called her early in the week and said she expected that Wes Farrell would begin calling his own character witnesses on Thursday or Friday and she would then be free to call Diane. Was she ready?

And then, last night—Thursday—Amanda had said she ought to come down to the Hall of Justice by noon. The prosecution would probably be calling her to testify about Mark Dooher's character in the early afternoon.

As it transpired, of course, Farrell had decided not to use his character witnesses, but there was no way for Amanda Jenkins to have gotten that word out to Diane Price before she left to come down. By the time the attorneys had come back to the courtroom from their extended meeting about Michael Ross in Thomasino's chambers, Sam and Diane were on their way.

So she pulled into the All-Day Lot—$5.00/No In & Out—and the two women sat for a moment in the car. A fierce, cold and blustery wind whipped trash up the lane of the parking lot—a milk carton bounced along and out of their sight like a tumbleweed.

"You ready to go out into this?" Sam asked her. She had her hand on the door handle, but didn't look as though she was prepared just yet. Huddled into an over-size down jacket, Sam looked tiny and vulnerable.

"I think the real storm's going to be inside," Diane said. "Are *you* all right?"

"Sure," Sam said, too quickly.

"You're nervous."

A nod.

"Don't worry. I won't blow this. I say what happened and they try to shake my story, which they won't be able to do, and then we leave and this whole thing is behind us, and they put that bastard in jail where he belongs." She looked over at Sam, still inside herself. "That's not it, is it?"

Sam shook her head.

"Wes Farrell?" Diane had learned all about Sam and Wes.

Another nod. "I'm going to hate him after he questions you. I know I am. That's all. And I don't want to." She blew out a quick breath. "It's just the end of something. The final end."

"I'll be gentle with him," Diane said, then patted the other woman's leg. "Let's go, okay?"

They crossed Bryant, leaning into the wind, and came to the steps of the Hall, where Sam held open one of the huge glass double doors and they entered into the cavernous open lobby.

Or not directly. First, a makeshift plywood wall funneled visitors toward a door frame, to the side of which sat a desk manned by two uniformed policemen. A couple of reporters had stationed themselves outside the courtrooms to be ready for just such arrivals, and they attached themselves to the two women, asking the usual inane questions as they fell into the desultory queue for the security check.

Diane was wearing designer jeans, a couple of layers of sweaters and a heavy raincoat, a large leather carrybag slung over her shoulder. Moving forward with the line of people entering the Hall, trying to respond politely to the reporters and stay close to Sam, it didn't register to Diane that the door frame was the building's metal detector until she was walking through it, setting off the beeper.

"Oh shit," she said as the policemen stopped them, took the carryall from her and put it on the desk and told her to step back through the entrance again. "No, wait." Reaching for the carryall, trying to take it back from him. "We'll just go back and put this in the car, I'll just . . ."

But it was too late. The policeman, alerted by the

weight of it, had already pulled it open and was reaching inside. "Everybody else! Hold it! Step back!"

"What?" Sam asked.

"You!" The cop had Diane by the arm and was moving her away to the side. "Get over there, put your hands against that wall. Do it! Now!" Then, to his partner, gesturing to the line forming behind the door frame. "Keep them back. Get on the phone and get a female officer down here."

"What is this?" Sam demanded. "What's going on?"

Diane started to turn around. "I know . . ."

But the officer yelled at her again. "Against that wall! Don't you move!" Then he lifted his hand out of the oversize purse.

He was holding a small, chrome-plated handgun.

At about the same moment, back in their office across the street, the mood had shifted from relief at getting a piece of Michael Ross to fury at Wes Farrell's decision to abandon his character witnesses.

Dooher was fuming. "What do you mean, you're resting? We've got to call Jim Flaherty."

Farrell was calmly shaking his head. "We're not calling Flaherty. We're not doing character."

"We have to do character, Wes. Character wins it for us."

"We've already won it. We don't need it." Farrell was giving it a more confident spin than he felt after the nearly disastrous testimony of Michael Ross, which in spite of his cross remained a serious evidentiary chip for the prosecution.

Wes wasn't going to tell Mark that the Archbishop had withdrawn as a witness unless he absolutely had to. The momentum had shifted, and Farrell's last and best hope was that he could save what he'd already accomplished. He still had a good chance to get Mark an acquittal. But he was holding all this close.

Christina was standing by the doorway. "I thought you could never get enough. You've said that a hundred times. And now we've just had a hit from this Ross character—I think we do need more, Wes."

"Well, I want to thank you both for your input, but unless you're going to fire me, Mark, this is my trial, and I'm done. We've won it. I've got a closing argument that's irrefutable. Christina, I'm sorry you don't get to cross-examine Diane Price. I'm sorry we didn't use you, and I believe you would take her apart, but I don't want any hint of bad character about Mark, not now. Even if we can refute. It's not worth the risk when we're so far up. You both have got to trust me here. I've done a pretty fair job so far. I promise you it's going to work."

But Dooher wasn't ready to give it up. "How long have you known this, that you weren't going to call Flaherty?"

"Frankly, Mark, I don't know. There was always that possibility, right from the beginning. I wanted to keep the door open as long as I could in case I needed him, but now it's my judgment that I don't. We don't."

Christina spoke up again. "I'd like to know where they got Michael Ross. What was that about? How could he have been where he said he was?"

"He wasn't," Dooher said flatly. "They made him up. Glitsky and Jenkins invented him."

Christina believed it, Farrell could tell. But it was more than any one witness or decision at this point— Wes knew that Christina had bought the package with Mark.

If the facts didn't fit, then the facts must be wrong.

As a defense lawyer, she was inexperienced; as a person, she was naive. And she made the novice's mistake. She confused "not guilty," a legal concept that meant the prosecution had failed to establish guilt, with "innocent," a *fact* of behavior.

But this was not the moment for these niceties. Farrell forced a relaxed tone. "How Ross got to testify is a long and tedious story about attorney duplicity that I'd be happy to recount for you at our victory celebration. But meanwhile, I'd like to put this thing to bed before Jenkins pulls any more quasi-legal shenanigans out of her bag of tricks—ones that might hurt us."

One last shot from the defendant. "You're sure we got it, Wes? This is my life here."

He forced himself to meet Dooher's eyes. "I have no doubts."

By the lunch recess, news of the arrest of Diane Price for carrying a concealed weapon had spread through the Hall, along with the myriad theories attendant upon any event of this nature: She had been planning to assassinate Dooher; she was going to kill herself as a last, desperate cry for help; or maim herself as a publicity stunt.

Diane's plea was that the whole thing was simply a mistake. She'd carried a gun for protection for years and years, since a few months after the rape—it was registered, even, though she had no license to carry it concealed on her person. She'd had no violent agenda. She simply hadn't realized that there was a metal detector at the entrance to the Hall of Justice.

This explanation was, of course, dismissed by every law enforcement professional in the building, and Diane was taken upstairs—Sam Duncan abandoned, scuffling to locate the Crisis Center's attorney. Diane spent three hours in custody before being cited and released on the misdemeanor.

Every person in the courtroom—the gallery as well as the principals—was aware of the drama that had occurred outside during the lunch recess.

With this as a backdrop, Amanda Jenkins stepped up and presented her closing argument. The facts, she said, spoke for themselves, and allowed for no other interpretation than that Mark Dooher had murdered his wife on the evening of June 7. The defendant had not been at the driving range when he said he was. They had a witness who'd positively identified his car near his house when the murder had been committed, another witness who'd been twenty feet from where Dooher was supposed to have been, and had never seen him.

Why hadn't he seen him? Because Dooher hadn't been there, ladies and gentlemen. He'd been home stabbing his wife, faking a burglary. The prosecution had shown the linear connection between the blood taken from Dr. Harris's office on the same day that Dooher had been there—indeed, within *minutes* of when the defendant had been in the *same examining room*. And then later this same blood, not even close to the most common type of blood, and tainted with EDTA, had been splashed on Sheila Dooher's bed and body. No one else but Mark Dooher could have done this.

The jury must return, Jenkins concluded, with a verdict of murder in the first degree.

Farrell stood as though lost in thought, scanning the yellow pages of his legal pad, on the table in front of him, for a last second before pushing back his chair and finally positioning himself in front of the jury box.

"Ladies and gentlemen," he began, then took another step forward and lowered his voice. This was now simply a talk with these jurors, whom he'd come to know. Intimate and familiar. "I remember that back in school, when I was first being taught how to write an essay, I had a teacher—Mrs. Wilkins—and she said if we only remembered three things about essays, we'd get an A in her class.

"First"—he held up a finger—"first you write what you are going to say. Next you say it. Then, number three, you summarize what you just said." He broke a smile, homespun and sincere. "I'm a bit of a slow learner, but I got an A in that course. And ever since, I've been comfortable with that essay formula. Which is why it's lucky I'm a lawyer, I suppose, because that's a little bit what a trial is supposed to be like.

"We've been here over the last couple of weeks listening to the evidence in this case, *trying* to see if we can resolve one question, and resolve it beyond a reasonable doubt: Does the evidence show that Mark Dooher, the defendant over there"—he turned and pointed—"that Mark Dooher killed his wife?"

Back to the jury, his voice now harsher in tone, though still at only the volume of whisper. "I'm going to let you in on something, ladies and gentlemen. It does not. Not even close. Let's look for a last time at what the prosecution has given you to consider, what they say they have *proven*." He stopped and looked back over his shoulder at Glitsky and Jenkins.

"A motive? Certainly, a man who apparently has been happily married for over twenty-five years to the same woman would need some overwhelming and immediate reason to decide to kill his wife in cold blood.

"The prosecution's theory is that Mark Dooher did it for the insurance money. Now, forget for the moment the fact that Mr. Dooher is a well-paid attorney, that he owns a house worth a million dollars, and that his retirement is secure. Forget all that and focus on this question: Where's the proof of this motive theory? Did the prosecution present any witnesses supporting any part of it? They did not. No proof. No witnesses. A bald assertion with no basis in fact."

Farrell glanced at the clock—3:15. He had a lot to say, but suddenly he knew with relief that he was going to finish today. It was nearly over. He went over to the table and drank some water, then returned to the panel.

"Now let's talk for a minute about the evidence of the crime itself, evidence found at the scene which they contend *proves beyond a reasonable doubt* an inextricable link between Mark Dooher and this murder."

He stood mute before the jury box, making eye contact with each juror, one by one. The process took nearly fifteen seconds—an eternity in the courtroom—the silence hung heavily.

Farrell nodded, including them all. "That's right. There is none. None. The kitchen knife with fingerprints on it? Those fingerprints were left by normal use around the house.

"The surgical glove? Where's the proof that it was Mark Dooher's glove, that he brought it to the scene? There is none because that didn't happen. No, this glove was brought to the scene by the burglar—by the murderer—and left there. That's all we know about it, and it says nothing whatever about Mr. Dooher.

"So we have no proof that Mark Dooher was at the scene of the crime, no direct or circumstantial evidence tying him to it. Next we must turn our attention to whether Mark"—Farrell began purposefully using

Dooher's first name—"whether Mark was even in the neighborhood. Mr. Balian says he saw his car parked a couple of blocks away when it should have been in the San Francisco Golf Club parking lot. But Mr. Balian also says he recognized a *brown* Lexus from diagonally across a wide street, in the dark." Farrell shook his head. "I don't think so.

"And Mr. Ross didn't see what he said he didn't see at the driving range that night, either." He put his hand on the bar rail in front of the jury. "You know, it's funny about people. You and me, all of us. You ever notice how sometimes we say something, and we're not too sure of it, but we say it anyway? Maybe something we've seen, or a story from a long time ago where we don't remember all the details so we kind of fill in what's missing with something plausible? I think we've all had the experience—after we've done this, especially if we've told the story more than once—of not being able to remember what parts exactly we filled in.

"That's what happened to Mr. Ross. I don't think he purposely perjured himself under oath here. No, he was at the driving range that night, or perhaps on some other night he was three mats from the end, and he remembered not seeing anyone at the last mat. But he told Lieutenant Glitsky it was this night, and he was stuck with that story."

"For those of you who might be familiar with Sherlock Holmes, Mr. Ross was the dog who did not bark in the nighttime. He saw no one. This testimony, even if it were true in all its details, does not possess the same authority as if he said he *saw* Mark picking his way through the hole in the fence. Perhaps Mark wasn't there one time when Mr. Ross looked up. Mark has admitted going to the bathroom and getting a Coke. *That* testimony was corroborated by the golf pro, Richie

Browne. *He says Mark Dooher was there the whole time.*
So let's leave Mr. Balian and Mr. Ross. The purported
proof they offer is fatally flawed."

Farrell let out a long sigh and gave another weary
smile to the jurors. "You've heard that Mr. Dooher carefully sedated his wife. Then, after killing her, he made
the scene appear as though a burglar had done it.

"Now, I ask you, if you were going to plan this
kind of elaborate charade, if it were your intention to
make it *look like* a burglar had been in your home, don't
you think you'd leave some sign of a forced entry? A
broken window? A kicked-in door? Anything? Ladies
and gentlemen, this theory defies belief.

"I don't know about you, but I kept waiting for
some witnesses to appear and say they'd seen Mark drive
up, enter the house, drive away, anything. But I never
heard that. Not one witness came forward to say that.
All I heard was Ms. Jenkins tell us she was going to
prove it, and I kept waiting, and the proof never came.
And you know why? Because it didn't happen.

"Now Judge Thomasino will be giving you jury
instructions, but I want to say a word about the defense's
burden of proof. *We don't have to prove anything*.

"And yet Mark Dooher chose to testify—to go
through three or four hours of Ms. Jenkins's questions—
so that he could tell you what he *did* do on the night of
June seventh.

"So what do we have? We have no *proof* of motive, we have no *proof* that Mark was at the scene of the
crime when it occurred, we have no *proof* that he was
even in the neighborhood at the time. In short, there is
no *proof* at all, much less proof beyond a reasonable
doubt, that Mark Dooher is guilty of this crime. There
are no facts that convict him."

Farrell was almost done. "Ladies and gentlemen,"

he said. "I'm a defense attorney. It's what I do for a living. I defend people and try to convince a jury that the evidence in a case doesn't support a guilty verdict."

He drew a breath. A trial was a war. You had to do whatever it took to win it. Now he'd gone this far and there was no turning back. He had worked tirelessly to convince the good people of this jury that he was a man of honor, worthy of their trust. And now he was going to lie to them.

God help him, he had to do it.

"This case is different," he said. "Once in a career, a guy like me gets a chance to tell a jury that his client isn't just *not guilty*, but that he's *innocent*.

"And that's what I'm telling you now—Mark Dooher is innocent. He didn't do it. I know you know this, too. I know it."

PART FIVE

44

THE WAY DOOHER SAW IT, HIS ACQUITTAL SHOULD have restored him to his accustomed power, influence and gentility. He'd been cleared of the charges, after all. That should have been the end of it and perhaps would have been if Wes Farrell had not led the charge of rats from the ship, adding to the illusion that it was, in fact, sinking.

He supposed it was because he had never cultivated friends. The way it had always worked was that people came to Mark Dooher. Not the other way around. They had always needed something he could give them—position, money, esteem—but he did not need them. He would give no one the satisfaction.

He had been the center of Sheila's life, providing her with a house and an income and children, but even in the early years she had never been his equal. That had been tacitly understood.

And Farrell? Until the trial, Wes Farrell wouldn't have dared presume that he was on the same level as

Dooher. The man's entire existence had been lived at a rung below Dooher's. His clearly defined role had always been as fawning admirer to whom Mark permitted easy access because Farrell amused him.

Flaherty? A friend? Hardly. The Archbishop was a man who needed Dooher's advice and guidance, and who paid for it. If he chose to believe that Dooher harbored any real affection for him, that was a need of his own nature, not Mark's.

Their social life had always been directed by Sheila. The occasional dinner in restaurants or at the Olympic, a night at the theater or a movie with long-standing acquaintances—that had been about the extent of it. Mark never thought he'd miss it and he didn't; at least not specifically. Dooher should have realized that Sheila's friends would shun both him and his new wife, but he didn't miss anyone's personal company.

There was an emptiness, though, a social void that filled him with a sense of isolation.

It wasn't just, he thought. The ostracism was as complete as it would have been if he'd been found guilty. He and Christina had married within a couple of months of the trial and now, between them, had no friends.

And very little business.

Flaherty had led that abandonment. Somehow, sometime during the trial, the Archbishop had lost faith in his innocence. He had taken no joy in his acquittal; hadn't even called to offer his congratulations. In the weeks after the trial, the legal work from the Archdiocese had slowly but inexorably dried up, and with it had gone the ancillary contracts from the network of agencies, charities, schools, and businesses that were one way or the other tied to the Catholic Church in San Francisco.

McCabe & Roth held on without the Archdiocesan billings for seventeen months, though the layoffs began almost immediately. First to go were the word processors. Then the attorneys began having to double up on secretaries. Next the junior associates started getting their notices. Morale went into the toilet. A splinter group of four senior partners left with their clients to form their own firm, getting away from the Dooher stranglehold.

Christina went back to work, but there was a lot of barely concealed resentment about her situation. Engaged, then married to the managing partner, she was avoided by the other associates and mistrusted by the partners.

Still, she was a game fighter and threw herself into her role of reestablishing her husband's credibility. She and Mark were together for the long haul. If none of the lead attorneys would assign work to her, then she would do business development, taking prospective clients to lunch or dinner, trying to help any way she could.

She fought the guilt that she had doubted him. Her actions must make that up to him. She would stand by him when the world had let him go. It was romantic and noble and filled her with a sense of mission and meaning. They would make what her parents had made —a life built on trust.

She told herself that she did not get pregnant to save the marriage. It had always been her dream to have children, a family, a normal life. But things with Mark had gotten difficult—his moods, darker than anything she had seen in their early going. But the failure of his firm, his power dissipated, that was devastating to a man.

* * *

A few weeks ago, it had come to a head.

"Mark, please."

"Just don't touch me, all right. It's not working. It's not going to work."

He violently threw the covers off the bed in frustration, then stood up and immediately snatched at his bathrobe, wrapping it around him. Turning, he grabbed the comforter from off the floor and threw it back on the bed, snapping at her. "Cover yourself, would you, for God's sake."

"I don't need to cover myself."

His jaw set, his angry eyes ran down the length of her body, over the protruding belly, the swollen breasts. She could not believe he could look at her like that. She loved the way her body had changed in the past eight months.

"This just isn't doing it for me right now," he said.

"What isn't?"

"Us, if you must know. You and me. All these doubts."

"What doubts? I don't have . . ."

"You don't talk about them, but I see them. You think I don't see what you're thinking? You think it turns me on to see you trying so goddamn hard?"

"I'm not trying anything, Mark. Come to bed. Just hold me. We don't have to do anything."

"*You* don't have to do anything. I *want* to do something, don't you understand that? But I can't. I can't with you! Nothing's happening."

He swore and stalked out of the room.

He hadn't felt any guilt or regret. When he got arrested, it actually played into his hands. Christina was sympathetically drawn to the grieving spouse, who was tragically and wrongfully charged with murder. She would help defend him.

It had been beautiful. He couldn't have planned it better.

But now Christina was ruining everything.

She pulled a flannel nightshirt over her head and came downstairs, turned on the reading light next to where he sat in the library, then crossed the room and lowered herself onto the couch. "I don't want to feel like it's not working with us when we're about to have this baby. I don't like you thinking I'm not attractive like this."

"My problem is not how you look. I said it upstairs. It's us. The way we are."

She settled back into the cushions. Her eyes flicked to the glass next to him, nearly empty.

"Yeah, I've been drinking. I might be drinking more. Is that a problem?"

She stared across at him. "Why are you so hostile to me? What have I done, except stand by you, support you? Don't you want this baby, Mark? Is that it?"

Defiantly, he drained the rest of his drink before he answered her. "No, that's not it." He got up abruptly, grabbed his glass and went over to the bar. He poured another stiff one. "I have always dealt from power, Christina. It's the only way I'm comfortable. What works is when you want me, and I see how you look at me now."

"I don't look at you any way, Mark."

But he was shaking his head. "You loved who I was when you met me, when I was running the firm, when I had a big dick . . ."

"You don't have to talk like that."

"I'll talk any way I want in my own house."

She shook her head and stood up, thinking she'd tried her best tonight. "Okay," she said, "but I don't have to listen to it in *my* house."

She was all the way to the door before he stopped her with a whisper. "Don't you hear what I'm saying at all, Christina?"

Taking a step toward him, she spoke evenly. "I don't recognize you, Mark. I know the firm's failing is hard and I don't know how you're dealing with it. But I'm not trying to take away any of your power. I've been here for you, I've kept trying even when . . ." She stopped.

"When what?"

"All right." A few more steps, up to his chair. She eased herself down on the arm of it. "Even when I found out you lied to me, even then."

Narrowing his eyes, giving nothing away. "When did I do that?"

She had to get it out. She'd come this far, maybe it would help. "I ran into Darren Mills a month ago, two months, something like that. Over at Stonestown. Remember Darren, your old partner?"

"Sure, I remember Darren. What about him?"

"During your trial, Darren wound up doing a lot of work down in LA with Joe Avery. They got to be friends."

"Good for them."

She ignored that. "Darren figured I'd be interested in how Joe was doing. He's still down there, you know. He got on with a new firm."

"I'm happy for him."

She paused. His venom was poisonous. She put her hand protectively over her stomach. "Darren mentioned Joe's transfer down to LA, how it had come on so suddenly." A beat. "You told me Joe's transfer had been in the works for months."

"I did?"

"Darren said that wasn't true. You sprang it on the Managing Committee a couple of weeks before it happened. It stunned everybody. Joe hadn't even been up for partner for another year, but of course they did what you told them they had to—rubber-stamped it."

Dooher pulled a stool around and sat on it. "That's my terrible lie? That's it?"

"Yeah, that's it. And it made me think . . ." She paused and started over. "It made me remember your explosion in the courtroom, when you blew up at Amanda Jenkins, and then saying it had all been an act."

"I got into the role." He shrugged. "And so what did the other lie—that whopper about Joe Avery—what did that make you think that you stopped yourself from saying just now?"

Swallowing, she met his gaze. He was unflinching, challenging her, casually sipping from his glass. He *wanted* her to get it out in the open. "It made me think you got rid of Joe so he'd be out of the way. You knew it would break us up."

"And then I could subtly court you? While Sheila was still alive? And if you responded, then I could kill her?"

She crossed her arms.

"Okay," he said, "let's say I did that."

"I'm not saying you did."

"Oh, but you are, Christina. That's exactly what you're saying. And if that were the case, then you were part of it, weren't you? And for a sweet person like yourself, that's hard to take, isn't it?"

He came off the stool, his hands in the pockets of

his robe, pacing in the area between them. "So let's say I did do it, let's say I killed Sheila because I had the hots for you—and get this straight, Christina, I did. And you knew it. You're not stupid. You knew it. So I killed her and now it's been almost two years and I got away with it. Now you tell me this: How does that change anything between us?"

"It changes who you *are*, Mark. It would change everything."

Hovering over her now, he shook his head. "No it wouldn't." He came down to one knee. *"I am the same person."*

She couldn't face any more of it, and she closed her eyes. "Tell me you didn't do that, Mark. Please. You're scaring me to death."

"And I suppose I killed Victor Trang *for practice*." He put his hand around the back of her neck. "It's your own guilt that's eating you up, Christina. Not mine. I don't feel any guilt."

"Did you do it?" she repeated.

"And the guy in Vietnam, too. And raped Diane Price."

"Did you?"

"What does it matter?"

"Please! I have to know."

"No," he said, "you have to trust me."

She took his hand away from her neck, holding it to keep it off her. "When I know you've lied to me? When you act so convincingly? When you're just so cruel? I need to know, Mark. I need to know who you are."

The eyes—at long last—softened. Shaking his head, he let out a sigh. "I don't even remember this lie about Joe Avery, Christina. I don't remember what it was about, when I told it, anything about it. If I told you a lie, I'm sorry. The act I put on in the courtroom was a strategic decision. The insane accusations got to me and I let myself lose my temper, which I normally hold in pretty good check. That's all that was."

"But were they insane, Mark? The accusations. That's what I'm asking you."

"How many times do I have to answer that question, Christina?" He hung his head. "God help the accused. It never ends."

"It can. It can end right now."

"What's it going to do for us? Or for me? I'll tell you again, no, I didn't do it, and then some other doubt will come up in six months or a year, or you'll hear some new story about something I did or didn't do in the Stone Age.

"No, Christina, what's happening here is I've got to keep proving myself to you, over and over again. And I'm going to tell you the truth—it's wearing me down. You're doing what Wes has done, what Flaherty did . . ."

"What did they do, Mark? What did they do?"

"*They abandoned me*, goddamn it! They didn't believe me, don't you see? They emasculated me. Except with you, it's more literal. That's what tonight was about, all these times it hasn't worked. I can't take your doubts anymore. What's happened is you cut my balls off."

"Mark . . ."

"No! We've taken it this far. I don't feel like I'm a man around you anymore. I'm afraid the smallest slip of the tongue, the tiniest slip in behavior, and I'm back on the block being scrutinized and judged—and *asked*—over and over again. Well, I can't do it. My body doesn't lie. I'm not loose. I'm not having any fun. Nothing's easy anymore. It doesn't feel like you love me."

He put his hands under her shirt and ran them over her belly, her breasts. She didn't want that—any part of it. What was the matter with him? Couldn't he tell that?

But he had just told her it didn't feel like she loved him anymore. And now, if she told him to stop, it would be worse.

She no longer felt she knew what the truth was anymore. Maybe the whole thing was her fault, her weakness in not being able to believe.

She understood why he wouldn't tell her again, once and for all. He was right—it wouldn't be once and for all. The last time she asked him, it had been once and for all then, too. The question had been asked and answered. How many times did she have to ask, and what damage did it do to him each time?

He was going to be the father of their child, and her own inability to trust was threatening all of them.

But it wasn't all her. She knew that. Something had darkened in him. His hands were still moving over her, his breath quickening.

Maybe the darkness had always been there and it had taken these troubles to make it visible. But the way he treated her now, talked to her, it was coarse. He had coarsened. She didn't respond to it and never would.

She felt his hands on her. He was strong and powerful and she realized that she was afraid. Her skin seemed to crawl under his touch. After all they'd covered tonight, she couldn't imagine that he felt amorous. He pulled her shift up, brought his mouth to her breasts.

God, what made him work?

He yanked at the rope that held his robe and it fell open. He was hard, protruding. He took her hand and put it on him, exultant at the simple functioning. "Here's something for you now."

He pulled her underpants off—quickly now, roughly—afraid that the moment would pass again.

No words. He was pushing her back into the chair, opening her legs. There was a savage set to his jaw, and emptiness in his eyes.

She could do nothing to stop him.

45

After the trial, Wes Farrell gave up for a long time.

He decided not to cut his hair again until something—anything—made sense. He stopped cleaning his apartment, not much of his forte anyway. Enrolling in night classes, he started taking history courses because everyone in them was already dead and couldn't hurt him anymore.

As part of his decision to quit the practice of the law entirely, he gave up the lease on his North Beach office. He located and reattached the ten pounds he'd lost for the trial, cut off his fancy mustache and mothballed his fancy clothes.

The world was a sham. People—particularly charming winners—were scum. Any form of idealism was delusion. Since a quick and painless suicide by, say, gunshot wound smacked of commitment, he elected to pursue the more leisurely course of gradual alcohol poisoning.

There had been a short window of opportunity right as the trial was winding down during which he considered calling Sam Duncan. After he'd read Diane Price's diary, he knew he'd been an arrogant fool and was wrong on all counts.

After he'd heard from Flaherty and decided to abandon the character issue, Wes realized he would not have to cross-examine Diane Price. He would not have to take her apart.

And *that*, in turn, might give Wes the chance to tell Sam that he'd come to believe her. He was a schmuck. He loved her. Could they perhaps try again?

But Wes wasn't Mark Dooher with his good timing and phenomenal luck. He was the punching bag for a hostile universe. The Diane Price fiasco with her rogue firearm took his play with Sam out of the game.

Since he was down anyway, Lydia chose this moment to confide to him the tender tale of her and Dooher's carnal union on the day of Sheila's funeral.

So Wes decided to sink forever into his quagmire of drink and despair over humanity. Lydia's story strengthened his resolve against women in general. He couldn't let himself forget that any commitment in the love area was bogus and suspect and programmed for failure. And he'd had enough failure.

In what he took to be a sign of his mental health, he forged a firmer bond with Bart, firing the graphic designer in his building who had been taking the dog out for walks. Wes started caring for Bart—albeit haphazardly—on his own.

The dark period lasted seven or eight months, but the race riots that nearly destroyed the city in the summer following the trial got his attention and he wound up being coerced by circumstances into helping a fellow student who was being framed for a racial murder, and making an unlikely ally in Abe Glitsky.

Finally, he'd done some good as a lawyer.

So he cut his long hair and broke out his old suits and started again.

And by then, time had healed some of Sam's wounds as well.

He put the full court press on her with apologies and flowers and apologies and dinners. And apologies. He was an insensitive non-nineties type of guy, but he was going to try and change. And he meant it.

Almost a year to the day after Dooher had been found not guilty, they moved together into the upper half of a railroad-style Victorian duplex on Buena Vista, across from the park of the same name, not two blocks from Sam's old place on Ashbury, not much farther from the Center.

They were sitting in striped fabric beach chairs on the tiny redwood deck that a previous tenant had built within the enclosure of peaks and gables on the rooftop. They were planning to barbecue large scampi on the hibachi when the coals turned gray. They were drinking martinis in the traditional stem glasses. The latest CD from the singing group Alabama wafted up through the skylight, the country harmonies sweet in the soft breeze.

Far down below and across the street, they could see the light green slope of the park, the strollers and Frisbee players, the long shadows, a slice of the downtown skyline beyond.

It was the last week of May. The weather had been warm for two entire days in a row—San Francisco's abbreviated springtime. To the west, behind them, a phalanx of fog was preparing for its June assault, and it looked like it was going to be right on time and the long winter that was the city's summer would begin on the next day.

As favorite topics of conversation, Mark Dooher did not make it to the Top 100 of their personal hit parade, so Sam had been avoiding it for several hours, but now she decided the moment was propitious. "Guess who I saw this morning?"

Farrell dug out his olive, sucked it, then tossed it over to Bart, who caught it on the fly. "Elvis? He *is* alive, you know. It was in the *Enquirer* at the counter, absolute proof this time, not like all those phony other times."

"You know what I'm looking forward to?" she asked. "No, don't answer right away because it kind of relates. I'm looking forward to someday I ask you a question like 'Guess who I saw today?' or 'You know what I'm looking forward to?' and you say, 'Who?' or 'What?' —whichever word happens to apply, you see, in that given situation. I think that's going to be a great day, when that happens, if it ever does."

Wes nodded somberly. "I'd pay you a dollar if you could diagram that sentence, if it was a sentence."

"That's what I mean," she said. "That's a perfect example."

"It is a problem," he agreed. "I must not be a linear thinker." Then, reaching and putting a hand over her knee, leaving it there. "Okay, who?"

"Christina Carrera."

She saw him try to hide his natural reaction. He took in the information with a slow breath, threw a look off into the distance, took his hand from her knee, sipped at his drink. "How was she?"

"She was pregnant."

"You're kidding, yes?"

"I'm kidding, no."

A glance, still guarded. "Wow."

"She came by the Center. No"—sensing the question he was thinking—"just to visit."

"Catch up on all those good old times?"

"That's what she said."

"How long did you believe her?"

"I didn't check my watch, but less than three seconds."

"Good," he said. "That was long enough. Give her story a fair chance. What did she really want?"

"Now, see, here—if I were you—I'd give you an answer like 'She wanted me to help her negotiate a new treaty between Hong Kong and China for the new millennium.' But I don't say stuff like that. Usually. I try to be responsive."

"That's because you're a better person than I am. So what did she really want?"

"I don't know for sure. Just to talk with somebody she used to know. Take a reality check. She was scared and didn't know how to admit it."

"I'd be scared too. Did you tell her she was smart to be scared?"

"No. That wouldn't have helped. We talked. Well, mostly I listened and she talked, pretending she really had dropped in out of the blue to say hi. She was in the neighborhood. And after a while the pretense kind of ran out of gas and she got to it."

Wes stood up and walked to the roof's edge, looking out over the park. "He beating her?"

She was next to him, an arm around his waist. "No. She says not. It doesn't look like it."

"How pregnant is she?"

"A lot. It looks like she's getting close. Then after a while, maybe an afterthought to be polite, she got around to asking a little about me, what I was doing, my personal life. I told her about me and you."

"Not all the good parts, I hope."

Sam squeezed against him, then lifted herself onto the edge of the roof. "When I mentioned you, it was like I threw her a rope. She said she'd looked you up, but didn't know what she could say. She didn't believe you'd talk to her."

Wes was silent. There was more than a little truth to what Sam was saying—he probably wouldn't have talked to Christina if she just walked in on him. During the trial, the players on the defense team had split up, obviously and cleanly—Wes on one side, Christina and Mark on the other.

Afterward, as his doubts about Dooher grew, Christina made it clear she didn't want to hear them. Her own agenda with Mark, her own priorities had taken over.

Then, when it was done, Wes had felt the tug of his misguided idealism again. He had tried one last time to get to Christina, to get her to consider, in spite of the not-guilty verdict, that their guy had done it.

Maybe his timing had been wrong—it certainly wouldn't have been the first time—but she was already wearing an engagement ring. That should have been his first clue. She had asked him for *proof*, for something new that they hadn't seen at the trial or during preparation for it.

And Wes had really blown it then, coming right out and telling her that Mark had *told* him . . .

"He *told* you? He admitted it?"

But Wes had to be honest. He always had to be honest. Someday, he was sure, it was going to do him some good. But this hadn't turned out to be the day. He said, "In so many words."

"You mean he *didn't* tell you and he *didn't* admit it? Is that what you're saying?"

At the time, Wes had ruefully reflected that she sounded like him on cross. So by having Christina watch him during the trial, cop some of his moves, he had probably helped turn her into a lawyer. He wished, hearing her now, that he could work up some soaring sense of accomplishment, but it just didn't come.

Instead, he admitted that Dooher had not admitted . . .

And that had been that. She wasn't going to consider it.

Farrell thought she probably wouldn't believe it if Mark himself told her. She'd worked herself up into being a true believer and Wes Farrell's niggling doubts only served to reinforce for her the fact that she and Mark were in this alone together.

She'd told him about *his* problem. He was jealous that Mark had come to depend more upon her than on him, that Wes's role in Mark's life was going to diminish, that . . .

He'd tried. He really had.

Sam took a breath. "So she wants to see you."

"I'll consider it," he said. "Okay, I have. No. I don't think so."

"She asked if I would talk to you."

"And you have." He walked to the other end of the tiny hollow in the roof. There was really nowhere else to go. He turned, back facing her. They were going to have to expand this deck, give him someplace to hide. "And what am I supposed to say to her that I didn't try to say last time?"

"I don't know. Maybe this time she'll be disposed to believe you."

"I don't care if she believes me! I don't care what she believes!" His volume was rising. He heard it and didn't like it. He didn't want to yell at Sam. He loved Sam. This didn't have anything to do with the two of them. He tightened down the control button.

"She's living with a murderer, Sam. What am I supposed to tell her, exactly? Here I am, listen. 'Hey, look, Christina, maybe it wouldn't be too good an idea if you kept living with your husband because, see—now how can I put a nice pleasant little spin on this for you? —he *kills people* once in a while. Not every day, you understand, and I'm not saying he'll kill *you*, of course, but just to be safe . . .' " He shook his head. "No, I don't think so."

He put his hand up to his forehead, combed his hair back with his fingers. "And after that, what's she going to do anyway? Leave?"

"She might. It might save her life."

"She could leave now. Save her own life. It's not my job. No part of it is my job. Shit."

Sam came toward him—she always did this because it so often worked—and put her arms around him. "I think she wants to know what you know, Wes, that's all. She's carrying his baby. That's a hell of a commitment. She can't just walk out. She's got to be absolutely sure."

"She'll never be sure, Sam. She knows everything I know already. It's all in her head, damn it." But his arms came up around her, his head down to the hollow of her neck.

"When?" he asked.

"I told her tomorrow morning," she said, smiling sweetly up at him, going up on her tiptoes to plant a kiss. "Would that be a good time?"

Glitsky had moved in his deliberative way back to the land of the living.

Nat, at seventy-eight, started studying to become a rabbi. He was doing aerobic walking from Arguello to the beach every single day and was never going to die, wasn't even going to age any further, and for this Abe was grateful.

Glitsky's oldest son, Isaac, was graduating from high school in a couple of weeks, and he'd turned into a reasonable approximation of a young adult. On the day after graduation, he was leaving on a bicycle tour of the West Coast with three friends. He planned to be gone for most of the summer and had been accepted at UCLA in the fall.

Jacob—his hip seventeen-year-old—had gone on what Glitsky thought had been a mercy field trip to the opera with his godmother, one of Flo's old college roommates. Over the howling derision of his brothers and his own misgivings, Jacob had spent an evening in San Francisco's grand hall. Then another. The experience—the grandeur, drama, emotion, tragedy—had transformed him. Before too long he was going down for Sunday matinees, standing in the back, buying discount tickets with his own money.

He'd started buying CDs. First the old duplex had been filled with the strains of the Three Tenors doing *songs*. But in short order he'd branched out into arias, then whole passages. He would study the scores, the librettos. He began taking *Italian*, of all things, as a special elective in school. Discovering that he had a rich baritone of his own, Jacob found an instructor who said it could be developed.

And the youngest boy changed his name. Living in the house of a half-black cop, the nickname O.J. had to go, so now he was Orel James, his given name. Every day, Flo's genes showed in his face, in the set of his eyes.

Orel was still having a difficult time. At school, he remained withdrawn. He did a lot of headphones time, his walkman. SEGA Genesis ruled the rest of his waking hours. And he'd developed a stutter.

His older brothers didn't play with Orel like they used to. Abe knew, heartrending as it was, that this was how it should be—everybody was growing up. The older boys had their lives. Orel wasn't their responsibility anyway.

It fell to Glitsky, no one else. He accepted it, and sometimes thought that somebody else needing him was what saved him, what pulled him through it finally.

He *had* to start coming home, to help Orel with homework, to go to parent conferences about his boy, to be free on weekends. Abe had played college football— tight end at San Jose State—and Pop Warner needed coaches.

Suddenly he found himself out among humanity. Fathers, women, non-cops, other children. This was disorienting at first, but then he and Orel would go out for a shake afterward and they'd have some things in common to talk about. Football, then—startlingly for both of them—what they were feeling.

He started making it a point whenever he could to be home in time to tuck Orel in at night, to sit and see Flo's face in his son's and realize part of her was still there, and listen to the stutter lessen as sleep closed in.

And then, gradually, starting to *hear* the boy himself, his own voice and identity, what he was saying—

his secrets and worries and hopes—and sometimes he didn't know what this feeling *was*—for his baby—it was so strong. Where before, he had barely known Orel.

Wondering—marveling—at the seeds that could spring up after the forest had been felled and cleared, he'd sit there, Orel sleeping with his breath coming deep, and he'd rest his hand on the boy's chest in the dark. Empty.

Filling up.

Now he was washing the dinner dishes, looking out his open back window into the Presidio National Park. A glorious evening, the sky above dark blue, almost purple. The day's remaining light had a peculiar reddish glow. Fog over the ocean.

The older boys, out doing important end-of-school teenage things, hadn't made it home for dinner. He heard Orel doing his spelling words with Rita, the letters coming out clearly, one by one. No stutter.

The telephone rang and he dried his hands, picking it up on the third ring, another change for the better. It used to be on one, always.

At home now, when the phone rang, it wasn't always for him. Girls would call for the boys. Also other guys. For years, Glitsky's greeting had been to growl his name. Now he picked up the receiver and said hello, just like a regular citizen.

"Abe?"

"Yeah."

"This is kind of an unusual call. A voice, as it were, from the strange and distant past. Mostly strange."

Glitsky, standing at his kitchen wall phone on this Thursday night, couldn't place it. He knew it, but not well. Whoever it was had his home phone number, so though mostly strange, it couldn't be too distant. Then the tumblers fell. "Wes?"

"Very good, Lieutenant. I'd even say excellent. How've you been this fine past year?"

"I've been good, Wes. What can I do for you?"

Farrell spent a couple of minutes running down some background on his meeting tomorrow with Christina Carrera. Glitsky listened without interrupting.

Glitsky had survived the political fallout from the Dooher trial, and over the past year and a half had distinguished himself in his job to the point where he felt relatively secure in it.

But Dooher was unfinished business. Any mention of him got all of Abe's attention right now.

Farrell concluded, "If she's getting ready to walk away from him, I'd like to give her a hand. It looks to me she's gotten to where she knows what he's done, but she still can't face it. She's going to want something more."

Glitsky was sitting on a chair at the kitchen table. "So what do you need from me?"

"I don't know. I thought you might have come across some evidence since the trial."

Glitsky was not unaware of the irony. The defense lawyer who'd convinced a jury that his client was not guilty was now asking if they'd turned up any new evidence to convince a colleague that he'd been guilty after all. "I gave everything to Amanda Jenkins, Wes. When Dooher got off, the investigation ended."

There was a pause. "How about Trang? That case is still open, isn't it? Technically?"

Glitsky admitted that it was, although by now it was what they called a skull case—long gone and all but forgotten. "Trang hasn't been taking up a lot of my time,

Wes. We got called off on that one, you may remember."

Farrell felt as though he deserved the rebuke, but he persisted. "What I'm trying to do," he said, "is give her a taste of what you've got, what you had."

"And then what?"

"I don't know. It might save her life."

"He threatening her?"

"I don't know. But I don't know if he threatened Sheila either. Or Trang. Threats don't seem to come with the package."

Glitsky knew what Farrell was saying. This man plotted and struck. He wasn't going to telegraph any moves. "So what do you want?" he repeated.

"Maybe your file on Trang? I never saw any of that. I don't know what you had."

Repeating it got Glitsky's blood flowing. Maybe they could still get this guy. Maybe Glitsky could close the circle once and for all with him. But, as was his way, he kept the enthusiasm out of his voice. "We had the same kind of circumstantial case we built for the trial. Conflicting witness interviews, a motive that only worked if you knew what you were looking for. We never found the bayonet."

"But you were sure? Personally?"

Glitsky went over the discrepancies between Dooher's version of his phone calls to Victor Trang on the night of his death, the computer files Trang had kept, and the interviews with Trang's mother and girlfriend. "All of that, taken together—I knew it wouldn't fly at a trial. We needed some physical evidence that put him in Trang's office. The closest we got to that was the cellphone trace. For me, it was enough. The DA didn't agree."

"You think it might be enough for Christina?"

Glitsky considered it. "I don't see how it could hurt."

After Wes had hung up, he walked into the living room where Sam was sitting in the window seat, staring out at the fog.

"Whoever wrote that stuff about little cat's feet?" she asked. "This stuff comes in on a steamroller."

Wes got to her and looked out the bay window. He could barely make out the lights directly across the street. "Glitsky says he'll send over some stuff, but maybe not by the morning."

"You know," Sam said. "I was listening to you in there talking to him. What was the moment for you, finally?"

He didn't have to think for long. "Diane Price. That diary. When it was obvious that *she* wasn't lying . . ."

She nodded. "You've still got that, don't you, somewhere in your well-organized files?"

"I never throw anything out, you know that."

She patted his cheek. "It's one of your many charms."

46

CHRISTINA ALMOST CANCELED.

The weather was terrible. Dense fog, forty-mile-per-hour gusts of drizzly wind, temperature in the low forties.

On top of that, the baby had kicked all night. She'd only slept three hours. She was exhausted.

Part of her wished she could undo having gone to see Sam yesterday. It put things in motion somehow, made her feel as though she had betrayed Mark. But living with him had become a daily exercise in controlling fear.

Day-to-day, Mark wasn't acting in a threatening way. He went off to his office—one room and a reception area on the sixth floor of Embarcadero One. He would call sometime in the late morning to check and see how she was feeling. Often he wasn't in the office in the afternoon—she didn't ask where he went.

He played golf, kept in shape at the squash courts, went to lunch with business acquaintances. His world hadn't ended. To the objective observer, he was back—almost—to his normal, charming, confident self.

Since their last episode, though, a fault line ran through their lives. She couldn't shake the feeling that Mark had manipulated her to a place where she didn't feel she could refuse to have sex with him.

Fear.

She realized that the nebulous worries and doubts had coalesced into real fear. The sex since then had been frequent, impersonal, so rough she was afraid for the baby.

He was her husband. You had to trust your husband.

She could leave. If it got any worse, she told herself she would do that. She would protect the baby—that was the greatest imperative.

But she kept trying to be fair. All of Mark's other friends had abandoned him. Could she join that parade?

She didn't trust herself, that was the problem. What if she was wrong? This could all be her own paranoia, the rush of hormones, another typical episode in her seemingly lifelong quest to have her relationships fail.

She *always* found an excuse, didn't she?

This was why she couldn't tell her mother, though they talked on the telephone three times a week. She could not bring herself to admit out loud that there was anything wrong in the marriage. She and Mark were happy happy happy.

She also couldn't afford to let her parents develop any doubts about Mark. She'd worked so hard to convince them that he was innocent. If this marriage failed, it would kill her mother. And Christina would appear a fool to her father.

So yesterday she decided she'd talk to someone she

liked, even though she knew that Sam didn't have anything approaching an objective view.

And when she'd found out that Sam and Wes Farrell were together, a couple, she let herself revel in the sense that, somehow, she could get the answer. Wes would . . . but again, what could he do?

It was a mistake. She knew what Wes was going to say. And once he did, once it got to that stage, there wouldn't be any more excuses. She was having a baby any day now. This was not the time.

She couldn't do it. She couldn't go. She would just call Wes and cancel and say she'd been having a bad day yesterday. That's what it had been.

Sitting on one of the stools by the marble counter in the kitchen, she got the number from the phone book and wrote it on the pad by the phone. She punched up the prefix, then stopped and hung up, watching the fog outside. The baby kicked inside her.

A tear coursed down her cheek.

Wes had rented a converted shopfront on Irving Street at 10th Avenue. Compared to his old office in North Beach, this one was a high-tech marvel in blond woods and glass block, skylights and decorative plants. He had a full-time, computer-literate secretary/paralegal named Ramon. He'd even broken down and decided an answering machine would be appropriate.

Wes was behind his desk, pretending to be taking notes from the Evidence Code. Christina sat in the teak and leather chair, reading Diane Price's diary. Other than obviously exhausted, Wes thought she looked—big surprise—terrific. She wore jeans, a pair of well-worn hiking boots, a heavy black sweater with a cowl neck.

He decided that Sam had been right about Dooher

not beating her, though perhaps, Wes thought—non-nineties insensitive jerk that he was—in some ways it might have been better if he had. He knew Christina was strong, intelligent and aware enough not to accept anything *overt* of that nature. If Dooher hit her, she'd be gone.

But Dooher wasn't overt. That was his thing.

He could tell when she finished the first half of the diary—where Diane was going out with Dooher the next night and she "couldn't wait." He imagined his own face had taken on the same confused expression.

She looked up at him. "It just ends."

"Keep reading," he said.

When she got to the next entry—the only other one—she sat still for a long time. Then she flipped the final pages, closing her hands over them finally, staring at the floor or somewhere just above it. She was finished.

He spoke carefully, quietly. "I don't think she wrote that as a publicity stunt for the trial. I think that's genuine."

Christina's head was bobbing, as though she were conferring with herself. "Something happened," she agreed.

He didn't push. "Anyway, I thought you should see it."

"Why didn't you show me this during the trial?"

A good question. He wasn't proud of himself and it showed on his face. "My first reaction was that if you read this, you wouldn't be as effective if you had to cross her. So it was need-to-know. Then, after Flaherty bailed on us, I knew we weren't going to do character, so Jenkins would never get a chance to call her. It became moot."

"But not for me, Wes. It must have been obvious I was getting involved with Mark. If I'd seen this . . ."

"You wouldn't have believed it," he said. "You would have called it a forgery or a fake of some kind. Think about it."

Silence.

"You remember that Mike Ross never caved under my pretty intense attack? You know why? Because he knew what he'd seen. He was facing Mark's tee and saw a lot of air where Mark should have been if he'd been there, which he wasn't."

She took a breath, blew it out hard.

"You want to meet this woman Diane? Talk to her? I know her pretty well by now. There's nothing flaky about her. Mark raped her."

The tears started again, without sound or movement of any kind. He figured it was as opportune a time as any. "I've got to tell you something else, Christina."

Her gaze came up to him, expressionless.

"On the day of Sheila's funeral, after everyone else had gone home, Mark and my ex-wife had sex on the floor in the living room of your house. So much for the grieving husband."

She took it calmly, as she had the rest, nodding. In shock.

"Wes's intercom beeped softly. He picked up his telephone. "I said no interr— who?" He sighed. "Okay, send him back."

Farrell stood by the door, holding it open.

Glitsky appeared in the hallway. "Sorry I didn't call, but I went in early and down to Records, found the file and had an appointment out here anyway. You said you needed it sooner, so I thought it would save time to run it by."

Farrell took the file, gesturing him inside. "I believe you know Christina."

She had tried without great success to fix her eyes. Glitsky, trained investigator that he was, saw the blotched mascara, the redness. "Am I interrupting?"

Shaking her head no, Christina looked up at him. "I don't know what to do," she said. "What's that file? Is that about Mark?"

"It's about Victor Trang." Farrell had the file in his hand and was moving back to his desk. "But if the lieutenant's got five minutes, he can probably do the short version."

It took more like a half hour. Glitsky had pulled over the other chair from across the room and sat kitty-corner to Christina while Wes perched himself on the end of his desk. When he'd finished, Abe spread his hands. "So unless you want to believe that Trang was laying this elaborate scam on his mother and girlfriend, creating bogus records in his own file that matched the exact times of *real* calls he got from Dooher, all the while knowing for a fact that he had turned down Flaherty's six hundred thousand dollar offer in the hopes of getting more . . ." He trailed off. The conclusion was inescapable.

"You're saying Mark killed him, too?" The eyes had dried by now, had taken on a glassy look that Glitsky had seen in survivors of hostage situations. In a sense, maybe that's what she'd been through, was going through still.

He nodded. "That's what I believe, yes. There is

one other thing you ought to know. It wasn't brought out at trial."

"Okay."

"There were very distinctive stripes in blood on both Victor Trang and Sheila Dooher. You can compare the crime scene shots. The killer of both of them wiped the blade on their clothes. And remember Chas Brown?"

She nodded. "Thomasino wouldn't let him testify?"

"Yeah, him. His story—the guy in Vietnam, Andre Nguyen? The first interview we did with him, he *volunteered* that your husband told him he'd wiped his bayonet blade off on Nguyen's pajamas. It's the same M.O. You can believe me or don't, but it's as true as anything gets."

Wes went on with the double-team. "One last thing, Christina, and I'm glad Abe's around to hear it. I've gone back over this case now nine ways from Sunday, and it was all by the book. All the reasons Mark gave us why Glitsky was somehow out to get him—we were just primed to believe them. We got sold a bill of goods."

Christina wasn't much in the mood for a lecture on how the justice system worked or didn't. On how she and Wes had been less than ept. She pulled down her sweater and got herself to her feet. "I want to thank both of you for your time," she said.

It was a dismissal. She was picking up her purse, grabbing her jacket from the peg next to the door.

"If you decide to leave him," Wes said. "Go someplace he won't think to look. And let us know, would you?"

She nodded, although she didn't really seem to be

in agreement. She was inside herself. Throwing them both a last ambiguous expression, she went out the door.

Farrell was back on the corner of the desk. "So what's she going to do?"

Glitsky shrugged. "I believe her exact words were that she didn't know. If she's got brains, she'll get out."

"I don't think brains is the problem. This was something I had a pretty hard time with myself, and she's pregnant with his baby. Thinking about it doesn't seem to help."

"Well, I hope it helps a little. I would hate to get another call about one of Dooher's wives." If Glitsky knew anything, he knew about murderers—the first killing was the hardest and if you got away with it, the second was easier. And if you got away with that . . .

But the topic rattled Wes and he stuck with it. "Why would he do that? Kill Christina?"

"I don't know," Glitsky said, "maybe he won't."

"But you think he might?"

Standing, Glitsky thought it was time for him to go. He didn't like dealing in hypotheticals. His job did not begin until something had actually happened. Until then, speculation wasn't much more than a parlor game. But he didn't want to alienate Farrell—he might need him after all. For the time being at least, they were on the same side, and Glitsky had the germ of an idea. "Yeah, I think he might."

"But why?"

"Why did he kill Nguyen, or Trang, or his wife? He didn't have to do any of those people, did he? So what's that leave? I'll tell you—he likes it. He likes tormenting you with it, he likes rubbing my face in it, he likes living with the fact that he's done it. Most of all, though, you want my take? *He likes the moment.*"

Farrell's shoulders were slumped, his hands clasped in his lap, and he nodded, agreeing. "The funny thing is, I've seen him that way. You'd think I'd have figured it out."

"Seen him what way?"

"I mean hurting people—his kids, Sheila, waiters, anybody. Those moments when he was in the middle of hurting somebody, you could tell there was some level at which he liked it. But afterwards he'd be so sorry, go back to the charming act." He shook his head, disgusted with himself. "Really, all you had to do to stay Mark's friend was never to get in his way. Don't cross him. Let him have whatever he wanted. Which between the two of us wasn't a problem. We wanted different things."

Glitsky moved toward the door. "Well," he said, "you know now."

Farrell took up the Trang file. "You want this back? I don't think Christina needs it."

"No. It's a copy. Why don't you look through it? Maybe your sharp attorney's eye will see something we missed. Although I doubt it." He grabbed the doorknob.

"Abe." One last thing. "Really. Is there anything we can do about her? I've got the same instinct as you do—let the thing work itself out—but Sam wants to help. She's not going to let it go."

Glitsky shrugged, glad it was Farrell's problem, his girlfriend's problem. "Here's the deal, Wes. He'll either leave her alone or he won't. I can't do anything until he does."

"I hate that part," Farrell said.

"If it's any consolation," Abe replied, "it's not my favorite either."

47

DOOHER SAW THAT CHRISTINA'S CAR WASN'T IN THE garage, but didn't think anything of it. It wasn't uncommon. She had a life—she wasn't a prisoner.

He let himself in through the side door and was immediately aware of the silence—a profound and ominous stillness. Standing there in the laundry room, by the alarm box, he listened—had the electricity been shut off?

He turned on the kitchen light. No, that wasn't it.

Silence.

"Christina!"

No answer.

Probably out shopping.

He had been thinking they'd go out to dinner. He'd gotten himself a decent referral from one of his old partners today. It looked like he was going to be getting work subbing on an asbestos lawsuit. If it came through, the job could be milked for a couple hundred hours.

Christina would be glad to hear about it. They'd celebrate. Get her out of the dumps she'd been in lately. It was really a pain, tell the truth, dealing on this level with female hormones.

He grabbed a beer from the refrigerator, twisted off the cap. Once Christina had this kid, he was thinking, he'd talk her into getting a nanny and put her back to work.

She was better when she worked, when he kept her busy. She was one of those women who wanted to please. You kept them focused on the trees, they never saw the forest that, basically, scared them.

Christina loved cutting the trees, though. She loved clearing the brush around the trunks, pruning the foliage. At the end of the day, Dooher would tell her what a good job she'd done, what needed to be done the next day. She'd been happy. And she loved him because he counted on her. He made her feel important, needed, fulfilled.

He could fix things between them, he knew he could. As a pure physical specimen, she was worth all the trouble, because she was who he deserved. She was the one he wanted.

So he'd tough it through the next couple of months, and she'd get back to the way she'd been when she'd been trying to save the firm. He'd get her back.

This interview today was a sign that things were turning around. His potential new client didn't mention his notorious trial of more than a year before. It was all fading into the background, where it belonged.

And about time, too.

Where was she?

He removed a frozen stein from the freezer, opened the plastic container of chocolate chip cookies. Poured his beer.

There was the pile of mail on the marble counter and he walked over to it, flipping through the usual bills and solicitations.

The telephone. There she was now.

"Hello."

"Mark, it's Irene." Christina's mother, checking in. "How are you doing?"

"Outstanding," he said. "How about yourself?"

She was great, Bill was great, the world was a beautiful place. Mark's business was going along fine. No, the weather here had turned cold again. Maybe he and Christina should come down to Ojai for a couple of days this month, get away from the gray. She was out shopping just now, but he'd tell her she'd called, and he was sure she'd get back to her later tonight.

He reached for the little green Post-it square next to the telephone and pulled off the top page, where there was a number in Christina's handwriting.

Popping the last of his cookie into his mouth, washing it down with beer, he went upstairs to get into something more comfortable.

Lord, it was a big house. Completely redone, of course, since Christina had moved in—more busywork, more trees to trim. There was no sign left of Sheila.

He looked in at the library, crossed the foyer, climbed the circular stairway. At the door to the bedroom, he turned on the light and stopped still.

Something here—as when he'd entered the house —something felt wrong.

The top to Christina's dresser had been cleared of all her bric-a-brac—their wedding portrait, pictures of her parents, the small jewelry box, a precious (to her) row of carved soapstone seals, her perfumes.

What the hell . . .

He grabbed the handles of the top drawer—her

underwear—and pulled it quickly out toward him. Then, more quickly, the next one down—pants. The next—sweaters and shirts.

Empty, or nearly so.

Empty enough.

He raced into the bathroom. Her toothbrush was gone, her combs. Wait wait wait, slow down.

She's having the baby, he told himself. She must have tried to call him and had run out of time. She'd driven herself to the hospital. That was it.

But he had had the cellphone with him all day. He would have gotten the call. Still . . .

He checked downstairs in the foyer closet. The small suitcase was gone. It was the one they'd packed for the delivery. All right, he thought. She's in labor. He'd call the hospital and get down there.

But something else struck him—the large suitcase was missing, too.

At the phone now, he called St. Mary's to see if she'd been admitted. No. Unwilling to believe anything else, he told himself again that she had to be in labor somewhere. He tried the other hospitals—Shriner's, the University of California Medical Center.

He punched the phone and waited while it rang. Irene Carrera answered again, but he'd just spoken to her and she'd known nothing. Surely, if Christina had been in labor and hadn't been able to reach him, she would have called her mother. He hung up without a word.

She'd left him.

The Post-it he'd stuck on the wall had a telephone number with Christina's handwriting. It might tell him something, might be someplace to start looking. He entered the numbers and listened to the message.

Farrell.

* * *

Okay, he told himself. Okay. Just think. She's gone, but it couldn't have been too long ago and it probably wasn't very far. And she hadn't yet told her mother, that was for sure, so she was staying close.

Maybe she was planning to call him, to give him a chance to talk her back.

She wasn't going to do that.

He'd have to find her and get her and bring her back. She was carrying *his* baby, goddamn it. Even if he didn't want it, it was his. And women just didn't walk away from Mark Dooher. He was not going to let that happen.

So she got Farrell's number, but hadn't called him, at least it hadn't been the last call from this phone. The redial told him that.

He was trying to figure it. The last call from this phone had been to her mother, but he had just talked to Irene, and she knew nothing. So what was going on? And where did Farrell come into it?

If she wasn't in labor—he shouldn't be kidding himself, she wasn't—that meant she'd at least looked up Farrell. It had to be for protection. From him.

He hit Farrell's numbers again. When the machine answered, he spoke calmly. "Wes, it's your old friend Mark Dooher. Would you call as soon as you get this message? It's very important, about Christina. If she's in labor and you know it, would you let me know. I'm worried sick."

Hanging up with exaggerated care, Dooher sat immobile on the kitchen stool.

Farrell, that ne'er-do-well busybody. Doesn't he know better by now—he ought to—than to go head up against Mark Dooher? If it came to a fight, Mark would destroy him. He always had, always would.

Christina hadn't been lying to Farrell and Glitsky —she didn't know what she was going to do. The only certainty was that she had to get away from Mark. She had to protect the baby.

She would stay near her doctor, Jess Yamagi. If he delivered the baby, it would be fine. It was about all she was sure of anymore.

She had checked into a motel room on 19th Avenue near Golden Gate Park, not far from the hospital. A kind of exhausted clarity had kicked in. She was too pregnant to get to her parents' house anyway, to do any real traveling at all. With the stress, she'd had contractions on and off throughout the day.

The thought of having to face her parents with another failure was almost worse than the failure itself. She would have to call them eventually to let them know, downplaying it at first to get them used to the idea, but it was going to be awful. It would have to be done—she knew that—but later.

She realized she didn't have any important phone numbers. The Duncan/Farrell home was unlisted. She had to call information for Farrell's number and left a message with him. The Crisis Center was also closed up for the night. She didn't leave a message.

The contractions were irregular, but they were continuing. She got into the bed, turned the television on, and pulled the covers up around her.

48

FARRELL HAD REACHED GLITSKY AT HIS OFFICE NEAR the end of the day, and told him he'd remembered something Abe hadn't known. It wasn't in the Trang file, but it might be important. About Jim Flaherty.

Since he'd made lieutenant, Glitsky had learned that it was bad luck to subvert the regular channels and lines of command. Credibility was all. If Abe called on the DA in his official capacity as the head of Homicide and requested a meeting, the DA had to know he wasn't trying to sell bingo tickets.

Glitsky first discussed Farrell's information with Dan Rigby, the chief of police, and Rigby told him that if the DA said it might go somewhere, he could move on it. Otherwise, it was a waste of company time. Having obtained Rigby's permission, Glitsky called the DA.

Which was why he was back downtown on this Friday night after a quick meal at home with Rita and the boys. He and Paul Thieu walked into the office of the new district attorney, Alan Reston. (Chris Locke, who had been the DA during the Dooher trial, had gotten himself killed—shot to death during one of the race riots that had rocked the city the preceding summer.)

Glitsky had come to admire Reston, a mid-thirties African-American. He was as political as Locke had been but, unlike Locke, had within this century put quite a few actual criminals behind bars.

Reston's face was black marble, smooth and unlined, under a closely trimmed Afro. His tie alone had more colors than Glitsky's entire closet, and the suit couldn't be bought for a week of Abe's pay. But he was a professional prosecutor, and for that, Glitsky could forgive the fancy clothes.

Everybody shook hands. The politician naturally remembered Paul Thieu by name, and he directed both the officers to chairs in front of his desk. He went around to his own seat and didn't waste any more time on amenities. The prosecutor made his appearance, a palimpsest. "What do you have?"

"How much do you know about Mark Dooher?"

Reston hadn't been in the city during the Dooher trial, so his recollection of it was vague. Glitsky went over the facts. Reston had his hands crossed on his desk and, listening, didn't so much as twiddle his thumbs. When Glitsky wound it up, he waited ten seconds to make sure he'd finished, then spoke. "And the point is?"

Paul Thieu popped in. "We never tried him for Trang, sir. Locke pulled us off the case, and Thomasino ruled any mention of our investigation inadmissible at the trial."

Reston looked confused. "Who's Trang?"

"Paul." Glitsky, stopping his subordinate. "The

point, Alan, is that this man's a multiple murderer and I'm afraid he's going to do it again."

Reston remained cool. "Well, then, isn't the usual procedure to wait until he does, then collect the evidence he's so kindly left us."

"Yes, sir, no question that is S.O.P."

Reston opened his hands. "Well?"

"Well, that brings us back to Victor Trang." He turned to Thieu. "All right, Paul. Now."

It was a little bit like turning a terrier loose. In under five minutes, Thieu outlined the entire history on the death of Victor Trang—the proposed settlement on the amended complaint with the Archdiocese, the computer notes, his mother and girlfriend, Dooher, the Vietnam connection, the bayonet—wiping the blood, the cellphone . . .

Again, Glitsky cut in. Paul could get a lot of information on the table in a hurry, but it could overwhelm, and Reston's eyes had begun to glaze. "We had a case building—circumstantial, but righteous. And then Locke pulled it."

"Why did he do that?"

"I think he did a favor for the Archbishop."

Reston frowned. "You're saying Chris Locke downloaded a murder investigation? That's a hell of a strong accusation, Abe, especially against someone who isn't around to deny it."

This response was expected, and Glitsky shrugged it off. "Locke told Rigby"—the chief of police—"that he wasn't going to try a circumstantial case against Dooher. He wanted to see physical evidence—the bayonet, an eyewitness or two, fibers or soils or fabrics, something."

This made sense to Reston. "He wanted to win if it went to trial. There's nothing sinister there."

"I understand that. And as it turned out, we got a

warrant and tore his place apart and didn't find anything."

Reston shook his head. "I'm afraid I don't see where this is going. You got some new evidence?"

Thieu, unable to restrain himself, up on the front of his chair. "The Archbishop. Flaherty."

"What about him?"

Glitsky: "He's the one who convinced Locke to back off. He talked Locke into keeping the Trang murder out of Dooher's trial. I talked to Dooher's old lawyer today—Wes Farrell . . ."

"A defense lawyer?"

"Farrell's a good guy. He and Dooher don't get along anymore. His news was that Flaherty went sideways on Dooher's character testimony. He found something out."

"You *think* . . ."

"We can find out. Flaherty's not a fan of mine or I'd ask him myself. Since the trial he's pulled the plug on all contacts with Dooher's firm. He should have led the cheering when Dooher got off. Instead, he cut him out."

"I'm listening."

"Ask Flaherty."

"Ask him what?"

"Ask him why he and Dooher aren't playmates anymore."

"And?"

"Then we know something, don't we? We've got new evidence. We try to build the case. We brought up all the files—you can check 'em out. A guy named Chas Brown . . ."

Reston held up a hand. "I will."

"Fine. And meanwhile we keep looking for the

good stuff. Above all, we take Dooher off the street again. Maybe save a life or two."

"Whose?"

"I don't know. His new wife's maybe. My guess is she's leaving him, and that's going to stir up the pot."

"Saving lives isn't the job, Abe."

"I never said it was, Alan. But wouldn't it be nice?"

"You want to get him, don't you? You got a hard-on for Dooher?"

But Glitsky had been down this road enough times. He knew where the potholes were. "I see a way to take a dangerous man off the street legally. It's a skull case we can close. That's all Dooher is. It's nothing personal."

Reston considered. "That's a very good answer." Telling Glitsky he didn't believe him. But he nodded. "Okay. I'll call Flaherty, see what he says."

It didn't take any time at all.

Glitsky and Thieu were talking over the relative merits of a no-warrant arrest—picking up a suspect without a warrant signed by a magistrate—and had pretty much reached the conclusion that in Dooher's case, it wouldn't be a great idea. Dooher wasn't acting like he was going to flee the jurisdiction. He'd committed no new crimes that they knew of. If Glitsky and Thieu just went in and arrested him on their suspicions, they'd open themselves up to charges of false arrest, harassment, police brutality.

On his desk, the telephone sounded. "Glitsky."

When he hung up, he told Thieu that it had been the DA. "Flaherty told Reston he's got no *personal* knowledge of any crimes committed by Mr. Dooher.

Emphasis added. If there's evidence he committed a crime, we ought to pursue it vigorously. His words."

Thieu broke a grin. "What do you say? Let's do that very thing."

At ten-eighteen, Sam had her feet up and was reclining in the BarcaLounger. She was vastly enjoying the political philosophy of Al Franken, laughing aloud every two minutes. Bart slept under the table and Wes was in a chair at that table perusing the Trang file— there *had to* be something in it.

The doorbell rang and Bart raised his head and barked. Wes looked a question over at Sam. "This time of night?"

"We don't want any," Sam said.

"I know."

He closed the Trang file and stood up. Crossing the living room, giving an affectionate tug on Sam's toe as he passed her, he got to the stairs and turned on the outside light.

Half of their front door was frosted glass, and a man's silhouette was visible behind it. Farrell paused with a premonition, then spoke to the door. "Who is it?"

"Mark Dooher."

He opened the door halfway, but kept a hand on it. The sight of Dooher, on his stoop in the fog, made his mouth go dry.

The damn physical reactions. His heart was turning over. "What do you want?"

"That's not the friendliest greeting I've ever heard, Wes. How about like 'How you been?' 'Long time no see.' " When Farrell made no response, Dooher cut to it. "I'm trying to find my wife. She here?"

"No, she's not here. Why would she be here?"

"She called you today." It wasn't a question. "You saw her. I think you know where she is."

"I don't have any idea where she is."

A coldness in the eyes. "I think she's here."

Behind him, Wes heard Sam's voice at the top of the stairs. "Who is it, Wes?"

Dooher's eyes narrowed. He tried to look up the stairs around Farrell. "Finally getting some, are you? She pretty?"

"Get lost, Mark. I don't know where Christina is. I didn't know she was leaving you, though I don't blame her. She got an earful of the evidence on Victor Trang today. I think it kind of bothered her." He turned around to Sam. "It's Mark Dooher."

"So you *did* talk to her?"

Damn. Farrell had to stop giving things away. He had to remember whom he was talking to. "How did you know where I live?"

A condescending smile. *"Parkers."*

Lord. Wes *was* pathetic. When the *Parkers Directory*—the lawyer's guide to other lawyers—had sent him their update form, he'd filled in his address here on Buena Vista. He hadn't opened his new office yet, hadn't wanted to lose any business.

Stupid.

Sam put her hand flat against his back. He hadn't heard her come down the stairs.

Dooher kept up with questions. "So what did Christina say? What did you talk about?"

"Soybean futures, Mark. Maybe some pork bellies. Famous killers we have known."

Dooher put his hand on the door. "You've always been a funny guy, Wes." He popped the heel of his palm against the frosted pane. "Where is she?" Another shot with his palm, rattling the window. Loud. "Where the fuck is she?"

Suddenly Sam was around Wes, slamming the door shut, turning the deadbolt. "Keep the hell away from here!" she yelled through the door.

Bart set up a racket and Wes leaned over, patting him, holding him by the collar, getting him under control. When he looked back up, the shadow was gone. He slumped against the wall. Sam had her back against the opposite wall. "I'm sorry," she said. "I just didn't want . . ."

"No, it's okay. He's gone now. That was a good move."

She came toward him, into his arms. "What did he want?"

"Christina's left him. He thought I'd know where she went."

"I don't want him coming around here."

"I don't either." They started up the steps, arms around one another. "You don't have to worry," Wes said. "He's just looking for her."

"I do worry. He didn't have to come by here. He could have called you at work tomorrow."

Wes thought about it. "He's not going to do anything to me. He doesn't perceive me as a danger."

"This was a threat. Him coming by here. He was threatening you."

"I don't think so. What for?"

"For talking Christina into leaving him."

"I didn't do that. She did that on her own."

"She did it on her own after she talked with you at your office. It's a fine distinction."

Wes shook his head. "There's no way."

She stared up into his face. "You want to promise

me one thing? You thought you knew him before. Remember that, would you? Remember that."

He kissed her. "Okay, I'll remember."

Ravenwood in the dark.

Slumped behind the wheel of his city car, Glitsky had the lights off but had left the motor running and the heater on. His hands encircled an oversize cardboard cup that had once held hot tea. The driver's side window was down an inch.

Across the street, Dooher's house appeared and disappeared in the shifting fog. Fifteen minutes before, Glitsky had knocked on the front door and returned to his car to wait.

He was thinking about Flaherty, wishing he hadn't come on so aggressively back long ago when he'd interviewed him. But then again, that's who Abe had been back then—a cop with a chip on his shoulder over Flo, over his life. Ready to explode at anybody, even people who might help him. Alienating everyone. Ineffective.

The Lexus pulled into the driveway. Glitsky got out of his car and reached the front door at about the same time a light came on in the back of the house. He pushed the doorbell and listened to the eight tones: *Lord we thank thee. We bow our heads.*

Another light inside, then overhead on the porch. When Dooher opened the door, Glitsky put a foot against it. "I thought you'd be interested to hear that we're looking into Mr. Trang's murder again. I wanted to give you the opportunity to confess to it now, save us all a lot of time and trouble."

"Get a life, Private." Dooher moved to close the door, but it wouldn't go.

Glitsky kept talking. "You've been through one

trial. You know the heck it plays with your life. You don't really want to go through that again. And I'm betting you don't get bail this time. Just a hunch, but I'd go with it."

"What the hell are you doing here?"

"I just told you."

"You got a warrant? You don't have a warrant, Sergeant, get off my property."

Glitsky moved his foot. "I'm going to take that as a 'no' on the confession, but you're making a mistake."

Dooher, disgusted, closed the door and turned out the overhead light. Glitsky, thinking he'd burned up his Friday night fun quotient, decided to go home. He was almost across the patio when the light came back on. He heard the door open, the commanding voice. "Glitsky."

Reaching inside his jacket for his .38—you never knew—he revolved halfway around. Dooher stepped out onto the porch. "It was you brought the Trang file over to Farrell's, wasn't it?"

"He asked so nice, I couldn't refuse."

"And you saw my wife?"

"Here's the thing, Mark. In my business, I generally ask the questions. You want to talk about Victor Trang, I'll listen all night long. But I've got nothing to say about your wife."

"You saw her at Farrell's. You know where she is now?"

"Another question about your wife." Glitsky tsked. "And here I thought I'd made it so clear." He shrugged. "Not that it hasn't been a good time, but I've really got to go. I don't have a warrant and I've been ordered off the property. Unless you want to invite me in?"

Dooher seemed almost to enjoy the moment.

"You're almost as funny as my friend Wes, you know that, Glitsky? And I admire that in a man. Really, I do. But you can't touch me. You should realize that by now. The fact is—you just don't seem to be able to do your job, do you? Though I guess being black and all, that's not much of a problem. You don't actually have to *perform*, do you? Actually get anything done?"

"Sometimes," Glitsky said, his scar tight now—he could feel it. "You might be surprised."

"Well, you do your best, then, would you. Give it your best shot. Or was that what you did with Sheila? No. That couldn't have been your *best* shot, was it?" Dooher took a few steps toward him, made his own tsking sound. "Oh, that's right. You'd lost your own wife back then, hadn't you? That must have been a hard time. That would explain why you couldn't touch me then either, why everything you did . . ." The voice got harsher, rasping. ". . . was such a total fucking waste of time. You were *sad*, weren't you? Poor guy. That was it. That was why you were so incompetent. See? There's always a reason if you look hard enough for it. I wonder what it will be when you screw this one up."

"It'll be fun to find out." Glitsky wouldn't take the bait. It did his heart good to see the real man for the first time. He half turned, then stopped, facing Dooher. "Oh, and hey, good luck finding your wife. I wonder why she'd leave you." A beat. "Must have something to do with *performance*."

Dooher couldn't sleep.

He kept coming back to Farrell.

What made a man valuable was imposing his will on the world he lived in. It was winning. Big risk, big prize. And he was the Alpha Male. He'd won. He'd beaten Glitsky, beaten Farrell, beaten the whole system. And it got him the mate he wanted, the prime female. And now he's supposed to feel *guilty*? Please. Peddle that twaddle to one of the sheep.

He kept coming back to Farrell, the whiner selling his loser's vision to Christina. By making Mark's guilt the big issue, he'd got her to leave him, tearing apart what Mark had *earned*.

Naked, he wandered through the big house—the library, the kitchen, the living room where he'd fucked Wes's wife.

He wondered if he knew. He should tell him.

Outside, it was freezing. But he liked it, liked the midnight stroll down his driveway without his clothes on. He was untouchable—he could do whatever he wanted.

He let himself into the garage. His M-16 was tucked into its shelf high up over his workbench and he took it down, unwrapping the cloth, shooting the bolt, sighting down the barrel, an idea forming.

But no, he couldn't use anything as obvious as a rifle that could be traced to him. He put the gun down on the workbench and picked up a crowbar, hefting it against his palm.

Doubts had tossed him from side to side on the bed for hours. Doubts about who he was. Doubts that he'd gotten himself to here by wanting too much, by lying, by lust, by murder, by all the cardinal sins. Now this—his world imploding, Christina leaving him—was his punishment.

And maybe he deserved it.

"Fuck that."

A violent shiver ran through him. He felt some coil release inside him and he brought the crowbar down in a deafening crash, shattering the wood, scattering hardware and the now-broken glass from the storage jars over the M-16 and the rest of the workbench.

Farrell was the prime mover here. He'd brought Glitsky back into it again after it should have been long over. Somehow Farrell had convinced Christina that she had to move out.

The self-righteous son of a bitch. Farrell, who'd never succeeded at anything, who believed in fair play and the goodness of man, was a slinking dog compared to the *men* who walked on this earth. How dare he presume to judge what Mark had done?

But now it was clear: Farrell wouldn't rest until he had brought Dooher down to his level.

He needed a lesson in where he belonged, in what his station was, in who made the rules.

Dooher wasn't going to let this continue. He'd take care of it in short order, set the world back straight.

Then go reclaim what was his.

49

DIANE PRICE VOLUNTEERED AT THE CENTER ON Tuesday nights and Saturday mornings. She picked up the phone when it rang at eight forty-five. "I'm looking for Samantha Duncan's number."

"I'm sorry," Diane said. "I can't give that out over the telephone, but I can call her and have her get back to you."

A frustrated sigh. "It's just I've been awake half the night and I'm starting . . . well, never mind. That would be good, if you could ask Samantha to call me." She gave her room number, the motel.

"And who should Samantha ask for?"

A long hesitation. "Christina Carrera."

"You're Mark Dooher's wife," Diane said.

"That's right." And clearly Christina had no idea to whom she was talking, who *Diane* was. She wondered briefly if she should tell her, then decided against it. What would be the point?

"Oh . . ." On the phone, the woman gave a low moan, followed by a succession of quick breaths.

"Are you all right?"

The breathing slowed. The voice was normal again. "I think I might be starting labor. Can you call Sam?"

"I'll call her right away."

Irene Carrera walked out onto the pool deck where Bill was taking his morning laps. She watched the effortless glide of his body through the blue water, then her gaze went up and out over Ojai—the peace of it, the order.

She pulled up one of the molded-iron chairs as Bill executed a swimmer's turn and headed back up to the deep end. She'd let him finish his workout, a few more carefree moments before she disturbed him.

Their daughter was in trouble again. Irene had just gotten off the phone with Mark. He told her he hadn't been completely truthful when they'd talked last night. Christina hadn't been home at that time. In fact, she hadn't come home at all.

She was staring again out over the serenity of her valley.

"What's that look for?"

She hadn't noticed that Bill had finished and was walking toward her, toweling off, his usual easy smile in place. There was no avoiding it. She had to tell him.

A puppet whose strings got cut, her husband slumped into another chair as she spoke to him. Irene continued. "Mark said she called him last night. Told him she needed some time to think, but wouldn't say where she was. She's hiding out."

Bill let out a deep sigh, staring into the space between him and his wife. "She's delivering his baby any time now and she's hiding out?"

Irene nodded. "Mark said she'd been acting unstable the last couple of weeks—skittish, crying jags, seeing ghosts everywhere . . .

"He called to ask us what we thought he should do. He sounded a wreck." Anguish, now. "Bill, why wouldn't she have called us?"

He barely trusted himself to speak. He would go up and find her. Somehow. Help Mark if he had to, though he'd never warmed to the man. "I don't know, hon."

"But wasn't it going so well? Hadn't she . . . ?"

Shaking his head, interrupting. "She didn't want us to know," he said. "She didn't want to disappoint us."

"So she won't call us?"

"She'll call." But his face betrayed his words.

"Bill?" She stood and came up next to him, put her arms around him. "I know what you're thinking, but we've got to keep Mark in this picture."

He said nothing.

"He's her husband. He still believes in her—I heard it in his voice. If we hear from her, we have to tell her that. You don't leave. You don't always leave."

"We don't know the whole story, Irene. Maybe Mark drove her in some . . ."

But she stepped away, fire in her eyes. "No! That's always been her excuse and . . ."

"It wasn't an *excuse* with Brian, Irene. The bastard was married to somebody else, knocked her up and dumped her. That's not an *excuse*."

"All right, but what about Joe Avery? What about all the other men?"

"Maybe they weren't good enough for her?"

She glared at him. "Spoken like a true father, Bill."

"What do you mean by that? I *am* her true father."

"And every time she left some man, it was always okay, because they weren't good enough for her. And every time, it broke her heart a little more, but it was okay, it was okay. She was still daddy's little girl."

"Irene . . ."

"No, listen. She's almost thirty years old. She's picked a good man, I'm convinced of that. A good man."

"I don't know that."

"Bill. You do."

"Then tell me why she's left him?"

"I don't know. But *he* called us. This isn't someone who's beating her. She's never said a bad word about him. He doesn't know what to do, so he comes to us. Doesn't that tell you something? Isn't that a good sign?" He didn't want to hear it, but it needed to be said. "Bill, she *married* him. It's time she learned that's where her life belongs, with her husband. Not with us. We love her, but she can't keep coming back to us. She'll never grow up. She'll never have a life."

They faced each other in the calm Ojai morning. Blue jays were fighting for territory in the air above them. One of the canyons off to their left echoed with the howl of a coyote.

They went on the assumption that you always made mistakes, which was how they thought they'd catch you.

Dooher had to admit that even he had made a few.

Well, to be honest, he'd made none with Nguyen.

But there had been a couple of small errors with Trang—the cellphone business, how could anybody be expected to know about that? But with Trang they'd only gotten as far as an investigation.

With Sheila, they got him all the way to trial, so by objective standards, he supposed he was slipping. He'd been forced to hurry his plans after Avery had gone down to LA. If he didn't move fast, he ran a risk with Christina. Someone else might have come along and distracted her and he would have been back to where he started. So he'd had to strike when he did.

But the lack of planning had showed.

The knives were one of the problems, though he favored a knife because you had control. You put it where it needed to go and held it there, feeling the life slip away, until you knew you'd done it.

But a knife was too much trouble. Too dirty. He'd had to throw the bayonet off the Golden Gate.

He thought he'd solved the problem with the kitchen knife, the gyrations with the blood and the glove and the botched burglary. But that had been close —his cleverness had nearly done him in.

He'd really learned a lot—the trial had been instructive that way. There were phone trails, paper trails, evidence trails, eyewitnesses, and trackers among the police for each of them.

So this time, from the moment he began to move, he wouldn't leave any hint.

Glitsky would know. How could he not know? But there would be nothing he could do.

He wasn't going to leave any messages on answering machines. All Saturday morning, no one answered at Wes and Sam's, and he hung up as soon as he heard the message begin.

After he'd made his decision last night, sleep came

more easily. Indecision was the ruin of lesser men. He'd set his body clock for around nine and called the Carreras down in Ojai. If he was going to locate his wife, he would need Irene.

Sam didn't pick up, and Diane Price called Christina back at her motel and asked if there was anything she could do. "How far apart are the contractions?" she asked.

"Not close. Seven minutes. They warned us about this in Lamaze. They won't admit me until it's two or three minutes. It's going to be a while."

"Why are you in a motel?" Diane asked.

"That's a long story."

"Is there anybody with you?"

"No."

"I could come."

"Why would you do that?"

"You used to volunteer at the Center here, too, didn't you? Us guys ought to stick together, don't you think?" Diane thought saying anything about the further connection between them at this moment would be counterproductive. She heard the breathing again. When it returned to normal, Diane spoke again. "I've been through this with two kids of my own, Christina. I could keep you company. We could talk. You need somebody with you. How are you getting to the hospital?"

"I don't know."

Diane made up her mind. "I'll be there in ten minutes."

* * *

Christina opened the door to her motel room. The woman was bundled for the chill—heavy woolen coat, enormous leather carryall, designer ski cap pulled down over dense graying hair. But she smiled warmly, projecting a calm confidence that Christina found comforting. She had beautiful gray-green eyes.

There was also something familiar about her. "Do I know you? How did you know I was Mark Dooher's wife?"

The smile remained. The eyes seemed to know everything. She didn't move forward, but seemed content to wait out in the cold until this was cleared up, until Christina had accepted it. She might not, after all, want her around after she knew. And that would certainly be understandable. "Sam said you were smart." A proffered hand. "I'm Diane Price. It's nice to meet you at last."

50

A T TWELVE FORTY-FIVE, WES PICKED UP ON THE SEC-
ond ring, heard Mark Dooher's voice. "I'm
going to start by apologizing."

He didn't reply. Dooher continued. "I was out of
line. I shouldn't have come by your house, made cracks
about your girlfriend." He paused. "Look, Wes, Christina ran out on me. I freaked out. I'm sorry."

"Okay, you're sorry. Nice talking to you."

He hung up.

"That was our friend Mark Dooher again," he told
Sam. "He said he was sorry. I told him I was glad for
him."

The subject made her nervous, but she played
along. "That wasn't what you said. You said it was nice
talking to him."

"It was," Farrell agreed. "We had a full and frank
discussion of the issues."

The phone rang again.

"Don't pick it up," Sam said.

But he already had.

"Wes! Don't hang up. Please. You still there?"

"I'm here. What do you want?"

Sam was telling him to hang up again.

"I need to talk to you."

"It must be your lucky day. You are talking to me."

"No. You and me. Privately."

Farrell's voice had no inflection. "I'll drive the hordes away from the extensions. We're talking privately right now. We can talk like this or you can hang up. Your call."

Dooher measured his silence. Finally, he produced a sigh. "I don't . . ." Starting again. "I need your help. Your legal help. I may want to talk to the police." Another silence to let the ramifications sink in. "I don't want to say anything specific on the telephone. You can understand that."

"You want to turn yourself in? Is that what you're saying?"

"I don't believe in telephones much anymore, Wes. You could work something out. I don't want to say anything else over these lines. I need to see you, is why I called. I need your help. I can't live with it anymore."

The Little Shamrock, the bar where Wes and Sam had met.

The fog obscured nearly everything outside the picture windows—across Lincoln, the cypresses were spectral shadows in the netherworld.

Sam sat across the table from Wes, holding both of his hands in both of hers. Neither had touched their Irish coffees.

That morning they'd bundled up and gone out early for an aerobic workout—a "power walk" from their

duplex to the beach and back. The Bay to Breakers race
—7.2 miles from the Ferry Building to Ocean Beach—
was in two weeks, and Sam ran it every year. Wes had
no desire to try to die crammed shoulder to shoulder
with ninety-eight thousand assorted crazed runners,
walkers, naked folks, cross-dressers and caterpillar floats,
but he didn't mind the exercise leading up to it.

They weren't talking about the race, though.

"Wes, I am begging you, please don't do this."

"He's going to give himself up, Sam. He wants me
to negotiate how it's done."

"Give himself up for what?"

"I don't know. Trang, maybe."

"I don't trust him."

But some part of Wes, evidently, still did. "I'm
surprised it's taken him this long. Christina left and that
made him see it."

"See what? That it's wrong to kill your wife? A lot
of people get that concept right away. You'd be surprised."

"He said he needs to talk, Sam."

"So do you really believe he's going to admit killing anybody? That he'll go to jail?"

"Maybe living with the guilt is a kind of jail."

"A motto for the ages, Wes, but then again, maybe
it isn't. Maybe that's not him."

"It's everybody. It catches up with everybody."

"Wes, listen to me. People *do* live with guilt. You
know this. You've defended criminals your whole life
. . . people don't care about guilt. They care about getting caught."

"Mark isn't most people. He's got a conscience."

"No he doesn't."

Farrell shook his head, sticking to his guns. "You
don't know him."

"I do know him. He's a killer."

"You didn't hear him on the phone. He needs help. I've got to help him."

"Somebody else can help him. Call one of your lawyer friends. Call Glitsky, he'll help him."

Farrell had to smile at that, though it wasn't much of a light moment. He squeezed her hands. "Sam, if he needs me, how can I not help him? What kind of man would that make me?"

"A live one."

Again, he shook his head, rolled his eyes. "Please."

"Please yourself, Wes. He's killed three people. Why wouldn't he kill you?"

"Why *would* he kill me? That's a better question." He pulled his hands away, looked at his watch. "I told him I'd be over there at three. I've got to go."

"Don't, please. For me."

He came around the table, put his arm around her shoulders and drew her to him. "Sam. Don't ask that. This isn't me against you. This is somebody I've known my whole life, reaching out to the only person he trusts, trying to save himself. There's nothing to worry about. I love you. I'll be home in a couple of hours. If I'm going to be late for any reason at all, I'll call. Two hours, max. Four-thirty."

He tightened his arm around her, but she resisted. "No. *No!*" Standing up, she pulled away, knocking over their table.

He watched her, half running through the bar, through the double doors, and out. Never looking back at him.

When she got home, she let the tears go on for a while. That's why she'd run—damned if she was going to use tears to make her point, to convince him to stay, although a part of her wished she had.

In the kitchen, drying her eyes on a paper towel, she noticed the message light flashing on her answering machine. Pushing the button, she heard Diane Price saying that she'd talked to Christina Carrera. She was in labor.

Since Sam wasn't home and Terri had come in for her shift at the Center, Diane was going to help Christina, maybe drive her to the hospital if she needed it. She'd call back when she had more information.

Sam glared malevolently at the machine. "Where is she, Diane? Where is she?"

But the machine provided no answer, and neither did Terri when Sam called back to the Center.

Paul Thieu was in a small internal room—no windows—in the Hall of Justice, where he'd spent most of the morning on the computer, hoping to find some heretofore unknown reference to Victor Trang or Chas Brown or anyone who'd known either of them. He didn't really know what he was looking for, but this was an unturned stone, and there might be something under it.

But so far—and it had been three hours—nothing.

Deciding to give it a rest for a while, Thieu got out of his program, blanked the screen. As far as he knew, he was the only person in the building who logged off the computer when he was finished using it. It was a small point of pride. He interlaced his fingers behind his head and leaned back, stretching.

Timing.

His lieutenant, Abe Glitsky—in on a Saturday,

pumped up—knocked on the doorsill, pulled up a chair. "Our plan won't work."

Glitsky had dreamed it up and run it by Thieu last night after he'd returned from Dooher's. The younger man had liked it.

They'd run a sting. Farrell was a real ally. He could reestablish his contact with Dooher and either wear a wire or, failing that, simply try to provoke him, as Glitsky had when he went to his house. Farrell would get him to say something incriminating. The veneer had begun to crack. They could get him.

But Glitsky didn't think so anymore.

"Why not?"

"Farrell is Dooher's lawyer. Anything they say is privileged."

Thieu had thought of this and sold himself on a rebuttal to it. "He won't take a retainer. He'll go to Dooher as a friend. The relationship won't be a professional one."

Glitsky told him this was wishful thinking. "Besides, if Farrell denies it, Dooher will say *he* was the lawyer and Farrell was *his* client. It won't get past the DA."

A scowl. "I hate it when you're right, you know that?"

"I don't blame you. My kids do, too. It's infuriating." Glitsky had become almost human. "There is something else we can try, a long shot."

"Is it legal?"

Glitsky's expression conveyed shock that Thieu could even think such a thing. "Forget what he says. Try to make him *do* something."

"What?"

"What physical evidence did we get with Trang? Clothes, the bayonet, shoes?"

"Nothing."

"Right. Which means? Tell me."

Thieu thought a moment. "I give up."

"It means he got rid of it. He stabbed the guy and held him close and he got blood on himself. Then he had to get rid of what he wore. No way around it."

Another bad idea, Thieu was thinking. "Abe, this was two years ago. Those clothes, all that stuff, is gone. Burned up, disintegrated."

"Not his Rolex. Not Sheila's jewelry."

Thieu kept shaking his head. The lieutenant must be tired. "You just said it. The Rolex was his wife's murder, the burglary. It isn't Trang. We can't touch it. That stuff's been pawned anyway."

"I don't think so, Paul. We looked hard when it was fresh. It didn't get fenced. He got rid of it."

"Which makes it gone, am I right?"

"But maybe not forgotten."

Farrell righted the table in the Shamrock. He went into the bathroom and got most of the Irish coffee washed off his pants. He hadn't intended for Sam to get so mad, for himself to get so defensive. They were both too hotheaded.

Dooher. The source of every fight they'd ever had.

Disgusted, he came out of the bathroom and pulled up a stool at the bar. He was going to have a long beer and chill out and be late for his appointment with Mark. Too bad. Let his ex-friend wait for once. He ordered a Bass and put a napkin on his lap, soaking up more of the damp.

The bartender's name was Moses McGuire. He was approaching his sixth decade with a new wife and a young child and seemed determined not to go placidly amid the noise and haste, remembering what peace there may be in silence. His nose had recently been broken for about the fifth time—some unpleasantness about a softball game—and he sported two black eyes and a bandage. During Farrell's blue period, as he called it, he had spent more time here with McGuire than he had at his apartment. With Bart, which had endeared Farrell to McGuire.

The Bass came sliding across the rail and McGuire leaned over, smiling. "Everything patched up between you lovebirds?"

Farrell sighed. "She's mad at me."

"I guessed that. I don't blame her. They're always right, you know. I don't know why we argue with 'em."

He sipped at his ale. "I know."

McGuire got called away on an emergency down by the picture window—Tommy, a fixture, had finished his fourth Miller's of the day and was slapping the latest empty on the bar.

There was more truth than Farrell wanted to admit in what McGuire had said. Which of course meant that there was more truth than he'd acknowledged in what Sam was saying.

Mark Dooher was a dangerous man who studied his prey. He knew Trang worked alone and would meet him alone. He'd known Sheila would never refuse a drink—even a mickey—that he put in her hand. He knew Farrell was an idealist who believed in the goodness of man, in confession's healing power, in forgiveness. He also knew he would come when beckoned.

So Dooher had beckoned, and Farrell was going.

51

DOOHER LOOKED WRUNG OUT, WITH BAGS UNDER HIS eyes and a deep pallor to his skin under an uncharacteristic stubble.

He wore a Sam Spade overcoat, an old felt hat and a pair of tattered running shoes. A grieving husband, he blew out in frustration. "Christina's got to call somebody, wouldn't you think? Who would she call?"

"I don't know. Not me."

Dooher stepped out onto his porch. "About last night. I don't know what to say."

Farrell waved it off. "We going somewhere?"

"There's something I want to show you. I bet your heater still doesn't work?"

"Good bet," Farrell said.

"We'll take the Lexus. That all right?"

"Sure."

They walked back down the driveway, past the infamous side door. Farrell let Dooher go into the garage. He waited outside, nervous. The garage door opened and Dooher backed out.

Sliding into the passenger seat, Farrell noticed that he'd put on his driving gloves, and cast him a sideways look. Dooher gave him a weak smile. "*Alea jacta est*, I guess."

The die is cast. They both understood the reference—Julius Caesar's words as he crossed the Rubicon, after which he would either rule Rome or be killed as a threat to the Republic. Dooher was saying he was crossing over, taking the irrevocable step—he was going to turn himself in. He put the car in gear and they began to move.

They drove out to the beach, up to Golden Gate Park, back halfway through it, then south on Sunset Boulevard, a straight and usually scenic shot to Lake Merced. Today, in the fog, the scenic aspect wasn't evident, but the road wasn't crowded and Dooher drove slowly, talking about the lives they'd lived together, trying Farrell's patience.

Finally he couldn't listen to it anymore. "I didn't come out here with you to talk about old times, Mark, to talk about us. You said you had something to show me. You want to tell me what it is?"

The ever enigmatic Dooher didn't answer directly. "I want you to understand what happened, Wes, that's what I want."

"What you want isn't a burning issue with me anymore. I'm not going to understand what you did. That's not going to happen."

Dooher kept driving, eyes on the road. "And what did I do?"

"You killed Sheila, Mark. You may have killed Victor Trang, too. Andre Nguyen. How am I supposed to understand that?"

"Did I ever say I had?"

"Fuck you, Mark. Let me out. Pull over."

But he didn't. He kept driving. "You think I did all that?"

"I *know* you did some of it, and any part of it's enough. Christ, you all but *told* me after the trial."

Dooher was shaking his head no. "You misinterpreted that."

"Bullshit!"

Shrugging, Dooher kept his tone relaxed. "You wearing a wire, Wes? Glitsky hook you up? That's why you really agreed to come today, isn't it? To set me up."

The great manipulator was wearing Farrell down. "There's no wire, Mark. I came because you called me and that's who I am," he said. "I didn't call you. You called me. You couldn't take it anymore, whatever 'it' is. Remember?"

Dooher spent a long time not saying anything, driving slowly through the deep fog. Finally, he sighed heavily. "What do I need to do? What do you want me to do? I want my wife back." There was real anguish in his voice. "I want you to forgive me."

Farrell asked him to pull over at a gas station just off Sloat Boulevard. They'd made a big circle from where they'd begun in St. Francis Wood. He had, he believed, forced the play, though it wasn't over yet.

He told Dooher he had to use the can. This wasn't true. It was nearing the time he'd told Sam he would be home, and he wasn't going to make it. He didn't want her to worry. "I know I said two hours, but I was late getting here . . . I had another beer is why . . . another hour, tops . . . no listen, it's perfectly safe, he's

. . . Sam! He's beaten." An earful. "I know that, too. No, we're . . . one more hour, I promise."

He had more to say, but she hung up on him.

Contractions every four minutes. Three centimeters dilated.

"Three? Only three? I've got to be more than three."

Diane was next to Christina in one of the labor rooms at St. Mary's, holding her hand, doling out ice chips. Jess Yamagi, Christina's doctor, checked the monitors, ignoring her outburst. "Everything's going along fine," he said, "but it's going to be a while." He gave her a reassuring pat and turned to Diane. "You okay with this?"

She nodded. "I'm here for the duration."

"You bring along any music?" Yamagi asked. "You could use a phone if you want. You're going to have some time, Christina, might as well enjoy it."

Another contraction began and Diane helped her breathe through it. Yamagi was frowning at the monitors.

"What?" Christina asked.

"Nothing. A dip in the baby's heartbeat. It's normal during contractions. We'll keep an eye on it."

Christina looked over at the beeping machine. "I'll take that phone now."

"Where are you, hon?"

"Mom, it's okay. I'm okay. I'm in labor. At St. Mary's. Everything's fine."

"Where's Mark? Is he with you? He called this morning. He's so worried."

"No, Mom. No. Mark isn't here."

"He said you'd left him."

She didn't have the strength to come out with all of it. She sighed. "Just for now, Mom. Until we figure some things out."

"Can't you figure them out together, Chris? Having a baby, that's a time you can't get back."

"I know that, but . . ." It was so tiring, trying to explain. "Mom, you have to trust me. Everything will be all right. I'll tell you all about it after the baby's born."

"But Mark, he deserves to—"

"Mom, please. Don't tell him. Don't say anything to Mark. Promise me."

Farrell's rising hopes when he'd called Sam had been dashed when he got back in the car. The critical moment—Dooher vulnerable—had shifted again.

Dooher had begun driving, heading north now. He had not yet confessed and Farrell was at the end of his tolerance. This wasn't going to work. Suddenly he saw it clearly.

Hard by the Golden Gate Bridge is a parking area favored by pedestrians who want to walk the three miles across it. Sepulchral in the fog, the place was otherwise deserted now in the late afternoon. A perennial gale battered the evergreens that bordered the northern lip of the lot, where below the trees, a cliff dropped nearly a hundred feet to the beach below.

Dooher parked the car, opened his door, and got out. Farrell sat a minute in his seat, then did the same. They heard the foghorns moaning deeply, the wind here on the headland raking the trees.

"What are we doing here?" Farrell asked.

"You'll see. This is it. What I wanted to show you. Come on, walk with me. Out on the bridge."

Farrell took a few steps, then stopped. "I'm not going with you, Mark. You can tell me here."

Dooher wasn't giving up. "I'm not going to throw you off, Wes. Is that what you're thinking?"

"I'm thinking that I'm done. I'm going home."

Dooher's face clouded. "What do you mean?"

"I mean I thought you needed me. I'd give you a chance. But you don't want a chance. You want me out of the way."

Dooher stepped close, hurt. "Wes, this is me, Mark Dooher. We've been friends since we've been kids. It's paranoid to think . . ."

"That's right. It may be."

"And you think I would . . . ?" Dooher couldn't even say it—it was too absurd.

"Over everyone's advice, Mark, I wanted to help you. Be your lawyer and maybe even your friend one last time. Now I've got to tell you. It's going to be over soon and you're going to need a lawyer and it's not going to be me." He hesitated, then came out with it. "Glitsky knows where you hid the stuff."

Dooher's face cracked slightly. He moved toward Farrell.

It was a flat and desolate stretch of bare earth—thirty yards deep by eighty in length—really not much more than a widening of the western shoulder of Lake Merced Boulevard, though hidden from the road itself by a stand of wind-bent dwarf cypress.

The Lexus inched forward over the area to where it dropped off steeply. Dooher pulled the car up near to the edge.

Here an eastern finger of the lake extended nearly to the fence that bordered it. Inaccessible from shore, it was rarely fished. It was also deep, the underwater topography continuing the steep slant that dropped off from the turnout. In the fog, the lake itself was only intermittently visible.

Dooher put the car into park, but didn't turn off the engine. Under his driving gloves, his hands hurt, but they were not bleeding. He got out and walked to the edge, looking out over the water, then around behind him. It was as it always was. No sign of anyone.

At the edge of the lot, the incline fell off at a good angle for perhaps forty feet of sedge grass dotted with scrub brush. Dooher picked his way down, hands in his pockets, crabwalking. When his head got below the level of the lot, the minimal road noise from Sunset dissipated, and he suddenly heard the lap of the lake water.

This was where he'd ditched the evidence.

Within twenty minutes, Dooher was back in his garage, placing the running shoes into the bottom of the grocery bag, then the gloves, carefully folding the old Sam Spade overcoat so that it fit. He put the bag onto the passenger seat of the Lexus and drove the half mile to Ocean Avenue, where he left it in the side doorway of the St. Vincent de Paul thrift shop.

Back in his kitchen, he realized he'd worked up an appetite, so he poured himself a glass of milk and grabbed a handful of frozen chocolate chip cookies, then went to the phone to call Irene Carrera, see if she'd heard yet from her daughter.

52

THREE GENERATIONS OF GLITSKYS WERE AT THE MOV-
ies watching *James and the Giant Peach* when
the beeper on Abe's belt began vibrating. He reached
over his youngest son and nudged his father's arm, holding up the little black box. "Back in five," he said. Nat,
caught up in the animation, barely nodded.

In the lobby, he faced the disorientation he'd always experienced when he saw movies in the daytime,
even on such dark days as this one. But his eyes adjusted
and he checked the readout, walked to the pay phone
and punched up the numbers.

"Lieutenant, this is Sam Duncan. Wes Farrell's
friend."

"Sure. Is Wes there?"

"No. That's why I'm calling. I don't know what
else to do. Mark Dooher called Wes earlier today and
asked him to meet with him." Glitsky was aware of the
muscle that began working in his jaw. "He convinced
Wes he was going to turn himself in."

"I know."

"What?"

"I knew that. He paged me and I called him back at some bar. He told me all about it. He's not back yet?"

"You let him go? How could you let him go? Mark Dooher's a murderer, and now . . ."

"He's probably still at Dooher's. He was meeting him there, right? Have you tried calling there?"

"I just did. There's nobody home, no answer. Wes said he'd be home in two hours. Then he called to say he was going to be later. It's been almost four hours now. That's why I called you. Something's happened. He would have called me again. He knew I was worried. He would have called."

Glitsky was silent for a long moment.

"Lieutenant?"

"I'm here. I'm thinking. Have you tried his office?"

An exasperated sigh. "I've tried everywhere, Lieutenant. Dooher called him and he went and . . ."

Glitsky chewed the side of his mouth another second or two, then made his decision. This time he was moving out before he was certain there had been a crime—if it *was* before. If it wasn't already too late.

Irene Carrera debated with herself over the right thing to do. The birth of a child was the strongest bonding experience a couple could have together. She was torn.

Distraught, Mark had called her again. Please, as soon as Irene heard *anything*, he'd implored her, would she call and let him know? He was desperate. He needed her.

And though Christina might not realize it herself, he told Irene, her daughter needed him, too.

It had ripped Irene up having to lie to Mark, not even to tell him that she'd heard from Christina. But what else could she do?

Irene wrestled with it, couldn't get it worked out. She wished Bill were here; they would come to the right decision together. She knew he'd be calling her when he got to San Francisco, but first he had to take the afternoon shuttle from Santa Barbara to LAX, then wait for his evening flight—he wouldn't get there until very late tonight.

Meanwhile, Irene knew that if Christina succeeded in excluding her husband from this moment of birth, there was a far greater chance that they would never be able to patch up whatever had come between them.

On the other hand, if Mark were there, with her— if they went through it together, husband and wife, it might be the very last chance for Christina's happiness. Even though it would be against her daughter's express wishes.

In the pink moment, Irene paced the ridge of her property overlooking the valley, agonizing over the greater good.

Glitsky left Orel with his grandfather at the movies and ran a block and a half to where he'd parked his city-issue car. He made it to Dooher's house by seven o'clock. He should have heard from Paul Thieu long ago. He tried to page him and there was no response.

What was going on? Where had everything gone wrong?

Glitsky didn't much care about probable cause anymore with Mark Dooher. He was going to take the man downtown on some pretext, get him off the streets before he struck again.

The house on Ravenwood was dark. Dooher wasn't there.

But Glitsky got out of his car, wanting to make sure. Crossing the front patio, getting to the porch, ringing the bell, waiting.

Empty.

There was no way he could explain away his actions to anyone if he was discovered. He would be reprimanded, perhaps fired.

He was wearing his own pair of gloves, standing inside a suspect's house. He had entered without permission and without a warrant and that was the plain fact of it. He was in the wrong.

The side door by the driveway had been left unlocked. So Dooher hadn't lied about everything during his trial. He'd testified—and standing under the cold and darkened portico Glitsky had remembered—that he tended to leave the side door unlocked when he went out, the alarm deactivated.

Now he stood in the kitchen where so long ago he'd sat and had tea with Sheila Dooher. When he'd come in, he turned on the light in the laundry and the overflow lit the counters dimly.

On the way here, he'd considered pulling over and making another call to Sam Duncan, bringing her up-to-date on Farrell. But there was no up-to-date with Farrell. He might be going to die, if he wasn't dead already. What could he tell her that couldn't wait another hour? Until they knew something?

But here, in the kitchen, it gnawed at him again. He remembered the last moments with Flo, where he hadn't been able to do anything, but had sat by the bed, holding her hand—perhaps she'd felt something, some pressure from him, some love, in the last seconds. Maybe it had made some difference.

Digging in his breast pocket, he fished out the piece of paper on which he'd written Sam's number. He'd at least tell her what he knew.

He crossed the kitchen in a few strides, stood by the telephone, hesitated briefly, then picked it up.

But instead of punching Sam's numbers, he noticed the redial key and, without really considering, pressed it.

There were eleven quick beeps. Long distance.

"Hello." A pleasant, cultured female voice.

"Hello. This is Lieutenant Abraham Glitsky, San Francisco Homicide. Who am I speaking with please?"

"Oh my God, homicide?"

"Yes, ma'am. In San Francisco. Who am I—"

"Is Christina all right? Tell me she's all right."

"Christina?"

"Christina Carrera, my daughter. Is she all right?"

"I don't know, ma'am. I hope so. Right now I'm trying to locate her husband, Mark Dooher. Do you know where he might be?"

"He said he was going directly to the hospital."

"The hospital? What hospital? Why was he going to the hospital?"

"To be with Christina. She's at St. Mary's, in labor. She's having her baby."

"And Dooher knows she's there?"

"Yes, I told him . . ." The voice had lost its modulation.

"When was this?"

"I don't know exactly. Maybe a half hour ago, not even that long. He called me again and I just thought . . ."

Glitsky didn't need to hear any more.

53

DIANE WAS IN THE POSTDELIVERY ROOM. SHE squeezed Christina's hand. "It's all right," she said. "You're allowed to cry. He's beautiful. Handsome, I mean."

"Beautiful," Christina said.

Jess Yamagi leaned over her, laid a finger against the baby's cheek, brought his hand up to Christina's shoulder. "I'm going to let you hold him for a couple of minutes, Chris, but his temperature is a degree or two low, which is perfectly normal. We're going to put him under the lamp and warm him up until he's stabilized."

"And then what?"

"Then we wash him off and bundle him up and bring him to you. Meanwhile, you get a little rest if you can." He squeezed her shoulder. "You did good, Chris. Great job. You, too, Diane."

Christina couldn't take her eyes from her baby, who seemed to be staring back at her. She'd always thought that infants were born with their eyes closed, but her son was wide-eyed, memorizing her.

A nurse appeared and showed Christina the little plastic hospital tag they put around the baby's ankle— "Baby Boy Dooher." Her husband's name startled her slightly, but the tag was already made up. It wasn't so important it had to be changed right away. "Everybody worries we're going to mix up their children in the nursery, so we show you this to put your mind at ease," the nurse went on.

"All the babies get one," Diane volunteered.

Christina was staring through the mist down at her son. "I'd know this guy anywhere. I could pick him out of a thousand other babies."

The nurse smiled again. "I know you could, sweetheart." Then, picking him up, "He'll be back in no time, don't worry."

It wrenched her to have the baby taken, but it wouldn't be for very long, it was a normal procedure. She turned to Diane, the rock, and squeezed her hand again, the fatigue kicking in.

She'd just close her eyes for a minute . . .

Like the rest of life, it was simplicity itself if carried off with grace and assurance. Dooher was the natural father of the child, the legal father. He had as much right to be here as Christina did.

"I'm sorry I'm so late," he said to the nurse at the admitting station after he'd presented his ID, proving that he was who he said he was. "I'm just in from the airport. I've been back east all week. I knew this would happen when I was out of town. I knew it. How is Christina?"

The nurse double-checked his ID, then Christina's

admitting record, verifying that yes, he was the husband, they lived at·the same address. They were careful here— babies had been known to disappear.

Looking up, satisfied, the nurse seemed to see Mark for the first time, the nervous father. "Your wife got moved to her room a couple of minutes ago, Mr. Dooher. Room 412, right down that hallway. She's resting now, doing fine. And congratulations, you have a baby boy."

Dr. Yamagi diagnosed the lieutenant to be on the edge of hysteria. His blue eyes were dilated in his dark-skinned face. An unusual combination.

But the man—Glitsky—wasn't here about genetics. He'd come in through the emergency entrance, always a fun place on a Saturday night. Probably so that he could park as close to the hospital as possible. Waste no time.

"Yes, I delivered the Dooher boy," Yamagi said, "maybe forty-five minutes ago."

"Is the mother all right? Christina?"

"Yes. She was, anyway. Why?"

Glitsky didn't answer that question. He had his own. "Have you seen the father? Mark Dooher? Has he been here?"

Yamagi shook his head. "No. Christina had a friend helping her. Diane." This name didn't seem to register.

"I'd like to see them. Talk to her."

"She may be resting."

Glitsky nodded. "I'll wake her up."

* * *

The doctor rode up the elevator with the silent homicide lieutenant. They passed the nurses' station without a word, and Yamagi escorted Glitsky into the maternity wing itself, past the double doorway that segregated the new mothers from the sick and the injured.

This was the happy part of the hospital, with bright stencils decorating the walls and the hallway filled with flowers and balloons and, somehow, a sense of optimism.

Glitsky noted it all, but little of it registered. Yamagi pushed open a door at the end of the hall— Room 412. The overhead light was turned off, but Glitsky recognized Christina in her bed, her eyes closed.

Under a directional light, another woman was reading *Modern Maternity*. She looked up when the men entered, breaking into a welcoming smile at Yamagi, then a questioning glance at Glitsky. She dropped her magazine into the carryall shoulder purse on the floor next to her chair. She stood up.

"Hi, Doctor. She's sleeping."

"No, that's all right, Diane. I'm awake." Christina was already pushing herself upright, getting ready to hold her son. "Is the baby here?" She opened her eyes, trying to get focused. She took in Diane and Yamagi, then blinked, as though having trouble with her vision. "Lieutenant Glitsky?"

He nodded. "Ms. Carrera."

"What are you doing . . . ?" She came straight up, grimacing with effort. "My son! Is my son all right?"

"He's fine," Yamagi answered reassuringly. "We'll have him in here in a couple of minutes."

Christina leaned back, relief all over her.

Yamagi came up to the bed. He held the switch to raise one end of it, propping Christina into a more comfortable position. "You get some rest?"

She nodded. "A little."

"You ready for your boy?"

"Please."

"Okay. I'll pass the word and they'll bring him along." Then. "Lieutenant, is everything here okay for you?"

Glitsky had already checked the corners. It was a private room with no place to hide. Mark Dooher wasn't here.

"Good." Yamagi looked at his watch. "Christina, be sure to ask for help if you need anything. They'll wheel in another bed if you want Diane to stay. I'll be back first thing in the morning. You want me to show you the way out, Lieutenant?"

Glitsky didn't like this. He didn't know what had happened with Farrell. Dooher knew Christina had come here, and yet—apparently—he hadn't. Something wasn't right, maybe a lot of things. "I'd like to stay on a minute. I have a couple of questions."

This wouldn't have been Yamagi's choice, but Christina read the indecision in his face and spoke up. "It's okay with me."

Yamagi yielded. "I'd appreciate it if you kept it short then. All of you."

As the door closed behind the doctor, Glitsky took a step toward the bed. "Have you seen your husband? I was sure he was coming here."

"Why would he be here? He doesn't know I'm here."

Glitsky considered that. He had to tell her. "Yes he does. Your mother told him."

A long, dead moment as it sank in.

* * *

Dooher didn't go right in to see Christina. He needed to see her, all right, to explain things, but he wanted to find his baby first. That would make it all clearer.

He looked through the glass and read the identifying tag. Baby Boy Dooher was under the warming light. A tiny red heart was stuck to his chest, keeping track of his temperature.

He pushed open the door to the newborn nursery. Inside, he stood quietly—the proud new father, overwhelmed with emotion, a little lost.

A pretty young nurse approached him. "Can I help you, sir?"

In the role, Dooher gave her his best smile, shading it with a touch of self-deprecation. "My new boy. I saw him through the glass in there. I just got here. I missed the birth. I wonder if I could just hold him a second? The Dooher baby?" He had his identification out again, and this nurse, too, looked it over, then handed it back to him.

But she was shaking her head. "It's against the rules, technically. I'm sorry."

He sighed, heartbroken, met her eyes. At home, he'd showered and shaved, then dressed with casual elegance. He looked good and he knew it. "Well, I certainly don't want to break any rules."

The nurse looked into the adjoining spaces, around behind her. She leaned in toward him. "I'll get you a mask," she said. "We'll make an exception. You'll have to wash your hands."

They were going to be bundling the boy up right now. His mother had asked for him. Would Mr. Dooher like to take the baby in to his wife?

"That would be great," he said. "I'd like that."

What he'd do, he thought, was act like she'd never left him, that it had never happened. He would let her know that he understood what had happened—her emotions had gotten the better of her and she'd given in to panic.

She'd be vulnerable right now and he didn't want to scare her away. He would be kind and gentle, solicitous. He had to prove to her that she could trust him. She had always been able to trust him. Whatever he might have done, he wouldn't do anything to hurt her.

But the situation would also work to his advantage. He'd walk into her room and she'd see him holding the baby. He had gotten to their son in the hospital without her knowing about it. She couldn't have stopped him, whatever she had done.

A message would get delivered there, now, wouldn't it? He wouldn't have to say a thing.

She would come back to him. They wouldn't ever have to mention these past couple of days. This was how training worked. There had to be periods of pain, of testing, of finding out how far the chain would go until you felt it choke.

Well, Christina had found out.

Dooher didn't remember the births or much of the infancy of his other children. He'd been putting in yeoman hours when they'd been born—in those days men went to work. They didn't change diapers.

So the size of this baby surprised him—so small, nearly weightless.

They had wrapped it tight, it arms cocooned in its blue blanket. The nurse he'd charmed earlier escorted him out of the nursery, reminding him to keep the neck supported, to cover the head and shield it from any drafts while they were in the hallway.

At the door to 412, Dooher turned to her. "Would you mind if I just go in alone and surprise her?"

Who could say no to such a reasonable request?

Christina was looking past Glitsky. The door was beginning to open and it would be the nurse with her—

No. This couldn't be.

In her dreams, something like this would happen. But this wasn't a dream.

Dooher stopped inside the door. "Well, look at this, a little impromptu party. Corporal Glitsky, of all people."

No one said a word. Dooher made sure the door was closed behind him. His eyes swept the room and alighted on Diane Price.

"Who's this?" he asked.

Christina spoke up protectively. "She's a nurse practitioner here, Mark. She helped with the labor."

Dooher accepted this. "Well, thank you very much." A shift of focus. "And how are you, Christina?"

She forced herself to speak calmly. "I'm fine, Mark. It went all right. No real complications."

"I'm glad." A pause. "Though it wasn't exactly how we planned, was it?"

"I'm sorry," she said. Her eyes never left her son. "I don't know what happened yesterday, Mark. I guess I lost sight of things for a minute."

"I guess so. That happens sometimes. Moments of stress." Another silence.

"Can I have my baby please? I have to feed it."

"Actually," he smiled at her, "it's not just your baby, it's *our* baby, isn't that right?"

"Of course, that's what I meant. It's our baby. I meant our baby." She held out her hands. "And he's hungry, Mark. Thank you for bringing him in, but I'll take him now, okay?"

He shook his head. "No, I don't think so. Not quite yet."

He didn't even recognize her.

Diane wasn't prepared for the wave of anger that swept over her. He looked—impossibly—the same as she remembered him from college.

And now he stared directly at her and saw nothing.

She wasn't there.

It all flooded back—the experience was etched in acid. Afterward, she had been curled up on the top of her bed, great pain down there. Too hurt for tears.

This couldn't have happened to her. Her blouse, torn open, had been still around her shoulders—a distinct memory. She remembered lying there in a fetal position, holding the scrap of her blouse collar in her fist, as though it offered some protection. He'd ripped the rest off.

He was pulling up his pants, tucking himself in. She could still hear the sound his breath had made. He'd said nothing.

When he looked down at her, just like now, she hadn't been there.

She found herself speaking in the same even tones Christina had been using. "The baby needs to be fed, sir."

He didn't like the diversion. Snapped at her. "I'm talking to my wife."

* * *

"The baby needs to be fed," Diane repeated.

This time Dooher glared at her. "Who are you? Do I know you?"

Glitsky broke in. "Give her the kid, Dooher."

A disappointed expression. "Not right yet, Private. Christina and I have a few things we've got to work out first." He turned back to her. "I want you back home."

Christina was glued to the child. "I was upset, Mark. With the hormones, I guess. I got scared. Of course I'll come back. You're the father. I'd never think of raising the boy without his father."

It seemed to anger him further. "You're just trying to get your hands on this baby, aren't you, Christina? You'd say anything now, wouldn't you?"

"No, that's not true. But the baby *is* hungry, Mark. He hasn't eaten yet."

Christina had reintroduced Diane to Glitsky, so he knew who she was. It would complicate matters if Dooher realized it. Glitsky had his gun inside his jacket. He'd drawn it only occasionally in his career, and had never fired it at a person.

If this turned out to be the first time, he wanted to know what was behind his target. He moved to his left.

"Stay where you are!" Dooher backed up a step. A wider angle on the room. "Whatever you're trying to do, it's a bad idea."

"I'm not doing anything."

"You're moving. I don't want you to move."

"And if I do, what then? Are you threatening to hurt your baby if I do, is that it?"

It didn't faze him. "I'm holding my child, Sergeant. That's all. What are you doing here?"

"I heard you were here. I wanted to talk about Wes Farrell."

A turn of his mouth. "I don't know anything about Wes Farrell."

The baby mewled quietly. Christina: "Mark, please. Let me hold him."

Glitsky looked to Christina, back to Mark. "Let her have him, Dooher."

He shook the baby, shushed at it.

"Don't shake him," Diane said.

"You shut up. I'm talking to the corporal here."

Diane saw it clearly. He was going to wind up killing the child.

"All right," Glitsky said. "Talk to me."

"I told you I don't know anything about Farrell. We were supposed to have a meeting today. He didn't show up."

Glitsky was impassive. "We found him. He wasn't dead. Not yet."

Christina was staring at Dooher. "Oh God, Mark, not *Wes*. Not your best friend."

Glitsky pushed at it. "You thought the fall finished him, didn't you?"

"I don't know what you're talking about."

The baby began to cry.

"Please, Mark, let me take him."

He shook his head at his wife, backed up another step, looking down at the infant. "Shh!" At Christina.

"Wes wasn't any friend of mine. He's the one who poisoned you about me, who made you leave me . . ."

"So you killed him," Glitsky said.

The baby wailed. "Shh!" More roughly. "Shhh!"

"Don't shake him, please. Don't shake him, Mark."

But he was back on Glitsky, holding the baby against his shoulder, both hands around the tiny body, shaking him up and down. "I thought you said he wasn't dead."

"When we found him. I said when we found him he wasn't dead." Glitsky played the trump. "We followed you to the lake."

"From where? Who did? What are you talking about."

"Give it up, Dooher. It's over. We know where to look. We're going to find everything, aren't we?"

"And then what? You find a bag of wet clothes, big deal. You can't connect them to me."

"I don't need to. I can connect Farrell to you."

Dooher shook his head. "You can't prove anything. Just like with Trang, just like with Sheila. That old proof keeps on fucking with you, doesn't it, Private? So Wes Farrell fell off a cliff. He died. So what?"

Glitsky's scar stretched white through his lips. "So he didn't die, that's what."

Dooher took in a breath. He nodded, bitterly amused. "As if Wes Farrell matters." He pulled the child closer to him, holding it with one arm, pointing with the other. "You think Sheila, Victor Trang, Wes Farrell —you think I feel *bad* for what happened?"

The baby began crying again and he pulled it roughly against him, pressing the infant's face into his body.

"Mark, please! You're hurting him."

* * *

Diane was in slo-mo. She stood up.
She lifted the purse from the floor.
"Sit down!" Dooher barked at her.
"No."
She took a step toward him.

Christina, pleading. "Please, Diane, no. Mark, just let him breathe. Let your son breathe."

Dooher pointed at his wife. "I had to have you, don't you understand that. After the trial, I told Wes I was sorry for what I'd put him through. If I'd made life hard for him, I'd make it up to him."

Christina had her hands out. The baby, the baby. Anything he said, just let her have the baby. "Okay, Mark, fine. We can talk about that."

He included Glitsky. "This nigger can't prove anything. They'll never convict me. We could start again, Christina. I could make it up to you. I could."

"Dooher!" Glitsky said. "Let the baby go."

Diane moved forward.

He glared across at her. "I told you to stop right there."

"Give me the baby," she said.

"Back off!" Dooher slammed a palm against the wall behind him. "What do you think you're doing?"

The baby got a breath and managed another piercing yell.

Dooher took it in both of his hands. He held it up in front of him.

He kept shaking it. "Shut up, damn it! Shut up!"

* * *

Diane Price dropped her carryall purse to the floor and lunged forward.

Glitsky started to react, reached inside his jacket. There was no time.

The gun was a metallic blur in her right hand moving toward Dooher's head. The sharp, flat report.

She let the gun fall. It clattered to the floor.

Diane grabbed for the child as Dooher collapsed.

The room hung for an instant in surreal suspension.

Glitsky smelled the cordite. His hand was still on his own weapon, but there was no need. It was over.

The baby began crying again.

Diane was bringing it over to Christina when the door flew open, a nurse and two attendants rushing in after the noise from the shot. They stopped in the doorway.

Diane laid Christina's son in her arms.

"He was killing the baby," she said. "I had to stop him."

That would be her story, Glitsky knew. It was a good one.

Her eyes pleaded with him. Did he understand what she was saying? "Guy says he's sorry and thinks that's enough? I don't think so."

Glitsky nodded at her. He was going to arrest her, but she posed no danger at the moment.

He held out a hand to stop the influx of other staff crowding to the door. He crossed the room and went down on one knee next to the still and crumpled body. Almost as an afterthought, he picked up the small gun.

He felt for a pulse. The throat at the carotid artery twitched once under his fingers. Then he felt nothing. He leaned over, closer.

"It's *Lieutenant*," he whispered.

54

AFTER HIS FIGHT WITH SAM, IN HIS HEART FARRELL had still wanted to believe that Dooher was turning himself in, that the guilt had gotten to him. But the more he considered it, the wiser it seemed to cover his bases, so he'd called Glitsky and the lieutenant had given him his marching orders.

In the event that Dooher did not confess, if the meeting began to look like an ambush, Farrell was to extricate himself as quickly as he could, remembering to drop the bait—"Glitsky knows where you hid the stuff." Thieu would be tailing them, so the threat to Farrell would be minimal.

Minimal. Farrell had liked that.

It was a gamble, but their only chance. If Dooher took the bait, if he went to make sure his hiding place was still secure, Thieu would follow. Dooher would lead them to the evidence. Thieu would call Glitsky when he'd found something.

And that's what had happened.

But not soon enough for Farrell.

They hadn't planned on the fog and they'd under-estimated Dooher's dispatch. Always stronger, faster, more determined than Farrell, Dooher had walked up close, concealing his intention, then come at him like an enraged bull. A blow to the solar plexus, then an-other to the face had driven Farrell backward, and Dooher had kept coming, forcing him off the pavement, onto the steep angle under the trees, all the way to where the land fell off and the air began.

Now, Monday, Thieu and Glitsky were playing lunchtime chess at one of the open tables on Market Street. The sun was bright overhead; the air still. Glit-sky was thinking mate in three moves, but his concen-tration got diverted when a bare-chested man in sandals and shorts stopped to watch the endgame. Carrying an enormous wooden cross, he just stood there looking on with his companion, who was a fashionably dressed businesswoman in her mid-thirties. The cross, Glitsky noticed, had a wheel at its base to facilitate pulling the thing along.

He moved his bishop and the man shook his head. "Blew it," he said, and moved on, pulling his cross, chatting with his friend. Daily life in the city.

Studying the board, Glitsky realized the man was right. Thieu made his move—one move!—and tried not to smile. It wasn't a really good try, though.

Glitsky started putting away his pieces. His brow was not clear. Throughout the game, they'd been dis-cussing their sting operation, how it had gone so wrong. "I still don't understand how you lost Farrell."

Thieu was holding the bag. "I didn't lose Farrell. I never had Farrell."

"You followed him," Glitsky said.

Thieu explained what had happened. "Two cars, Abe," he said. "We always tail with two cars. You know that. We waited by the lot by the bridge when they pulled in there. When the Lexus pulled out, I followed Dooher down to Merced. There was nothing to call you about until we found the bags. The guys in the second car didn't find Farrell right away and they had better things to do than report to us, like get him out of there, try to keep him alive. What I'm curious about is the Price woman."

"After this," Glitsky was laconic, "odds are she'll get her movie deal."

"Not precisely what I meant, Abe."

"I know, Paul. I know what you meant."

They crossed Market, negotiating a stalled Muni bus spewing out a stream of unhappy campers. When they had forded it, Glitsky told Thieu that the DA hadn't yet decided on the charge for Price. "My guess is Reston will go with manslaughter, she'll plead and get some community service. Maybe not even that if I have any real influence, which I don't."

"Community service for *killing* a guy?"

"Using deadly force, Paul, to save a life. The situation called for it. I was there. He was going to kill the baby. That's what I'm going to say. It's what Price's lawyer is going to say. It'll fly."

Thieu was skeptical. "How was Dooher going to do that, exactly? Kill the kid, I mean. Did *he* have a gun, a knife? What was he going to do?"

"He was shaking it. Kills infants every day. You know that, Paul. We've got that nice poster on the column—'Never, *never*, NEVER shake a baby!' I'm sure you've seen it."

"So she had to shoot him dead?"

Glitsky shrugged. "Must've seemed like a good idea at the time."

"You're cute with those tubes coming out of you."

"Mmmmfff."

"I know, I agree. Oh listen, I brought you a present. You can pin it on your 'Take me drunk, I'm home' shirt." Sam fished in her purse and pulled out the button. She turned it to face Wes. It read, "What if the hokeypokey is what it's all about?"

Two weeks later, Christina was on the deck of her parents' home, breast-feeding William. Her father was coming out of the house with a tray of food.

"Your mother will be along in a minute," he said, sitting down on one of the wrought-iron chairs, "but I wanted to tell you something—she feels so guilty about telling Mark you were at the hospital. It's been paralyzing her."

"She did what she thought was best, Dad."

"You know that. I know it. She did it, though. I think it feels different."

Christina looked out over the valley. "She didn't trust me. She didn't believe what I told her."

Bill was all agreement. "That's true. She feels terrible about that, too." He leaned forward, his voice soft. "I'm just trying to tell you her intentions were the best." He put a paternal hand on her knee. "I've got to ask you to let her share her grandson, Christina. You can't go on punishing her. You've got to trust her again. Let her hold him."

"I can't."

"I think you can. She loves you, Christina. I love you, too. This is something you can do."

She blinked a couple of times. William gurgled and she looked down at him. She had finished nursing. She took a moment fixing her swimsuit, her eyes down.

"I can't do anything. All I've done is cause you both pain. Now I'm hurting Mom and I can't make myself do anything else."

"I'll say it again. You can."

She forced herself to breathe. "No, Daddy, it's more of the same. I mess my life up and then I do it again and again and again. Now I'm a single mother with no job and no career and you're taking care of me again."

"That's what we do, Christina. That's what parents do. You followed your heart."

But she was shaking her head. "I didn't. I followed some dream, to be like both of you. And I'm not really like either of you. I've got all this *stuff*, this baggage. A woman's role, a mother's role, a daughter's role—roles define everything I am, so I'm not anything anymore. I'm just not carefree."

Bill's elbows were on his knees. He canted forward in his chair. "I know that. It's a different world than we grew up in, your mother and I. Maybe it's better, I don't know, worrying about so much, trying to do right on so many levels."

"But I haven't done right. I'm guilty about everything. I'm all lost."

Bill took her hand. "You guilty about William here?"

She looked down at the boy. "No."

"You know where you are with him?"

"Yes. Definitely."

He sat back in his chair, took an olive and popped

it. "You're going to make mistakes with him, you know. Just like your mother did with you about telling Mark. Like I did, too, lots of other times. Still do. We make mistakes."

"But . . ."

"No buts. That's the way it is. Guilt isn't going to help—William or anybody else. It hasn't helped you. Let it go. Start over."

"That's just it. I don't know if I can."

Irene opened the French doors and came down the steps onto the deck. She pulled up a chair and smiled a practiced smile. Christina could see that she'd been crying, had tried to hide the traces. "You two having a nice talk at last?" she asked. "Oh, these are excellent olives. Have you tried these, Christina?"

She was sitting up, emotion ripping through her. She could feel the invisible chain tying her to her son. How could she ever loosen it? He was anchored to her.

She swung her legs over the side of the lounge. "I'm taking a dip, Mom. Do you want to hold William?"

She held her baby out and her mother took him. The chain hadn't broken—she'd let him go and they were still connected. Her mother's eyes brimmed over again.

Christina walked to the pool and stood at its edge. It was the pink moment.

Special preview from
John Lescroart's novel

THE MERCY RULE

available now from Delacorte Press

PROLOGUE

T HE PAST KEPT UNRAVELING, TANGLED IN AN ENDLESS present.

Afternoon sunlight slanted through the open window, warming the skin of the old man's face, throwing into bright relief the two-day gray stubble. Salvatore Russo reclined in an ancient Barcalounger that he'd pulled over to catch the rays. God knows, balmy weather was rare enough in San Francisco. You took it when you could.

He had his eyes closed, remembering another sun-dappled day. But to Sal it didn't feel as though he were remembering it. It was more immediate than that. He was living that long-ago moment all over again.

Helen Raessler was nineteen and the light shone off her honey-colored hair. She was lying on her back on the sand on a dune at Ocean Beach. Even now he could feel the warm sand. They were sheltered by the contours of the land, by the surrounding sedge.

In spite of the difference in their backgrounds Sal

knew that Helen loved him. She loved his big hands—already heavily callused from work and from baseball—and his thick hair and powerful chest. He was twenty-five.

No, he *is* twenty-five.

He pulls away from their kiss so that he can see her perfect face. He traces the line of her jaw with his workman's hand and she takes it and brings it down over her sweater to her breast. They've been seeing each other for a little more than a month, and the heat between them has scared him. He's been afraid to push her, physically, in any way. They haven't done even this yet.

They are kissing again and a sound escapes her throat. It is hunger. He can feel the swollen nipple under the fabric of the sweater. He realizes that she has purposely worn no bra. A gull screeches high overhead, the waves pound off in the distance over the dunes, the sun is hot on him.

And then his shirt is open and her smooth hand is under it, pinching at his nipple, drawing her nails down his side, his belly. He pulls away again to see her.

"It's okay," he says. "I'll stop."

"No."

His hand has found her and she nods.

Hurry. She pulls at his belt and gets it undone.

She wears only a short skirt and it is up near her waist now and he is on top of her, her panties moved to one side.

She arches once into him. There is a moment of resistance, but she pushes violently then—once—with a small cry, and he is in her and she sets him, and the world explodes in sensation.

Opening his eyes, he looked down, surprised and absurdly pleased with his erection.

Well, what do you know? he thought. Ain't dead yet.

But the thought, as they all seemed to, fled. As did

the tumescence. His headache returned—the sharp, blinding pain. Frowning, he brought his hands to his temples and pressed with all his might.

There. Better. But, Lord, he could certainly do without that.

He looked around. The room was furnished in Salvation Army. Sal's lounger had bad springs and canted slightly to one side, but it was comfortable enough. Over the sagging green couch hung a piece of plywood upon which, sixteen years ago, Sal had watercolored his old fishing boat, the *Signing Bonus*. The grain of the wood showed through the faded paint, but in the right light—now, for instance—he could make out what he'd done.

There was a coffee table in front of the couch and a couple of pine end tables, scarred with cigarette burns and water stains, on either side of it. The wall-to-wall carpeting was worn to its threads.

But Sal didn't need much, and he had more than most of the other people who lived in this building. A corner that got some sun. The place was small, okay, but had three legitimate rooms, this one and the kitchen and bedroom, plus its own bathroom. What the hell more did anybody need?

There was still most of a bottle of Old Crow next to a half-filled tumbler on the low table and Sal leaned forward, picked up the glass, and smelled to see what was in it. He didn't remember pouring any of the booze, but that's what it was, all right. He drank it off, a mouthful.

Something was nagging at him. What day was it? He ought to get up, check the calendar in the kitchen. He was supposed to be somewhere, but damned if he could remember.

He closed his eyes again. The sun.

On his face, making him squint against it. He's on the third-base side, a weekend day game at Candlestick, and everybody's shocked it's so nice out. Where's the wind? The

*whole family's down on the field—Helen's holding his hand
and smiling, proud of their oldest, Graham, out in the middle
of the diamond now, by the mound, getting his fifty-dollar
U.S. savings bond for winning his age in the finals of the
city's hit-and-throw contest. Kid's only eight and hits a hardball a hundred and fifty feet off a tee.*

He's gonna be another DiMag—you wait and see.

*Six-year-old Deb holds her mom's other hand and, em-
barrassed at being out in front of thirty thousand fans, holds
on to her old man's leg at the same time. Her little brother,
Georgie, begs himself a shoulder ride and now bounces up
there, bumping his heels against his dad's chest, holds on to
his hair with both hands, pulling. But it doesn't hurt. Nothing hurts.*

*Sal's got Helen and he's got the kids. His own boat. He's
his own boss. The sun is shining on him.*

But it's gotten cold. He should get up. Dusk was coming on and where's the day gone?

He walked over to the window and pulled it down
against the breeze, sharp now. He could see the fog curl-
ing around Twin Peaks.

Straightening up, he stopped still, his head cocked to
one side. "God damn it!" He yelled it aloud and raced
into the kitchen. The day was circled on his calendar.
Friday!

Friday, you fool, he told himself. Business day. Customer day. Make-your-rent day. Keep your life together
the one day you've got to!

"No, no, no!" Yelling at himself, stomping on the
floor, furious. He swore again, violently, then kicked at
the chair near the table, but it just sat there, obstinate.
So he grabbed the back of it and sent it flying across the
room, where it slammed into the cabinets, cutting new
gouges into the pitted wood.

He left the chair where it was on the floor, then stood a long moment, forcing himself to calm down, to think.

This was one of the signs, wasn't it? He'd warned himself to be sure to recognize them when they got here, and now he wasn't going to go denying them. His mind was going to leave him someday—inevitably—and in the lucid moments he was clear on his strategy. He wasn't going to go out mumbling with shit in his diapers. He was going to die like a man.

He had the syringes, the morphine. He still knew where they were. Thank God for Graham—his one good son. The one good thing, when he looked back over it all.

He would call Graham. That's what he'd do.

He walked back through the living room. How had the window gotten closed? He was sure he'd been sitting in the chair and then he'd remembered it was Friday and he'd gone into the kitchen. . . .

All right. The syringe. He remembered. He could still remember, God damn it.

But then he saw his watercolor and stopped again, lost in the lines he'd painted so long ago, trying to render his old boat. A foghorn sounded and he stared at the window again—the closed window. He stood in the center of the room, unmoving. He had been going somewhere specific. It would come to him.

Another minute, standing there, trying to remember. And another blinding stab of pain in his head.

Tears ran down his face.

The vials—the supply of morphine—were in the medicine cabinet with a couple of syringes, and he took the stuff out and laid it on the dresser next to his bed. He went back to the kitchen. Somebody had knocked the chair over, but he'd get that in a minute. Or not. That wasn't what he'd come in here for.

He'd come in to check . . . something. Oh, there it was. The fluorescent orange sticker taped to the front of the refrigerator. Opening the freezer, he found the aluminum tube where he kept the doctor's Do Not Resuscitate form. It was still inside the tube, where it should be, where the paramedics would look for it. The form told whoever found him to let him alone, don't try to help him, don't hook him up to any damn machines.

He left the form in the freezer. In his bedroom again, he gathered the other paraphernalia and went back into the living room, where he laid it all out on the coffee table next to his bottle of Old Crow.

The window drew him to it. The thin ribbon of light over the fog. He sat himself on the couch and poured himself another couple of fingers of bourbon for courage.

He hadn't heard any approaching footsteps out in the hallway, but now someone was knocking on his door.

Suddenly he realized he must have called Graham after all. To save his life for this moment. It wasn't time for him to die yet. It was close, maybe, but it wasn't time.

He *had* called Graham—he remembered now—and his boy had come and they would find some way to work it all out until it really was time.

Dignity. That was all he wanted anymore. A little dignity. And perhaps a few more good days.

He got up to answer the door.

1

D ISMAS HARDY WAS ENJOYING A SUPERB ROUND OF darts, closing in on what might become a personal best.

He was in his office on a Monday morning, throwing his twenty-gram hand-tooled, custom-flighted tungsten beauties. He called the game "twenty-down" although it wasn't any kind of sanctioned affair. It had begun as simple practice—once around and down the board from "20" to bull's-eye. He'd turned the practice rounds into a game against himself.

His record was twenty-five throws. The best possible round was twenty-one, and now he was shooting at the "3" with his nineteenth dart. A twenty-two was still possible. Beating twenty-five was going to be a lock, assuming his concentration didn't get interrupted.

On his desk the telephone buzzed.

* * *

He'd worked downtown at an office on Sutter Street for nearly six years. The rest of the building was home to David Freeman & Associates, a law firm specializing in plaintiffs' personal injury and criminal defense work. But Hardy wasn't one of Freeman's associates. Technically, he didn't work for Freeman at all, although lately almost all of his billable hours had come from a client his landlord had farmed out to him.

Hardy occupied the only office on the top floor of the building. Both literally and figuratively he was on his own.

He held on to his dart and threw an evil eye at the telephone behind him, which buzzed again. To throw now would be to miss. He sat back on the desk, punched a button. "Yo."

Freeman's receptionist, Phyllis, had grown to tolerate, perhaps even like, Hardy, although it was plain that she disapproved of his casual attitude. This was a law firm. Lawyers should answer their phone crisply, with authority and dignity. They shouldn't just pick up and say "Yo."

He took an instant's pleasure in her sigh.

She lowered her voice. "There's a man down here to see you. He doesn't have an appointment." It was the same tone she would have used if the guest had stepped in something on the sidewalk. "He says he knows you from"—a pause while she sought a suitable euphemism. She finally failed and had to come out with the hated truth—"your bar. His name is Graham Russo."

Hardy knew half a dozen Russos—it was a common name in San Francisco—but hearing that Graham from the Little Shamrock was downstairs, presumably in need of a lawyer's services, narrowed it down.

Hardy glanced at his wall calendar. It was Monday, May 12. Sighing, he put his precious dart down on his desk and told Phyllis to send Mr. Russo right on up.

Hardy was standing at his door as Graham trudged up the stairs, a handsome, athletic young guy with the weight of this world on his shoulders. And at least one other world, Hardy knew, that had crashed and burned all around him.

They had met when Graham showed up for a beer at the Shamrock. Over the course of the night Hardy, moonlighting behind the bar, found out a lot about him. Graham, too, was an attorney, although he wasn't practicing right at the moment. The community had black-balled him.

Hardy had had his own run-ins with the legal bureaucracy and knew how devastating the ostracism could be. Hell, even when you were solidly within it, the law life itself was so unrelentingly adversarial that the whole world sometimes took on a hostile aspect.

So the two men had hit it off. Both men were estranged from the law in their own ways. Graham had stayed after last call, helped clean up. He was a sweet kid—maybe a little naive and idealistic, but his head seemed to be on straight. Hardy liked him.

Before the law Graham's world had been baseball. An All-American center fielder at USF during the late eighties, he'd batted .373 and had been drafted in the sixth round by the Dodgers. He then played two years in the minor leagues, making it to Double-A San Antonio before he'd fouled a ball into his own left eye. That injury had hospitalized him for three weeks, and when he got out, his vision didn't come with him. And so with a lifetime pro average of .327, well on the way to the bigs, he'd had to give it all up.

Rootless and disheartened, he had enrolled in law school at Boalt Hall in Berkeley. Graduating at the top of his class, he beat out intense competition and got hired for a one-year term as a clerk with the Ninth Circuit Court of Appeals. But he only stayed six months.

In early 1994—the year of the baseball strike—about two months after he passed the bar, he quit. He wanted, after all, to play baseball. So he went to Vero Beach, Florida, to try out as a replacement player for the Dodgers.

And he made the team.

At the Shamrock he'd made it clear to Hardy that he'd never have played as a scab. All along, all he'd wanted out of the deal was for the Dodgers to take another look at him. The fuzziness had disappeared from his vision; he was still in great shape. He thought he could shine in spring training, get cut as a replacement when they all did, but at least have a shot at the minors again.

And that's what happened. He started the '94 season with the Albuquerque Dukes, Triple A, farther along the path to the major leagues than he'd been seven years earlier.

But he couldn't find the damn curveball and the new shot at his baseball career, upon which he'd risked everything, lasted only six weeks. His average was .192 when he got cut outright. He hadn't had a hit in his last seven games. Hell, he told Hardy, he would have cut himself.

Graham had a lumberjack's shoulders and the long legs of a high hurdler. Under a wave of golden hair his square-jawed face was clean shaven. Today he wore a gray-blue sport coat over a royal-blue dress shirt, stonewashed jeans, cowboy boots.

He was leaning forward on the front of the upholstered chair in front of Hardy's desk, elbows on his knees. Hardy noticed the hands clasped in front of him —the kind of hands that, when he got older, people would call gnarled—workingman's hands, huge and somehow expressive.

Graham essayed a smile. "I don't even know why I'm here, tell you the truth."

Hardy's face creased. "I often feel the same way myself." He was sitting on the corner of his desk. "Your dad?"

Graham nodded.

Salvatore Russo—Herb Caen's column had dubbed him Salmon Sal and the name had stuck—was recent news. Despondent over poor health, his aging body, and financial ruin, Sal had apparently killed himself last Friday by having a few cocktails, then injecting himself with morphine. He'd left a Do Not Resuscitate form for the paramedics, but he was already dead when they'd arrived.

To the public at large Sal was mostly unknown. But he was well known in San Francisco's legal community. Every Friday Sal would make the rounds of the city's law workshops in an old Ford pickup. Behind the Hall of Justice, where Hardy would see him, he'd park by the hydrant and sell salmon, abalone, sturgeon, caviar, and any other produce of the sea he happened to get his hands on. His customers included cops, federal-, municipal-, and superior-court judges, attorneys, federal marshals, sheriffs, and the staffs at both halls—Justice and City—and at the federal courthouse.

The truck appeared only one day a week, but since Sal's seafood was always fresher and a lot cheaper than at the markets, he apparently made enough to survive, notwithstanding the fact that he did it all illegally.

His salmon had their tails clipped, which meant they had been caught for sport and couldn't be sold. Abalone was the same story; private parties taking abalone for commercial sale had been outlawed for years. His winter-run chinooks had probably been harvested by Native Americans using gill nets. And yet year after year this stuff would appear in Sal's truckbed.

Salmon Sal had no retail license, but it didn't matter because he was connected. His childhood pals knew him from the days when Fisherman's Wharf was a place where men went down to the sea in boats. Now these boys were judges and police lieutenants and heads of departments. They were not going to bust him.

Sal might live on the edge of the law, but the establishment considered him one of the good guys—a character in his yellow scarves and hip boots, the unlit stogie chomped down to its last inch, the gallon bottles from which he dispensed red and white plonk in Dixie cups along with a steady stream of the most politically incorrect jokes to be found in San Francisco.

The day Hardy had met Sal, over a decade ago, he'd been with Abe Glitsky. Glitsky was half black and half Jewish and every inch of him scary looking—a hatchet face and a glowing scar through his lips, top to bottom. Sal had seen him, raised his voice. "Hey, Abe, there's this black guy and this Jew sitting on the top of this building and they both fall off at the same time. Which one hits the ground first?"

"I don't know, Sal," Glitsky answered, "which one?"

"Who cares?"

Now Sal was dead and the newspapers had been rife with conjecture: early evidence indicated that someone had been in the room with him when he'd died. A chair knocked over in the kitchen. Angry sounds. Other evidence of struggle.

The police were calling the death suspicious. Maybe someone had helped Sal die—put him on an early flight.

* * *

"I didn't know Sal was your father," Hardy said. "Not until just now."

"Yeah, well. I didn't exactly brag about him." Graham took a breath and looked beyond Hardy, out the window. "The funeral's tomorrow."

When no more words came, Hardy prompted him. "Are you in trouble?"

"No!" A little too quickly, too loud. Graham toned it down some. "No, I don't think so. I don't know why I would be."

Hardy waited some more.

"I mean, there's a lot happening all at once. The estate—although the word *estate* is a joke. Dad asked me to be his executor although we never got around to drawing up the will, so where does that leave it? Your guess is as good as mine."

"You weren't close, you and your dad?"

Graham took a beat before he answered. "Not very."

Hardy thought the eye contact was a little overdone, but he let it go. He'd see where this all was leading. "So you need help with the estate? What kind of help?"

"That's just it. I don't know what I need. I need help in general." Graham hung his head and shook it, then looked back up. "The cops have been around, asking questions."

"What kind of questions?"

"Where was I on Friday? Did I know about my dad's condition? Like that. It was obvious where they were going." Graham's blue eyes flashed briefly in anger, maybe frustration. "How can they think I know anything about this? My dad killed himself for a lot of good reasons. The guy's disoriented, losing his mind. He's in awesome pain. I'd've done the same thing."

"And what do the police think?"

"I don't know what they can be thinking." Another pause. "I hadn't seen him in a week. First I heard of it was Saturday night. Some homicide cop is at my place when I get home."

"Where'd you get home from?"

"Ball game." He raised his eyes again, spit out the next word. "Softball. We had a tournament in Santa Clara, got eliminated in the fourth inning, so I got home early, around six."

"So where were you Friday night?"

Graham spread his Rodin hands. "I didn't kill my dad."

"I didn't ask that. I asked about Friday night."

He let out a breath, calming down. "After work, home."

"Alone?"

He smiled. "Just like the movie. Home alone. I love that answer. The cop liked it, too, but for different reasons. I could tell."

Hardy nodded. "Cops can be tough to please."

"I worked till nine-thirty. . . ."

"What do you do, besides baseball?"

Graham corrected him. "Softball." A shrug. "I've been working as a paramedic since . . . well, lately."

"Okay. So you were riding in an ambulance Friday night?"

A nod. "I got home around ten-fifteen. I knew I had some games the next day—five, if we went all the way. Wanted to get some rest. Went to sleep."

"What time did you go in to work?"

"Around three, three-thirty. I punched in. They'll have a record of it."

"And what time did they find your dad?"

"Around ten at night." Graham didn't seem to have a problem with the timing, although to Hardy it invited some questions. If his memory served him, and it always did, Sal had apparently died between one and four o'clock in the afternoon. This was the issue Graham was skirting, which perhaps the police were considering if they were thinking about Graham after all. He would have had plenty of time between one o'clock and when he checked in to work near three.

But the young man was going on. "Judge Giotti, you know. Judge Giotti found him."

"I read. What was he doing there?"

Graham shrugged. "I just know what everybody knows—he'd finished having dinner downtown. He had a fish order in and Sal didn't show, so he thought he'd check the apartment, see if he was okay."

"And why would the judge do that?"

The answer was unforced, Graham recounting old family history. "They were friends. Used to be, anyway, in high school, then college. They played ball together."

"Your father went to college?"

Graham nodded. "It's weird, isn't it? Salmon Sal the college grad. Classic underachiever, that was Sal. Runs in the family." He forced a smile, making a joke, but kept his hands clamped tightly together, leaning forward casually, elbows resting on his knees. His knuckles were white.

"So. Giotti?" Hardy asked. Graham cast his eyes to the floor. "You weren't *his* clerk, were you?"

The head came back up. Graham said no. He'd clerked for Harold Draper, another federal judge with the Ninth Circuit.

"I guess what I'm asking," Hardy continued, "is whether you and Giotti—him being your dad's old pal and all—developed any kind of relationship while you were clerking."

Graham took a moment, then shook his head. "No. Giotti came by once after I got hired to say congratulations. But these judges don't have a life. I didn't even see him in the halls."

"And how long did you work there?"

"Six months."

Hardy slid from the desk and crossed to his window. "Let me be sure I've got it right," he said. "Draper hired you to become a clerk for the Ninth? How many clerks does he have?"

"Three."

"For a year each?"

"Right. That's the term."

Hardy thought so. He went on. "When I was getting into practice right after the Civil War, a federal clerkship was considered the plum job of all time right out of law school. Is that still the case?"

This brought a small smile. "Everybody seems to think so."

"But you quit after six months so you could try out as a replacement player during the baseball strike?"

Graham sat back finally, unclenched his hands, spread them out. "Arrogant, ungrateful wretch that I am."

"So now everybody in the legal community thinks you're either disloyal or brain dead."

"No, those are my *friends*." Graham took a beat. "Draper, for example, hates my guts. So do his wife, kids, dogs, the other two clerks, the secretaries—they all really really hate me personally. Everybody else just wishes I'd die soon, as slowly and painfully as possible. Both."

Hardy nodded. "So Giotti didn't call *you* when he found your dad?"

Graham shook his head. "I'd be the last person he'd call. You walk out on one of these guys, you're a traitor to the whole tribe. That's why I came to you—you're a lawyer who'll talk to me. I think you're the last one who will."

"And you're worried about the police?"

A shrug. "Not really. I don't know. I don't know what they're thinking."

"I doubt they're thinking anything, Graham. They just like to be thorough and ask a lot of questions, which tends to make people nervous. This other stuff with your background might have made the rounds, so they might shake your tree a little harder, see if something falls out."

"Nothing's going to fall out. My dad killed himself."